FELONY

AT 40,000 FEET

Dear Curt:
I hope you enjoy my
writing as much as I enjoy
yours.
Best Wishes,
Jerry Norcia

A NOVEL BY

JERRY NORCIA

For quantity pricing or comments, please e-mail:

Jerry@jerrynorcia.com

PUBLISHER'S NOTE:

This is a work of fiction. Names, characters, places, and incidents either are the product of the author's imagination or are used fictitiously, any resemblance to actual persons, living or dead, business establishments, events, or locales is entirely coincidental.

ISBN: 978-0-615-67599-2

Printed and bound in the United States of America
by Maverick Publications • Bend, Oregon

Dedication

to Mary Ellen Watson.

When I lost interest and couldn't write another word, Mary Ellen asked for more. "I'm enjoying your story," she would say. Without her encouragement this never would have been printed. She's been a dear friend.

Jerry Norcia

Acknowledgments

A special thanks to all those friends who labored through my first drafts and made meaningful suggestions. To protect their anonymity, I shall not name them here, but you know who you are. I am very grateful to these friends.

Kim Petersen, a terrific writer and friend. Kim is presently teaching Science and Business in China. Kim has made more than great suggestions, he's given me ideas and encouragement. He is a good editor.

Of course my wife Barbara, what she's had to put up with, mostly the back of my head as I sat staring at the computer expecting the words to pop out.

Cover design by Gary Asher, Maverick Publications.

Prologue

October 25, 1979

The conflict with Renee weighed heavily on Grant's mind as he ascended the 747's spiral staircase to the upper first class lounge. Under the command of Captain Steve Como, flight 96 from Honolulu seemed longer than usual to Inflight Supervisor Grant Guidera. Unable to clear his mind, Grant felt emotionally drained as he slid into a single window seat breathing in the aroma of the rich leather. He fastened his seat belt preparing for landing; these moments alone after a busy flight of sales and passenger contact were normally a relaxing reward, not today. He looked around the empty lounge and tried to pretend this was his own private jet. All he needed were the kind of friends he imagined he'd have with that kind of money, and never again having to deal with the likes of Renee.

During flight, this lounge bustled with first class passengers who were now on the main deck preparing for landing. The cockpit door was only a few feet in front of where Grant normally sat to watch the California coastline and San Francisco Airport come into view. It was an especially beautiful day with a heavy fog layer directly over the airport that promised a thrilling descent and landing. He put on a passenger headset and tuned to channel 9, anticipating the excitement of an instrument approach. He was just in time to hear Bay Approach hand his flight over to the San Francisco tower: "Universal 96 heavy contact San Francisco tower on 120.5. Good day, sir."

Captain Como repeated, "Contact tower, 120.5, 96 heavy. Good day, sir." Grant pictured the captain turning the dial to change frequencies. Como came back, "San Francisco tower, Universal 96 heavy with you at 9,500 for 28 left."

"Universal 96 heavy, you're cleared for the ILS on 28 left, please expedite, you have Lufthansa traffic on final. Lufthansa 2121, please slow to your final approach speed."

1

Although Grant was a private pilot, he continued to be amazed how the captains could remember so many instructions and repeat them word for word. The fully loaded 747 entered the thick cloud layer as Grant stared out the window. His stomach leaped with excitement as the plane broke through the cloud layer and he saw the runway with less than a 200-foot ceiling. He could feel the confidence in Captain Como's voice as he called the tower, "San Francisco, Universal 96 heavy has runway 28 left in sight, landing."

The plane touched down at the very beginning of the runway and Grant felt his seatbelt strain as the captain applied reverse thrusters while gently lowering the nose to the runway. Turning smoothly onto the high-speed taxiway, Grant was sure they had cleared the runway in plenty of time for the approaching Lufthansa aircraft. He heard the tower direct his flight to contact ground control on 121.8.

***In the cockpit**, the captain changed frequencies and started to say something to the flight engineer, but stopped short when the engineer furrowed his brow and covered his lips with his forefinger. With his free hand, the engineer scribbled a note on his clipboard and handed it to the Captain. "What's this about?" Como asked. After reading the engineer's note, he crumpled it and tossed it flippantly over his right shoulder in the direction of a garbage bag taped to the engineer's table. While Grant had been listening to communications between the tower and his flight, he was surprised that channel 9 went silent. The cockpit had to be talking to someone, but who? Captain Como came over the PA system, "Ladies and gentlemen, we would like to ask that you please remain seated."*

Grant was surprised to hear the captain on the PA system. While the announcement wasn't out of the ordinary, it was not usually made by the captain. He couldn't help but wonder what was going on. When Captain Como came on again and told the passengers they would be parking at the company ramp area because of a maintenance problem, Grant figured it was just another airline trick not to tie up one of the busy gates.

Detoured to the ramp area, the 747, guided by a mechanic, slowly rolled to a stop. While the engines wound down, Grant looked out the window and saw portable stairs being put into place at the main cabin door. Cars with flashing lights surrounded the plane with several men standing alongside. Grant wondered what all the commotion was about; he was sure the flight attendants were going to need his assistance with the passengers. In fact, he was surprised he hadn't been advised of this unexpected turn of events.

Heading down the spiral stairway, he saw the first flight attendant disarming the emergency slide at the main cabin door. She gave a thumbs up through the small window, signaling the mechanic it was now safe to open the door. A few passengers rose from their seats, prompting Grant to grab the nearby mic: "The seat belt sign is still on. Please, everyone remain in your seats!"

Two heavy-set men dressed in dark gray suits appeared in the open doorway. Both wore mirrored sunglasses—oddly unnecessary, Grant thought, since the bright sun of Honolulu was hours behind them.

Renee pointed to Grant. "That's him!"

The men walked over to Grant. "FBI. Put your hands on top of your head." One of the men reached up, grasped one hand and placed it firmly behind Grant's back and then did the same with the other hand, placing them both in handcuffs. The other man cleared his throat. "You have the right to remain silent..." Astonished passengers sitting by the door watched Grant being taken off the plane in handcuffs.

The two men took Grant to a waiting car at the bottom of the stairs. In a state of shock and disbelief, Grant felt someone's hand push his head down, stuffing him in the back seat. He turned and looked out the back window. Two flight attendants stood on the stairs outside the cabin door; one had an unmistakable grin on her face: Renee. That bitch. At that moment, Grant's dream job had turned into a nightmare.

Chapter 1

Grant sat in the back seat of the cruiser, his jaw hanging open in disbelief. Two official looking men stood by the stairs as the passengers deplaned and directed them to a roped off area. Grant saw Brian showing an agent his identification. They walked together to the forward cargo area, had a brief conversation and then parted. It was starting to get crowded with all the people getting off the plane. Brian blended in with the crowd and as he got close to the car where Grant was sitting, winked and put his finger up to his lips. One agent got in the back seat with Grant and one in the driver's seat. Brian's gesture had given Grant a little confidence and he decided to act innocent.

"What the hell is going on?" Grant demanded. Neither man responded.

Brian didn't appear concerned as he walked back towards the plane and talked with one of the agents. Both men looked toward the car. "What could they be talking about?" Grant wondered. He knew he needed to play this out and act indignant. There was a car waiting to take Captain Como and the crew to flight operations. Another car took Donna and Renee toward the terminal, weaving among the baggage carts. Donna and Renee got out and walked with two agents to the elevator. Grant's driver pulled up to the same elevator and waited for it to come back down. Grant could see the ramp guys staring. He was embarrassed to be seen in handcuffs.

The three men rode the elevator to the top floor, where Maryann was waiting to take them to a conference room. Grant saw Renee and Donna deep in conversation with an FBI agent. Maryann stopped and asked him, "Is it really necessary to keep Grant in handcuffs?"

One agent looked at the other; the first nodded his head, and then removed the handcuffs.

Grant demanded, "Who the hell are you and where is your identification?"

They each reached for a wallet and showed him a small identification card with a picture and bold letters, FBI.

"So what do you want?" Grant asked.

"We think you know what we want. We're having the passengers check their bags for contents."

"All the bags? That will take hours."

"No, just the bags in the forward cargo pit."

Grant turned to Maryann and said indignantly, "Maryann, if Renee is causing all this trouble because I went in the cargo pit, she should have her ass fired."

"So you did go in the forward cargo pit?" Maryann queried.

"Of course I did, there's no secret about that."

"For what purpose did you go in there?"

"Mr. Lasswell, the onboard courier, asked me to check on his courier boxes." After Brian's eye contact and signal on the ground, Grant was confident that the two of them were on the same page with this whole mess.

Maryann asked, "Why didn't you tell Renee what you were doing?"

"I didn't think I needed to explain anything to Renee. I've tried talking with her since her last hearing, but she made it clear she didn't want to talk to me."

One of the agents was in the back of the room talking on his radio. He was asking about the suitcases and then the courier boxes. Grant was sure this was it; they must have found him out. Grant still felt he should continue to play his indignation out to the end. The second agent walked over to where the first agent was standing, they spoke softly, but Grant could still hear them.

"The courier said everything was in his boxes and there was no evidence of tampering. Of the suitcases checked so far, there was nothing amiss. They think some of the passengers are at the next baggage carousel getting their checked bags. The front pit had last minute bags and some that were too big to carry-on. That Lasswell fellow said he asked Grant to look at his courier boxes. He said the guys were manhandling them when they put them onboard in Honolulu."

Grant tried not to show how relieved he was. The second agent asked, "So, where does that leave us?"

"Well, there are still some bags that haven't been claimed."

There was a call on the radio for one of the agents in Maryann's office. He walked outside the office and when he returned, he said, "Grant we would like you and Donna to come with us to the baggage area."

Grant walked out of the office with Maryann and looked over to where Renee and Donna were sitting. Renee didn't look too happy and that was a comfort to Grant. The two agents escorted Donna and Grant into the elevator. It was uncomfortably quiet standing next to a sulky Donna.

Grant couldn't help himself. "Where are we going?" He was feeling more confident since he was pretty sure he was out of the woods.

"I want you two to see if you recognize someone," one agent said.

The elevator led to the baggage claim area. There were still a number of people milling around and looking through suitcases. One of the agents in the baggage area motioned for them to follow. He turned and walked into the baggage claim office. Grant stopped and let Donna walk in first. She gave him a chagrined smile. Grant walked in behind her; sitting in a chair by the desk was Mr. Chin. Grant smiled at Mr. Chin, but he didn't smile back.

The lead agent asked, "Do either of you know this man?"

Donna didn't, but Grant said, "Yes, that's Mr. Chin, why?"

"He seemed to be lost and when a passenger agent asked if she could help, he panicked and got upset. The baggage supervisor called for an interpreter. He doesn't seem to have a ticket or any identification. How could he have gotten on the plane?"

Donna responded first, with a puzzled look on her face, "I don't remember taking his ticket and I think I would have."

"That's because the passenger agent brought him onboard early while you were in first class." Grant explained, "The passenger agent told me about him and pulled his ticket."

"There was nothing on the manifest about a pre-board or a passenger needing special assistance. Don't you think I would have said something in briefing?" Donna questioned.

"I wasn't in briefing, so I thought maybe you already knew about him."

Grant wasn't sure what the problem was; there were lots of passengers who didn't speak English. The interpreter/passenger agent, Andy Park, showed up and seemed as happy to see Mr. Chin, as Mr. Chin was to see him when he heard Andy speak Chinese. They talked briefly, and Mr. Chin took an envelope out of his small carry-on case and gave it to Andy who looked through it. "Well here's his passport, visa and ticket stub." Andy looked at Grant and the agents. "I was supposed to meet the flight and escort him. Of course I was waiting at the terminal and was just told of the diversion. There is nothing wrong here."

Grant looked out the large office window toward the carousel and saw the last of the passengers showing their baggage stubs and leaving the area. Grant's stomach jumped. He did a double take when he saw two familiar suitcases with their identifying strings sitting on the carousel, obviously unclaimed.

He tried not to pay attention to the lone bags and asked the FBI agent, "May I go now? I have reports to fill out and I will need your names." The agents once again showed Grant their identification cards. He took down their names and felt smug while doing it.

"You and the stewardess can go; we'll call you if we have anything else," the FBI agent said.

Grant and Donna headed toward the elevator, but Donna slowed her pace, dropping behind. Grant was sure she needed to go up to the office, but he wasn't sure she wanted to get in the same elevator with him. When the door opened, Grant held it for her. "Are you coming Donna?"

"Sure, if you don't mind riding in the same elevator with me."

"Well, you are a pain in the ass."

"I had that coming," she said sheepishly.

"You're not a pain in the ass. I just can't believe you fell for Renee's crap."

"I should have known better, but she was so convincing."

"I'm going to talk with Maryann and see what, if anything, we're going to do."

Grant was extremely worried about the two unclaimed bags. Under the circumstances he wasn't sure if they would just be put aside. This was going to be a waiting game. He needed to pretend as though he didn't know what was in the suitcases. If anything came up, he was prepared to act just as shocked as anyone.

Grant and Donna got off the elevator and walked toward Maryann's office. Renee was coming out, looking displeased. Grant wanted to yell a litany of names at her; instead he said, "Renee, we'll be talking about this soon."

"Fuck you!" Renee turned on her heel and stormed off.

Grant knew with her attitude the situation would be going in his favor. He went into Maryann's office.

"Well Grant, you sure keep things exciting around here. And somehow, Renee is always involved."

"What are you going to do about her?"

"What are you going to do about her is more the question." Maryann rebutted.

"I don't believe under the circumstances, I should be the one to do anything," Grant retorted with conviction.

"I'll give it some thought and get back to you. It's been a long day. Why don't you do your basic flight report and go home. You can write a more detailed report and get it back to me in a day or two."

Grant completed his report and headed for the crew bus. Donna was standing at the bus stop as well. They were both slightly uncomfortable still—Grant because in his heart he knew she was more right than wrong.

If it weren't for those unclaimed suitcases, he would be home free. "Maybe they will just put them in the rack with the other unclaimed baggage," he hoped. The biggest problem was going to be getting the claim check out of the small pocket on the side of each suitcase. Grant needed to figure out how to proceed.

Once home, relief settled over Grant as he lost himself in thought, sipping on his bourbon and watching planes land. Unfortunately, it was short-lived. He had too much on his mind to really enjoy himself. Grant knew that this was no way to end his career helping Brian run drugs. He needed to do something with those two suitcases.

Grant knew it was much too late, but he called Pat anyway. To his surprise she was home.

"It's really you, not the machine?" Grant asked.

"It's really me. Is this really you or a message?"

"I'm sorry to be calling so late, but I just wanted to hear your voice and leave a message. Were you sleeping?"

"Actually no, I'm doing some stitchery and just relaxing. How about you?"

"I just got home from working 96."

"You just got home! Did you have a delay?"

"I guess you could say that. It's too much to tell you over the phone and it's getting late. Do you have some time off? Maybe I could come over tomorrow."

"I have four days off. Why don't you come early? We can have lunch at Zack's, and later I'll make us a nice dinner."

"I can't wait. See you tomorrow. And honey, I've missed you."

"I've missed you too. Good night."

Grant was afraid to call Brian not knowing if his, or Brian's, phone was bugged. Grant's paranoia suddenly made him fear that the FBI was just giving him false hope and rope enough to hang himself.

It was now past twelve o'clock. The doorbell rang and scared the shit out of Grant. He went down expecting the FBI, the DEA, or maybe the ATF to be beating down his door. He looked through the peephole. It was Brian but too dark to see him well. Grant opened the door to find Brian slumped against the wall with his head down. When Brian brought his head up, Grant was shocked to see that his face was a bloody mess. Grant helped Brian into the house and led him upstairs.

"What happened to you?"

"Max and Roberto happened. I went straight to the warehouse with the courier truck. Sure enough the jeweler who wanted his courier box was there waiting and that was fine, but when I left Max and Roberto showed up. One of them said, 'You better have our packages.' I asked them if they had been at the airport and seen all the FBI agents. They said, 'Yea, so what, where's our stuff?' I called them dumb bastards and told them the suitcases were at the airport like always. I figured they would have claimed them. That's when they started hitting me. I don't know what they are going to do." Brian noticed the full highball glass sitting on the end table. "That looks good."

Grant made Brian a double and helped him clean up his face with a damp washcloth. Fortunately, Brian's face wasn't as bad as it first appeared.

"What now?" Grant asked.

"I'm not sure. If Max and Roberto get the bags, it'll be fine. If the Feds look in the suitcases first, who knows what they'll think. I'm sure they will think of every scenario, but I don't think they can prove anything. I had the courier boxes cleaned. I'm sure there are no traces of coke."

"Have you talked with Vicki?"

"I called her from my office before I headed out. She asked how the trip went. I told her fine and that I would tell her all about it tomorrow. Who knows if anyone was listening? She'll be home tomorrow at 3:25 on flight 180."

"Brian, this isn't looking good. I want out, now more than ever. What are you planning to do?"

"I'm not sure. The guys in Honolulu actually offered me enough for my business franchise, but I wouldn't want them working with the legitimate customers I have. Personally, I would like to sell the business to someone who is smart enough to not do something stupid, like shipping drugs."

"Look, why don't you spend the night here? Do Max and Roberto know where you live?"

"They most likely do, but I better go home anyway just in case. I have a good security system with cameras around the property."

Brian soon left, and Grant poured himself another drink. He was just too wound up to sleep. Those damn suitcases and Renee weighed heavily on his mind. He knew better than to drive to the airport, especially after drinking, but he couldn't get those suitcases off his mind. Maybe, just maybe, he could pull something off; at least just take a look around. Against his better judgment, he drove to the airport. Since it was so late, he parked right outside the baggage area where the limos usually parked. There was one lone limo with a sleeping driver in the front seat.

Grant had his identification badge and a couple of stories ready depending on whom he might run into. The baggage area and carousels were empty of people and luggage. He wasn't sure if the missing bags were a good sign or bad omen. Grant wasn't familiar with this part of the airport, so he started looking around. He walked into the back room and there were the suitcases, chained to a luggage rack with a couple of other unclaimed bags.

He felt relieved just knowing they were there. He would have felt better, however, if he had the key to the chain that kept them secure. In any case, this was his chance to get the claim checks from the outside pocket of the suitcases. That alone would be a small victory.

Grant could never get over how quiet the airport could be in the early or late hours. He was leaning over the suitcases fumbling through the side pockets looking for the claim checks; suddenly, Grant heard an unexpected voice from behind and instinctively his torso and head flinched in response.

"So Grant, what do you think you're doing?"

Chapter 2

October 1971

T oday was different. Unlike most mornings, when Grant would swear at the alarm, hit the snooze button and roll over, he was anxious to start this day. After eleven years as a reluctant mechanic, Grant knew this job interview could very well be the key to a new beginning. Before today, he only dreamt of getting one of the most sought after jobs in the airlines, the position of friendship service director. If hired, he would be onboard Universal's 747 and DC-10 airplanes doing what he liked most, flying and talking with people. Grant felt he had earned this opportunity after working so many special assignments at the maintenance base.

Wanting to look his best, Grant combed his dark blond hair until it lay just right. His teeth were bright and straight and his hazel eyes had a clear, friendly sparkle. Other than raw hands and fingernails from trying to remove any sign of grease, he didn't look too bad for a thirty-five-year-old guy. He smiled at himself in the mirror, feeling self-confident at that moment, but stopped short of wishing himself good luck.

As much as Grant wanted this dream job, he wanted more than anything to please his sister, Gina. He wanted her to be proud of him.

The ringing phone snapped Grant back to reality. He quickly dried his hands and then answered the phone.

"Hi honey. I wanted to wish you luck today."

Grant cradled the phone on his shoulder and fastened his watch. "Thanks, Mom."

"I know someone who works at Universal. Do you want me to talk to him about your interview?"

Another one of her barroom acquaintances, Grant was sure. "No mom, please," Grant begged, "I earned this interview and I don't want anyone ruining it for me."

She clucked her tongue. "Remember what I've always told you, it's not what you know, it's who you know."

Grant loved his mom, but after his parents divorced her drinking and hanging out in bars was difficult for him to accept. Grant was eleven when they split; by eighteen, joining the Air Force seemed the best solution. Grant had dated the same girl for two years and got engaged just before he joined the service. But then, he still believed that loving one woman would be enough. In contrast, his father, Pete, fancied himself as a ladies man. He relished being seen with attractive woman.

It wasn't long after Grant joined the service that his fiancé stopped writing. Finally, a letter arrived that took Grant from elation to devastation when he read; "Perhaps when I tell you I'm getting married April 7th, you'll understand why I haven't been writing. I'll give the ring to your mom." He couldn't believe his eyes. It was the only thing he had to look forward to—marrying his high school sweetheart. Out of desperation Grant called his dad. Holding back tears, he had told his dad about the letter, hoping his father would provide some words of comfort. There were none to be had. Grant's father advised his heartbroken son, "those fucking broads are all alike." Grant knew in his heart that his dad wasn't right, but had never forgotten those words.

Gradually, Grant became his father. He would drink a little too much and impress his friends by dating attractive women. Grant grew to enjoy attractive women and how they helped him forget the remnants of his broken heart. After leaving the service, Grant continued his promiscuous lifestyle, contrary to his inner feelings. Drinking, sex, and beautiful woman seemed more of a reward than those years of faithfulness.

Grant never did well in school, but made up for that shortcoming with clever moneymaking ideas, ambition, and sometimes, taking risks.

Grant didn't want to take any risks with his interview though, and with that in mind, he and the knot in his stomach arrived forty-five minutes early to the San Francisco International Airport for his interview. He loved the sounds and hubbub of the airport; people running to catch their flights, the loud speaker announcing flight arrivals and departures and people's names being paged. Grant saw an elderly woman having a difficult time with her bags and asked if she would like some help. She was a bit dubious until she saw he had a Universal Airlines identification. Her warm thanks convinced Grant he belonged in the public arena for Universal Airlines. He still had plenty of time to show up for his appointment at the Aloha Room on the B Concourse.

✈ ✈ ✈

Grant sat in the dimly lighted Aloha Room. In his new suit, dress shirt and paisley tie, he stood out from the Honolulu-bound passengers in their Hawaiian attire.

Two dark figures entered from the bright lights of the concourse. They hesitated, letting their eyes adjust. "This has to be them," Grant thought. He took advantage of that moment to quickly wipe his damp right hand on his pant leg, before standing to greet them. Both men wore Universal identification badges on their short-sleeved shirts. The taller of the two extended his hand. "You must be Grant. I'm Bill Byrne."

Grant, noting just a hint of an Irish brogue, shook Bill's hand, "Nice to meet you."

"This is my colleague, Ron Mason."

Grant nodded and reached his hand out to the shorter man standing behind Bill. With a manila file in his hand, Bill pointed to the door. "Let's go to my office, I believe it will give us a little more privacy."

They walked past the few people meandering around in bright shirts waiting for the announcement to board their Honolulu flight, and Grant wished he were one of them. The three men took the elevator to the second floor and Bill's office.

Again, Grant wiped his palms on his pants as he sat down in front of Bill's desk. Ron sat to one side of the desk.

Bill cleared his throat. "Grant, tell us, how much do you know about our inflight program?"

Grant swallowed the lump in his throat and silently willed the butterflies in his stomach to settle down. "I know it's a very special position dealing with the passengers onboard our flights. I understand the flight crew is an important part of encouraging our passengers to come back. In fact, I understand a big part of the job is to convince passengers with returns on other carriers to change their tickets onboard."

Ron and Bill glanced at each other. Ron leaned forward. "How could you know all that from working at the maintenance base?" He asked in a perplexed tone.

"As part of the employee sales program, I worked with a lot of people from inflight service, customer service and flight operations. We visited each other's departments to get a better idea of how we could make all employees feel they are an important part of Universal. I learned a lot from that program."

Bill shuffled through the manila file and pulled out a report. "Though impressive as your knowledge of our service may be, we can't dismiss the bad marks against you. You took an excessive amount of sick leave while working in the maintenance department."

"I understand, but if I might say…" The ringing phone startled Grant. Bill excused the interruption and answered it. Grant took a moment to think about what he was going to say when Bill got off the phone. He took a deep breath, glancing from Bill to Ron and then to the large window in Bill's office.

Bill had a spectacular view of the Universal ramp and the airplanes being readied for their busy day of carrying passengers to destinations around the world. It all started and ended right in front of his window. Ramp workers and mechanics scurried around the planes. There were fuel trucks, tugs with long trains of baggage, and second officers walking around the huge jets as part of their contractual obligation, so the passengers looking out the windows would see their plane being checked over before flight.

Grant turned back to see the color drained from Bill's concerned face. Bill loosened the knot in his tie before speaking into the phone. "Yes sir, I understand."

Grant looked nervously at Ron and saw that he had a puzzled look. Ron flicked his pen up and down on his leg watching the expression on Bill's face.

Bill held the phone to his shoulder and shuffled through the papers in a file, which Grant assumed was his work record. Bill held up a letter and scanned its contents, then turned his chair toward the window behind him. "Yes, I will…Of course I will." The call ended and Bill swung his chair back around.

"Sorry for the interruption." Bill cleared his throat, his eyes darting to Ron.

Ron stopped flicking his pen and sent Bill a questioning look. Collecting the scattered papers of Grant's file, Bill looked at Grant. His expression was unreadable.

Grant's stomach tweaked. He wiped his sweating hands on his pants again and searched his mind for any connection between the phone conversation and the interview. He found none.

Bill tucked the papers back into the file. "Now, where were we?"

Grant, taking this as his cue to finish, leaned forward. "I believe I was telling you about the sick leave I…"

Bill held up his hand. "It's irrelevant. Just know that we'll fire you if that happens here."

Grant swallowed but didn't say anything.

Bill looked at Ron. "Do you have anything further for Grant?"

"Well, yes…" Bill frowned and jerked his head towards Ron. "Actually, no. No, I think that's about it."

Bill stood. "Well, Grant, it's been nice meeting you, do you have any questions?"

Grant knew he should have had some good questions, but he couldn't think of any just then. Tension weighed heavily on his mind, blocking any coherent question. "No, I think I'm well acquainted with the position and hope you'll consider me."

Ron was the first to hold out his hand.

Grant wanted so badly to wipe his hand on his pant leg again, but to his relief his hand was dry as he shook both of their hands and thanked them.

After Grant left the office, Ron pulled back a chair and sat. He waited for Bill to say something, but nothing was forthcoming. Bill kept busy putting Grant's file back in the envelope, while obviously avoiding eye contact with Ron. "What's going on?" Ron asked.

"Ron, I want to give this Grant kid a chance, I'm hoping you feel the same about it," Bill said, as he got up and walked to his window. He appeared distant as he waited for Ron to say something. Ron almost pressed Bill about his behavior, but finally said, "I better get back to my office, give me a call and we'll work this out."

"I'll call you later today," Bill said, almost looking apologetic.

Chapter 3

After three of the longest days Grant could remember, he received a call from Ron Mason. Grant had the job and a date to report to the office. He couldn't remember ever feeling so excited about anything. He couldn't wait to call his sister with the good news. Gina was a successful doctor who had always done well in school. Grant loved her dearly. After hanging up, he recalled how as kids, they had to sit in the car outside the bar where their folks stopped in to drink with their friends. Gina studied and did homework. She would also read to Grant until he became impatient and would go inside to see what was going on. With little success, she tried to encourage Grant to work harder to get good grades. Without saying anything to Grant, she was concerned about two things; did he have what it would take to be in management and would he be careful working around so many beautiful stewardesses?

The news of Grant getting the onboard position traveled fast through what was affectionately known as Universal's "bamboo wireless." Enjoying his first breakfast as a friendship service director, Grant got a call from John Cross, who he'd met during the employee sales program and they had become fast friends.

"Congratulations Grant. I heard you got the latest opening for the FSD position."

Grant gulped the rest of his tea. "Thanks John. I just found out yesterday. When did you hear about it?"

"Are you kidding? I think we knew before you did. I'm really happy for you, but I think there is something you should know."

"What's that?" Grant pushed his dish aside and listened intently.

"There were a few people from customer service who had their names in for that opening, some from San Francisco passenger service and some from other domiciles. In any case, a few of them are upset that a mechanic from the maintenance base got it."

"Why are they upset?"

"They think because they have more experience in dealing with the public, they should have been chosen first."

Grant paused a moment, but he was too excited to let this news bring him down. He thanked John for the heads up.

Enjoying the drive to work was a new experience for Grant. He was especially pleased to be passing the maintenance base where for many years he punched a time clock and crawled around greasy airplanes.

With a big smile and more than a little apprehension, Grant reported to the inflight office where Dakota Mills—a secretary with long raven hair—greeted him. Along with a cherished key card to the crew parking lot, Dakota showed him a mailbox that already had his name on it. Then she gave him a briefcase and all the materials he would need onboard his flights, including ticket stock to write new tickets.

"You also have an appointment to get fitted for a uniform." Dakota added.

Grant took the appointment card from her manicured hand. "Thanks."

To his delight, there were no demands on his writing or other intellectual skills in the two-day class on writing tickets and sales techniques. No matter how often he checked his mailbox, there was always something new waiting to be read. While checking mail after his last class, Dakota approached him.

"Grant, I have you set up to go on two training flights—one with Pete Loyola and another with Dave Holt. The flights will be Monday to Pittsburgh with Pete and then on Thursday to Honolulu with Dave. These are two of our best friendship service directors."

Monday was an evening flight on a DC-8 to Pittsburgh. As early as Grant had arrived at the office, proudly sporting his new uniform, Pete was already there.

Grant saw Pete's nametag and held out his hand. "Hi, Pete, I'm Grant Guidera."

Pete shook his hand, and then gave Grant a crooked smile. "How did you get this job?"

Grant cocked his head. "What do you mean?"

"I mean what does a mechanic know about public relations?"

Grant smiled back, not sure if Pete's plastered smile meant he was kidding or if he was harboring ill feelings. "I don't know anything. I thought you were supposed to teach me."

With that Pete laughed. "We'll be on a DC-8 this evening," Pete said, "so it's important to stay out of the flight attendant's way when they're doing their cocktail and meal service."

With Grant in tow, Pete walked to the podium and said hello to the agent checking in passengers. The agent gave Pete some papers and then Pete walked toward the enclosed, telescoping Jetway that connected the airport terminal to the aircraft. He motioned with his head for Grant to follow.

It was difficult for Grant to contain his excitement as they walked together down the Jetway, both in their powder blue blazers and gray slacks. Before they entered the plane, Grant glanced through the cockpit window at the pilots inside. The captain took a brief look in Grant's direction, smiled and continued his pre-flight. Onboard, a flight attendant was checking her supplies in the front galley.

The flight attendant lit up when she saw Pete, giving him a hug and asking, "Where have you been? I haven't seen you in awhile."

Pete smiled and said, "They're keeping me busy and now I'm trying to teach this mechanic how to be a friendship service director. Connie, say hi to Grant."

"Hi Grant. What's he talking about, a mechanic?"

"I used to be a mechanic at the maintenance base. Pete doesn't think a mechanic can do his job." Pete and Grant exchanged smiles. "Nice to meet you, Connie."

Pete and Grant walked to the back of the plane and introduced themselves to the flight attendants in the coach section. Pete showed Grant where to stow his briefcase for takeoff. Connie came over the PA system, "Okay folks, we're starting to board."

"Come with me," Pete motioned to Grant. They went to the first class section and sat across from each other at a lounge table just opposite the main cabin door. Nicely dressed passengers boarded the plane with their carry-on luggage and garment bags; most returned Connie's greeting as she took their tickets.

After ten passengers or so, she paused and passed the tickets over to Pete. He looked through them, putting some aside, he told Grant to write down the passenger's name, seat number, and on which return flight they were scheduled. After Grant wrote down the information referred to as tips, the tickets were given back to the agent, the door was closed and the engines came to life. The flight attendants went through their safety demonstration.

"Here's what I want you to do," Pete said. "Put this list in order so you're not running up and down the aisles. Put the people who have returns on other airlines first. The ones that have an open return will most likely come back with us anyway. Let me know when you get that done."

Pete turned and walked away, leaving Grant to finish his task. After being in the air about fifteen minutes, the seat belt sign went off. Connie made a brief announcement informing the passengers they could now move about the cabin. Then Pete picked up the mic.

"Good evening ladies and gentlemen, my name is Pete Loyola. I'm onboard your flight this evening to help you with any ticketing questions and provide information about ground transportation in Pittsburgh. I'm also training a new friendship service director. His name is Grant. One or both of us will be available in your cabin this evening. Have a wonderful flight and thank you for flying Universal."

When Pete got back to his seat, he smiled at Grant. "I want you to make the announcement on the way home." Grant swallowed and stared at Pete. Making the announcement wasn't something Grant had expected, at least not this soon. "Look at Mr. Blakely's return," Pete continued. "He's coming back next Tuesday on TWA. Check the Official Airline Guide and see what flight and equipment we have around the same time."

Grant shook his head to focus on the task before him. "I found a flight leaving a half hour later on a DC-10. He is currently scheduled on a 727."

"Okay, go ask him if it would be convenient for him to come back a half hour later. And don't forget to mention our plane is a DC-10."

Grant closed the OAG and, eager to please Pete, made his way to coach. "Hi Mr. Blakely," Grant held out his hand, "I'm Grant Guidera." They shook hands and Grant continued. "I see you're coming back on TWA at 4:30 on Tuesday. I was wondering if you would be interested in our five o'clock DC-10 flight?"

Mr. Blakely set his drink on the tray in front of him. "In fact, I prefer that flight. I don't know why my secretary put me on the 4:30."

"If you'll give me your ticket, I'll change it for you and be right back."

"Thanks. I'd appreciate that."

Grant took the ticket to their table and started to change it.

Pete grinned. "Well, you just made your first sale, good job. Did you ask him if he wanted a special seat assignment?"

"No, I didn't."

"Well, go back and ask him if he'd like an aisle or window seat."

Grant wished he hadn't had to be reminded, but for the most part he felt he'd done a good job. By the time they were done with their list, they'd convinced most of the passengers who were coming back on other airlines to return on Universal.

Grant closed his briefcase. "I think I did okay, didn't I?"

"You did okay, for a mechanic," Pete said with that crooked smile on his face.

With one successful trip under his belt, Grant met Dave Holt for a 747 flight to Honolulu. Dave was a charming guy with a definite air of confidence and sleek composure. In his presence, Grant felt a bit apprehensive because of Dave's obvious self-assurance.

Grant sat next to Dave at the briefing. There were fourteen crewmembers, which included two Hawaiian stewards. After discussing the meal service, the first flight attendant introduced Dave, and in turn Dave introduced Grant as a trainee.

Dave ran his hand through his cropped, sandy hair. "If you don't have any questions, let's go onboard." With Grant in tow, Dave walked into the cockpit. When the captain looked back, Dave said, "Captain Schiltz, I'd like to introduce you to Grant Guidera. I'll be training him on this trip."

Captain Schiltz, half standing so as to not bump his head on the overhead console filled with buttons and switches, held out his hand. "Welcome aboard Grant. Feel free to come up anytime and say hello."

Lost for words, Grant tried to contain his excitement at the opportunity to stand in the cockpit, where everything happened. When they left the cockpit, closing the door behind them, Dave walked into the lavatory and came out with a handful of paper towels. He took off his jacket and unbuttoned his shirt. Not looking the least bit embarrassed, he put some of the towels under his left armpit and then his right.

He looked at Grant. "I get so nervous meeting people, if I didn't do this, I'd soak through my shirt and jacket."

Hiding his disbelief, Grant felt a wave of confidence come over him realizing Dave was human after all.

The upstairs first class lounge had a table for two on the left side and a table for four on the right. There was a large lounge seat in the very back shaped like a semicircle with a table in the middle. In case of a full plane, most of the upstairs seats could be used. The seats facing sideways were marked: "Not to be occupied during takeoff and landing."

Dave looked around and explained to Grant, "After getting all my tips I come up here and work on them before the seat belt sign goes off. If you don't have any questions, let's go down and get our tips."

The boarding went smoothly, and carry-on luggage was handled in a timely manner. The aisles were wide enough so passengers could pass others who were still stuffing their belongings into the overhead bins.

Trying hard to get all the tips written down, Grant barely noticed the flight attendants coming into the cross aisle where he was working. One smiled at Grant on her way to first class. He smiled back and turned to get a second look. "No," he thought, "don't screw this up," reminding himself he was lucky to have his job.

Passenger boarding slowed to a trickle and so did the tickets with possible tips. Grant took a moment to peek around the corner and look down the aisle to the rear of the plane. It was a long way to the back from where he stood. By this time, most of the passengers were in their seats. The flight attendants were passing out pillows and closing the overhead bins.

The passenger agent was coming down the Jetway with a long piece of paper in her hand. It turned out to be the final manifest with the seat assignments. Passengers who needed to be found during the meal service were listed too: kosher, special diet meals, etc.

"Ladies and Gentlemen," the agent said into the mic, "This is your final boarding announcement. This is flight 97 bound for Honolulu. If there is anyone onboard who is not going to Honolulu, this would be a good time to deplane."

She said it with a mischievous smirk and a little bounce that brought a few chuckles. She told Dave to have a good one, and then closed the door. Shortly after, the tug connected and started to gently push the plane back from the gate. Dave turned to the first flight attendant, a slim brunette with a sporty wedge cut. "Donna, we'll be upstairs if you need us." She nodded and Grant followed Dave up the spiral staircase.

The engines spooled up and the plane lumbered down the runway, rapidly picking up speed. Grant definitely had a different perspective sitting in the first class lounge. Even so far forward, Grant could still hear the landing gear come up and lock with a dull thud. They were on their way, and Grant could see the maintenance base where he once worked. He smiled to himself. Those days were over.

It was a bright day with a thin layer of low clouds. Grant could feel the large 747 climbing to meet them. He could almost feel the cold he was sure was contained in the clouds. As fast as the plane punched into the clouds, they were out, and the sun shone extremely bright. He had to squint and turned away to see Dave taking out his briefcase. Sitting across the lounge table from Dave, Grant felt a sense of importance. He took out his OAG and a piece of paper, and wrote down a couple of tips to work on. Like a kid seeking parental approval, Grant wanted Dave to see he was doing things without being told. As Grant had expected, Dave's announcement was smooth, friendly and professional and he too mentioned that Grant was onboard as a trainee.

With tip sheets in hand, both men went down the spiral staircase. The seat belt sign was still on, but the flight was smooth and the flight attendants were already up and preparing for their cocktail service.

Finally, Grant decided to take a break and walked into the first class galley area where Dave and Donna were laughing and talking while she worked. The elevator came up from the first class lower galley, called the pit. An attractive flight attendant came out of the elevator wearing an apron. Grant stepped back to give her space.

"I won't bite," she said with a smile.

Grant smiled back, but before he could think of anything clever to say, Donna interrupted. "Vicki, did you meet Grant?"

"No, but I saw him in briefing. Nice to meet you, Grant."

After they exchanged hellos, Vicki asked, "Donna, do you want some more pupus for first class?"   "Maybe some more macadamia nuts and that should do it for now."

As Vicki got in the elevator, she turned to Grant. "Would you like to take a look at the galley?"

Before Grant had a chance to answer, Dave said, "Go ahead. When you come back up, meet me in the upper lounge."

It was a small two-person elevator and Grant wasn't sure which was the right way to face. He didn't dare stand face to face, it was too close, so he stepped in and turned his back toward Vicki. It was a short ten feet down to the galley. When Grant opened the door to get out, Vicki asked, "Is this your first time in the galley?"

"No, I did some work in the galley when I worked back at the maintenance base, but this is my first time inflight."

"Let me show you around. On this side are the hot entrees and over there are the cold dishes and trays." Vicki started working as they made small talk.

She couldn't have been more pleasant, but Grant, not wanting to overstay his welcome, said, "Well, thanks for showing me the galley Vicki. I'd better get back upstairs now."

"Come back later if you want," she said with a smile. "It was nice meeting you, Grant."

Donna was still in the main deck galley when he got out of the elevator.

"What did you think?" she asked.

"Fascinating, but it sure looks like a lot of work. Vicki seems to know what she's doing."

"I love working with her. She knows what I need up here before I even have to ask."

During the movie, Grant walked through the coach section. This was the job and surroundings he knew he would come to love.

Two Hawaiian stewards added a splash of adventure to the Honolulu flights. An announcement made by one of the Hawaiian stewards was an indication the flight was almost over: "Aloha, and good afternoon, ladies and gentlemen. Welcome to our beautiful islands. My name is Daniel Kakua. In Hawaiian, Daniel is Kaniela. I was born and raised on the island of Oahu. It's always a pleasure to welcome visitors to my islands. I would like to tell you a little about my home.

"On your left is the big island of Hawaii. This is the home of one of the largest cattle ranches in the United States, the Parker ranch. For those of you visiting this island, don't miss the fish auction in Hilo. The next, smaller island is Molokai. I'm sure many of you have heard about Father Damien and the leper colony. There are still many of the descendents from the original members of that colony living on the island. If you go to Molokai, I suggest the mule ride to the bottom and the beach area.

"We'll be landing shortly, so be sure and check your seat belts. Again, thank you for flying Universal and welcome to my islands. By the way, for those of you who didn't have time to exchange your money, I can do that for you now. I'll give you one of ours for two of yours. Aloha."

The announcement drew a big laugh. The change from somber passengers departing San Francisco to eager arrivals in Honolulu was extraordinary. People were already unwinding from the rigors of their lives back on the mainland. Of course, a few Mai Tais didn't hurt.

Dave and Grant sat in the upstairs lounge.

"Do I need to be doing anything, Dave?"

"No, just enjoy the view."

On the way to the Marine Surf Hotel, Grant sat by a window in the crew van watching the camera-toting tourists walk in and out of shops along Kalakaua Avenue. Walking into the hotel lobby, and pointing to a couple of padded doors, Dave said, "If you're up to it meet me at Jamison's in about thirty minutes?"

"I'll see you there. Thanks."

Grant turned down the air conditioner in his room, paused to revel in the fact that he was indeed in Hawaii, changed out of his uniform and then left for Jamison's to meet Dave. It took a moment to adjust his eyes to the darkness in the bar. After a moment, he saw Dave with his hand in the air. As Grant slid into the booth, Dave passed a piece of paper saying, "This is the local number to call in sales. I didn't want to waste your time sitting with me while I called in today's sales. Use this number whenever you're here. It's faster than the listed one."

Dave toyed with his cocktail napkin and awkwardly said, "Grant, I think you have a knack for this job. I also think you have some disadvantages. I don't think it's anything you won't overcome, but well, there are some people out there just waiting for you to mess up. They didn't like you getting this position in the first place, but I think they'll change their minds when they find you're doing a good job."

"What kind of things would they expect me to do wrong?"

"Being single, it's easy to get involved if you're not careful. A few guys have gotten a reputation for that and they didn't last long."

"I'm aware of that and have given it a lot of thought. So, you don't date flight attendants?"

"I'm not going to say that, but you have to be careful. You'll just have to make your own rules." Dave finished his drink and said, "I hope you don't mind, but I have some things to do. I'll see you in the morning at pickup."

Grant assured Dave that he appreciated his candor; it must not have been easy for him.

Later, Grant wandered out alone to do a little sightseeing close to the hotel. He found a shopping area that sold fake Rolex watches and puka shell necklaces. He bought one of each for Gina.

On his way back to the hotel, Grant came across a narrow alley. It looked intriguing, before he realized it, he was halfway down the alley looking at trinkets in the stands of the street vendors. There were homes down the alley and small children running back and forth. One house had loud pop music emanating from it. People sat on the porch smoking and drinking. Grant couldn't tell what they were drinking, but he could sure smell what they were smoking.

A couple of the locals made remarks and laughed. Some waved, and Grant waved back. The house looked inviting and the people friendly. But this was Grant's first long haul and he needed to rest, so he headed back to the hotel.

Grant lay on his bed and thought about his conversation with Dave. He couldn't imagine having to go back to being a mechanic for behaving inappropriately. He hated the greasy flap wells and stinking fuel tanks where he'd spent far too many days as a mechanic. There was no question, he would have to park his testosterone at the airplane door. "No sex, no flap wells" would be his new self-imposed mantra.

The next morning, Grant was in the lobby early waiting for pickup. Dave and Donna came out of the elevator together. Much to Grant's surprise, Dave was wearing civilian clothes.

Anticipating Grant's question, Dave said, "Why not? You're working the trip home, and I can sit in first class and have a glass of wine." Dave didn't even go to the briefing. Donna introduced Grant as the FSD, much to his pride.

After the briefing, Grant knew there was no hurry for him to get on the plane. He spent his time getting familiar with the Honolulu office. He walked to a large window and watched their 747 on the ramp just in front of the office. Several planes from other countries sat in front of the international gates.

While he looked out the window, a Loomis armored truck pulled up on the right side of the 747 by the forward cargo pit. Two beefy guards got out and opened the back door. A man in civilian clothes stood next to them, watching. He looked somewhat out of place in his suit and tie. The guards unloaded a large box, and with the help of the ramp crew, put it in the cargo pit. The truck pulled away from the plane but remained close by on the ramp, leaving one guard, the man in the suit, and a Universal supervisor at the door to the pit. They all stayed until the door was closed. The Universal supervisor escorted the man in the suit up the outside stairs to the Jetway connected to the plane.

As Grant boarded the plane, Donna asked, "Grant, if you're going upstairs, would you please show this gun permit to the captain? I got it from Mr. Lasswell, the courier, and then got busy. I'm sorry."

"Of course, no problem."

The cockpit door was open, and Grant walked in. "Hi, Captain Schiltz, did you want this gun permit?"

"Yes, Grant, thank you." Captain Schiltz wrote down the seat number and Lasswell's name.

When he took the permit back to Donna, she asked if he could return it to Mr. Lasswell in 22C.

Grant recognized Mr. Lasswell, not from seeing him out the window before the flight, but from somewhere else; he just couldn't quite put his finger on it. With other people, he'd learned it was easier to ask rather than to wonder for days, but with a passenger he didn't think it would be appropriate. "Mr. Lasswell here's your permit."

Mr. Lasswell took it and looked at Grant's nametag. Smiling, he extended his hand. "Thank you, Grant."

Grant shook Mr. Lasswell's hand and excused himself as passengers began boarding. Grant stayed busy most of the flight making his sales. When he stopped by Dave's seat, Dave gave Grant a thumbs up and said, "Good announcement."

Grant smiled but didn't stay. He wandered by the main deck galley during the movie, then decided to go down and say hello to Vicki. The elevator was there so he got in and pressed the button. When the door to the pit opened, he didn't see Vicki anywhere. He got out of the elevator and closed the door. He waited briefly for her to return. When she didn't show up, he got in the elevator and went back up.

"Where's Vicki?" Grant asked Donna.

"Isn't she in the pit?"

"No, I was just down there."

"I'm sure she won't be gone long. Did you need her for something?"

"No, just killing time during the movie."

After landing, Vicki walked up to get her suitcase from the first class closet, and was on her way out when Grant waved to her.

"How come you didn't come down for something to eat?" she asked.

"I did come down to say hello. You weren't there."

Vicki looked a little flush and said, "I must have been up in the blue room. Well, it was nice flying with you."

"You too, Vicki, hope to see you again."

Dave walked off the plane with Grant, and told Donna he would see her in the office. As they walked down the concourse to the office, Dave said, "I really think you have a handle on this position. How do you feel about it?"

"I feel pretty good now, more comfortable with my announcements. But I'm still not sure about writing new tickets."

"You'll do fine. Why don't you go home? I'll check in at the office."

"How will I know when to come in again?"

"Don't worry, Dakota will call you."

Chapter 4

Grant couldn't wait for a call. He was pumped up from the previous flight. He almost couldn't sleep. He decided to stop by the office and was greeted by Dakota's smiling face. "Good morning, Dakota."

"Good morning, Grant."

Dakota turned to answer the phone. Grant admired her hourglass shape. She had a spectacular figure.

Ron peeked out from his office. "Grant, come see me when you have a minute." Grant stepped into Ron's office. "Dave tells me you're ready to get out on your own. Do you feel comfortable with that?"

"I think so. I'm sure I'll learn more as I go, but feel I can work a flight by myself."

"We usually like to give at least one more training flight, but we're a little shorthanded and I want to keep these flights staffed. The passengers have come to expect friendship directors onboard. In fact, I'd like you to take the all-nighter to Pittsburgh this evening. Can you do that for me?"

"Sure, I'd be happy to."

"It leaves at 11:30 getting you in around 6:30 their time. So go home and get some sleep and be back here by 10:30."

The first flight attendant, Debbie, greeted Grant at the cabin door and invited him to follow her to the back where another flight attendant was doing an inventory of the liquor. "Grant, I'd like you to meet Martha."

"Hi, Martha. How are you?"

"Not great, I hate this fucking trip."

Grant was glad she looked away after her remark. Had she not, he was certain she would have seen the dumbfounded look on his face. Grant went to his place at the first class table to make up his tip sheet. From time to time he looked up and smiled at the boarding passengers.

An hour into to the flight the service was completed and Grant worked on his sales. Before long, the lights were turned down and the steady drone of the engines lulled most of the passengers to sleep.

Grant sat down on the jump seat next to the buffet and watched Debbie and Martha pick up glasses. He sighed. This was going to be a long night. When Martha finished cleaning the buffet area, she came over to Grant and said, "Move over," and sat next to him. Her pleasant scent clashed with her earlier harsh words. Grant had dated girls who talked like her, but this wasn't a date. He reminded himself to be professional and pretended to look over his paperwork, while Martha thumbed through her Cosmopolitan. It was obvious she didn't want to talk. He realized this was a job around beautiful women, so he needed to set some ground rules; don't be aggressive, don't be pushy, and don't make sexually explicit innuendos. That only left the possibility that a flight attendant might make an obvious first move. Then what? If the office found out, he'd be back at the maintenance base in some dark, messy flap well.

Grant shook his head. He was over thinking it. Martha wasn't trying to get in his pants—she was thumbing through a magazine. He went to the cockpit to kill some time. The bright red and amber lights on the instruments transfixed Grant, as did the lights on the ground. The guys didn't say much, making it a peaceful place to take a break.

It was a short ride to the airport Howard Johnson's or Ho Jo's as the crew liked to call it. The cabin crew went into the lobby where the desk already had their keys prepared in envelopes. The cockpit crew waited until all the flight attendants and Grant had gotten their keys. Before leaving the lobby, Martha asked if anyone wanted to have breakfast. Grant was the only one interested.

"Meet me in the restaurant. I'll save you a seat," Martha said.

Grant went to his room and changed into a pair of comfortable jeans and shirt. He found Martha sitting at a table with a cup of coffee and sat across from her. She still had her uniform on but looked different in this light. She had white, unblemished skin, which softened her angular features.

They chatted about their backgrounds. Martha came from a nice family, was outspoken, but friendly, and well educated. She seemed impressed that Grant had worked his way up from being a mechanic. She offered to pay for her own breakfast, but Grant insisted on treating her. He had enjoyed spending time with her.

They walked up the stairs to the second floor. Martha unlocked her door, then turned to Grant. "I'm not too sleepy, do you want to come in and watch Good Morning America?"

"I should call in my conversions."

"Can it wait an hour?"

Grant fidgeted with his room key. "I better not. I'll see you at pickup."

Martha shrugged and opened her door. "Suit yourself then."

The flight home had a light load with few sales and lots of time to talk with passengers. Grant had a cup of tea in the galley, while Debbie and Martha sat on the jump seat reading after their service was completed. Most of the passengers were either reading or dozing.

Debbie looked up and asked, "Do you fly Honolulu much?"

Grant blew on his tea. "I did have one Honolulu trip just two days ago."

"Did you have any of the hookers on your flight?"

"What do you mean hookers?"

"Were there any Pan Am girls on your flight?"

"I think there was one. Why?"

"Because I hear a few of them are subsidizing their income on layovers."

"Are you kidding me?"

"No, I'm not. I heard it from one of my roommates who flies Honolulu."

"Do they give employee discounts?" Grant asked, hiding his smile behind his teacup.

Martha laughed. "What do you care, you wouldn't do it for free."

Obviously Martha had told Debbie about Grant not accepting her invitation to watch TV in her room. Debbie looked uncomfortable and got up to do a cabin check.

Grant put his cup down and glared at Martha. "What's that about? Are you referring to this morning?"

"What do you think?"

"I don't think I want to start a relationship just yet."

"Neither do I. It would have just been sex. Do you have a problem with that?"

"I didn't know an invitation to watch Good Morning America was an invitation for sex. I feel pretty lucky to have this job, and I don't want to screw it up by trying to get laid."

"Well, good for you. You're the only one."

"Are you telling me some of the other guys are sleeping with flight attendants?"

"That's what I hear, except for some of the married ones."

"That's what you hear or that's what you know?" he asked sarcastically.

Martha stood up and moved closer to Grant. "Both." Then she turned around and followed Debbie.

Grant was surprised to see his mailbox half full. He'd been gone less than a day. He walked to Ron's office and knocked on the open door. Ron was working on a large schedule he had on an easel.

"Come on in Grant, I'm putting some schedules together. Do you think you would be comfortable with a Honolulu trip?"

"I think so," Grant said, unconvincingly.

"I could set up another training flight if you'd like."

"No, I really think I can do it."

"I could use you on 181 on Saturday coming back on 97 on Sunday."

"Doesn't the 181 crew work the red eye flight 22 coming back?"

"They do, but I like to see our people get more rest than the crew gets on that trip."

"I'll be here."

"Check-in is at 7:30. Thanks Grant."

Grant approached the crew elevator and found two flight attendants wearing colorful Hawaiian dresses waiting as well.

"Are you working 181 to Honolulu?" Grant asked.

"Yes we are," one of them answered. "What trip are you working?"

"Same one," Grant said as they entered the elevator.

When the elevator door opened, Grant said, "I'll see you in briefing. I'm Grant by the way."

"Nice to meet you Grant, I'm Barbara."

"And I'm Pat," the other said. They exchanged smiles.

It was easy for Grant to spot the Honolulu briefing, as the room was crowded with flight attendants dressed in their colorful Hawaiian uniforms. No one seemed to notice Grant as he entered the room. The supervisor did most of the talking, much to the displeasure of the crew. The supervisor briefly introduced Grant and only Pat's friendly smile stood out as he caught her eye. He smiled back and his heart leapt.

Grant sat in the upper lounge and waited for take off. He watched out the window for the tug to hook up. A hearse pulling away from the forward cargo pit made him queasy, which he soon forgot when he felt a small bump as the tug hooked up to the plane. The engines started up and he could only imagine what was going on behind the closed cockpit door.

As the plane pulled onto runway 28 right, Grant looked down the entire length of the two and a quarter mile-long runway. The nose was almost to the other side of the runway before the captain turned to line the 747 up with the centerline. The plane started to gain speed; the acceleration was so strong it forced Grant back in his seat. The tires thumped over the cracks in the runway as they gained momentum. Before the 747 was abeam the main terminal, the nose lifted, followed shortly by the main landing gear. A solid thump indicated the wheels were up and locked.

The giant 747 started a shallow left turn but not until it had passed the Golden Gate Bridge. Grant had crossed it many times, but none of those crossings were comparable to this. The plane gently climbed to a cruising altitude of 40,000 feet.

Before getting organized, Grant decided to go down and see Pat. He'd liked her from the moment they'd met. He got in the small elevator and went down to the lower galley. Pat was pushing buttons and setting up carts, her chestnut hair pulled back into a ponytail.

Grant cleared his throat to get her attention. "Is it okay if I sit back here and get prepared? I'll stay out of your way."

Pat flashed him a warm smile. "Sure, and you're not in my way. I'll be caught up in a minute."

Grant sat back for a few minutes and admired Pat as she went about her work. He had finally managed to focus on his tip sheet when he heard barking. Pat caught his puzzled expression and without being asked, she explained, "There's a dog in the forward cargo pit. You can slide open the aluminum door and take a look if you want."

Grant opened the door and stepped through. A dog kennel stood just inside the pit with a note on top that read: "My name is Sky and I'm very friendly." It also had the name of a passenger. The pit was dark, and as Grant's eyes adjusted, he was taken aback to see a dark wooden coffin on the other side of the kennel. Looking back to Sky, he touched the dog's nose and spoke soothingly before exiting and closing the door.

Pat looked up when Grant came back. "What's the matter, did you see a ghost?"

"Almost, there's a coffin in there. I knew they put them there. I just didn't want to know about it. I better get back upstairs and start working first class."

"Sure, scare the hell out of me and leave. You better come back and check on me."

"I will."

"Promise?"

"Yes, I promise."

Grant stepped out the elevator just as the inflight supervisor, Gloria, brushed past him. He could overhear her telling Joanne that the second coffees weren't done in the proper time frame. Joanne didn't say anything at first and then asked Gloria exactly what she wanted her to do.

"Have a couple of carts come down the aisle with second coffees."

"Why can't we just take coffee orders and bring them on trays? Not that many people have second coffees."

"We need to do it like the service procedures call for."

Grant finished his ticket sales in the upper lounge, and then he went down the staircase to the main deck. Gloria was ensconced on the jump seat, taking notes.

"How's it going?" she asked. "Making any money?"

"Not enough to pay my salary so far."

"I'm sorry if I seemed short back there. It's not easy enforcing company rules. I just can't turn my head when some flight attendants don't want to follow serving procedures. The fact is, I'm thinking of going back to being a flight attendant myself."

"I thought being a supervisor was a good job?"

"It could be, with the right crews. Some flight attendants just don't want us onboard."

Grant gave her a sympathetic smile. With thoughts of Pat still lingering, he went to the pit for a visit. Pat was busy cleaning and Grant could tell this wasn't a good time. "I'll see you upstairs after we land."

She smiled. "Hope so."

After most of the passengers deplaned, Grant said good bye to the pilots and walked off with Barbara and Pat. "It was nice meeting you both. I wish you were going back with me tomorrow."

Grant was into his third drink at Jamison's when an attractive girl in a beige dress sat next to him. She frowned and tapped her little feet nervously.

Grant kept looking around the room hoping to find a familiar face. Finally, the girl leaned toward him, her neckline billowing to give Grant an enticing view of her generous bosom, and discreetly asked, "Excuse me sir, are you looking for a little company?"

Taken aback, Grant sputtered, "Why are you asking me that?"

She pushed back her dark hair. "You just look lonely."

Her profession dawned on him, but he couldn't stop himself from asking, "Do you work for Universal?"

"What?"

"Did you come to Universal from Pan Am?"

"What the hell are you talking about?"

The bartender saved Grant when he came over and motioned with his head toward the door. The girl grabbed her change and said, "I'm Marleen, I'll be across the street or at Mateo's if you want some company."

The bartender blurted after her, "And stay out."

Feeling dumb and alone, Grant decided to go watch television in his room. As he was leaving Jamison's, he saw Vicki sitting with someone he didn't recognize at first. With a second look, he realized he had seen the man and Vicki sitting together on his first Honolulu trip.

Grant pushed the button and the elevator door opened. His heart skipped a beat when he saw Pat.

"Pat, what are you doing here? I thought you were deadheading home."

"Only one of us could deadhead home and Barbara wanted to get back."

"If I can buy you a drink, we'll talk about Sky and the coffin."

"I'm still trying to forget about that."

"Come on, let's grab something to eat."

They walked into Jamison's and to Grant's pleasure Pat reached for his hand. "Sorry, I didn't want to lose you in the dark," she said.

"And I thought you were starting to like me." Pat didn't see the smile Grant had on his face.

The pair were hardly settled in their booth when the cocktail waitress, Lonnie, came to their table. Lonnie was an exotic-looking native of Hawaii with long dark hair and sparkling teeth. Grant had met her on his training flight. Dave had explained to him it would have been futile to pursue anything with Lonnie. Others had tried, and were politely rejected. Grant left her good tips and kept his distance.

"Hi Grant, you weren't gone long. What would you two like this evening?"

"What are you having?" Pat asked Grant.

"I like their Manhattans."

"I'll try one of those too."

"Two Manhattans, coming up."

"What did she mean, you weren't gone long?" Pat asked.

"I was in here having a drink before I decided to go upstairs."

"You were here all alone?"

"Most of the time, except for when a hooker tried to pick me up."

"What happened to her?"

"The bartender kicked her out."

"How did that make you feel?"

"What are you, some kind of psychology student?" They laughed as Lonnie arrived with their Manhattans. Grant held up his drink. "Cheers! It's been nice flying with you."

"You too." She took a sip of her drink. "Wow! This is strong, but tasty."

"That was a nice surprise seeing you come out of the elevator."

"I wasn't as surprised to see you. I knew you would be staying here."

She must have thought about him too, Grant surmised. They were almost finished when Lonnie returned.

"Can I get you another round?"

"I'm not sure," Grant said, looking at Pat. "Do you want another?"

"I should eat, but maybe one more. These are good. Have you eaten already?"

"Actually, no, I was going to have an artichoke later. But if you're hungry, I'll take you to dinner."

"Where were you going for an artichoke?"

"Here, they're delicious and almost a meal in itself."

Lonnie came back with their drinks. Pat was enjoying hers, but Grant could tell she should have something to eat. She nibbled the cherries in her drink, along with his while they flirted.

"Why don't we go someplace and get something to eat?" Grant asked.

"I think that artichoke sounds tasty. Let's do that. Besides, I had a big lunch on the plane."

Grant motioned politely to Lonnie, who came right over. He ordered two artichokes and two glasses of white wine. He was feeling the Manhattans on his empty stomach and he could tell Pat was too.

"Two artichokes and two white wines coming up," Lonnie said.

Vicki and her male companion got up and were leaving by the door leading out to the street. She looked over, but before Grant could smile or wave, she looked away.

"Hmmm," he mumbled.

"What's the matter?"

"I had a trip with that flight attendant who just left. I think she recognized me, but she didn't wave or say hello."

"You mean Vicki?"

"Yeah, do you know her? When did you see her?"

"I saw her in the lobby earlier and then sitting over there with that courier guy."

"You know him?"

"Not really, but he's been on a couple of my flights. I've had to ask him for his gun permit for the captain."

Two huge artichokes arrived with the white wine. Pat and Grant dipped the leaves in a butter-mayonnaise-garlic sauce. Between bites, Grant asked, "Tell me all about Pat. Where do you come from? Where does your family live? How did you become a flight attendant?"

"That's a lot of questions." She took a bite. "Let's see, I'm from Saratoga, California, and my dad worked for the railroad. I used to baby-sit for a neighbor who was a captain for Universal. He said I should apply to be a flight attendant and gave me a good recommendation. Other than the irregular days and hours, I love it."

"Any boyfriends in your life?"

"Not now, I did date a guy who had a Monday through Friday job. With my schedule, it just didn't work."

"Just one more, I promise." Grant wanted to know all about her. "Where do you live?"

"I live in Sausalito with a nice view overlooking the bay."

"Sounds beautiful, I love Sausalito. Do you ever go to Zacks?"

"When friends come to visit, we go there or Scoma's. There are a lot of great places to eat and drink."

"I used to go to Sally Stanford's Valhalla restaurant. Have you been there?"

"Yes I have, but I'm now getting worried about you and prostitutes."

They laughed and Grant said, "Sadly, I was too young for Sally's hay day. It was intriguing seeing Sally Stanford sitting at the end of the bar. It's almost hard to believe she was such a famous madam."

"I hear she's running for the city council. Maybe someday she'll be our mayor."

They sipped the wine and ate every bite of the artichokes. Grant enjoyed the conversation and the laughter as much as the food. He asked, "What trip are you working tomorrow?"

"The 9:00 A.M. with a 7:15 pickup. In fact, I better get some rest. Didn't you say you were working 97 at 1:30?"

"I am, but I wish I was on your flight."

"Why is that?"

"I could come down to the pit to see you."

Pat blushed. "Since you won't be on my flight, and I most likely won't be working the pit, I'll make you a deal."

"What kind of a deal?"

"If you walk me to my room, I'll give you a hug."

"If I can't be on your trip, that'll have to do."

Grant raised the tab and caught Lonnie's attention. Pat put her small purse on the table and took out her wallet. "Here, let me chip in."

"No way, it's my treat."

"This could become a very expensive habit if you do this on every layover."

"I won't. But I have enjoyed your company."

When they got into the elevator, Grant asked, "What floor, ma'am?"

Pat smiled and said, "Three, please."

"Me too, we have a lot in common."

At this point, Grant wasn't sure what to think or do. He could still feel the drinks and wondered how Pat felt. The food helped a little, but it didn't make all the thoughts racing through his head any clearer.

"Here we are," Pat said.

"Well then, I've earned my hug."

Pat opened the door, turned on the light, walked in a few steps and turned around. Grant followed and put his arms around her. Her thick brown hair was aromatic and its gentle touch on his face excited him. He kissed her gently on the cheek. She reached over his shoulder and pushed the door with just the right momentum. It closed without slamming. She put her arm back around him. He kissed her cheek again and slowly pulled back. They gazed deeply into each other's eyes, then kissed passionately.

It was an evening of incredible passion and it felt so natural. They lay on top of the sheets and he took in her firm, perky breasts and narrowed waist, accentuated by the flair of her hips down the length of her supple legs. He started feeling a little awkward and fell shyly silent. He propped himself up on one elbow and looked into Pat's warm blue eyes. She was so wholesome and radiant. They smiled and kissed again.

"I would like for you to stay, but I have an early wake up call. And you would have to get up and go to your room anyway."

"I wouldn't mind staying, but I better let you get some rest. Besides, I snore sometimes. May I call you some time?"

"I'd like that." Pat got up and put on a red robe. She wrote her number down and handed it to Grant with vigor. He left after one last kiss.

Grant went to bed thinking of Pat. He had been with his share of women, but this felt different. The evening had been magical. He wondered if it would become something more.

The next day at briefing, the only person Grant recognized was Vicki. Not knowing any one else, Grant went down to the pit to visit Vicki during the inflight movie. He wondered if she would say anything about being in Jamison's. When he entered the pit, Vicki wasn't there. He assumed she was up using the blue room. He decided he'd just wait awhile for her to come back. He looked around, got some leftover snacks and sat on the jump seat. He didn't give it much thought when someone pressed the elevator button and it went up, thinking it must be Vicki. Grant was startled when the aluminum door to the forward cargo compartment rolled open and Vicki came out, a stunned expression on her face when she caught sight of Grant. Just then the elevator started back down. Neither of them had a chance to say anything before Karen got off the elevator and came into the pit. "What's left over? I could use a bite."

Vicki showed Karen the food that hadn't been served. Karen asked Grant if he wanted to share a meal. He told her he had just finished and was going back upstairs. Vicki looked down and cast her eyes away. Grant wondered what she had been doing in the cargo pit. If she was just curious, why didn't she leave the door open? He put these questions out of his mind and focused on the rest of the flight.

Grant went to the office after landing and was surprised to be the only one there. He checked his mailbox and found two letters attached to a picture of an orchid and a handwritten note: "Grant, this letter speaks for its self. You are making a good impression with our customers. Keep up the good work, Ron."

There was a light tap on the open door, and Grant turned to see Vicki standing there looking a little frazzled.

"You got a minute?"

"Sure, have a seat. What's going on?"

"I just wanted to tell you why I was in the cargo pit."

"I'm not sure it's any of my business, but I am curious."

"Maybe not, but you're in management and I want you to know."

"What do you want me to know?"

"I have a bad back. The doctor gave me a prescription for some pain killers. I brought another suitcase with me because I was buying a lot of gifts. When I was packing for the trip, I put the medicine in the wrong suitcase. When I came down the Jetway, the agent offered to put my extra bag in the forward pit. Anyway, my back was killing me, and I was in there looking for my bag and the pills."

"That's quite a story."

"What do you mean by that?"

"Just that, it's quite a story."

"You don't believe me?"

"I didn't say that. It's just an interesting chain of events."

"Well, I better get going. I just wanted you to know."

"Thanks for coming by."

It seemed the more Vicki talked, the shakier her story became. Grant didn't know what to think, but he knew it didn't feel right. He thought she should have cut her losses when he said it was none of his business.

Grant continued going through his mail. There was a sealed envelope with his name on top. "Dear Grant, Hope you had a nice trip home. I just wanted to say I enjoyed our time together. I hope you didn't get the wrong idea. I don't normally behave like that. I'm not sorry I did, but just wanted you to know. I guess I could blame those great Manhattans, but that wouldn't be true. Hope to see you on another trip. Maybe we'll run into each other at Zack's or Sally's. Affectionately, Pat."

The note made Grant's day. He definitely had feelings for her and maybe, just maybe, she felt the same.

Chapter 5

T he next three months were terrific. Grant's only regret was that he and Pat hadn't gotten together again.

Grant received 22 more complimentary letters—called Orchid letters in the flight industry. He made friends with hotel people, bartenders, waitresses, and, of course, flight attendants. He felt secure in his position. So when Grant walked into the office early for a Pittsburgh flight with a 33-hour layover, he was surprised to see Ron, Bill and a couple of long time friendship service directors in a deep conversation. It was far too early to see them in the office. Bill, who was standing at the front of the table, saw him first. "Grant, come in and have a seat." No one said anything. Grant wondered what was wrong.

Catching Grant up to speed, Bill explained, "I was just telling these guys the inflight program is in for a big change. Behind the scenes, we have been fighting to see which department will be accountable for onboard management. We have been going around with upper management for months on this one, and inflight services won out. The inflight program will be administered under the umbrella of inflight services. There has been a lot of dialogue at all levels. Most importantly, there are those who no longer want two management people onboard. Initially, the supervisors were onboard to keep the service procedures consistent. When it appeared most flight attendants knew the service, they started doing inflight evaluations on the flight attendants. This is something they want to continue, along with sales."

Grant was in shock. He looked around the table and saw the same look reflected back at him. Bill went on. "Bob Bittman will be meeting with all the friendship service directors. There will be three meetings to accommodate those of you who are working trips. The first meeting will be the day after tomorrow." Bob Bittman was the vice-president of customer service. The friendship service director program was under his department's organization.

When Bill was done, the men got up and walked into the mailroom. Dakota obviously knew what was going on. Her usual smile was gone and had been replaced with a glum look. Nobody said anything. Grant tried to look through his mail but couldn't grasp what was happening or going to happen.

One of the friendship service directors, Rob, addressed Grant, "What trip are you flying?"

"I have the Pittsburgh trip with the 33-hour layover."

"That's the reason I came in early. I was wondering if you wouldn't mind trading with me."

"I thought I was the only guy who liked that trip."

"You are, but I need to see my folks. They live just outside of Pittsburgh."

"What trip do you have?"

"Honolulu 181, coming back on 97 tomorrow."

"Sure, I'll trade with you. That way I can go to the first meeting on Tuesday."

"Are you in a big hurry for the bad news?"

"Maybe they will change their minds by then. I don't think they can get rid of this program."

"Grant, you're in denial big time."

"I love this job."

"I think we can kiss this job goodbye."

Grant went to the Honolulu briefing room. He was early for the briefing. There were only three flight attendants in the room. Grant sat at the big round table facing away from the door. A pair of soft hands covered his eyes. "Guess who?"

"Pat is the only one I can hope for." It was her. He got up, turned and gave Pat a warm, intimate hug. The room was starting to fill so Grant told Pat he was going to sit in the back and make room for the flight attendants. His beating heart confirmed his thrill at seeing Pat again. To top off his excitement, Pat seemed more than pleased to see him as well. Grant felt he had been killing time with his romantic interludes, waiting for the right woman to come along, he wondered, could this be her.

Grant walked to the plane with Pat. He was glad he had left a couple of messages on her answering machine and some notes in her mailbox. As they got on the plane together, Pat said, "Just like when we met, I'm working the pit and have to go check the buffet and get the pre-departure ready for first class. Come down later and have a snack."

"And a hug too?"

She smiled. "Of course."

Judy Grimes was the inflight supervisor. Grant had flown with her before and knew she was liked by most of the flight attendants. He tried to put the meeting with Bill in the back of his mind but it was no easy task. He wondered if the inflight supervisors would be affected as well.

Grant got all of his tips written down and headed up to the lounge for departure. No matter how many times he'd done it, he just loved the San Francisco departure. They took off on runway 28 right and made another perfect left turn over the Golden Gate Bridge. This was something he would never take for granted. The flight was barely over the rugged, uninhabited Farallone Islands when Judy startled him by sitting down across from him. "Mind if I join you?"

"Not at all. Let's sit at the big table."

"Can I get you a cup of coffee?"

"Make mine tea."

She made Grant a cup of tea, set it on the table, and sat down with her coffee. "So, tell me, how hard is it to sell tickets?" Judy asked.

"Why do you ask?"

"Haven't you heard? They're combining our two jobs."

"I just did this morning but had the feeling I was hearing it before it was public knowledge."

"That's what I thought too, but not so. I think most of the supervisors know, at least the ones I've talked with."

"How are they dealing with it?"

"Some are going back to flying. They don't want to have the pressure of making sales. They don't want to deal with rejection."

"Maybe that's why guys are good at this; we're used to rejection. I know I am."

She laughed lightly and twitched her nose. "That's not what I heard."

"What do you mean, that's not what you heard? What did you hear?"

"I heard you don't get rejected all that much, nor do you reject."

He wasn't sure what to say. He'd always been more than discrete. "What exactly are you talking about?"

"Don't get your feathers up. What do you think is going on out here? You are well liked but a little naïve."

"Why, because I'm concerned about losing this job?"

"It's no different for any of us. Obviously, as a supervisor, I have to be a lot more careful than when I was a flight attendant, but I like a good time, too."

"I just never heard anything said about me before. I'm surprised."

"I've never heard anything bad, so I wouldn't worry about it."

"What else have you heard? About our jobs."

"Just that they are going to combine our jobs and the new position will be under inflight service."

"What are you going to do?"

"That's why I was asking about selling. I think I want to stay."

"If you want to give it a try, I'll show you what to do."

"What do you mean, give it a try?"

"Mr. and Mrs. Belton in 2A and B have a return on TWA next Tuesday. I'll tell you what to say and you can try to get them to fly back with us." Grant showed Judy the Universal flight leaving a half hour earlier that the Belton's could catch. The flight was a 747 instead of the L10-11 with TWA. "Talk about our upstairs lounge. Give them a free pass for a one-time visit to the VIP Club. There's a good chance they'll come back on Universal. Tell me, how many of the supervisors do you think will give up this job if they had a choice?" Grant asked.

"I heard around five so far. What are you going to do?"

"I don't know yet. We're having a couple of meetings next week."

"Would you want to be a supervisor?"

"If that's the only choice I have to keep flying. Is it very difficult?"

"You have to know a lot about the contract, appearance standards, and service procedures. And you'll have to write letters if a flight attendant needs one in her file."

"What kind of letters?"

"For example, if they use too much sick leave, get an onion letter, don't meet uniform standards, the list goes on."

It didn't sound like it was an easy job to Grant, but it looked easy watching supervisors on the plane. He let Judy talk to the Beltons and he did the rest. He was starting to feel his days were numbered. He would almost rather die than go back to the maintenance base. He's had a taste for the first time in his life, of looking forward to going to work.

The flight was going smoothly, other than moments of panic about the tenuous status of his job. After getting all his conversions, and congratulating Judy on hers, he went down to the first class pit to see Pat. There was one flight attendant finishing her meal. She left shortly after he arrived. Pat and Grant looked at each other, smiled, walked together, and hugged. Grant leaned back, looked at her, and they kissed. He didn't intend for it to be so passionate, but it was wonderful.

"You must think I'm terribly easy, don't you?" Pat asked.

"Do you think I'm terribly easy?"

"Yes."

"Well, at least one of us is right."

They heard the elevator coming down and stole one last quick kiss. It was obviously an overture of something to come later. Pat's demeanor endeared her to Grant. Judy stepped out of the elevator, and Grant took that opportunity to thank Pat for the snack he never had and left.

The flight cruised along. Grant walked around the plane and paid a few visits to the cockpit and around the cabin. He really didn't know what to do after he had all his conversions. Grant always felt comfortable and enjoyed talking with people but didn't know if that had a value to the company. People said it did. If so, why am I and the other friendship service directors possibly on our way out, he wondered.

Grant went back to the pit to visit Pat. She had a way of making him forget his worries and she was quickly becoming etched onto his consciousness. When the elevator door opened, it looked like Pat had everything organized. He couldn't wait to touch her, hold her, kiss her—it felt so right. They kissed, as if for the first time.

"Why don't you come to the baggage area on the Wiki Wiki bus and ride to the hotel with me?" Grant suggested.

"I need to go to the crew desk for just a minute, and I can meet you there."

"Okay, I'll wait for you."

The baggage area was empty by the time Pat showed up. They found a cab and got in the back seat. Pat looked unbelievably fresh for having just worked a trip in the overheated pit. He gently, but firmly, took her hand, raised it up to his eager lips and kissed it. He couldn't get enough of her. He felt she wanted him as much as he wanted her. They kissed again.

Grant and Pat knew it was obvious to those sitting in the lobby that they came in the same cab. The windows were large and looked onto the street in front of the hotel. They both knew people sitting in the lobby but the curious looks they were expecting never came. In the elevator Grant asked, "Why don't you stay in my room?"

"I'd like that, but I have a 10:30 pickup this evening."

"I know. If I went to your room, I would have to go back to mine anyway."

"If you don't mind me waking you for my pickup."

"Just kiss me goodbye before you leave."

They went to Grant's room and before the door had closed he had pulled Pat into his arms. They made love and afterwards, fell asleep in each other's arms. Their nap was brief, just enough for them to desire each other again. They showered and went for a bite to eat. They lay down so

Pat could get some rest after lunch but there was no way they could just go to sleep. Their embrace was warm and their nerves prickled at the slightest touch. It was the most romantic lovemaking Grant had ever had.

Later, Grant and Pat discussed the possibility of him having to go back to the maintenance base. She seemed to think it wouldn't happen. He admired her optimistic outlook, but didn't feel as confident.

Pat's alarm went off at nine o'clock. They made love one more time and then Pat took a shower while Grant dozed off. He woke to see her dressing. She looked radiant in her green, yellow, and red kimu. She came over to kiss him goodbye. Grant reached out to pull her onto the bed.

"No, let's not start this," Pat protested.

He smiled and sat up. "Let me walk you down."

"I thought you were trying to be careful not to be seen with hot little flight attendants."

"First, I don't think of you as a 'hot little flight attendant.' You are, but I don't think of you that way. I just don't want anyone to get the wrong idea about you. Or us."

"You can stay here if you want or come down. It's not a problem for me."

"Perhaps I should stay here. I don't want to complicate anything."

"Whatever you feel most comfortable with."

Grant kissed Pat in the hallway while waiting for her elevator. Pat wore her hair down. Grant could smell her, just like he could when they were making love.

Grant felt terrible about the way they had parted. He felt he was trying to protect her, but from what he wondered. Was he really trying to protect himself from looking like he was dating a flight attendant against all good advice. Considering how he felt about Pat, he was almost willing to take that chance. He continued to think about it as he walked into Jamison's. Lonnie was sitting next to the waitress station, so he sat on the other side.

"Hi Lonnie, are you working this evening?"

"Hi, Grant. No, I'm out on the town this evening. When did you get in? And where are all those pretty girls I usually see you with?"

"I got in this morning and leave tomorrow afternoon. The crew I flew in with is just now leaving."

Jamison's was quiet. Grant bought Lonnie a drink and had his usual Manhattan while he stewed about Pat. His guilt grew as he saw the crew bus pull away from the alley. So what if people knew about he and Pat.

Grant thought about the meeting the day after tomorrow. What was going to happen with his position? He just couldn't believe it might be over. He tried to put that thought behind him and had a few more drinks. He had far too much on his mind.

"So Lonnie, is this a bus driver's holiday for you?"

"What's a bus driver's holiday?"

"I think it's when a bus driver goes for a ride on his day off. In your case, when you come to the place where you work on your day off."

"I'm just stopping by before going to a party."

"Hope you don't drink too many of those tequilas before you drive."

"Actually, I came in a cab and the party is just down the alley. Maybe you'd like to come with me? You don't have to stay and it's only a short walk back."

"Sure, sounds like fun."

Grant sucked down the rest of his Manhattan and ate the cherry. He was starting to get hungry.

"Are you hungry, Lonnie?"

"A little, but I'm sure they'll have some pupus at the party."

They walked out the front door and down the stairs to the alley. Grant saw the hooker standing across the street and remembered how he had thought she was an ex-Pan Am flight attendant.

With her hair worn casually down, Lonnie looked nice in her form-fitting Hawaiian dress.

To Grant's surprise, they stopped in front of the same house where people had yelled something to him the first time he was here. Loud music was playing and a lot of people mingled on the porch. A bit apprehensive, Grant followed Lonnie up the stairs to the front porch. Several people smiled and greeted her.

"Hey, Lonnie, who's your Haole friend?"

"This is Grant Guidera, he works for Universal."

"Aloha ahiahi, I'm Keoki, George where you come from. Your name is Keli in Hawaiian." Keoki beamed, he was obviously proud of his Hawaiian genealogy and the knowledge of translating from English to Hawaiian. Lonnie hugged him and laughed and he instructed her, "Go on inside and get some maik'i pakalolo."

The house was bigger than it looked from the outside. There was a lot of smoke coming out the open front door, through which they walked to see people sitting on the floor around the room. As noisy as it was, Grant could make out the rattling of a bamboo curtain leading to a room with a dim red light inside. The kitchen was just across from the red light room.

"Didn't Keoki say there was some food inside?" Grant asked.

Lonnie laughed, "No, he said there was some maik'i pakalolo."

"Sounds like food to me."

"I guess you could eat it, but these people are smoking the good marijuana—that's what it is."

"Oh okay. I'm just a dumb Haole, but I think I'd rather have something to drink."

"I'm sure they'll have some wine in the kitchen."

Lonnie led Grant into the crowded kitchen and worked her way towards the sink, where a bar had been set up. Grant poured a large glass of white wine and leaned nonchalantly against the blue-and-white tiled wall to take in the scenery. Lonnie asked if he'd be all right and said she wanted to mingle. Grant didn't have a problem being left alone and lost himself to his thoughts. He looked around and saw a few available-looking girls. At this point, it didn't matter. Pat was heavy on his mind.

Grant walked through the bamboo curtain and looked around the dimly lit room. His stomach jumped, and he sucked in his breath when he saw Vicki sitting on the floor, totally engrossed with Brian Lasswell. Neither noticed Grant. They had their own little group, passing around a joint. Grant didn't want to be seen by them. It had been over three months since he'd had that uncomfortable conversation in the office with Vicki.

Grant found Lonnie talking with a small group and caught her attention. When she came to him, he asked, "If you're all right and don't mind, I think I'll head back to the hotel after I get a bite to eat."

"Is there something wrong? You look upset."

"No, I'm just a little drunk and a lot hungry. I'm going to get some sushi. Do you want to go?"

"I think I'll stay here, I don't have to work tomorrow. When are you coming back to town?"

"I'm not sure yet. Thanks for bringing me. I had a nice time." Grant hugged her and walked out. He said goodbye to Keoki on the way down the stairs.

"All right Keli, come again next time you're in town. You have some pakalolo?"

"Next time, thanks."

Grant enjoyed the warm night air. He was sobering up as he walked into the sushi bar. The staff bowed slightly and sang out their greeting: "Irashaimasen."

Grant sat back in his chair and felt the tension from seeing Vicki at the party subside. He picked up his drink, and turned his attention to the street, watching the tourists and locals mingle. Marleen caught his eye as she paused on the corner and he wondered why she became a hooker, with her attractive face and killer body. As he mulled this over, his sushi arrived and he dove in with a ravenous appetite. Grant finished his sashimi and California rolls, sopping up the last of the wasabi-soy sauce mix with his last bite. He got up and said, "Sayonara" as he pulled open the door. The sushi chef and waitress bowed their heads and replied, "Itarashai," meaning, "take care" in Japanese.

As Grant started walking toward the hotel, Marleen saw him and crossed the street at an angle to intercept him. "Hi there, would you like a little company?"

"As tempting as that is, I think I'll pass this evening."

"I could show you a real nice time."

"Maybe another time."

Grant fell asleep thinking of Pat, wondering how she felt about him.

The next day as the crew bus started pulling out of the alley someone yelled, "Wait!" The flight crew all turned to see Vicki running down the stairs, her blonde locks bobbing. She was a mess. She got on the bus with a quick "Thank you" to the driver. She flashed an embarrassed smile to the other flight attendants as she walked toward the back of the bus. She seemed nervous.

The briefing was led by Carolyn who closed the meeting, saying, "The only thing significant on the manifest is an armed courier in 27B; his name is Mr. Lasswell." A couple of the flight attendants glanced Vicki's way. Vicki didn't acknowledge them with any kind of reaction. Then Gloria, the supervisor, said something about the service procedures, which was greeted with a collective group groan.

Onboard, entering the buffet area, Grant could see Carolyn was visibly upset. He wasn't sure if he should stay or leave. He didn't want her to think he didn't care, so he stayed. He stood back feeling helpless, watching her throw things around and shoving carts into the elevator.

"Vicki's getting worse each trip," Carolyn complained. "I used to love working with her, but she's fucking up the entire service."

Gloria walked into the buffet a moment later. She instantly noticed that something was amiss. "Carolyn, is something wrong?" Gloria asked.

"I just got a little behind. It'll be fine." Carolyn pushed the button for the elevator and it came up with the same cart she had just sent down. Carolyn didn't say anything, but Grant could tell she was upset about the cart. Gloria took the cart out and got in the elevator, telling Carolyn to send the cart down. Once Gloria removed the cart from the elevator, she came back up and asked, "Where's Vicki?"

Carolyn replied, "I thought she was down there, maybe she went to the blue room while I was in first class."

Gloria left the buffet without saying a word. Carolyn was wiping the counters when the elevator went down, startling both her and Grant. They were even more surprised to see Vicki coming up. She rushed out, saying she needed to go to the blue room.

"How the hell did Gloria not see her?" Carolyn asked.

Grant thought he knew the answer to that one, but shrugged his shoulders and left the buffet. When the flight was over, Grant stood alongside Carolyn and bid farewell to the passengers as they deplaned.

Grant went to the office, checked his mail, and called in his sales. In his mailbox was an official notice about the up coming meetings. They were going to have two each day for the next three days. Grant anxiously looked through his mail for a note from Pat. He had a sinking feeling but there it was—a small envelope among all the junk mail. "Grant, I enjoyed our trip together, hope to see you soon." It was short, but oh-so-sweet.

Pat's brief note was one bright spot among Grant's negative feelings as he left the office. He walked past the inflight office and saw the door open to the large supervisor area. Gloria was sitting in a cubicle with Vicki, who appeared to be crying. Grant wasn't sure who to feel sorry for, Gloria or Vicki. Being a supervisor couldn't be easy.

When he got home, Grant poured a straight shot of bourbon into a glass of ice. He took his shoes and tie off, sat in a soft armchair, and looked out his window over the San Mateo Peninsula. With the time change, it was around 10:30 P.M. and the lights were beautiful. He sat for some time and watched planes take off and land. He could see planes leaving from both San Francisco and the Oakland Airports. He truly enjoyed the great view from his house.

Grant didn't set the clock but still woke up in plenty of time for the first meeting. He took a shower and made some toast and tea, then called Pat, only to leave a message on her machine.

Arriving early, Grant went to the office to check his mail. It seemed everyone who wasn't going on a trip had the same idea. There was a lot of hand shaking; Bill and Ron came out of their offices. It was evident they were trying to keep an optimistic outlook. Bill walked to the door, turned and said, "Let's go to the manager's meeting."

Bob Bittman towered over the conference table at six-foot-five. He was a friendly, upbeat kind of guy. The fact was, if Grant didn't know Bob was a vice-president, he never would have guessed it.

Bob was standing in front of the room, greeting everyone who walked in. There were about twenty-five people sitting in the room—some in their powder blue uniform jackets. Finally, Bob looked around, sat down and said, "I guess we better get started."

A late arrival showed up, saying, "Sorry."

"That's okay, get the door behind you. By now most of you know why we're here. I guess it's no secret there has been an internal battle going on for several months. It has become apparent that two management people onboard our airplanes are no longer necessary. I can't argue with that now, although I did a few months back. Once the decision was made, the question became which department would manage the program. Needless to say, I felt that we—customer service—should, and I believe we made a pretty good case to that end. I'm sorry to say, the decision didn't go our way.

"I've been so proud of all of you and our program. I even brought a number of the many orchid letters we received from passengers to some of the meetings. But the real problem became how to define the new position and what sort of selection process to use. Combined, there are over seventy supervisors and friendship service directors presently on flying status. The new position will be given new responsibilities and job description. There will be interviews and thirty-five people will be selected. While customer service will no longer be accountable for the new program, we will help to define it. It appears the focus is more on management than sales, but those things can change."

A dark cloud had descended on the room. Some of the newer friendship service directors had just relocated to San Francisco from other stations. Bob said the company would do their best to accommodate them with a position at SFO. Many were downright pissed off and weren't bashful about expressing their opinions. Grant tried to be philosophical about it, hoping that maybe he would be selected for the new position.

After the meeting, Bob approached Grant and shook his hand. "Grant you've done a good job here. At least if you don't get the job, you will get a pay raise when you go back to being a mechanic. I understand the union got them several raises since you've been here."

"If nothing else, I've learned that money isn't as important as being happy," Grant replied.

✈ ✈ ✈

It was early afternoon, and Grant didn't have a clue where to go. He left the parking lot feeling depressed and indecisive. He found himself going out 19th Avenue toward the Golden Gate Bridge, which, when completed in 1937, was the largest suspension bridge in the world.

He stoically drove across the 4,200-foot main span of the bridge and parked in the north side observation area. It was a spectacular view, but he was unsettled. He drove aimlessly toward Sausalito and pulled into Valhalla's parking lot. He entered the atrium area dividing the restaurant from the bar and chose the bar. The matronly Sally Stanford was sitting in her barber chair at the end of the bar, conversing with the bartender. When Grant sat, she smiled and indicated Grant's presence to the bartender.

"What can I get for you today?"

"I think I'll have a Manhattan."

"Good choice. One Manhattan coming up."

It only took one Manhattan for Grant to realize he came this way for a reason. Maybe, just maybe, Pat would be home. He needed to talk to someone, but he didn't want to drag Pat down. Pat's phone was ringing. "Please be home. Pick up. Pick up," he pleaded softly in the empty phone booth.

"Hello, this is Pat. I'll be out for a short while. Please leave a message and I'll get back to you."

"Hi Pat, sorry I missed you. I should have known better than expect to find you home." Grant knew that sounded kind of desperate, so he continued, "I was just here in your hometown visiting Sally at the Valhalla. I was hoping you could come down for a drink."

Grant left the booth feeling even sorrier for himself. He had a few more drinks and tried to discretely observe Sally. He imagined how much she must have seen in her life. She was a plump woman who appeared to have made a good life from her high-class brothels. "Hell, if judges, politicians and other rich and famous people went there in the good old days, why not me?" He answered his own question, "I know why. I couldn't afford it then, and I can't afford it now." He had a few more drinks and feeling a little adventuresome, moved down toward Sally and asked, "Do you mind if I join you?"

"Of course not. What's your name?"

"I'm Grant, and I just love this place."

"Thanks Grant, I'm guessing you've been here before?"

"I've been here a few times and have always had a good time. Of course you are known for providing a good time."

He could tell Sally didn't find that amusing but was kind enough not to get upset. She exuded warmth. She even asked Grant what he did for a living. He wasn't sure what to say, he didn't want to bore her with his concerns. He told her he was an onboard PR person for Universal Airlines. She seemed duly impressed, and it pleased him that she seemed to be a genuinely interested.

Grant sat and pretended that he didn't need to keep talking nonstop. It was killing him. He wanted to talk, but doubted there was anything he could say that would interest Sally. Grant's eyes wandered around the room and from time to time he would make small talk with Sally. He looked up each time the main door opened, hoping to see Pat. The bright daylight pouring in silhouetted each figure. Magically, Pat finally appeared, still in her uniform. Grant's heart leapt at the welcome sight of her.

"Hi mister, are you looking for a good time?"

"Maybe, are you one of those Pan Am girls?"

They both laughed. He asked her what she was doing in her uniform. He thought maybe she was leaving on a trip.

"Actually, I just got back. I called to check my messages and heard you were here."

"You were just on a trip, why another so soon?"

"A friend called and needed a trade. I worked 181/22."

"You want to sit in a booth and have a drink?"

"No, I don't dare drink in uniform. In fact, I shouldn't even be in here."

"Are you hungry? We could go to the restaurant section."

"I am, but I'd rather go home and fix us something." Grant introduced Pat to Sally as if they were old friends. Pat seemed duly impressed, but suspected Sally was just being a good hostess/owner.

They left in Pat's car, after she convinced Grant that he shouldn't be driving. It didn't take a lot of convincing. He knew he'd had far too many.

Pat's apartment was only eight blocks from Valhalla. The street was narrow and most of the homes had garages that hung over the hill. The view of the bay and Sausalito from outside her apartment was breathtaking and her apartment was advantageously situated and designed with large bay windows to maximize the vista. Pat proudly showed Grant around her apartment.

Grant wandered through a set of large double doors to her spacious bedroom, which was decorated with distinctive style. He felt he should take off his shoes so as not to soil the plush white carpets, but he didn't. The large windows overlooking the Sausalito harbor were framed with delicate floral curtains. The wicker table and chairs in front of the window were an ideal place to sit and enjoy the view. At the top of the windows under the valance were dark shades to keep out the brightness, for a weary flight attendant sleeping off an overnight flight. Grant could tell a great deal of time and thought had gone into the decor, from the tasteful pictures of far away lands she must have visited, to the hand crochet doilies on her night stand. Her king size bed, with its black-and-white patterned bedspread complemented the picture frames on the wall. Against the headboard were rows of faceless Amish pillowcase dolls.

"I'm so impressed. You have a beautiful apartment."

"Thanks, I love it here."

Pat prepared some pasta el pesto and steak malinase. Then they sat with a glass of wine and relaxed. She surprised Grant when she asked, "How was the meeting today?"

"I didn't think you knew about it. Did I tell you?"

"The supervisor on my flight was going to their meeting this afternoon. She's pretty upset about the entire thing. And besides, you left that message on my machine. How are you feeling about it?"

"I'm not sure. I was just getting comfortable with handling the job, and now it's almost gone. I would love to be a fly on the wall at the supervisor's meeting."

"Maybe you'll get selected for the new position."

"That's possible, but I understand there's a lot to learn. I'm not sure I'm up for all that contract crap, along with hearings and letters. I talked with Gloria Carson the other day, and she said there's a lot to it. She doesn't mind that part, but she's afraid of the sales part."

"So, you see, you have that part down. I know you can do it. Besides, you don't have to have been a flight attendant to be a supervisor."

"That may be true, but I don't think it would hurt at this point."

Pat and Grant had a nice evening together but he was sure she must be tired from her trip. She offered to let him stay, but he felt in control and wanted to go home—he just wanted time to think. She drove Grant to his car at the Valhalla parking lot and left him with an affectionate kiss.

After arriving home, Grant went up to the third floor of his house and made a drink he didn't really need. He sat there looking out at the airport and worked at feeling sorry for himself. It didn't take much. He was damned good at it. "Let's see," he thought, "I worked hard to get this job. I'm good at it and now I might lose it. Poor me. Bullshit, I will learn to live with whatever it is I have to do." His gaze wandered out the window at the string of planes lined up to land. He went to bed feeling better. He was sure his last drink gave him some much needed courage; he went to sleep hoping it was still there in the morning.

The phone startled him at 8:15. Dakota was on the line. "I'm sorry Grant, did I wake you? I thought you got up early."

"I usually do, I surprised myself when I looked at the clock. What can I do for you?"

"Ron wanted me to call and tell you that you have an interview time at the Roadway Inn and you'll be taken off of your Pittsburgh trip."

"They're not wasting any time. How fast is this all going to happen?"

"Fast, your interview is at two o'clock on Wednesday."

"Who's doing the interviewing?"

"Mostly people from inflight service. Bill and Ron will be there also. Unfortunately, they don't feel their input will mean much. I think it's more of a courtesy than anything."

That wasn't good news. Grant was sure Bill and Ron would have given him a good recommendation.

Wednesday came all too fast. Grant was familiar with the Roadway Inn because he had gone there for drinks on Fridays after work when he worked at the maintenance base. The bar was just to the left, off the lobby. It had large double doors that were always open. He could see a combination of supervisors and friendship service directors sitting inside. He thought it took a lot of nerve to be drinking on the day of an interview. Turns out, the ones who were drinking already had had their interviews. After a few drinks, the interviewees took turns recalling the questions they were asked. "Would you have a problem with disciplinary actions? Do you feel you have the skills to discuss job responsibilities with flight attendants? Do you have communication skills as far as writing reports and answering passenger letters? Could you work side by side with crewmembers and still be objective?" Grant didn't think he had any of those skills. He was sure this would be the end.

Grant went to a room on the second floor at two o'clock sharp. The door was open. There were five people sitting at a long oak table. To Grant's disappointment, Bill and Ron were not two of them. He was feeling queasy. Grant gave a light tap on the door and the three people not looking his way turned and acknowledged his presence.

"Grant, come right in. Have a seat." It felt and looked like a parole hearing. Grant wished he had an attorney to argue his case. Jackie from

Inflight Service made sure everyone was introduced. They exchanged smiles and hellos. Jackie continued, "Let's get started. Do you understand why we're having this interview and the new position?"

"Yes, I've been to our office meeting. I do have a few questions, if I may?" Grant was trying to be proactive and show an interest in the new position.

"Of course," one responded. "We want a two way exchange, what questions do you have?"

"I was wondering what the main priorities would be onboard the aircraft? Will it be sales or supervision?"

"Good question," Karen said. "What do you feel would be most important?"

"Answer a question with a question," Grant thought. "What the hell, I'll go down talking." He responded, "I would have a difficult time making that decision. I've seen both the need for supervision and sales, especially if you consider passenger contact sales."

Jackie said, "I've shared a number of letters you've received from both passengers and management people who were onboard your flights."

"I was very impressed with what I read," Karen said. "You are obviously very good with passengers and crew members. I also see where a group of flight attendants wrote a rather special letter on your behalf."

If they were looking for someone to be an onboard asshole, that letter was going to be his kiss of death. It was, of course, well intended, but it shouted, "This guy would not cause us any problems."

That fact didn't go unnoticed by Karen. "Grant, do you think you would have a difficult time disciplining people who hold you in such high regard?"

Grant mumbled, "I can't see that being a problem." He was lying and hoped it didn't show. He was asked most of the other questions he learned in the bar and then the interview was over.

It was a short ride home, after which Grant sat for hours staring out his window. He could actually see the Roadway Inn and wondered what was taking place after the interviews, when the phone rang. It was Dakota. "What are you doing at the office so late?" Grant asked.

"I'm doing a lot of re-scheduling. Can you work a trip to Pittsburgh on Friday?"

"Of course I can, which one?"

"Flight 86, returning on 89, with the 33-hour layover at the Carlton house."

"Okay, I'll see you on Friday."

The trip left at nine, Grant was in the office by seven. He was surprised to see Dakota sitting at her desk so early. She made a heartfelt attempt at a good morning smile. A couple of guys were checking their mail with glum looks on their faces. It just wasn't the same office, so full of personality and humor not all that long ago. Grant was sitting at the table reading his mail when he felt a hand on his shoulder. It was Ron. "Got a minute?" he asked, nodding towards his office.

Grant followed and took a seat while Ron lit up a cigarette. "I've got some bad news. Very few of our people got the new job. It seems the hiring board is leaning more toward supervision than sales. We could have guessed it was going that way since inflight service will be in charge of the new program. Actually, it's not all that new. They'll continue with what they've been doing all along, adding sales to the list. We can't see where that will make a lot of money for the company, but it was their choice."

Grant, grasping for straws, asked: "Is there a chance they might reconsider if the new program doesn't work out?"

"I doubt it. They wouldn't want it to indicate they made the wrong choice. We think they did, but that's irrelevant." Grant was taking the news poorly, as Ron continued, "This will be your last trip. You will be off all next week and report back to the maintenance base the following Monday. I want you to know, while I was personally hesitant to hire you, I was wrong. You've done a great job here and everyone knows it. They just didn't seem to think our people would have made good supervisors."

Grant felt sick to his stomach. He couldn't believe this was happening. Just the thought of going back to the maintenance base made him feel ill. Almost as an afterthought Grant asked, "What about you, Bill, Dakota and everyone else?"

"Bill will be a manager in customer service and I'm going to a new computer department. Some of the people from other stations are going back if they so choose. If they want to stay here, we'll find a place for them. Look at the bright side—you will actually get a pay raise. The mechanics have gotten several raises since you've been here."

"They keep telling me that, but I can honestly say I could care less about the money. I just loved this job. Anyway, I better get ready for my trip." Grant added, "My last trip."

Grant tried to call Pat and then Gina. He needed to tell someone that his worst fear had materialized. He left them both messages and left the phone booth feeling even emptier inside.

He went to the briefing room for his DC-10 Pittsburgh trip. There was only one flight attendant sitting there reading her mail. She looked up and said, "Hi Grant, you mean we get both you and Shanda?"

"Is Shanda Simms working this trip too?"

"Yes, she's been on this line all month. It's been a lot of fun."

Shanda was a shapely blonde with an aura of likeability because of her giggle and the deep dimples that formed in the middle of each cheek when she did so. She was a well-liked and practical supervisor, not a stickler about the service procedures. Shanda was a touchy-feely person, and Grant liked that. He recalled one time when he was sitting at the computer, she walked up behind him, put both her hands gently on his shoulders, and asked if he would pull up some information for her. He tried to act cool as if he hadn't noticed her hands while he fumbled with the keyboard getting her request. Her touch was arousing and she was close enough that he could smell her long blond hair and feel the warmth of her breath on the back of his neck. She thanked him and sauntered away leaving Grant breathless. He turned to see her looking back, smiling. Grant had never forgotten that encounter.

The room started to fill with the rest of the crew. The flight attendants smiled generously when they saw Grant. Shanda came in with a smile and flashing dimples, cranking the male pulses in the room up a notch. She sat before looking up and seeing Grant sitting in the back of the room. He was flattered when she said, "Grant, are we lucky enough to have you going with us?"

"I think I'm the lucky one. I haven't seen this many smiles all in one place in a long time."

Before she could reply, in walked a male flight attendant a few minutes late. "I'm sorry, this is the first time I've been late all month." Some laughed and some groaned, but no one could resist Daniel's smile. His steely blue eyes and chiseled face made for a good-looking guy, and by all accounts, he was also a good flight attendant. Grant knew that combination helped him get away with just about anything.

Shanda tried to look stern and said, "Have a seat."

Diane, the first flight attendant, gave out the assignments. She gave Grant a copy of the manifest. There was nothing special to note----it would be an easy flight.

Diane asked, "Does anyone have anything else?"

Shanda said, "There'll be a going away party in my room tonight."

Grant thought, "How did she hear I was leaving?" He was surprised and delighted at the same time.

Then Diane asked, "Who's going away?"

Grant was getting ready with a humble unassuming little speech when Shanda said, "I am."

A wave of confused mumbles went around the room. Everyone was dumbfounded, including Grant. Finally the room became quiet, and Diane asked, "Where are you going?"

"Back to being a flight attendant, so I really won't be going away. I just won't be a supervisor."

Grant couldn't believe Shanda hadn't gotten the job. There is no way a businessman could turn her down if she asked them to give up another carrier's ticket and come back on Universal. Sales wouldn't be a problem for Shanda. It made him feel less depressed knowing someone he felt was more than qualified also didn't get the job, but still he was puzzled.

Other than Grant's cloud of depression, it was another pleasant flight. The crew seemed to be in a good mood as they waited for the crew bus and Shanda seemed especially happy.

Shanda and Grant waited for the others before putting their bags in the lower compartment of the bus. It was a large bus for just the fifteen of them. Most of the flight attendants had paired up, so Grant followed Shanda to the very back of the bus.

He hesitated but asked, "Aren't you upset about not getting the new position?"

"I guess I would be, if I wanted it."

"What do you mean, if you wanted it?"

"At times this job has been difficult enough: reports, hearings, disciplinary situations. I just had enough without having to sell tickets. I didn't interview for it."

"I guess if I could be a flight attendant, I would have done the same thing. I don't have that choice, so it's back to the base for me."

"You didn't get the job?"

"No, and as a matter of fact, this is my last trip."

"I can't believe that. Well, yes I can—you just didn't go to the right parties."

"What do you mean?"

"I'm willing to bet I could tell you who got the job."

"So tell me, who do you think got the new job?"

"Unfortunately, I've been to a few parties and seen some of the friendship service directors out in the yard smoking dope with people who could have helped them get the job."

Grant sat back and looked out the window as they arrived in downtown Pittsburgh. He tried to enjoy the ride to their hotel. Glancing at Shanda with her long blonde tresses, her eyes closed, and full lips glistening made the trip a little more pleasant. They got to the Carlton House and Grant let Shanda get out of the seat first so he was the last one off the bus. One of the flight attendants hung back and seemed to be waiting for him.

"Grant we're going to chip in and buy Shanda a going away gift. Do you want to contribute?"

"Sure, what are you going to get her? How much do you need?"

"We're going to get her something cute she can open at the party."

Grant gave her some money and then some extra for food and drinks.

Their rooms were primarily on the same floor. As far as crew rooms went, these were top of the line. They had refrigerators, cooktops and a large counter. The thick velvet curtains were perfect for keeping the light out on bright mornings.

Grant took a shower and put on his nicest layover clothes. He went to Shanda's room, just down the hall. The door was ajar, but he still gave a courtesy tap before walking in. There were more people there than just the crew. Everyone looked a lot different in casual clothes with their hair down. All but Daniel—he had on a pair of jeans and a scrub shirt from a hospital. It didn't matter what he wore he always looked good. There had been times when flight attendants had confided in Grant that they found some pilot or some male flight attendant attractive and Grant couldn't see it, but he could see where they would find Daniel attractive. He had straight white teeth, and thick, swept-back dark hair.

Grant kissed a few girls on the cheek on the way in and headed for the section of counter being used as the bar. He turned from making his drink to see Shanda walking up. She gave him a friendly hug and a kiss on the cheek. He said, "Nice party."

"Thank you for chipping in."

"My pleasure, I'm going to miss these people."

"They were shocked when they found out you didn't get the new position."

"How did they find out?"

"I told a couple of them earlier. Hope you don't mind."

"No, it's just not my favorite subject."

Shanda grabbed a plate of cheese, crackers, and appetizers and served the people sitting around the room in chairs and on the beds. The room was a good size, with a table and two chairs in front of a large window looking out to the cobblestoned streets of downtown Pittsburgh. Grant pulled out a chair under the small writing desk that was sitting in a corner. It was a great spot to sit and people watch.

One of the flight attendants gave Shanda a gift wrapped box with a card, declaring: "This is from all of us." Shanda sat on the edge of one of the beds and opened the card first. It was a "Good luck in your new career" card. Everyone laughed at that. Shanda opened the gift-wrapped box next, to a lot of cheers. She held up the top to a sexy pair of baby doll pajamas with matching bottoms.

After the party, Grant's room seemed larger and lonelier than ever. He poured himself a glass of white wine and sat on one of the king size beds. He left the television off and just sat there brooding. He was on his second glass of wine when the phone rang. Much to his surprise, it was Shanda.

"The last one of the kids just left and it's still early, why don't you come over and we can have a drink together?"

Not wanting to seem too eager, Grant said, "Give me a few minutes." He put his shoes on and brushed his teeth. The toothpaste clashed with the lingering flavor of wine. Grant went down the hall to Shanda's room and knocked lightly. To his shocked surprise, she opened the door wearing the sexy baby doll pajamas. Just looking at her took his breath away. Her hair cascaded over her bare and enticing shoulders. If he could have kept the surprised look from his face, it would have been an Oscar winning performance.

"What do you think?" Shanda asked coyly, standing aside to let Grant in. He couldn't think of anything to say that might sound even a little bit witty or coherent. She closed the door and walked to the counter. Her ample breasts swayed revealingly under the silky material. She turned and asked, "What would you like?" Grant couldn't hide the dumbfounded look on his face.

"I'm sorry. Did I shock you wearing this?" She pulled Grant into her arms. It was an invitation Grant could not refuse. They stood there embracing. Grant couldn't believe this was happening.

"Grant, let's make this a going away party we'll never forget." Shanda led them backward toward the bed while slipping the top of her baby doll pajamas over her head. The drinks kept Grant from feeling guilty, but they didn't help the next morning when he thought of Pat.

After the trip Grant walked into the dimly lit office as he had done so many times before, only to find his name had been taken off the mailbox as if he had never existed.

Chapter 6

The next week Grant went back to the maintenance base. His glum, dark outlook was only interrupted by an occasional date or visit with Pat. But they didn't connect as much as he would have liked, and he became disheartened. Besides seeing Pat, the only other bright spot was when Gina invited Grant to have lunch with her and Randy, her new boyfriend. Randy was a law student and his father, Steven Barrett, was an Assistant Attorney General. Randy was from a well established family, which pleased Grant, who knew how much Gina deserved a man like him. The three met at the Airport Hilton. Grant had taken the day off to meet Randy and was pleased to see a good-looking six-foot tall man with a slender build, sandy hair parted to the side and wire-rimmed glasses. Grant liked him immediately, and it seemed to be mutual. Grant could tell Gina was pleased they got along so well.

Back at the maintenance base, Grant was up to his ass in hydraulic fluid and grease when Butch Hammond walked into the area where Grant was working. Butch's eyes widened with surprise as he asked, "Grant, what are you are doing in coveralls?"

"Didn't you know? They combined the supervisor and friendship service director positions and unfortunately, I wasn't selected."

Butch grumbled, "Hmm, sorry to hear that." He put the stub of an unlit cigar in his mouth and walked away. Grant was pleased to see what he perceived as concern.

Two days later, Grant's supervisor called him into his office after a morning meeting. The supervisor had a grin on his face as he said, "You have an interview on Wednesday at 10:00 A.M. with Ann Grover. She is the operating manager for inflight services."

Grant wondered why he had another interview with inflight services. They had already rejected him once for the new position. Whatever the reason, Grant made sure he was ready for this interview. In the past months, he had given a lot of thought to his other interview and what he should have said. He wouldn't make the same mistake again.

But Grant didn't need to worry. Ann could have given lessons on how to get a person to talk too much. She was a pleasant woman with a good reputation as an operating manager. She would ask Grant a question, then sit back and look at him. He would answer the question, thinking he had said enough. Ann would just keep looking at him. Thinking she wanted more, he would go on and on. Once he realized he had said far too much, he stopped, but she was still just looking at him. Grant started to wonder if maybe she was daydreaming. He sat there and waited. Finally, it seemed that Ann realized he'd stopped talking and broke her silence.

"Well Grant, I think you'll do fine as one of our new supervisors. We just need to set up a time for you to report. You'll have two weeks training on the flight attendant contracts and service procedures, maybe a brief refresher on ticketing. Welcome back."

Grant knew something didn't seem right—it was as though she hadn't given it any thought. But it didn't matter. He had his job back. Grant couldn't wait to tell Gina. He called her apartment and was surprised when a man answered the phoned.

"Hello, who's this?" Grant asked.

"Grant, who do you think it is?"

"Sorry Randy, I didn't recognize your voice at first."

"I better be the only male voice who answers this phone. I'm getting very serious about your sister," he chuckled. "She's cooking, but I can take over if you need to talk to her."

"Thanks Randy, just for a minute if you don't mind."

"As much as she loves you, I wouldn't dare say no. Here she is, take care."

"Grant, what's going on?" Gina asked.

"I wanted you to be the first to know. I got the supervisor's job."

"I'm so happy for you! I just knew they would choose you when they had an opening. When do you start?"

"I have a couple of weeks training before they give me a flight schedule."

"Grant, I don't mean to be redundant, but don't take advantage of that position, please. Don't be Dad."

Grant could hear Randy in the background, "Don't listen to her. Have some fun."

"Don't listen to him, Grant. Stay in touch, and let us know how it's going."

"I will Gina. I'll let you get back to your cooking. What are you making?"

"Stuffed zucchini and pasta and peas."

"You're making me hungry. I love you Gina."

"I love you, too. Be good."

Next, Grant called his mom. He didn't see her very often, but he tried to call from time to time. He could seldom catch her home in the evenings and usually tried to call in the late mornings. After divorcing his father, Grant's mom had started dating much nicer men who took her places like the Olympic Club and the Tiburon Yacht Club. Somehow, even at their young ages, Gina and Grant knew their mom was socializing with a much higher class of men than their dad. Grant was hoping he would catch her before she went out.

"Hi Mom."

"Grant, how are you?"

"Well, right now I'm pretty excited. I got the new job as supervisor."

"That's nice Grant. I'm glad you're happy. What else is new with you?"

Her lack of enthusiasm took the wind out of his sails. "Nothing much I guess. I start classes on Monday for the new job."

"Well, pay attention. School work was never your strong suit."

"Yeah, that's the part that has me concerned. I'll try hard."

"I'm sure you will, but remember, sometimes it's not what you know, it's who you know."

Grant wasn't sure what she meant. "I've heard that before Mom. Well, I better get going. I love you."

"I love you too Grant. Just remember that—I love you."

The excitement of the new job evaporated quickly and was replaced with disillusionment. Grant had only one dual-training flight to New York, so as far as job priorities were concerned, it depended on who he talked to. Supervisors who were comfortable with sales focused on getting conversions; those not comfortable with approaching passengers, spent their energy supervising. It didn't take long before those concentrating on sales got in trouble for not supervising and the supervising types got in trouble for having low sales.

As a supervisor, Grant flew with the same crew all month. His first trip of the month was to Chicago, Universal's headquarters—not a great trip, as all too often there would be company officers onboard. On this trip, there was a director from the maintenance base. Grant always made a point of greeting company officers. Most were very nice, but this guy had a reputation for being a jerk. To make matters worse, he had been married to a flight attendant who had dumped him. He motioned for Grant to come to his seat.

"Grant, I think you need to have a talk with the flight attendant collecting tickets. She looks terrible and needs makeup."

Not wanting to look like he hadn't noticed, Grant lied and said, "I've already taken care of that."

"What did you do?"

"I didn't think I needed to come and tell you what I was doing as a supervisor. It's been taken care of."

Grant was pissed off. He knew it would be unprofessional, but he wanted to start his conversation with the flight attendant by saying, "The asshole in 1C, a director from the maintenance base, told me you needed makeup." But Grant thought better of it. He waited until he could get her alone. He had to admit she looked pretty washed out. With his stomach in a knot, he said, "Shelley, do you think maybe you could use a little more makeup?"

Shelley spun around on her heals and headed to one of the aft lavatories. Feeling terrible, Grant stood outside the door for over half an hour. Finally, Shelley came out still with tears in her eyes.

Grant asked, "Would you please tell me, is there a better way I could have told you? I wasn't trying to make you cry."

"What do you expect? You told me I look like shit."

"I never said anything close to that. Now tell me, how, in your opinion, could I have said that in a nicer way?"

Shelley went on to tell Grant how some guy broke up with her best girlfriend and she was up all night before the trip listening to her friend. Grant, not realizing using sick leave would have been contrary to company policy, suggested that maybe she should have stayed home.

"Yeah right, then I would be called in for using too much sick leave."

Being a supervisor was not going to be easy. The next morning at the layover hotel, Grant dressed and got ready to go, walked out of his room when another door opened. It was Shelley, who was also heading for the elevator. They stood there for a couple of seconds before she said, "I hope you noticed. I have makeup on today."

If she'd put makeup on, he couldn't tell. Grant told her she looked fine.

Grant's first flight to Honolulu was intimidating. Many of the Honolulu flight attendants had been outspoken about their displeasure with having supervisors onboard, and the supervisors knew it. The strict supervisors seemed to have control, but Grant knew he was way out of his league. He would be on this line all month with the same flight attendants. He had to put his reservations aside if he was going to have any luck. To his pleasant surprise, Donna was the first flight attendant and Vicki was also on the trip. Not to his surprise, Vicki was working the pit position. It was a friendly atmosphere and as usual, Donna did a nice job in the briefing. She was kind enough to ask Grant if he had anything to say. Unprepared, he mumbled, "It looks pretty much like you have it under control. I'm sorry, I don't think I'll be much help with the service. I'm still learning."

Grant overheard someone sarcastically say, "Surprise, surprise."

He continued with, "Let me know if there's anything I can do to help."

The flight crew boarded the flight and Grant did what he was the most comfortable with, getting his tips and selling Universal. As usual during the flight, he went down to the pit. Vicki was in the process of sending up the main course for first class. She came over and gave Grant a hug.

"It's good to see you again. I'm really glad you finally got the new job."

"It's good to see you again. I can't tell you how much I've missed flying."

"So, what do you think of being a supervisor?"

"I'm not sure. It's just not the same. I love flying and being on a flight crew, but I don't feel as welcome. What's going on?"

"Good perception on your part. There are a lot of flight attendants who don't want supervisors onboard. You really are caught in the middle."

"In the middle of what?"

"The middle of a big battle. There are a lot of flight attendants who believe they should be in charge. They want to be called chief pursers as opposed to first flight attendants, and they want the supervisors off the plane. Maybe I'm speaking out of turn, but you seem to have a lot going for you. Brian might take you on as a courier, if you are interested. They do pretty well. You wouldn't have to give up this job—just start out on your days off. If that works out and this job doesn't, you'll have something to fall back on."

"Are you and Brian still dating?"

"Yes, we are. I think we'll be getting married."

"Congratulations. The job sounds interesting. I wouldn't mind talking to him about it."

"I'll talk with him and maybe set something up. I better get these meals out."

"Thanks Vicki, I'll talk with you later."

The next day Grant went to the forward pit to visit Vicki and get a bite to eat. She was already done with the meal service and putting things away.

"Hi Grant, are you hungry?"

"I'm starved."

"I talked with Brian last night and told him you might be interested in his company. We're going out on his boat this Wednesday, and he told me to invite you if you're off."

"I'm off, and I'd love to."

"Bring a date, and meet us at Oyster Point Marina, slip B-13 around 9:30. We'll have to watch for you, the gates to the slips are usually locked. If something comes up and you can't make it, here's my number."

"Thanks," Grant said taking the slip of paper from Vicki, "I'm sure I'll see you on Wednesday."

Grant called and left a message for Pat about the Wednesday boat trip. Their conflicting schedules had made it hard to see each other, but it was worth a try. He beamed when she called back and said she could make it.

On Wednesday, Pat drove to Grant's house and they drove together to the Oyster Point Marina. Vicki and Pat exchanged some airline talk as they walked up to a beautiful 48-foot Bayliner. Grant couldn't hide how impressed he was. "Maybe this courier business could be the start of something," Grant thought to himself. Brian was on the flying bridge and came down to greet them.

"Welcome aboard you two, glad you could make it," he smiled.

"Thank you for inviting us, what can I do to help?" Grant asked.

"After I clear the dock, you can pull in the bumpers."

It was a clear chilly day with lots of promise for sunshine as they left the harbor and headed north under the Bay Bridge. Vicki and Pat were chatting in the galley, Brian and Grant sat on the bench seat on the flying bridge. The girls came up the stairs with coffee and tea.

Brian looked at Grant, "These girls never stop serving."

"We were born to serve," Pat quipped as she sat next to Grant and gave him a soft kiss on the cheek. They both smiled.

They had all been enjoying the faint gnaw of the salty air for a couple of hours when Brian interjected, "Hope you're all hungry, we have reservations at the Dock." That brought a few hungry smiles.

After a breakfast of the Dock's famous Eggs Benedict and Bloody Marys, the foursome re-boarded Brian's beautiful boat. Grant noticed the envious glances of the other patrons sitting on the restaurant's open deck; shamelessly, he basked in it.

It wasn't long before Brian said to Grant, "Take over and go where ever you want."

"Can I go under the Golden Gate Bridge?"

"Sure, anywhere you want."

Grant cruised under the world-famous suspension bridge and looked up. It was both an awesome and a dangerous feeling being below the bridge. Grant turned the large boat around and looked at the picturesque bridge, the city skyline, and the historic island of Alcatraz.

They cruised into the Sausalito harbor and Pat pointed to where her apartment was. Grant asked, "Can I pull into the Valhalla and buy you guys a drink?"

"Sure," Brian replied and helped Grant gently ease the boat up to the pier.

After drinks at the Valhalla, Grant turned down Brian's offer to drive some more. He wanted to sit on the lower deck with Pat. "Honey," he said, "This is just too perfect of a day. I can't believe how much he must make in the courier business."

"Well, it seems he works hard and spends a lot of time on airplanes and away from home."

"Pat, you just described our job; and we don't make that kind of money."

"Maybe it just looks good. You never know what people have to go through."

Brian cruised up the Oakland Estuary to Jack London Square, and Vicki said. "Pat, let's go look around and let the guys talk."

Pat grabbed her coat and followed Vicki after kissing Grant. Brian and Grant sat on the flying bridge having another drink. Grant thought it had to be the fresh sea air that kept him from feeling the effects of all the drinks he'd had.

Brian said, "Vicki said you might be interested in a courier job."

"Actually, I said I would be interested in having a backup position if this supervisor job doesn't work out."

"There's no reason you can't do both. You could work your regular days and then on a few of your days off, you could work for me."

"With my office days and flying, I don't have a lot of those days off. In fact, it's been keeping Pat and me from getting together more often. I would like to know more about the job though. What kinds of things do you accompany on your flights?"

"I ship cash, bonds, gold, diamonds—too many things to mention. Let me ask you something, is this conversation between us, can I trust what I tell you not to leave this boat?"

Not expecting what Brian was about to tell him, Grant said, "Sure. Of course, it's between us."

"Along with my courier business, I've been bringing in a more lucrative cargo. It's not legal, but it's a real moneymaker and almost too easy. It's just a matter of getting in the forward pit and changing some things from the courier boxes to a couple of suitcases."

"Brian, I promised, I wouldn't say anything and I won't, but I don't think I want to hear any more. I've worked too hard to get this job and I don't want to lose it."

"Well, you think about it, and if ever you become interested, let me know. I like you and I'm sure you would be the right guy for what I'm doing. Keep in mind, the pay is fantastic and the job is easy." Grant was feeling uncomfortable as Brian pulled the boat back into Oyster Point. It was truly a great day on the water and he liked Brian. He tried to put the conversation out of his mind, but it wasn't working. Fortunately, Brian didn't seem upset or concerned that Grant wasn't receptive to his "business opportunity." Grant couldn't help but to wonder how much of a moneymaker it really was.

Pat was quiet all the way home. They were the good kind of tired as they sat upstairs looking out the window at the beautiful bay where they had just been. Grant asked Pat why she was so quiet.

"I was just wondering what happened."

"What happened when?"

"After you and Brian spent some time on the boat alone, things seemed different. I can't explain it."

"Can you keep what I'm going to tell you a secret?"

"Sure, of course I can."

"I mean it, you have to promise."

"Of course I do."

"Well, it seems Brian doesn't just ship bonds, diamonds and gold. He evidently ships something else of value. I'm guessing it has to do with drugs. I told him I didn't want to know anymore than he had already told me. He seemed all right with it."

"I guess that explains a lot of things: his home in Hillsborough, her BMW, their boat, and the list goes on."

"So, do you think I should compromise my job and become a rich international whatever-it-is he does?"

"I don't think so. I kind of like you the way you are. We don't get to see each other much, but at least you're not in jail. How much did he offer you?"

"I didn't let him get that far. Should I have?" Grant said with a smile.

"No, of course not, but you have to be a little bit curious. I am."

Grant made Pat a nice dinner, and since they both had the next day off they shared a romantic evening. Grant woke early and looked over at Pat, who lay with the blanket pushed to the side. "How beautiful she would look in a Hillsborough home," he thought. He pulled the blanket over her and fell back to sleep.

Grant and Pat were awakened by a call from the crew desk. "Grant we need you to work a trip to Philadelphia, layover and deadhead to Chicago the next day. You will either be reassigned or deadhead home from there."

"These are supposed to be my days off."

"Yes, and I'm sorry. We'll try to get you some days off at the end of the month to make up for this. We need you to check in at 1:00 this afternoon."

Unenthusiastically Grant agreed, "Okay, I'll see you then."

Pat just smiled and laughed, "Welcome back to the glamour of aviation."

After checking with the crew desk, Grant went to the briefing room. He was a lot more comfortable with the domestic crews. They were younger and didn't seem to mind having a supervisor onboard. Many were like Grant—they were just happy to have the job, and he loved their enthusiasm. It seemed most of them were on reserve and this was some kind of special, last-minute trip. It was a pleasant briefing and the trip went well. Grant was pleased to have made a lot of conversions.

The crew was checking in at the Wyndham downtown hotel when Grant announced, "The first round is on me." He felt good about the crew and the trip.

An energetic red-headed flight attendant named Betty lamented, "And me without any layover clothes."

Grant offered to loan her an extra shirt he had, and another flight attendant had a pair of pants she could borrow—just enough so she wouldn't be recognized as a Universal flight attendant. Grant was hoping to build a reputation for being fair and fun to fly with and that he appreciated hard-working flight attendants.

There were eight of them sitting around a beautifully set table. Grant told the waitress to put the first round of drinks on his tab. The rest would be separate checks.

Betty hadn't had half of her drink when she started talking about the company, the crew desk, and anything else she could think of to complain about. She was like a different person. Grant tried to listen and act interested. He even asked a few polite questions. She became even more agitated and started on about how crappy the company was. Several of the flight attendants rolled their eyes and shook their heads. Finally, when Grant couldn't stand it anymore, he interrupted, "You know, this is a beautiful restaurant. We have nice people here and lots to drink. Why don't we enjoy this and talk about the company some other time?"

The table fell silent and Betty's face went as red as her hair—not from embarrassment Grant suspected, but because she was pissed. Everyone tried to enjoy the dinner, but after that, it was awkward.

The next morning most of the crew had deadhead clothes on, except Betty. They checked in at the crew desk and got their deadhead tickets. One of the junior flight attendants got a ticket for coach, since first class was full. Grant gave her his first class deadhead ticket. He knew she appreciated it.

Grant wound up sitting in the fourth row of coach, very close to the flight attendant who was doing her safety demo. He picked up his safety card to encourage the other passengers to do the same. Rita, the flight attendant doing the demo, was attractive enough to capture every male passenger's attention. She had large, dark almond eyes judiciously accented with mascara and eyeliner. Her slim figure pleasingly filled out her well-tailored uniform. When she faced aft, Grant noticed she was chewing gum, not graciously, but like a cow chewing her cud. To make matters worse, she canceled out her physical charms by exuding boredom. It was one of the longest safety demonstrations Grant had ever witnessed.

Onboard confrontation with a flight attendant was something Grant tried to avoid, but he knew he couldn't overlook this matter. With his stomach in a knot, he tried to think of the best way to confront Rita. When the seat belt sign turned off, he got up and went to the back of the cabin where she was getting ready to do her service. Grant excused himself and showed her his company badge. "I don't know if you realized it, but you were chewing gum during safety demonstration. I'm sure it's easy to forget you have gum in your mouth, but you need to think about it."

Rita didn't say anything, just looked a bit surprised. As far as Grant was concerned the matter was over and done with, so he went back to his seat. A few minutes before landing, Rita came to Grant's seat with a grin on her face. "The Captain wants to see you after we land."

"Thank you." Grant assumed the captain had gotten a message from the crew desk with some kind of assignment. He waited until most of the passengers were off the plane and walked into the cockpit. "Hi Captain, I'm the supervisor. You wanted to see me?"

"You're damn right I do. I'm getting sick and tired of you people ruining our flights. We don't need you onboard, upsetting the flight attendants."

Grant was taken back. "That's not my intention. Just tell me the flight attendants have your permission to chew gum during their safety announcement."

The captain paused and averted his gaze elsewhere. He changed the subject, still berating Grant.

Grant pressed, "Do the flight attendants have your permission to chew gum?"

The captain rambled on about supervisors destroying workplace harmony. Grant waited until he was done before leaving the cockpit. Grant saw the offending flight attendant standing nearby.

"Come with me to the office," Grant ordered.

The pilot overheard and asked Rita, "Do you want me to come to the office with you?"

She nodded and said," Yes."

Grant and the pilot went to the duty supervisor and Grant told his story. The captain immediately launched into his pleasant workplace diatribe, so Grant interrupted him to ask if he was giving the flight attendants on his airplane permission to chew gum. There was no getting an answer out of him. The pilot told the flight attendant to get in touch with him if she needed to and left. Grant noted her name and file number and tried one last time to make her see that she had caused a small thing to turn into a big deal. She fired back, telling Grant she heard he had caused trouble at dinner the night before. It turned out the little redhead from that dinner was a union rep and had gone into the cockpit to tell the captain about the dinner table situation the night before. She was using the arrogant pilot in an effort to make Grant look stupid and get back at him in the process.

Later, the pilot took it upon himself to go to the office in San Francisco and complain about Grant. One of the secretaries overheard the pilot telling the operating manager how Grant had disrupted his flight. She told Grant what the operating manager said to the captain, "If you were talking about anyone other than Grant Guidera, I might just listen to you. Grant is one of our best liked and most reasonable supervisors."

That was enough to send the pilot out red-faced. Grant smirked when he heard that, just wishing the egotistical bastard had said whether or not it was okay with him if his flight attendants chewed gum. The sad part was, Grant later found the captain was the kind of pilot he admired. He flew antique planes on his days off. He was involved with aeronautical clubs and organizations.

Being a supervisor was just not as pleasant as sales. The whole incident made him think of Brian and his offer. Grant knew if the job continued like this, he would need a way out.

Grant flew again on Sunday to Honolulu. He was flying with his regular crew except for a couple of flight attendants who had traded out of the trip. Unfortunately, one of the replacements had a reputation of causing problems for the supervisors. Renee was infamous among the supervisors for her onboard antics. As part of the first flight attendant's responsibility, Universal required a marketing announcement after each flight had landed and was taxiing to the gate—something simple like: "Thanks for flying Universal Airlines, please keep in mind our partners in travel Host Hotels and Top Rate Rent-A-Car." The rumor was that Renee refused to make the marketing announcement. A supervisor told her it was required and she would be charged with insubordination if she refused, so, she started her announcement with, "I'm making this announcement because my supervisor is making me."

Grant knew Renee from years prior when she was the roommate of a friend's girlfriend. She had even been out on Grant's boat when he was a mechanic. Because of that, he didn't think Renee would be a problem for him. Before the flight, they exchanged stories about her girlfriend who had since left the company and a few memories of their day out on the boat. Grant figured he was home free.

Grant was making a lot of conversions and staying out of the way of the flight attendants. He visited Vicki in the pit and thanked her again for the nice day out. Brian had told her about their talk and she said, "Don't totally put aside Brian's ideas, you never know." Grant agreed and offered to buy her a drink if she was around Jamison's that evening.

Grant went back upstairs and was walking down the coach aisle when a passenger asked Grant if he could help her with a question. He sat next to her and put his OAG on the tray table to look something up. Renee came down the aisle and a passenger a couple of seats up asked her a question. While Renee was leaning over, talking to the passenger, a man sitting one row in front of Grant lightly tapped Renee on the shoulder. Renee snapped around and barked, "You touch me again and I'll punch you in the mouth!"

Grant couldn't believe his ears. Renee headed toward first class and Grant excused himself and caught up with her. "Renee, let's go upstairs."

She followed Grant up the spiral staircase to the first class lounge. He didn't really have time to think about what he was going to say. Fortunately, there were no passengers in the lounge.

Grant asked, "What was that about back there?"

"I don't like being touched. People shouldn't be touching us."

"First, I saw him tap you on the shoulder—he didn't touch you in an inappropriate place or in an inappropriate manner. I can't make you do it, but I think you owe him an apology. You could just tell him he startled you."

"I'm not telling him anything."

"Okay, here's what I'm going to do. I'm going to put on my flight report what happened and that I discussed it with you."

"Do whatever you want. I don't have to be touched by passengers. If you give me a letter, I'll grieve it."

"I didn't say I was going to give you a letter. I'm going to put it in my flight report and file it like I do all flights. If a letter comes in from that passenger, then this situation will be covered. Still, if I were you, I'd apologize."

"Is that so? Why aren't you sticking up for me?"

With that she left. Grant couldn't help but to think, "This is no way to make a living." Part of him liked the supervisor title, but the unnecessary nonsense that went with it was taking its toll. Grant took it upon himself to go to the aggrieved passenger to apologize on behalf of the airline.

The stresses on Grant's psyche made it difficult to enjoy the steward's, "Welcome to my island" announcement. The ride to the hotel was uncomfortable. Renee was telling anyone who would listen about her exchange with the passenger. Grant couldn't help but to think the poor bastard was most likely still in shock.

While the crew checked in, Grant asked Donna if she was going to Jamison's before dinner. He told her he was meeting Vicki and hoped she could make it, his treat. She agreed to meet them at five o'clock. Donna was there before Vicki. Grant was surprised to see she was alone and asked where the other flight attendants were.

"I'm meeting them in the lobby at six and we're going to Chucks for dinner. I didn't think you would want Renee here."

"So, you heard the story?"

"I heard Renee's version. So what really happened?"

Grant told Donna the entire story, including his attempt to reason with Renee. He was doing her a favor after all. Since he witnessed the entire exchange, he should write her up for her actions. Grant was pleased that Donna agreed he was being more than fair.

Grant changed the subject and told Donna about his day out with Vicki and Brian. Donna told him how much Vicki had improved since the tension he had witnessed between them. Vicki came in and joined them. The two women chatted about the service before Donna left to meet her dinner companions. Vicki and Grant were alone. They had a few drinks and talked about their day on the bay.

"Brian is coming over on a later flight, maybe we can get together." Vicki suggested.

Grant had had just enough to drink and that was all the encouragement he needed to talk. Vicki was a good listener. After listening to his tales of despair, she said, "Grant, you really need to reconsider Brian's offer. At least listen to him."

"I think I'm about ready. I really need another job, and I don't want to go back to the base."

"Actually, you would need to stay with this job, but it would really become worthwhile."

"It couldn't hurt to know more about it. Can you explain to me what you know?"

"I think it would be better if you talk with Brian. Maybe on tomorrow's trip I could show you what we do. Why don't you meet us here around 9:30 this evening. He should be here by then."

Grant walked to the little sushi shop and had his favorite sashimi and a couple of California rolls. After his snack, he went back to the hotel, laid down, and watched some news. He woke in shock to the phone ringing.

"Grant, where are you? Its 10:00 P.M. Brian and I are waiting for you."

"I'm so sorry. I'll be right down." He ran a comb through his tousled hair, tucked in his shirt, and headed for Jamison's. Brian and Vicki accepted his apologies. It wasn't long before Vicki excused herself.

"Grant, Vicki said you might have second thoughts about my business."

"Actually, I just wanted to know more about it."

After reminding Grant to not say anything to anyone, Brian stated, "As you may have guessed, it's cocaine." Grant looked afraid to listen. "Just hear me out. In Colombia cocaine costs $1,500 US per kilo, or about 2 lbs. On the mainland, San Francisco for example, it's worth between $35,000 and $50,000." Grant's face wore a mixed expression of being impressed and surprised. "Americans spent some $36 billion on cocaine in 1970 alone, that's six times GM's profits for the same year, and they are a Fortune 500 company." Brian finished by saying, "I don't take the risk of selling retail, but I have a very busy wholesale business."

Still with his eyes wide open and sober, Grant inquired, "So, where would I come in?"

"I have a regular route from Honolulu to San Francisco. Not to mention other cities." Vicki came back and slipped in next to Brian who continued with his story. "I mostly ship bank papers, gold, and sometimes pearls from the Orient. My secure courier boxes go directly from the bank or wholesale jewelry outlets to the plane. In the regular baggage area there are drug sniffing dogs and random bag searches. My courier boxes are exempt from that area. What I use are oversized courier boxes. Depending on what I'm shipping, I put anywhere from two to four keys of cocaine in a box."

"So, why do you need me? It sounds like you have it all worked out."

"Almost, but here's the deal: I need someone on the plane to take the coke out of the courier boxes and put it in empty suitcases in the same cargo pit."

Grant glanced at Vicki. He knew now why she was in the forward pit those couple of times when she seemed to have disappeared. She smiled back sheepishly. Grant looked at her and then Brian. "So why do you need me? It seems things are going along fine."

"It's been a coincidence that you have been on so many of my flights and also Vicki's. There are a lot more shipments that need the same thing done when neither of us is on the flight."

"Who does your part if you're not here?"

"First, I'd like to know how interested you are. I would give you $1,000 per kilo to move them from the courier box to a suitcase."

"So, I could make up to $4,000 per trip?"

"Yes. Multiply that by six or eight trips per month on a good month. Sometimes it's only one kilo per trip, so at least six or eight thousand per month."

"How risky can this be?"

Vicki spoke up. "The worst thing I've encountered is someone coming down the elevator into the galley. One girl stayed so long I just came out of the cargo hold and told her I was looking for the suitcase I checked because of my pain pills." Grant smiled at her. She had told him the same story. "Why don't you come down to the pit tomorrow and I'll show you exactly what I do"

"What's the best time?"

"Actually, during the meal service is best in some ways. Definitely not during the movie—the pit gets crowded during the movie"

"So, Grant, are you interested?" Brian asked,

"I'm not sure just yet, but I want you to know I will keep this between us."

"Will you come to the pit tomorrow?" Vicki asked.

"I will, but if you'll excuse me, you've given me a lot to think about."

Vicki gave Grant a hug and Brian shook his hand. It was getting late and he did have a lot to think about. "What is there to think about besides the potential for $25,000 to $45,000 per month?" He jokingly thought to himself, "With that kind of money I could put out a contract on Renee and Betty."

The next morning Grant went to Jolly Rogers for breakfast. Looking around, he saw Donna sitting with two other flight attendants and Renee. Grant's stomach twisted at the sight of Renee. He smiled at Donna as he walked by and joined Vicki and Brian sitting in a far corner. They had a nice breakfast together, but didn't discuss the courier business. Brian and Vicki expressed how much they enjoyed Pat on the boat outing. They were curious to know how serious a pair they were. Grant explained that they really liked each other but had a hard time finding time to be together. "We date different people, so I guess we aren't all that committed. But I really enjoy being with her. Maybe someday," he said hopefully.

In the lobby waiting for the crew bus it was uncomfortable for Grant to be anywhere near Renee. She was laughing and joking to unimpressed flight attendants. He was sure she was ridiculing him and their talk in the upper lounge. Donna wandered over and said, "You are sure getting cozy with Vicki and Brian lately."

"Yeah, I really enjoy their company. In fact, I took a date and went out on their boat last Wednesday. We had a nice day, the weather was perfect."

"I saw some pictures of the boat, looks like Vicki is marrying into money."

"It looks that way. Let's face it, he has a good business."

"Where is Vicki? The bus will be here any minute."

"I'm sorry, I should have told you. She went with Brian and said she would meet us in briefing."

While Grant was talking with Ruby about crew scheduling, he could see out of the corner of his eye the Loomis truck pull up to his San Francisco flight. Grant's heart skipped a beat knowing what was on that truck.

It was a flight like any other flight, except for Grant's nervous anticipation. He did his conversions and talked with passengers. Finally the meal service was winding down and the carts were being sent to the pit. Grant told Donna he was hungry and was going down for a bite to eat. Vicki was busy putting the carts and leftover food away. He could tell she was anxious to get this over with, a feeling Grant shared. She left some carts sitting in the pit, not on their usual tie-downs. She took a quick inventory. "That's most of them." She picked up the phone and asked Donna to hold the rest of the carts until she called for them.

"Come with me." Vicki went to the aluminum door and twisted the handle, slid the door open and looked back. "Grant, leave the elevator door open so they can't use it. They'll call if they get desperate."

Vicki motioned for Grant to follow her. She had a flashlight and looked around the pit area. They both tripped over suitcases on the way to the courier boxes. She leaned down and turned a combination on the first courier box. She pointed with the flashlight, "Pass me that suitcase with the pink string on the handle."

Grant was surprised at how light the suitcase was. Vicki told him the combination was 7-4-7. He dialed it in and opened the luggage. Not surprisingly, it was empty. She passed him one of the tightly wrapped packages, then another. There were two in that one box. Vicki locked the courier case back up and turned the combination on the suitcase after closing it. A voice came over the speaker wanting the elevator door closed and Vicki went flying out of the cargo hold, waving for Grant to follow. "We'll get the other one later." It was all a frightening rush for Grant. He smiled and Vicki said, "That's why we make the big bucks."

Just one cart was sent down, then Vicki and Grant went back in the cargo hold and repeated the process, this time putting the packages in a suitcase with a chartreuse string. There were four packages in all. Grant realized that could have been $4,000 in his pocket for those horrifyingly short few minutes. He went upstairs thinking it might not be so difficult. Grant walked back in coach and joined Brian who had three seats to himself. Brian asked, "How's it going? Selling lots of tickets?"

"Yes, I am." Grant lowered his voice. "I'm doing pretty well and so is Vicki."

Brian got Grant's meaning and gave him a thumbs up. They made a little small talk and Brian told Grant he would call. Grant explained he had a couple of days off before his next trip.

Brian called the next day and asked Grant if they could meet at the Airport Hilton around noon for lunch, Grant agreed. When he walked into the dimly lit room, he found Brian and Vicki sitting together at the back of a large plush booth. Grant slid in next to Vicki and said, "I wasn't born yesterday! I always take the seat next to an attractive woman."

They had a laugh, and Brian said, "Vicki said you were a big help yesterday."

"I'm not sure about that, but I was certainly frightened enough for the two of us."

"I wasn't expecting you to be much help at all." Vicki admitted.

With that Brian pushed an envelope across the table to Grant. "This is a little something for you, open it later."

"I wasn't expecting anything."

"And we weren't expecting you to help, so we're all happy. Here's the thing—I need to know how interested you are. As you know, there's a lot of money in it. I just need a commitment from you. What do you think?"

"It does look good, and so does the money. Would you mind if I think about it?"

"No of course not, but I would like to know within a couple of weeks."

Grant thanked them both for lunch. He couldn't wait to see what was in the envelope. He got in his car, drove to the end of the parking lot, stopped and opened the envelope. There were 10 one-hundred dollar bills. Grant thought that was awful generous for five minutes work.

Grant gave Brian's proposal a lot of thought on the way home. He felt they trusted him but could have gotten other people to do the same thing. Maybe they already had. Grant tried not to think that he would be letting down his family who had supported him in getting the job in the first place. But then he thought of the Universal CEO who left the company with over 50 million dollars worth of stock, and he was only there three years. Was anyone disappointed in him? Grant doubted it. If everyone else was getting theirs, why not him? Grant tormented himself trying to make a decision. He knew his sister Gina would be ashamed of him for even thinking about it.

The phone rang and Grant was surprised to hear Gina's voice on the other end. She was usually busy and he normally called her.

"Hi Gina, what a nice surprise. How are you?"

"Not too well, Grant, I have some bad news." She hesitated, "Mom passed away this morning." There was silence on Grant's end. Gina waited. "Grant, are you all right?"

His voice trembling, Grant said, "I can't believe it. What happened? How did she die?"

"She had a stroke last night. Dad called me this morning. He asked me to call you. He didn't want to have to tell you. I tried to call you earlier, but I got your machine. I didn't want to leave a message under the circumstances. You and I will have to make arrangements for Mom's funeral service."

With tears in his eyes and a broken voice Grant said, "Let's make it a nice service. Can we do that?" His grief was evident in his voice.

"Of course we can."

Grant, Gina and their dad sat in the front row of the large funeral parlor. The bronze and silver casket was surrounded by beautiful flowers on tripod stands. The somber, olive walls held a hundred colorful wreaths hanging on hooks. The priest gave a moving eulogy. Grant could only think of the good times. He and Gina held hands as they watched people walk past the open casket to say their goodbyes. Some knelt and said a prayer. Their dad just sat there; he was lost to nostalgia. Most of the people stopped by the front row to offer their condolences. Gina, Grant and Pete explained to each other their relationship with the various people who came by. Gina pointed out her friends from the hospital, there were also mutual friends of Pete and Nadine's from the old days. Grant saw some of his friends walking past the casket. Some stopped by their front row seat, others just smiled. Grant looked towards the casket and he couldn't believe his eyes. Butch Hammond was standing in front of the casket. He lingered longer than most.

Grant looked to Gina and Pete. "I can't believe Butch Hammond came to the service. He's a vice-president at Universal."

Pete turned to him, "You got to be kidding. He and your mom were, let's just say, good friends."

"What the hell are you talking about?" Grant asked.

"When Gina was around three years old, your mom and I separated for a couple of months. She was going out with him. I think they've stayed friends. I heard she was seen with him at the Olympic Club."

Grant looked at Gina, who was slowly nodding her head in affirmation. Grant wasn't able to comprehend. Butch walked past him and touched him on the shoulder. Grant just sat there wide-eyed. He couldn't put a thought together. He sat there alone while Gina and Pete got up and talked with people as they were leaving. The sight of Grant sitting alone in the empty parlor staring at the open casket brought tears to Gina's eyes. She sat next to him, but didn't say anything.

Grant broke the silence, "Gina, you knew about mom and Butch Hammond?"

"Not everything. She told me that she had had a date with some guy who was a vice-president at Universal. She mentioned his name a couple of times."

"That's it. That's all you know?"

"What else is there to know? Why are you so upset about it?"

"Did you know he was the vice-president who gave me a letter of recommendation when I was interviewed to be a friendship service director?"

"I remember you telling me about the letter, but I don't think you told me his name. I think I would have remembered. I still don't understand, why that would upset you?"

"I thought I earned that job. I believed it was all the work I did with base tours, the ESP program and everything else."

"Grant. I'm sure that was it. So what if he helped you a little."

"I'll tell you what; mom was right. It's not what you know, it's who you know."

Gina put her arm around Grant's shoulder. "Grant, I'm sure you're doing a fine job. I'm sure your boss knows that too."

"So why wasn't she here?"

Gina didn't say anything else. They just sat there looking at their mom.

Grant knew he was using this new knowledge about his mom and Butch Hammond as an excuse, but he was definitely going to work for Brian. On his first trips working for Brian, Vicki was flying the same schedule. Grant agreed to help her, as two people made switching the contents an easier task. Vicki even agreed to split the money with him. Grant couldn't stop thinking how difficult it might be for him to work alone. He gave it a lot of thought. It was a big concern for him.

On the last trip of the month there was a letter in Grant's mailbox, which read: "Grant, would you please come to my office after your trip?" His heart skipped a beat and he was almost relieved to read the next sentence. "We need to talk about an onion letter regarding Renee Burkhart."

Grant would have to defend his actions as a supervisor, he was sure of it. He went to Maryann's office the next day and tapped on her open door.

"Hi Grant, come in." Maryann seemed to be in a good mood considering the open letter on her desk was obviously waiting for him. She handed Grant the letter and told him to close the door and have a seat.

The letter was from a Mr. Cole and explained exactly what Grant had witnessed on his flight with Renee. The letter was well written; he was obviously an educated man who hadn't missed a thing. That type of letter held a lot of credibility. Grant especially liked when Mr. Cole described Renee's reaction: "She turned and with a beastly shriek declared 'If you touch me again, I'll punch you in the mouth.'" The letter also noted that Grant had apologized for Renee's actions.

Grant wasn't sure what to do. Maryann had a smirk on her face that could have been mistaken for a smile. Grant didn't want to chance smiling back. "It's well written and totally accurate."

"Did you discuss this with Renee?"

"Yes, and I put it in my flight report."

"But you didn't put anything in her file saying you spoke to her about this incident."

"I guess I could put it in her file if you want."

"I think this is a lot more serious than noting in your flight report that you had a discussion with her. She should have been given a letter of warning and possibly been suspended. It's now a little late for the suspension. With this letter, she definitely deserves a reprimand in her file." Maryann admitted to Grant that she had flown with Renee. She knew Renee had changed a great deal over the years and become difficult to deal with.

Grant left Maryann's office not looking forward to the letter of warning he had to put in Renee's personnel file. He would also have to notify her of the letter. Writing the letter was no easy project. First, Grant wrote a rough draft and showed it to John Cross, who re-wrote it. Then, he took it to personnel to make sure it was legal and that he had explained all Renee's rights as an employee. It was a good letter but not because of Grant's supervisory skills. Maryann gave the final okay to put the letter in Renee's file, and a note and copy to Renee directly. Maryann also informed Grant he needed to respond to the passenger's complaint letter.

That evening, Brian called and suggested he and Grant get together for a drink. They met at the Airport Hilton. To Grant's surprise, Brian had a copy of Grant's flight schedule with dates, flights, and times. Before Grant had a chance to ask, Brian said, "Vicki picked these up for me. There are only two trips on your schedule that I need you. I think it will be five packages each trip so you'll still turn a good profit. I'm concerned though, about one thing. How you will be able to get in the forward pit if there's a flight attendant working there, any ideas?"

"Truthfully, I'm worried about that too. What would happen if I couldn't switch the packages?"

"It would cause a lot of confusion. First, if the suitcases were empty the recipients would go into shock. Then I would have to try and remove the goods from the courier boxes back at our warehouse, which is a bona fide risk. We have security guards who meet these boxes and know nothing about what was in them prior to landing. I can handle most of them, but I can't plan for every likelihood. Do you think it's going to be a problem for you?"

"I've been thinking about it a lot. I thought I could send the pit person to the cockpit with coffee for the crew. Maybe tell the pilot to keep her there for a while or maybe just tell her I'm looking for a passenger's suitcase which has their prescription in it. I have over four hours to get it done. I should be able to do it." Grant knew Brian sensed his tentativeness.

Before Grant could say anything else, Brian suggested, "Let's do this: Vicki can trade into your next trip, she can work an aisle position. Someone else will be working the pit, but you do what you think you need to do to exchange the packages."

"What good will Vicki be, if she is working the upstairs aisle?"

"Just in case you can't get it done your way, she can help somehow. Maybe tell the pit person to take a break, whatever it takes. If you can get it done without her help, we'll know it can work. Let's just call it a trial run."

Chapter 7

Grant's first trip for Brian was the following Wednesday. He was working flight 97 to Honolulu and returning on 96. Grant wasn't surprised to see Vicki in the briefing room when he walked in. He sat next to her, and they made small talk like the friends they had become. Alana was the first flight attendant, but Grant wasn't sure who was working the pit. It was a good briefing, and Alana was kind enough to ask if it was all right to use a three-cart train. Grant had learned a bit about the service and was proud to announce that he liked the three-cart train as opposed to the two. He was especially pleased not to have responded with a blank look on his face as he had so many times in the past.

Connie, a stout, shorthaired brunette was working the pit. Connie seemed friendly and conscientious. Since he was unfamiliar with her, Grant made a point of visiting her more than he normally would have. He told her he would be buying drinks at Jamison's for anyone in the crew who would like to join him and made sure she knew she was invited.

Brian had flown over to Honolulu the day before and made plans to meet Vicki and Grant at Mateo's for dinner. After meeting several of the crewmembers for drinks at Jamison's, Grant excused himself, paid the bar tab and headed to Mateo's. After giving Grant time to take a few sips of his Manhattan, Brian asked, "So Grant, how do you feel about this?"

"I'm nervous, but having Vicki onboard will help. I also invited Connie, the pit person, out for drinks."

"How do you think that will help?"

"I'm not sure just yet, but I think we've become friends of sorts."

The next morning, Vicki rode in with Brian, which made Grant feel apprehensive and alone on the crew bus. Alana did a short but complete briefing. After the briefing, Grant went to the office and made small talk with Ruby. Grant glanced out the window and his stomach did a flip at the sight of the Loomis truck pulling up to the forward pit. Ruby noticed the look on Grant's face and turned toward the flightline in confusion.

"What's the matter Grant? You look like you've seen a ghost."

"I almost did, you should have seen that last plane bounce."

"I see some pretty bad landings from time to time."

Grant was pleased with his recovery from his poorly concealed apprehension. Grant and Ruby exchanged farewells, and Grant went down the escalator and onto the Jetway. He was sure he had been more enthusiastic going for a root canal appointment. Alana was collecting the tickets and would pass them to Grant from time to time. Grant experienced further apprehension when he saw Brian come onboard. They smiled and said hello. Brian seemed comfortable and Grant could only hope he looked as calm. Grant didn't want the fact that he was a nervous wreck to show. "This," he thought, "is more nerve-wracking than a job interview." Grant recalled all the times he had encountered Vicki in the forward cargo—she was always cool with a ready explanation. She was also concerned enough to cover her ass by going to his office to explain her actions. This was Grant's opportunity to make a lot of money. He needed to be as cool and confident. But he couldn't remember ever feeling so shaky.

Grant waited until the cockpit turned off the no smoking sign, indicating the flight was above 18,000 feet and the cockpit was no longer off-limits. Until the no smoking sign turned off, no one was allowed in the cockpit. There was too much communication with air traffic control to allow for distractions. Grant went into the cockpit and chatted with the pilots. Before Grant left, he asked if they would like him to have some coffee or drinks sent up. They looked pleasantly surprised and ordered a guava, a coffee and an ice water.

Grant went down the spiral staircase and directly to the pit. Connie looked relaxed and in control. She had loaded the meals in the ovens on the ground, sent up the liquor carts for first class, and then set the time and turned on the ovens. He knew this was a slack time for her during the cocktail service.

"Connie, would you mind taking the pilots something to drink? The captain wanted a guava and the others guys a coffee and an ice water. Also, would you mind helping Alana by setting up in the first class lounge?"

"I don't usually do that, but for you…"

She smiled and went about getting the cockpit order ready. Grant told her he hoped she didn't mind, but he was going to organize his tips using one of her counter tops for his papers. She smiled and said, "Make yourself at home." With that she went up the elevator.

Grant opened the elevator door so no one could come down and went to the sliding door into the forward cargo hold. His heart was beating fast and he needed to use the lavatory but he just wanted to get the exchange over with. The door was tight to open and took some pulling. The courier boxes were toward the front of the cargo pit. Overly conscious of his racing heart, Grant tripped and stumbled over suitcases. He fumbled with his flashlight, whose beam was much too small for this large dark area.

He found the suitcase with the pink string and pulled it with him toward the courier boxes. Then he saw the chartreuse bow on the other suitcase off to the right. A warm flush enveloped him, beads of sweat formed on his forehead. In his haste, he tripped and fell. He left the one suitcase close to the boxes and went for the other. He got it in his hand and swept the area with the light, trying to find a clear path back to the courier boxes. Adrenaline was doing all his thinking. He got to the first courier box and went to work opening it. He was graceless while holding the flashlight and trying to open the first suitcase. Grant lifted the lid of the first box. There were three packages sitting on the top and separate metal containers on the bottom. He put the three packages in the first suitcase, thinking of the $150,000 street value.

"Hey, what's going on down there? Close the door, I have carts to send down." Alana's voice blared over the intercom.

Grant closed both lids in a panic, without locking them, and went aft to the sliding door. He grabbed the phone expecting to hear Alana but no one was there. He held it to his ear, knowing it was ringing upstairs. With the phone in his hand, he closed the door to the cargo pit. It took a few minutes for Alana to answer. Grant dusted off his uniform from his fall.

When Alana finally answered, Grant went on the offensive. "What took you so long to answer?"

"I was picking up in first class. Why is the elevator not working?"

"The door was ajar, I just closed it."

"Let me talk to Connie."

"She's setting up the first class lounge. Just send the carts down and I'll take them off the elevator."

"Why is she doing that? She's supposed to stay in the pit unless I ask for her help."

Grant felt droplets of sweat roll down the nape of his neck. "There were some people going up there, so I asked if she wouldn't mind when I saw she wasn't busy."

The elevator came down with a cart. Grant removed it and sent the elevator back up. His heart rate slowed as he got the situation under control. He removed a couple more carts, sending the elevator back up each time. The next time the elevator came down, Connie was on it and she didn't look happy. She explained that Alana told her not to leave the pit without having someone take her place. Grant apologized for the trouble he caused her and left. He tried to smooth things out with Alana but she seemed less than enthusiastic about listening to his explanations.

Grant was doubtful this arrangement would work out. He didn't know how to get the attendant out of the pit. Even if he could make it work, he couldn't do it with the same flight attendants more than once. He walked back to coach and looked around for Vicki. He could tell it wasn't a good time. They were getting ready to do the meal service and once they got the carts in place, he would be stuck back there. He left in frustration. There was still plenty of time, but he wanted to be done with it.

Grant took a moment to compose himself, walked into first class to get some conversions and then to the upper lounge. It wouldn't be long before the first class meal service started. There were two couples in the lounge. He knew what seats were empty downstairs, but he didn't know who was sitting in which seats. Only one couple had returns that needed his attention.

"Hello, Mr. & Mrs. Coleman?"

"No, we're the Hansens."

From across the cabin, a nondescript man sitting with his dozing wife raised his hand to get Grant's attention. "I'm Mr. Coleman."

Grant apologized to the Hansens and went over to the Colemans. His sales performance was suffering. On the other hand, he was going to start making some real money. He made the conversion, and they had a pleasant conversation. Not wanting it to be too obvious that sales were his only motive, he went back to the Hansens and spent some time with them. Near the end of their conversation, Mr. Hansen mentioned that their daughter was a flight attendant with Universal and asked if Grant knew her. Grant didn't know her because she was based in Chicago. Grant kicked himself. That was a real amateur mistake—the manifest, had he looked at it, was very clear regarding the presence of a company employee or relative. Grant justified his error with the more pressing task at hand.

If this were a job interview with Brian, Grant was sure Brian wouldn't be impressed with his performance so far. The time was going by too fast, and Grant was starting to panic. He went looking for Vicki who was in coach picking up trays. He caught her eye and motioned with his head for her to come up front with him. She gave him a nod and continued picking up trays. Under his breath Grant muttered, "Come on Vicki, that wasn't a friendly nod hello." He needed help—so much for remaining cool. He turned and looked into first class and saw they were in the middle of their meal service.

Vicki startled Grant when she came up from behind, "What's the matter?" He whirled around, flustered. "Grant, what's wrong? You're sweating. Your hair is a mess, go look at yourself."

He told her the entire story and she told him to calm down. He hadn't realized his nerves were so obvious. Vicki calmly told him, "You go down to the pit and wait for me."

Grant complied and was happy to see that Connie didn't appear to be upset with him. She even offered him some pupus. His queasy stomach instructed him to say no thanks. The elevator came down with Vicki onboard. Grant felt like the cavalry had arrived.

Vicki made a little small talk with Connie and took some snacks to nibble on. She told Connie, "Why don't you go upstairs and help pick up, and I'll put the carts away while I'm down here having my break."

"Sure, if you don't mind. I'm sure Alana would appreciate the help."

Connie went up the elevator and Grant told Vicki how amazing she was. Grant went straight to the door and into the forward pit. He heard the elevator coming down and closed the sliding door behind him. He could only hope it wasn't Connie wondering where he disappeared to. He didn't hear anyone talking so he was sure it was only a cart being sent down. He stumbled toward the courier boxes and suitcases. "What a sight," he shook his head looking at the unlocked box and suitcase. He first locked the courier box and then the suitcase. Grant then opened the other courier box and the suitcase next to it. There were three more packages of tightly-wrapped cocaine. He switched them from the box to the suitcase, closed both and turned the combination tumblers.

On his way out, Grant tripped and fell next to the sliding door. He was sure it couldn't be heard considering the noise from the 550-mile per hour slipstream. He picked himself up, dusted off his uniform, and opened the sliding door a crack to look into the galley. It flew open, scaring the hell out of him.

Vicki was laughing and said, "So, did you fall down in there?"

"Yeah, how did you know?"

"I heard you. I've fallen a few times myself. I've ruined a lot of nylons that way."

"I'm not sure I'm cut out for this crap."

"You're doing fine, but we really need to talk with Brian. It's too difficult for one person to keep this up and not get caught."

Connie sent a few carts down and then came down herself. After she thanked Vicki for helping out, Vicki and Grant went up in the elevator together. They agreed to meet later in the flight and make plans to talk with Brian. During Grant's walk around the plane he passed Brain's seat and ever so slightly nodded his head and smiled. Grant was sure Brian understood the cloak-and-dagger nod.

Vicki was busy most of the flight and she and Grant never had time to talk again. She just whispered, "I'll meet you upstairs in the office."

Grant stood with Alana and said goodbye to the people as they deplaned. He was feeling more comfortable; the anxiety of his earlier adrenaline attack had subsided and he was going to be six-thousand dollars richer "Well, maybe three-thousand," he thought. He knew he would share his earnings with Vicki. He knew they were both more comfortable sharing the money and the responsibility of switching the contents of the courier boxes. It was a lot less stressful for the two of them to work together.

Grant went up to the office and checked his mail. There was an envelope from Maryann. The note read, "Grant, Renee has grieved the letter of warning and we need to set a hearing date. I've looked at your schedule and you have a couple of days off next week. Which is best for you: Thursday or Friday? You might also want to come by my office beforehand, so we can discuss this."

"Swell," he thought, "there go my days off."

Vicki walked up. "What's the matter, you look upset?"

"I have to go to a hearing next week. I really hate this part of the job."

"Brian had to go to the warehouse and said he could meet with us in an hour at the Airport Hilton. Can you make it?"

"Sure, I just want to change out of my uniform and drop a note to Maryann." Grant quickly wrote a note telling Maryann that Friday would work best for him and that he would stop by on Thursday to discuss the hearing.

Grant drove into the Airport Hilton parking lot just in time to see Brian walking with a couple of guys to his car. They were both large, sinister-looking men. One had a shaven head and a tattoo on his neck. Grant thought how unpleasant it would be to meet those guys in a dark alley. They gave Brian a small package, talked briefly, and left without shaking hands. Not wanting Brian to know he had seen them, Grant sat in his car until Brian walked into the front lobby.

Grant went into the lobby and headed straight for the bar area. Brian was sitting alone in a dimly lit back booth. He looked up and smiled as Grant approached his table. Brian stood up and they shook hands. The waitress stopped at their table and Brian ordered for all of them as Vicki slipped into the booth next to him. When the waitress left, Brian said, "I just talked with the pickup guys. Everything's fine. Good job, Grant."

Since it didn't seem to be a secret, Grant asked, "Are those the two guys I saw you talking with in the parking lot?"

"Yeah, they take turns picking up the suitcases while the other guy stays in the background just in case. They're nervous that maybe someone knows what they're doing and might try to follow them or steal the suitcases, typical paranoid drug dealers."

"They sure looked mean to me."

"I think they could be if they had to be. The bald guy used to be a semi-pro wrestler. He still uses his wrestling name—Max Payne—and the other guy goes by Roberto. They're okay to deal with and they always pay after they pick up the cases."

"Frankly, I wouldn't feel comfortable dealing with those guys."

"I think their boss keeps them in line and pays them well. If he can trust them, so can I."

"Who's their boss?"

"Grant, that isn't important or necessary for you to know."

Grant was a little stung by Brian's short remark.

Just when Brian was about to apologize for his shortness, Vicki chimed in, "Brian, we need to do something about moving things from the boxes to the suitcases."

"In what way?"

"I've come close to getting caught. Once by Grant of all people, and I don't think Grant would have been able to switch the contents today without my help."

Grant chimed in, "I couldn't agree more. It took both of us to get it done today."

"So, what would you suggest?"

"Grant and I don't mind sharing the $1,000 per package, but I don't think we can fly together every trip. Maybe we could find another flight attendant to work with us? Why not make it two supervisors and two flight attendants?"

"We'll discuss that another time. First, I want you to know, I'm going to raise your share to $1,500 per kilo since it looks like you'll be sharing it. The street value is going up and I can get it from the dealer."

Vicki and Grant talked about bidding the same line, but there were two problems with that. First, supervisors didn't bid by seniority, they bid by rotation. All the supervisors were on a list and worked their way to the top.

If Grant was at the top he could bid any trip and be sure to get it. But if he was far down on the list, he still had a chance to get what he wanted, but it wasn't a sure thing. The other problem, which was less concerning, was if Vicki couldn't get the pit position. She was sure that even if she couldn't, she could always find a reason to let the pit person take a break.

"If we found another supervisor or flight attendant, we could rotate with them," Vicki proposed.

Brian was reluctant about recruiting another flight attendant. "It would be a delicate situation finding someone we could trust, and things are going well enough as is. Let's think about getting another flight attendant some other time."

Vicki and Grant agreed, and made plans to meet in a couple of days to work out their schedules.

Thursday arrived, and Grant went into the office to talk with Maryann. He didn't bother to make an appointment. If she was busy, he had plenty of office work to do. He walked past Maryann's office and looked in the open door. She looked up and motioned him in. "Close the door behind you. I've set the hearing for 10:00 A.M. tomorrow. I've looked at your letter again, and it's good. There are no mistakes the union can use to have it thrown out. I'm guessing this is your first hearing?"

"Yes it is, and I'm not really sure what to do. There is no way she doesn't at least deserve a letter of warning in her file."

"While that may be true, I'm sure the union representative will ask why you didn't put a letter in her file before this; if you thought it was serious enough in the first place."

They talked about the hearing in detail before Grant left. He felt comfortable since Maryann was also the hearing officer. He wondered if it was a conflict of interest for her and thought maybe she should recues herself. But on the other hand, he knew he needed all the help he could get.

Grant showed up at 9:30 the next morning and checked his mail. While he tried to act nonchalant, he was actually a nervous wreck. Walking around the office, Grant wondered if anyone knew there was going to be a hearing. He was sure Renee hadn't missed her chance to tell anyone within earshot.

Maryann was startled when Grant knocked on her open door. "Come on in. Are you ready for the hearing?"

Before he could respond, there was a knock on the door and Maryann and Grant looked up. "Good morning. Please come in," Maryann said.

Grant almost choked when he saw Betty, the redheaded union rep with Renee. Formally, Maryann started, "We're convening this hearing regarding a letter of warning placed in Renee Burkhart's personal file by Grant Guidera. It was placed there in response to a passenger's complaint letter. Would you like me to read the letter? "

Betty said, "No, that won't be necessary."

"Okay then, why don't you start by explaining the grounds for your grievance."

Betty presented their case while Renee sat there with a smug look on her face. "We feel first and foremost that Mr. Guidera should have in fact, come to the defense of Ms. Burkhart. For a member of management to just sit there and let a passenger paw a flight attendant is inexcusable."

Grant spoke up, "Wait a minute, that's not…"

Maryann jumped in, "Grant, you'll have your turn. Now let Betty finish."

Betty continued: "For him to witness this man touching Renee and then to have the nerve to suggest that she apologize is unacceptable. If Mr. Guidera truly felt Ms. Burkhart was so wrong, why didn't he do something about it immediately?"

"It's because I was…"

Maryann spoke up, "Grant, I told you. You'll have your turn."

Betty concluded, "We feel this letter should be removed from Renee's file as it's only there because Mr. Guidera was told to put a letter in Renee's file. He was there and saw everything and didn't believe Renee deserved a letter then or he would have given her one. This letter was given to her because a passenger who got his feelings hurt made a big stink. Renee didn't want his hands all over her and stuck up for herself."

Maryann inquired, "Grant, why didn't you give her a letter of warning before?"

Grant was getting frustrated. He sarcastically remarked, "Is it my turn to talk?"

"Yes."

"I was sitting one row back of Mr. Cole helping a lady with a ticket. Renee came down the aisle and a lady on the other side of the aisle from Mr. Cole raised her hand to get Renee's attention. Renee leaned over to assist her. Mr. Cole, after waiting a minute, tapped her on the shoulder very lightly. It seemed to startle Renee, and she swung around and hollered, 'If you touch me again, I'll punch you in the mouth.' Needless to say, this turned a lot of heads. I couldn't see Mr. Cole's face, but I'm sure he didn't look happy. Wanting to give Renee the benefit of the doubt, I tried to have a talk with her."

Betty jumped in, "Didn't you tell Renee that you wouldn't give her a letter of warning?"

Grant said, "Excuse me, Maryann can I finish?"

"Just let Betty finish what she was saying."

Grant couldn't believe he had lost his turn already. Betty went on, "And the reason was that you didn't think it was important enough? And didn't you tell her you would just mention it in your flight report?"

"Is it my turn again?"

With Betty and Renee looking smug and Maryann trying to look authoritative, Grant went on, "I told Renee I didn't think she was touched in an inappropriate way or place, and that she should apologize. She had a bad attitude about the entire situation. Looking back, I think she should have been suspended. I tried to give her a break and a chance to realize what she had done. I will never make that mistake again."

Sensing Grant was finished, Maryann queried, "Do either of you have anything else?"

Betty summed up the situation smugly, grating on Grant's last nerve. "We ask the letter of warning be removed from Renee's file. Mr. Guidera didn't feel it was important enough to give her a letter in a timely manner since he didn't think the situation required more than a mention in his flight report. If he did think it deserved more and didn't do anything at the time, then he was in-fact derelict in his duty as a supervisor. We think the only reason the letter of warning was issued is because he was told to write one after Mr. Cole's letter came in. More importantly, Mr. Guidera should have protected Renee from being groped by a passenger."

Maryann asked, "Grant, do you have anything else?"

"Yes, I have to agree with Betty, I was derelict in my duty. I tried to give Renee the opportunity to put a stop to further problems by apologizing to Mr. Cole. That still may not have helped. When I talked with Renee and witnessed her bad attitude, I should have taken her out of service and had her sit down. I should have then given her a Letter of Charge and had her suspended. I made a terrible mistake in judgment and gave a break to the wrong person. That's the only point I will concede: I was derelict in my duty."

Maryann adjourned the hearing and said she would have an answer in a few days. As Renee and Betty left the room, Maryann motioned for Grant to stay. She looked at Grant, "So Grant, did you learn anything here?"

"I'm not sure. You didn't seem to be on my side, why is that?"

"You made a lot of mistakes with this situation, and I can't condone you doing a poor job in front of the union. Like you said, you should have given her a Letter of Charge, especially since her attitude was so bad at the time. And then trying to cover your ass by putting this in your flight report hoping to bury it in the files? I'll let the letter stay in her file, but I hope you've learned from this one."

"I've learned Universal has some pretty undesirable flight attendants."

Maryann shook his hand indicating their meeting was over. Grant walked into the crew desk area and saw Betty and Renee talking and laughing with some flight attendants. He walked out thinking, "They wouldn't be laughing if they knew the outcome of the hearing." He wished he could be there when they found out. He was also sure this job didn't pay enough to put up with the likes of Renee and Betty.

Chapter 8

G rant got to the top of the bidding rotation, which made it easy for him and Vicki to bid the same flights. They flew together for three months, averaging four flights a month. Multiply that times four kilos per trip at $1,500, grossing $72,000 to split between them.

Things were going easier for Vicki and Grant as a team. In fact Grant thought things were going so well it was almost too good to be true. Not surprisingly, they were becoming confident and comfortable. They found the best time for Grant to come down was during the cocktail service. It seemed fewer people, if any, would go to the pit during that time. Grant would go down the elevator and with barely a hello to Vicki, who was usually busy setting up carts. He would go directly to the sliding cargo door and enter the cargo hold. They had even established a simple method of communicating. If Grant heard the elevator he would wait by the door to hear two knocks from Vicki letting him know she was the only one there.

Today, Grant closed the door and turned on his flashlight. Sometimes, like today, there was a coffin in the pit, which always made him uncomfortable. At least this time Grant didn't have to go past it to get to the courier boxes. He exchanged the packages and if the elevator had come down, he waited for Vicki's all clear knock. He came out and headed toward the elevator. He had to get it off his chest. "There's a coffin in there."

"Thanks, that's all I need to think about."

"Sorry, it was too creepy for me to keep to myself."

With the coffin off his mind, Grant went back to coach to see Brian. Grant shook his hand as he would any passenger. Brian asked Grant to join him for the sake of any passengers who might have been looking. Grant sat and smiled to Brian that familiar, mission accomplished smile. Grant noticed flight attendants starting to move around the cabin a little more than normal. They were moving carts aft toward the coach galley area. Grant was getting ready to excuse himself to see what was going on when the captain came over the PA system.

"Good afternoon folks, this is Captain Robertson. I'm sorry to say we're having a hydraulic problem with one of our engines. I promise it's nothing to worry about as far as safety goes. This 747 can fly on two engines if need be. Since we are not past the point of no return, I should say the halfway point, we will be turning back to Honolulu. Again, this is not a safety problem. I've asked the flight attendants to prepare the aircraft for landing. I'm sorry for any inconvenience. I'll keep you posted and thank you for your understanding."

Grant excused himself from Brian and went forward to talk with Nancy, the first flight attendant. "So, what else did the captain say?"

"He said he would be talking with maintenance and keep me posted."

"I didn't hear you make an announcement. How did the crew find out?"

"I just told them to pass it on. There's no big hurry and I didn't want to alarm anyone."

"That was good thinking. Let me know when you hear something. I'll have a lot of misconnects I'll need to work with."

It was a little premature to start looking up alternate flights since Grant needed an estimated time of arrival into San Francisco before he could be of any real help. He went down to visit Vicki who was busy putting away the liquor carts. Nancy came over the intercom, "Vicki, would you please make a double scotch for Mr. Nervous in 2B? Thanks, and if Grant's down there, would you tell him there are some passengers asking for him."

Grant went up and thanked Nancy, feeling slightly embarrassed. He knew he should have been more on top of customer concerns. He walked into first class and found a lot of people who were concerned about their connections in San Francisco. To alleviate the premature questions that were sure to come up, Grant picked up the PA. "Ladies and gentlemen, this is your Inflight Supervisor Grant Guidera. I am aware that many of you have connections in San Francisco. At this point, we don't have an estimate of the time that will be required to fix our problem. As soon as we have that information, we can better make arrangements for alternate connections."

The flight was still over an hour out of Honolulu and well above 18,000 feet. Grant called the cockpit and asked if he could come up. The second officer answered the phone and said it was okay, but they were doing a lot of talking with engineering in San Francisco. Grant was astounded they would be talking all the way to San Francisco and not Honolulu. He knocked lightly on the cockpit door, heard it unlatch and went in. Tom, the second officer, held his finger over his lips to be quiet. He then pointed to the headset hanging by the jump seat and motioned for Grant to put it on. Grant could hear someone talking with the captain. "Captain, we're going to run this by the Pratt and Whitney company-representative and get back to you, San Francisco maintenance out."

The Captain sat back and looked a little more relaxed. "Grant, how's it going back there?"

"Not bad so far, they seem to be taking it pretty well. Do you have any idea how long it will take to fix the problem and be on our way?"

"We're not sure yet, they think it's a pump problem with the indications we've given them. We've isolated that engine in case there's a leak out there. We might have to get on the ground before they can really tell what's going on."

The guy from maintenance came back over the headset: "96 heavy this is San Francisco maintenance."

"Go ahead maintenance."

"The factory rep thinks it's a bad impeller in the pump. They have a new pump in Honolulu, but there have to be some checks made first. We're talking about switching planes when you land."

"Won't moving all the baggage and cargo take a long time?"

"It will take less time than waiting for the engine check and even then there might still be a problem. This is our best bet, time wise. Please contact Honolulu scheduling on your company frequency. Good luck, San Francisco maintenance out."

The captain turned around in his seat and said to Grant, "I guess that's it. You might want to tell the crew what's going on. We'll have to change the buffets and switch the cargo."

With those words, Grant's stomach cramped and his heart skipped a beat. He went back to coach and over to Brian's seat. He sat down and very quietly told him, "We are going to switch planes."

Brian must have seen the worried look on Grant's face and spoke up before Grant had a chance to say anything more. "Grant, I'll need to be out on the ramp and escort my courier boxes to the other plane. If we're getting another crew, I'll need to show my arms permit to the captain."

"Sure, that shouldn't be a problem. Why don't I move you closer to the door, so you can be the first one off. Depending on time, I think we'll be keeping the same crew. They should still be legal for the trip home."

The fact that Brian didn't seem worried calmed Grant down. Passengers kept inquiring about their concerns and Grant couldn't help but wonder if they had listened to his announcement. He went to the nearest PA and made another announcement. He felt he had been clear the first time and knew it was redundant to the ones who did listen. When giving the same announcement the second time, some of the passengers smiled and gave Grant a look of understanding.

After Grant finished his announcement, the captain came on, "Hi again folks. This is the captain speaking. I understand your concerns and promise to keep you informed. After talking with engineering we've decided it would take less time to change planes than to wait for this one to be repaired. Fortunately, we do have another plane that is ready to go. When we arrive back in Honolulu, we will need time to change the cargo from this plane to our replacement. With any luck, that shouldn't take more than an hour, and we'll be on our way. Again, we'll keep you informed and thank you for your understanding."

The captain's announcement made it official. Grant, still trying to comfort the concerned passengers, made another announcement. "Hi again folks, this is your supervisor, when we get under way, San Francisco passenger service will know our arrival time and make arrangements for those of you who will miss your connections. Thank you and we will keep you informed."

The crew prepared for landing and Grant moved Brian to the front of coach next to the door. The captain parked at an open gate to unload the passengers and baggage. When the Jetway pulled up, there was a knock on the door and Nancy gave the agent a thumbs up after disarming the emergency slide. There were a couple of agents and a supervisor standing on the Jetway. When the door opened, the supervisor came onboard and made an announcement giving the new gate number for their return flight. Grant told the supervisor he was going to escort Mr. Lasswell down the Jetway stairs and stay with him on the ramp.

Brian and Grant walked down the stairs, around the nose of the plane. A belt loader and a well-used forklift arrived at the front pit, along with a tug and container cart for the loose suitcases. Brian and Grant looked at each other with some anxiety. By rights, Brian could only act interested in his courier boxes. The big guys working the ramp weren't always that careful with luggage, so it was reasonable to be apprehensive. A couple of them flipped their kneepads around for protection and rode the belt into the pit. The coffin was the first to come out followed by the well-marked courier boxes. The coffin was loaded onto a lowboy truck at the bottom of the belt and pulled away. The tug driver jumped off to help load the courier boxes. "Okay," he said, "just walk along side and we'll take these right over."

Grant didn't know what to say, but Brian spoke up. "Thank you so much, but let's wait until you have a full load, I'm in no hurry."

The driver indicated his appreciation and helped fill the tug with the other baggage. Brian and Grant just watched while the bags were transferred. There weren't too many and Grant spotted the pink and chartreuse strings marking the bags of value as they were moved. Grant asked the tug driver if he could drive slowly so they could keep up alongside. Fortunately, the replacement plane was only three gates away. Grant was nervous watching the suitcases bouncing along and could just picture one of them toppling off and spilling their valuable contents on the ramp. They were nearly to the new gate when a cop with a dog came to the cart and motioned for the driver to stop. Holding the dog back, he walked to Brian and Grant. Noticing Grant's badge, he motioned to Brian and asked, "Who's this?"

"This is Mr. Lasswell. He's a courier."

Just then the dog started barking and tugging on his leash. The dog led the officer right to the suitcase with the chartreuse string. Grant's heart started pounding and his palms became sweaty.

Brian, trying to sidetrack the cop, intervened. "Excuse me officer," he said holding out his gun permit. The cop looked at Brian, then the dog and Grant. He looked confused. He didn't seem to know which was more important.

"I think my dog smells something."

Grant said, "Look, we just landed because we had engine problems, this luggage, including these bags, have already been through security."

"I still think he smells something."

"Does your dog's nose ever give you a false positive?"

"Very seldom."

"Well, this must be one of those times. Look, we would have to find the passenger to get these bags opened. It's your choice if you want to be responsible for delaying this flight any longer."

The officer looked puzzled and reached for the walkie-talkie on his shoulder. Before the officer could say anything, Brian held out his gun permit again, and said, "Would you please look at this so I can put it away?"

The dog stopped barking and sat down. Grant said, "Officer, we need to do something, either let us get the plane re-loaded or call someone. I don't want to be responsible for any further unnecessary delay."

Grant's heart was in his throat. He knew this was their last chance to bluff the cop or get caught. The dog sprawled lazily next to the baggage cart, panting lightly. The confused cop relaxed too. "Okay, go ahead." The dog barked once as Brian, Grant and the luggage tug left and headed for their plane.

Grant made a lot of money working with Brian and Vicki. For the most part, the only times he felt any guilt was when he thought about Gina. He knew she would have been disappointed in his choice of a new venture.

It had gotten almost too easy. There were a few times when a flight attendant had seen Grant go down to the pit and thought she was losing her mind when she followed shortly after and Grant wasn't there. Vicki would tell her he had only been there for a minute and had just left.

More pressing on Grant's mind was the infrequency with which he saw Pat. They knew it was unusual to have schedules that were so opposite. He sometimes worried Pat wasn't trying, but would then question if, maybe, he was the one not trying hard enough. When they were together, their time was special to him. Grant knew it was for Pat as well. But it had nearly been a month since they had seen each other. Grant had come to depend on a phone message or a note in his mailbox, but that didn't seem like enough. It didn't seem to be a relationship—not one they could enjoy.

While Grant's romantic life may have been disappointing, financially he was booming. He had wisely been investing in stocks and real estate along the way.

As expected, Grant was on the reserve list for a month. On his first reserve day, he was called for a New York trip. He walked into briefing ready for a change and a lot less stress. But the sight of Renee sitting there was the end of that idea. Luckily, Shanda was the first flight attendant. Grant had never forgotten their night together in Pittsburgh. He wondered if she ever thought about it. As he sat next to Shanda he could feel something stirring inside again. "Grant, it's so good to see you again," Shanda said with a wide white smile. It was a cute smile.

Grant was thrilled when he found Renee was working the first class pit He wouldn't have to worry about her in the main cabin, around passengers.

Shanda asked if Grant had anything to say at the end of the briefing. Jokingly he said, "I wouldn't dare try to make suggestions with Universal's best ex-supervisor as the first flight attendant." That got a few laughs and an unpleasant look from Renee.

Grant felt uncomfortable being in the same room with Renee, never mind on the same plane. "Thank goodness she will be in the pit," Grant thought again. He was sure she would be telling her side of the story to a captive audience coming for meal breaks. They would have to listen while they ate and they might be convinced that the situation was his fault. Grant fought back his worries and his insecurity because he was confident that most people knew her reputation.

Before passenger boarding, Grant was standing in the buffet getting ready to write down his tips. Renee opened the elevator door to the pit, avoiding eye contact with Grant. Against his better judgment, he suggested, "Renee, I would like it if we could put that letter behind us and move on. We were friends once and this is no way to have to work."

"I don't need to put up with your kind, and we were never friends. We just had friends in common." With that she closed the door and went to the pit.

Shanda stopped by Grant, having overheard her remark. "I heard what happened between you and Renee. I don't have to tell you how I feel about her, but for now I need to work and get along with her. I've been there, and I'm on your side."

"I appreciate you saying that. If you don't have any plans in New York, maybe I could buy you a drink at the Back Stage?"

"I'd like that, but let me see how things go. If some of the flight attendants have plans it wouldn't look good if we just went off together. I'm sure you would be welcome."

"Not if Renee has anything to do with it, let me know later."

It was a smooth flight and Grant kept himself busy with passengers in the first class lounge; they were a nice bunch, and as usual, they weren't bashful about drinking early in the day. A few of them invited Grant to join them at their table. He stayed for some time before going downstairs to check the deli service. He admired Shanda's work in first class. He knew she was providing the special service the passengers had come to expect. She was definitely a first class kind of person.

Grant was getting hungry, but he would rather have starved than go to Renee's pit, so he went and snacked on some of the deli leftovers in coach. Grant was relieved the flight attendants were so friendly to him. He was paranoid about Renee spreading her poison and infecting the rest of the crew. If she had talked to them, they didn't appear to give it much credence. Their friendliness put Grant in a good mood, and he told the three flight attendants in the aft pit that he would buy the first round of drinks when they arrived and asked them to tell the others when they came down for break. He was sure Renee wouldn't show up, and hoped Shanda would feel more comfortable joining him.

The flight crew was staying at the Park Sheraton Manhattan, which had a nice bar. There were two gleaming limos waiting for them outside the boarding area. Grant swiftly got in the front seat of the first limo. As he hoped and expected, Renee got in the second limo. Grant broke the silence in the limo with his invitation: "That was a nice trip. I'll buy the first round for anyone who would like to meet for a drink an hour after we get in."

A few of the flight attendant's mumbled thanks and others replied: "See you there." Grant was happy when Shanda, sitting way in the back, said, "Bribing the crew with drinks? I'll be there." That got a few laughs. Grant sat back and enjoyed the rest of the ride from the airport.

Waiting at the hotel desk for his room keys, Grant overheard Renee asking a couple of girls if they wanted to meet for a drink and maybe dinner. Not knowing any better, one of them said, "Dinner sounds good. We're going to meet in the bar and Grant is going to buy us a drink. We can talk about dinner then." Renee made a remark that Grant couldn't overhear. He was sure it wasn't something that would have pleased him.

Grant called in his sales, took a shower, and headed out. He saw three of his flying partners sitting at a large table and almost didn't recognize them. It never ceased to amaze him how attractive they were out of uniform and their hair down.

The rest of the crew came in together. Shanda sat next to Grant, and much to his surprise, Renee came in and sat at the far end of the table. As the waitress was taking orders, Grant told her to put everyone's first drinks on his tab. When the waitress got to Renee, Grant saw her put money on the table and tap it with her finger, much like the guy who tapped her on the shoulder, only harder. The two girls sitting next to her looked a little surprised at what she must have said.

A couple of the girls held up their glasses and said cheers. Renee glared Grant's way and said something to the girl sitting on her left. Shanda put her hand on Grant's leg. He wasn't sure if that was a sign of support or affection. It felt good and brought back fond memories of their Pittsburgh layover.

Shanda had agreed to go to the Back Stage if Grant invited the rest of the girls. He announced, "If any of you would like to go to the Back Stage, first drinks are on me. You'll need to share a cab going and coming." A few people asked what kind of a place it was, and he explained that after the theaters closed for the night, a lot of the performers would go to the club and take turns singing to unwind after their performances on Broadway. On a previous visit, Grant had been sitting with a flight attendant when a couple of well-coiffed ladies came to their table and asked if they could sit in the other two empty seats. Grant and his date agreed and later found out they were sitting with world famous opera singer Beverly Sills. Grant didn't have a clue as to who she was at the time, but Beverly's young companion wasn't bashful about explaining, Grant later saw Ms. Sills on a television show.

Grant explained it was a good idea to get there before the shows let out so they could get good seats. Six of the crew were eager to go. Grant was encouraged when he saw Renee stay behind with two other girls. As usual, the sight of six attractive, tall women standing up caused heads to turn. Grant enjoyed the envy of the male patrons.

Getting a cab was no problem in New York, but the driver wouldn't let seven of them squeeze into one—not even with a bribe. They met in front of the club and went in together. Gerald was greeting patrons at the door and Grant was pleasantly surprised that Gerald remembered him from past visits. "Grant, what have we here, more beautiful girls, how do you do it?" Grant introduced Gerald to the girls and asked for a couple of tables. The club was dark, and Gerald put a pen light up to his broad nose and said, "Right this way." He reminded Grant of Rudolph the Red-nosed Reindeer as he walked them to their table. He always thought it was crude, but funny at the same time.

"How's this?" he asked, "Great view of the piano." There were two tables close together. Shanda tugged on Grant's sleeve and whispered, "There's Rita Moreno." Trying to act sophisticated, he said, "Say hello Rita." He said it loud enough that Rita heard him. She turned and said, "Hello Rita," with a smile.

Two of the girls were sitting with Grant and Shanda. The other three sat at the adjacent table and were soon joined by some guys that Gerald brought over. Anyplace else and that wouldn't have been acceptable, but on a couple of occasions Grant had gotten seats the same way. Everyone was having a good time. The club was filling rapidly. The pianist was playing, and soon patrons were singing. Grant didn't recognize any of the entertainers, but they were fantastic. They must have been young unknown talents.

The crew was having an enjoyable time, but it was getting late. One of the guys from the other table came over and started talking with the girls at Grant's table. Evidently he was on a soap opera and the girls were thrilled. Grant couldn't help but notice that Shanda hadn't completely shed her supervisory past as she seemed overly concerned about the other flight attendants. She relaxed when she realized the others were just having a good time. As if to overcome the noise, Grant got closer to Shanda and whispered in her ear.

"As your supervisor, I would like to talk to you about your attitude. It will be an informal hearing in my room. Wear your negligee."

She laughed and said, "I didn't think you were the type to take advantage of your position."

"I just want to help you become a better flight attendant."

They laughed and surprisingly, she kissed him solidly on the lips. It was a quick one, but Grant looked around to confirm none of the other crew had seen his delight. They didn't seem to notice. Grant asked, "Are you hungry?"

"I could eat something. Why don't we ask the others if they're ready to leave?" Shanda asked. Much to Grant's pleasure they all wanted to stay.

Grant waved down a cab, "Stage Deli, please." Shanda smiled, touched the back of his hand and gave him a kiss on the cheek. "You can do better than that."

"Grant!" she protested. Just then the cab pulled up to the Stage Deli.

It wasn't crowded. The low background buzz was a pleasant contrast to the loud and brash Back Stage. "Look!" she gasped. "There's Rodney Dangerfield."

Grant and Shanda shared a sandwich and walked back to the hotel. They kissed on the elevator, and he wondered if security watched what was going on, the thought excited him. He knew if anyone was watching, they would have been jealous. They arrived on the seventh floor and got out of the elevator. There was an awkward moment until Shanda suggested, "You have a nicer room. How about I get the bottle of wine I have in my room and come back for a nightcap?"

"Okay, only if you promise not to try anything."

Shanda laughed as she opened the door to her room. Grant entered his room, turned on the television, pulled back the bedspread, got a couple of glasses and put them on the table by the window. There was a light tap on the door and his heart jumped. He opened the door and Shanda entered. He hadn't noticed that she had her company raincoat on, until it lay on the floor. She was wearing the same baby dolls she had worn in Pittsburgh. Her blonde tresses spilled over her shoulders concealing her left breast, but her right breast rose enticingly under the thin material. "Okay, did you want to talk to me about my attitude?"

"You get more beautiful and exciting each time I see you," Grant told her. He pulled her into his arms, kissed her cheek tenderly and then her lips.

"Can a girl get a glass of wine around here?" Shanda said with a twinkle in her eyes.

"Forgive me. Of course she can."

He filled the two glasses. They sat, and drew a breath.

"That was a fun evening," Shanda said.

Cleverly Grant replied, "It's not over yet. Let's pull the covers back and watch a little television."

Shanda pulled the covers back with one hand, while holding her glass in the other. As she lay back with the pillow propping up her head, the bottom of her baby doll pulled down a bit, revealing her flat abdomen and the whirlpool of her navel.

"Wait, don't move," Grant commanded. He grabbed the bottle of wine and playfully poured some in her navel. She just giggled as he put the bottle back on the nightstand and began to lap the wine. The merriment continued into the early morning.

The next day, the crew had the six o'clock flight to San Francisco. There were two white limos waiting outside the hotel to pick up the crew. The first one filled up and unfortunately, Renee wasn't in it. The rest of the waiting flight attendants got in the second limo.

Grant finally asked, "Has anyone seen Renee?"

One girl answered, "I had dinner with her last night."

"Did she say anything about not being here or that someone would be driving her to the airport?"

"No, we had dinner at a French restaurant and met a couple of guys, but we came home together."

Wanting to have a good witness, Grant asked, "Shanda, would you mind going in and calling her room or asking if she's checked out?"

"Okay, but don't leave without me."

"I promise."

The driver was getting impatient and asked how long they would wait. Grant told him they needed to get to the airplane, and if she wasn't in her room they would only wait ten minutes for her. Shanda jumped in the back seat, "Renee didn't answer and the clerk said he couldn't give checkout information about a guest."

Grant went to the desk and told the clerk he needed to find out if Renee Burkhart had checked out, and he needed to know now. The clerk looked at Grant's company badge and finally checked in the computer.

"No, she hasn't checked out."

"What's her room number, I need to call."

"We can't give out that information."

"What's the matter with you people? I'm her supervisor."

"I'll dial her room sir, pick up that phone." The clerk said, pointing to a black phone at the end of the counter. Grant picked it up and heard it ring eight times. Grant thanked him. As far as Grant was concerned, he did all he could and had witnesses. It was almost fifteen minutes past pick up time when he jumped in the front seat of the limo, next to a frustrated driver. "That's it. Let's go."

The ride was quiet for the most part. One girl wondered out loud what could have happened to Renee. Grant wondered if he should have had someone go to her room and make sure she wasn't lying dead on the floor. That thought brought a little smirk to his face that he couldn't fight back. He was ashamed of the thought and turned his head to the right and looked out the window. He didn't want it to show.

The limo arrived at Kennedy and the driver jumped out to get their bags and help the girls out of the back. The crew from San Francisco's flight 22 was waiting by the curb for the limo. Grant walked over to the supervisor, apologized and explained why they were late.

She smiled and said, "Renee Burkhart. I'm glad she was on your flight."

There weren't briefing rooms in New York, so the flight crew went straight to the gate area. The gate agent said he was sure the cleaners were done and told them they could do their briefing onboard. He gave a copy of the manifest each to Shanda and Grant. Grant took a moment to call the crew desk and ask for a replacement for Renee, He explained that she was a no-show. The crew was briefing in the upstairs lounge when he got onboard.

Grant wrote down all his tips as usual and was headed to the upstairs lounge. He took one last long look at Shanda. She was captivating.

The passenger agent came onboard and made his final announcement. As the doors were closed, Grant told Shanda he would be up in the lounge getting his tips organized.

Grant enjoyed sitting in the dimly lit lounge and watching the people in the terminal watch the plane. He glanced down the left side and saw the Jetway pulling back from the door just before he felt the tug hook up for push back. He saw Renee standing next to the agent driving the Jetway. She was frantically waving her arms and looked as though she was hollering. He was sure the engine noise was drowning out her voice. It didn't appear they were going back to pick her up. Grant didn't want to bother the cockpit—the pilots might have been receiving their clearance or flight plan. He had to admit, if that were Shanda out there, he would have done all he could to get them to go back. But Renee didn't deserve a break and especially not from him. He had tried that once and it had come back to bite him. This was going to be serious. She wasn't just late; she had missed the flight entirely. Grant was sure she would file some kind of a grievance when she got his letter of charge.

Other than thoughts of Renee and the paperwork he needed to file, it was a nice flight home. Among the crew during breaks, Renee was the topic of conversation. Grant didn't dare join in.

When Grant checked his mail, he felt a pang of guilt when he saw a note from Pat. Afraid Pat might somehow see it, Grant put Shanda's phone number in his pocket before reading her note. It was a warm, loving note that made him feel even guiltier. He would have called her right then, but the note said she was leaving on a trip. His guilt was nearly suffocating.

Grant went to the office around 10:00 A.M. the next day to start the paperwork on Renee. There was a note from Maryann: "Please stop by my office to talk about Renee."

Grant knocked on the open door.

"That was fast. I just put that note in your box."

"I was trying to get here before you had to leave a note."

They had a long conversation about Renee and the situation. Maryann heard through the duty supervisor that Renee had to catch a flight to Chicago and then the all-nighter to San Francisco. Renee told the duty supervisor she thought her pickup was at four and that she must have been in the shower when and if anyone called.

Maryann asked, "So, what do you think you should do?"

Grant was sure she wanted to see if he had learned anything from the last episode. "I don't know. I'd like to fire her ass."

"Be serious and stop dreaming."

"Well, at least a letter of charge and considering her record, maybe a suspension?"

"That could be defendable considering the other issues in her file aren't dependability-related."

Maryann had Renee's file on her desk and asked Grant to look through it. Renee had been written up for her marketing announcement. Then there was Grant's letter of warning and one other incident where she was late for a trip.

Grant made his recommendation, saying, "I think she should get a letter of charge putting her on probation for six months, specifically because this is the second issue with her dependability. The letter will state that if she has another infraction related to attitude or dependability, she will be suspended."

"I think you're on the right track. Why don't you draft a letter, run it by personnel and show me the finished product."

Grant drafted a letter with the help of a couple of supervisors. They were good at writing letters and particularly enjoyed helping with this one since they also were not fond of Renee. He took the letter to personnel and then showed it to Maryann, who was very impressed. He sent Renee a copy to her home and explained that he also put one in her file.

Chapter 9

The following morning, Brian called and asked if Grant could meet him at the Airport Hilton for coffee. By this time, Grant considered Brian a friend. Over coffee and tea they small-talked about Grant's real estate and stock investments. He had two rental houses. It was nothing compared to Brian's portfolio, but Brian was impressed with how well Grant had invested.

"If it's possible, I could sure use your help on a Honolulu pick up." Brian said.

"I'm on reserve. I might not get a Honolulu trip. I'm actually on my first of three days off."

"Okay. Well if you do, will you call me? I have a good feeling about it."

"Of course I will, but I don't want you to depend on me. What about Vicki, would she be there too?"

"We'll work that out." Brian seemed a little despondent. Grant was starting to feel uncomfortable. They finished their meeting, walked out together and shook hands good-bye.

When Grant got home there was a message on his machine: "Grant, this is Joe please call the crew desk. We need someone to deadhead to Honolulu this evening on flight 129 leaving at 7:25 P.M. and cover the afternoon Honolulu to SFO return tomorrow."

Grant called Joe to say he could make it and then Brian. "Hi Brian, I have a Honolulu trip tomorrow."

"Okay good. Vicki will be working as an extra coming home on flight 96 and deadheading over tonight on the same flight as you. I'll be with her." Grant hadn't told Brian what flights he would be on, but Brian knew. Brian had more connections than Grant had realized.

Grant had an aisle seat in first class on his deadhead over. The window seat was empty. Vicki sat in coach with Brian. It really didn't matter to them—the drinks were always free when you knew the flight attendants. Grant slept a few hours when he wasn't thinking of when and how to end his risky relationship with Brian. Doing the right thing and Grant's ambitions were no longer compatible. He was thinking all too often about Gina and what she would think of his behavior. It wasn't a pleasant thought.

Grant was just waking up when he heard a sweet voice behind him say, "Hi handsome, can I buy you a drink?" It only took a second to realize it was Pat. His heart was racing as he moved to the window seat so she could sit with him.

"Why didn't I see you?" Grant asked.

"Because I'm working the pit and just now found out you were here. I shouldn't tell you this, but one of the girls came down for a bite to eat and said, 'I saw that nice supervisor Grant sleeping in first class.'"

"Nice and supervisor aren't two words we normally hear in the same sentence."

"What are you doing on this trip, taking a little vacation?"

"No, actually I'm working 96 back tomorrow."

"Me too, that explains it. Our supervisor is deadheading back on 22 this evening, something to do about an office meeting tomorrow."

Grant spent the night in Pat's room. In the morning they had breakfast at the Jolly Rogers with Brian and Vicki. Brian and Vicki finished first and excused themselves. Grant didn't know when, if, or what he should tell Pat about working for Brian. They finished their breakfast and walked back to the hotel. There were a lot of flight attendants coming and going on the short walk, so they didn't hold hands. They were trying to keep their relationship private as much as possible.

"Grant you're being curiously quiet. What's on your mind?"

"Let's talk upstairs in your room."

Grant didn't say any more and they rode the elevator without saying a word. Pat anxiously opened her door and sat on one of the king size beds. Grant sat on the other, facing her. "I almost don't know where to begin. Actually, I should begin at the beginning. You were there. Remember our day on the boat with Brain and Vicki?"

"Yes, what about it?"

"Remember how he offered me a job?"

Pat was grasping at straws and finally said, "You mean you're involved in his drug trafficking scheme?"

"I am, but I won't be much longer. I've made a lot of money. I've invested it well and I'm looking for a way out."

"I don't know what to say. You mean a lot to me, more than I realized. I was hoping you were feeling the same."

"I do, but this is separate from us. I can't get out right now. In fact, there is a shipment on our flight today. I have to get in the pit and change some packages around."

Pat's eyebrows arched, her eyes squinted, her lips pursed, and her face became red. "So, you got on this flight knowing I was working the pit?"

"No, I swear to you. I didn't know you were going to be on this flight."

"How did you think you were going to get past whoever was working in the galley and into the cargo pit?"

"I've done it before, it's not easy. Vicki would come down and offer to give whoever was working a break and that's when I would exchange the packages."

"Grant, why don't you go to your room and get ready, I have a lot to think about."

Grant picked up his suitcase and headed to the door. He didn't think a parting kiss was in the cards, so he didn't try. He was concerned, but mostly hurt that she actually thought he was taking advantage of the fact she was working the pit position on his flight. She should have known, he loved her far too much to put her in that position. After being with Pat, he realized just how much he had missed her and his feelings for her were stronger than ever. He had to admit he was truly in love with her and the drug smuggling and encounters with Shanda would have to stop if they were going to have a future.

Grant finished showering and went to the lobby. He didn't know if he should knock on Pat's door and decided it was best not to push her. There were a few other crewmembers waiting for the bus. They were glad to see Grant. He didn't feel like talking, so he sat on one of the large sofas and looked at some company mail he hadn't read.

Pat came out of the elevator and went to check out. She stopped to chit-chat with a couple other flight attendants, then walked directly to Grant and sat fairly close. He looked up to see Pat's head tilted and a compassionate smile on her face. They didn't say anything; they didn't have to.

Grant couldn't wait to be alone with Pat. He was still concerned about her feelings, both about their relationship, and his work with Brian. After takeoff Grant made his announcement and then went back to coach. On the way to where Brian was sitting, not wanting to look obvious, he stopped to talk with a few passengers. Grant shook Brian's hand as if they had just met. Brian invited him to sit and opened his ticket wallet to show Grant a note: "Everything is set, how about you?"

Grant got up and said, "That connection shouldn't be a problem at all." They shook hands again and Grant headed toward the forward pit, only to be stopped a couple more times. He felt he was being a bit short with the passengers, but was anxious to talk with Pat.

Grant got in the elevator and was getting ready to close the door when the first flight attendant pulled it open and asked if he would have Pat send up some more champagne. He pressed the down button but left his stomach in the upper galley. Pat was loading the ovens and glanced at the opening elevator door. Grant had barely closed it when Pat came to him with outstretched arms. They hugged and said nothing.

"Where is the champagne I asked for?" a voice came over the intercom.

"Sorry, I forgot to tell you." Grant said apologetically.

Pat picked up the phone and said, "It's on the way, sorry."

Grant wasn't sure how to handle the situation.

"Grant, just do what it is you have to do. Close the door behind you and listen for the elevator. The only one who knows you're down here is the first flight attendant and she won't be coming down anytime soon."

With that Grant gave Pat a kiss on the cheek and went into the forward cargo pit. The courier boxes and suitcases were easy to get to and it only took a few minutes and he was done. Since he hadn't heard the elevator, he came right out.

Pat looked surprised, "Is that it? Are you done?"

"Yep, and I just made six thousand dollars."

"We'll talk about this another time. I need to get these meals out."

They kissed, and Grant went up to the upper lounge to make his conversions. Grant was writing a ticket and suddenly, was overcome with guilt. This was not something he wanted to get Pat involved with, not if he truly loved her.

Grant made three more lucrative trips before getting a note from Maryann about Renee: "Grant, Please stop by within the next couple of days. I want to get this Renee thing off my desk." He stopped by Maryann's office and she looked frazzled.

"Needless to say, Renee wants to grieve your letter of charge. I had a talk with Betty and told her you wanted to suspend Renee. I told her the letter of charge with six months probation was my suggestion. In essence,

I told her I did Renee a favor and that if she insisted on continuing with the grievance I wouldn't have much choice other than to hear the grievance and barring any new evidence, possibly suspend her. Plus, I told her I would be less inclined to interfere with a supervisor's recommendations the next time."

"So you got out of a hearing by telling her I wanted her suspended, and you're the good guy?"

"Pretty much, but I'm still not sure what she's going to do. She could be really difficult and say that I had obviously made up my mind before hearing her grievance. I'm just hoping they think I'm doing them a favor."

Grant was upset with Maryann's action, but glad there might not be a hearing. As far as he was concerned, Renee should have been fired some time ago. He just didn't like how Maryann was cutting down her workload at his expense.

While Grant and Pat spent time together, it didn't seem their schedules or their relationship was on the super highway to heaven. Grant knew Pat didn't approve of his activities, and she was often reserved when they were together.

Six months later, Grant was $90,000 richer. He bought a home in Hillsborough and purchased a considerable number of shares in start-up Silicon Valley companies. Grant rented out the Hillsborough home and hoped to remodel it someday before he moved in.

Grant was proud of his investments, but was still troubled about his method of making money. With guilt constantly weighing on his shoulders, his increased drinking was becoming a problem too. He realized he needed to make some tough changes in his life. He liked the fact the other supervisors and flight attendants were impressed with his success. But he knew it wasn't from hard work or any talent he had—he just let people think he was good at investing and fixing up homes. Grant never told anyone about the Hillsborough home. It was enough he had four other homes already.

Unusual as it was, Grant and Pat both had the weekend off. Grant needed grounding and he decided to plan a dinner for Gina and Randy. First, he had to call Pat. "Hi honey. If they can make it, I'm trying to put a dinner together for Gina and her boyfriend Randy this weekend. How does that sound?"

"That sounds great. I'll come over and we'll make a great dinner. I would love that."

Grant called Gina immediately.

"That would be perfect. We are free. It will be nice to see Pat again. What can I bring?"

"Just bring Randal, sorry Randy."

Grant called Pat back and couldn't hide his enthusiasm. "Hi honey, the dinner is on. Let's get together and plan something special."

Pat and Grant decided on a Chinese theme dinner. Pat made egg rolls, pot stickers, sweet and sour shrimp, and hot and sour soup. Pat set the large table upstairs, wanting to enjoy the view and impress Randy. They had drinks at the bar and discussed the view. It wasn't the best neighborhood on the peninsula, but it had one of the best views around. There was Crystal Springs Reservoir, the bay, the airport and Oakland on the other side. Pat and Gina got along well together, as did Grant and Randy.

Gina asked Grant about his houses, and if being a landlord was difficult. Grant kept his answers brief, and it was obvious he was avoiding the subject. Pat looked at Grant. She knew why he wasn't talking about his houses. She also hoped Gina and Randy would mistake Grant's not wanting to talk about his houses as modesty. Aside from that discomfort, they enjoyed a wonderful dinner and evening together. When the evening was over, there were hugs all around.

Grant and Vicki had another trip together the following Friday. They were on flight 97 to Honolulu with a return on 96. Brian was on the same flight. It was a light load so Grant had time to stop and talk with Brian. Brian just wasn't himself, and it was an uncomfortable conversation. Grant wanted to ask Brian to meet so they could talk, but he decided better of it.

At the hotel Grant called in his conversions, took a shower and called Vicki's room to see if Brian was there. Brian always got a room at an adjacent hotel, but spent a lot of time with Vicki at the crew hotel. Vicki picked up the phone on the first ring, "Brian?"

"Sorry it's just me. What's going on?"

"We had a little argument on the way in, and I feel badly."

Not wanting to be nosy and yet willing to listen, Grant said, "I'm sure you two will work it out. Is it personal?"

"He's under a lot of pressure to sell his Loomis franchise, and it's getting to him."

"Does he want to sell it?"

"Yes and no. He's concerned what might happen if he does and how it will be run. The guys who are interested want to continue to ship drugs and use the courier business to do it."

"I don't know about you, but I wanted to talk to Brian about getting out anyway. How do you feel about it?"

"I've had enough and so has Brian. We have enough income from legal investments and could do fine."

"So, what's the problem?"

"These guys know about you and me and our involvement. They think we go along with the business. If we don't, they say they can get others. That's the problem—our names could come out if they make a mess of it."

"Why don't I give Brian a call and go over and visit for awhile."

"Please call me as soon as you're done."

Brian also answered on the first ring.

"Hi Brian, can I come over and talk with you for a few minutes?"

"Not right now. I'm going to be meeting Vicki for drinks and dinner." Brian didn't sound right.

"I've talked with Vicki, and she's going to give us some time to talk."

"This is not a good time, I'm getting ready, and I have calls to make. Can we do this later? Why don't I give you a call or leave a message later?"

"Okay, but I really need to talk with you."

"I'll call."

Grant didn't feel right about the conversation. He wasn't sure if Brian was being rude or had too much going on. In any case, it wasn't like Brian. Grant decided to go over and knock on his door. When he got to Brian's floor and the elevator door opened, Keoki and two large Samoans were standing on the landing. Grant was getting ready to say hello to Keoki when he realized Keoki didn't recognize him. Grant nodded and walked off. He went to Brian's room and listened before knocking. He could hear water running. Brian looked through the peephole.

"Grant, go away. I'll talk to you later."

"I'm not going anywhere. Open the door."

Brian finally opened the door. He was a mess, his shirt was open and Grant could see welts on his upper body. "What do you want Grant?"

"What happened to you?"

"This is none of your business. I'll handle it."

"Brian, we're friends. What's going on?"

"I guess you have a right to know. It's been too good to be true. The guys I've been shipping for want to buy me out."

"That's almost what I wanted to talk to you about. Personally, I have enough money and investments. I don't want to keep this up. I owe you a lot for what I have, but I really want out. And let's face it Brian, you have a lot more than me. I know it's none of my business, but why not sell and get out?"

"I would in a heartbeat … to anyone but those dumb bastards. They'll fuck it up, get caught and start naming names. They know a lot more than I care to admit. If we could leave clean, I would be out of here. I have Vicki to think of and our future together."

"How are they going to mess it up? Let them have it."

"Grant, I've spent time with these people and see the kind of people they deal with. I see them down at the alley house with other supervisors and flight attendants. They are trying to get things in motion with all the wrong people. And sadly, those people now know about me, Vicki, and I'd bet, even you."

"Did they try to get you to sign anything?"

"No, this" Brian said, gesturing to his chest "was just a friendly reminder they want me out."

"What are you going to do?"

"I'm not sure just yet. I told them I have some things to work out back in the mainland, and I'd let them know. I need some time to think."

"I want to help you if I can. But I also really want out. It looks like this is a good time for just that."

"Don't say anything to Vicki if you see her. I want to surprise her. We're going to her favorite seafood place for dinner. I'm going to tell her that we'll be getting out, but it might take awhile. I want her to quit flying so we can enjoy each other. I'll work on the rest later. And Grant, thanks for caring. Let's get this trip over with and really think it out when we get home."

Grant went back to the Marine Surf and headed straight to the bar. Lonnie was her charming self, but had very little time to talk. Grant couldn't get a seat next to her station, but she came by when she could. Grant distracted himself, watching a couple of ex-Pan Am girls sitting in a booth with a couple of guys. He couldn't believe they would risk being so obvious if those were paying dates. Grant knew he was being unfair. Not all the Pan Am flight attendants were working on the side. By the end of his first drink he was relaxed and felt he would be able to make a clean break from the drug smuggling.

Lonnie asked Grant if he wanted to walk down the alley with her to the house party when she got off. He begged off, in no mood to see Keoki or his two big friends. They might just recognize him this time. Grant was sure when he first met Keoki, he was stoned. That would explain why Keoki hadn't recognized Grant by the elevator. Grant told Lonnie he would see her on his next trip and went to the little sushi bar for dinner.

Chapter 10

October 25, 1979

It was an early night and Grant woke feeling rested and happy with himself. He had breakfast at the Jolly Rogers and sat with a couple of flight attendants going out on the earlier trip. Brian and Vicki didn't always eat at the Jolly Rogers, so Grant didn't give it much thought when he didn't see them.

Grant got on the crew bus last and sat on the bench seat in back. There was the usual chatter and Donna asked, "Grant, have you seen Vicki?"

"She most likely rode in with Brian. He usually drops her off before turning in his rental car, then he meets up with the armored truck."

Grant's good feeling didn't last long. When he walked into the briefing room, he saw Renee sitting there and his mood worsened. She looked just as disappointed to see him.

"What are you doing here?" he asked, not trying to hide his feelings.

"Vicki is in the hospital and they pulled me off the earlier trip to work her position."

He couldn't believe what he was hearing. He left the briefing room and went straight to Ruby's desk.

"What happened to Vicki? Do you know?"

"A nurse called from the hospital—they had to pump her stomach. They want to keep her overnight. They think it was some kind of a shellfish poisoning. She's okay now."

"Why Renee, weren't there more junior people on that trip?"

"There were, but she volunteered to stay. I forgot you two had a history. Too bad she didn't ask me to look and see who the supervisor was. I'm sure it would have changed things. I'm sorry Grant."

"It's not your fault, you didn't know."

Grant caught Donna before she went into the briefing room. "Donna, Vicki's in the hospital with food poisoning. She's okay, but won't make the trip. Renee Burkhart volunteered to work this trip from the earlier one. If you can, keep her from working the pit."

"She's the senior flight attendant, and if she wants it, she'll get it."

"Okay, but do your best for me. I'm going down to see the courier."

"You mean Brian?"

"Yes, I'm sorry, Brian. I keep forgetting how many people know him."

Grant went down the Jetway and then down the stairs to the ramp. Brian was standing outside waiting for the ramp guys to put his courier boxes in the forward pit.

"Brian, what happened to Vicki?"

"What are you talking about?"

"You don't know? She's in the hospital with food poisoning. Don't worry, she'll be okay, but they're going to keep her overnight. "

Brian's mouth hung slightly agape and his eyes looked frozen open. "My God, she said she wasn't feeling well and wanted to go to her room. I offered to go with her, but she said she would be fine. I called her early to see if she wanted breakfast, but she wanted to stay in bed. She said she would see me on the plane." Brian looked impatiently at the boxes being loaded. "Grant, where is the nearest phone?"

Grant took Brian to the pilot's lounge and got him an outside line. When the hospital operator answered, he asked for Vicki O'Donnell's room. Brian was relieved when Vicki answered the phone, "Why didn't you call me?"

When Brian got off the phone, Grant approached him. "We've got another problem. Renee Burkhart might be working the pit."

"What's the problem? You've been able to switch the bags when someone besides Vicki was working."

"I guess you wouldn't know. I've written Renee up several times. And the last time the operating manager told Renee I wanted to suspend her. I'm concerned that anyone who knows me would be surprised to see me go down to the pit with her there."

Grant escorted Brian up the outside Jetway stairs and onto the plane. Grant was anxious to see where Renee was working. Just as he was closing the Jetway door, he looked back and saw a passenger agent coming toward the cabin door with an Asian man.

"Grant, I'm going to pre-board Mr. Chin. I've already pulled his ticket. Is that okay?"

"Sure, that's fine with me."

Donna was checking safety equipment in first class. She came walking back to Grant.

"I'm not sure why you didn't want Renee to work the pit, but she insisted. I would think you would be happy not to have her in the cabin."

"I just like to be able to go into the forward galley for a break."

"Well, I tried. You'll just have to make the best of it."

"You're right, thank you. It was just a shock to me."

Grant realized he'd made too big of a deal out of Renee working the pit. He didn't want Donna questioning what he was doing. He needed to think the situation over. Just then a flight attendant from coach came to Grant.

"We have a seat duplication."

"Did you look at both of their boarding passes?"

"One is a Chinese man who doesn't speak English or seem to have a boarding pass."

Grant walked back with her to see a man standing in the aisle by Mr. Chin, who was seated. "I'm sorry sir, we're getting ready to close the door and there are a lot of open seats. Would you mind sitting in one of them?"

The man was very nice about relocating and Grant told the flight attendant to give him a complimentary headset and drinks. Grant looked back at Mr. Chin who sat with his head held low, eyes darting back and forth nervously. Grant just smiled and did a slight bow. Grant didn't want to attempt to ask him for a boarding pass or ticket stub. It would have been too hard to explain. The passenger agent came onboard and gave the final departure check. Grant half wondered if Mr. Chin was on the wrong plane. If the passenger agent hadn't brought Mr. Chin on, Grant might have looked into that possibility.

Grant sat in the upper lounge during take off. But today he just wasn't enjoying it like he had in the past. Grant agonized about dealing with Renee and switching the packages. He took a Valium to calm himself down. Grant's tip sheet was a mess, and he only got half the possible conversions. He went through the motions and greeted the first class passengers. He walked back into coach toward Brian's seat. Brian nodded his head for Grant to come sit with him.

"Are you okay?"

"I'm a wreck. Let me ask, what would happen if we just didn't switch bags this trip?"

"Don't even think about it. It would have the guys in the baggage area going nuts over empty suitcases. There is just no way this time. Grant, just do it. I have enough problems without this."

"I'll do what I can, but it's not going to be easy."

Grant wandered around the plane making small talk, just watching and waiting for the first class service to get close to desserts and liqueurs. That would be the best time to get Renee out of the pit. He walked up to Donna in the galley. "Donna, the aft pit has four people down there and a couple waiting to go. Could you ask Renee to come up and help with second coffees and liqueurs?"

As she reached for the phone to the pit, Donna said, "Grant, you're a pain in the ass."

She pressed the phone button, "Renee, would you mind giving us a hand with second coffees and liqueurs? We have people all over the place."

Grant couldn't hear what Renee said, but the elevator came up and she got out. She was pleasant to Donna and asked where she wanted Renee to help. "How about the upper lounge and also check with the crew to see if they want anything."

Renee looked at Grant, but right through him. She left the area heading for the lounge.

"Thanks Donna." Grant smiled.

She smiled back, "You're welcome, and you're not a pain in the ass."

Grant got in the elevator. His heart was beating so fast he thought about taking another valium. There was no time for it, he just needed to hurry. He went straight for the cargo door, opened it and realized he had forgotten his flashlight. He grabbed one that was attached to the wall for emergencies. He had to break the plastic strap to remove it. He didn't care; he needed to get this done. He opened the sliding door and scanned the cargo pit with his flashlight. He started close to the door hoping the courier box wasn't too far forward. No such luck. Grant slowly moved the beam of his flashlight further forward and saw one of the suitcases, and then the second one, but no courier box. He continued scanning forward until he spotted the familiar box. His heart was pounding as he navigated through the maze of lose suitcases on the cargo compartment floor. He grabbed the first suitcase, then the next, tripping and falling as he worked his way toward the courier box. His vision was obscured as he held the flashlight and one suitcase in the same hand. He finally reached the courier box. The sound of his heart pounding and the noise from the 550-mile per hour slip stream drowned out the sound of his thoughts. "This shouldn't take long, just concentrate," he told himself.

Grant nervously opened the two suitcases, then the courier box. He grabbed two packages from the courier box and put them in the suitcase with the chartreuse string tied to the handle and then set it aside. He did the same with the second suitcase and tried to place it away from the first case and the courier box. He was closing the courier box when he saw a shadow in his peripheral vision. He turned his head to get a better look, but couldn't tell who was standing at the door opening. The light from the galley streaming into the darkness of the cargo pit only allowed him to see a silhouette. He knew he needed an explanation. He headed toward the opening, tripped and fell, only to find Renee glaring at him. Grant tried to appear nonchalant as he exited the cargo pit, closing the door and twisting the handle to the locked position.

"What the hell are you doing in there?" Renee demanded.

"I needed to check something."

"You don't belong in there. What were you checking and why did you take the emergency flashlight from the wall?"

Grant was ready. "As if it were any of your business, I was asked by Mr. Lasswell to check on his courier container; and I'll write up the damn flashlight."

Grant knew Renee had seen the dampness on his forehead as he got into the elevator. He was relieved and newly concerned at the same time. He had gotten the job done, but had loose ends with Renee. "Maybe she will just let it go," he hoped to himself.

Grant hurriedly went to coach. He stopped at Brian's row, looked both ways and sat down in the empty seat next to him.

"Brian, I need to talk with you."

"What is it Grant? You look like a mess, calm down."

"Renee just saw me in the pit by the courier box."

"What did she say?"

"She just ranted and raved and told me I had no business in there."

"What did you tell her?"

"I told her you had asked me to check on your courier container."

"So, I don't see a problem, do you?"

"There is no telling what that bitch might do."

"Grant just relax, you are making too big a deal out of it."

Grant didn't see Renee step into the main galley to talk with Donna. He was too deep in conversation with Brian.

"Donna, I'm going to the cockpit to report Grant." Renee said.

With a questioning look, Donna asked, "Report Grant, for what?"

"He was going through luggage in the cargo pit."

"Did you ask him what he was doing in there?"

"Of course, and he gave me some lame excuse. Would you please cover for me while I'm gone?"

Reluctantly, Donna agreed.

Renee knocked on the cockpit door and entered when she heard it unlock. Captain Como looked back and not seeing any coffee, turned back around in his seat.

"Captain, I need to report something."

"Report what?" Captain Como asked.

"Grant was in the forward cargo pit going through suitcases. I think he was stealing things."

Renee's story drew a look from the co-pilot and raised eyebrows from the engineer.

"And what do you want us to do?" Como asked with a questioning expression on his face.

"I think you should report him to the company; don't you talk to the company?"

"Sure, but not about this sort of thing."

Renee didn't look ready to leave without some kind of solution, so the captain told her, "I'll have the engineer report this the next time we're talking on the company frequency." That seemed to satisfy her and she left. The Captain shrugged his shoulders and went back to his checklist.

After finishing his conversation with Brian, Grant went to the upper first class lounge to talk with a few passengers in hopes of forgetting about Renee. Finally, Donna made her pre-landing announcement, requesting everyone to return to their seats. Grant remained and strapped himself into his favorite seat by the window for landing. He enjoyed listening to the communication on channel 9 between the tower and his flight. Grant relaxed into his seat and a wave of relief came over him as he spotted the airport coming into view. "Thank God," he thought, "this flight is almost over."

Chapter 11

Grant knew he should never have left the house after drinking so much. Resolving the issue with the suitcases was overriding his better judgment, that and all that bourbon.

"So Grant, I said what do you think you're doing?"

Grant wheeled around to find Andy Park, the passenger agent/Chinese interpreter, standing behind him with his hands in his pockets.

"Andy, what are you doing here so late?"

"I'm on overtime. The real question is what are you doing here? And what are you doing with that suitcase?" Andy had a grin on his face, and didn't let Grant respond. "So Grant, do you want to hear a story?"

"What kind of story?"

"I was working lost and found earlier this evening and two druggy looking guys came here looking for a couple of suitcases. One guy said he lost his claim checks. I asked for his name and flight number to check the manifest. He said his name was Lasswell. I asked him to spell it, and guess what, he spelled it L-a-s-w-e-l-l, with one 's.' There was a Lasswell on your flight, but it sure wasn't him, the Lasswell on your flight was a courier. This guy couldn't spell his own name and didn't show up until hours after the flight arrived. Real quality guys too. The bald one was one mean looking dude." Grant was sobering up fast.

"What's your point Andy?"

"My point is this; they described those suitcases to a T, including the ribbons tied to the handles. I told them there were no bags fitting their description and that I couldn't look further without a claim check."

"So where are you going with this?"

"You must think I'm one dumb Korean."

"I thought you were Chinese."

Andy grinned, but didn't let that stop him. "I guess you didn't know, us baggage guys can open just about any suitcase. We do that a lot when they sit here too long. We try to find something inside to identify the owner."

"I'm impressed with your talents Andy, but I'm just looking for a passenger's lost bag."

"Knock off the bullshit Grant. You smell like booze, and I've looked in your bags of interest. I'll bet it's worth a fortune on the street."

Grant was beginning to panic and wasn't sure which way to go. "Andy, you saw all the FBI agents here today. This is what they're working on. They asked for my help. I'm supposed to be keeping track of these suitcases."

"Okay then, I'll just follow procedures and report this to the airport police. I've reported a few joints before, but this is a real haul."

"What the fuck do you want, some money, some of the coke, what?"

"Calm down Grant. I don't want any of those things. I want to help you and maybe you could help me."

"Help you with what?"

"Let's go someplace and talk. I get off in 30 minutes, how about the Hilton coffee shop?"

Grant knew he didn't have much of a choice and agreed to meet with Andy. Grant turned to leave when Andy said, "You forgot something." Grant turned back to see Andy lean down and unlock the chain through the bags. "You forgot your suitcases."

Grant wanted to hug Andy. He picked up the suitcases and confirmed he would meet Andy at the coffee shop. Grant didn't think he had time to take the suitcases home before meeting Andy and decided to chance leaving them in the trunk of his car. Grant was in the coffee shop fifteen minutes before Andy showed up. He got a booth away from the few people who were there and ordered a drink, just getting his order in before last call at 2:00 A.M. He sipped his drink wondering what Andy had in mind. Andy didn't want money, any of the coke, "and hell, he could have taken it all if he wanted to. What could I do for him?" Grant wondered, "What does he want?"

Brian relaxed after leaving Grant's and having a drink. It was a short drive from Grant's to his beautiful Hillsborough home. Brian pressed the remote and the two large gates swung open. Out of habit, Brian pulled in and watched the gates close in his rearview mirror. He pressed another button on the remote, one of the three garage doors opened and he drove in. Brian got out of the car, set his bag down and unlocked the door leading to his kitchen. The last thing he remembered was flipping on the light switch inside the door.

When Brian came to, he was lying on the parquet floor in front of the sofa. His feet and hands were tied and his head was throbbing. There was blood on the floor where he had rolled over.

"Wake up asshole. You didn't think you saw the last of us did you? Are you ready to tell us where the bags are?" Max Payne stood over him.

"I told you what happened to the bags; they're at the airport."

"We went to the airport. The guy said he didn't see them and couldn't look further unless we had the claim checks." Max and Roberto were desperate and extremely dangerous. And they were smart enough to get past Brian's security gate, into his house, and split his head open.

"I'm sure it was a misunderstanding. Let me help you find them. But this is no way to do it."

Max kicked Brian in the abdomen. Brian tried to roll away and Max kicked him in the back for his efforts. Max's smile revealed how much he was enjoying it. These weren't the same staged kicks he gave his wrestling buddies, these were real.

Roberto leaned over Brian, "You can bet your life you're going to help us. Just remember, that's exactly what you'll be doing if you lie to us—betting your life."

"I won't be able to go to the airport or do anything if you keep this up."

"You don't need to go anywhere to help us. You're going to make a few calls and get this straightened out."

"Call who?"

"Your airline friend; or your girlfriend, what's her name? Vicki?"

"If you just let me go and leave me alone, I'll do whatever I can to get the suitcases back. If I can't do that, you don't have to pay. Let me call Romano. He'll understand."

"We're here because Romano told us to do whatever it takes to get his suitcases."

"I don't think he meant this way."

The two goons exchanged puzzled expressions. Then Max and Roberto started kicking Brian again. Brian writhed with pain. He curled into a fetal position, using his forearms to protect his face. "Now, we're going to untie your hands, and you're going to call your airline friend."

Roberto untied Brian and set the phone on the coffee table. Max pulled Brian's battered body upright into a sitting position against the sofa and pushed the coffee table against his chest. Blood streamed from both nostrils and Brian's left eye was swollen shut. His lower lip was split and blood stained his teeth. It ached for him to rest his arms on the table. It was painful just to reach for the phone. Max handed Brian the remote phone from its cradle. Using his thumb, Brian went through the directory to Grant's number and hit the dial button. Brian got a sick feeling when he heard a recording.

"Hello, you've reached the home of Grant Guidera. I'm sorry I'm not here to answer your call."

"Come on Grant, pick up." Brain muttered.

"Please leave a message and I'll get back to you as soon as possible." Brian hung up the phone without leaving a message. "He's not home. I'll have to try again later."

"It's one o'clock in the morning, he better be home." Max threatened.

Roberto grabbed the phone and hit the re-dial button. "This time if he doesn't answer, you better leave a message and hope he calls back, soon." He handed Brian the ringing phone. Brian waited but he got the same recording.

"Grant, I need to talk with you. I really need your help. Call me." With that he pressed the off button and set the phone down.

"Why didn't you tell him it was a matter of life or death—yours?" Roberto said with a grin on his face.

"Because the FBI questioned him, and we're not sure if they're on to us. They might have his phone bugged."

Max and Roberto looked at each other, not knowing what to do next. They only knew one thing to do.

Andy walked into the coffee shop and immediately saw Grant. "I'm sorry I kept you waiting. I wanted to change out of my uniform." The waitress came right over when Andy sat down. Andy ordered a hot tea. It was a brief waiting game. Finally, Andy spoke. "You know that Chinese guy who was on your flight today?"

"What about him?"

"The reason he looked so scared was because he's here illegally and thought all the commotion was about him. I explained it wasn't. He wasn't sure who to trust."

"He had a passport and visa. The passenger agent in Honolulu brought him on. I assumed everything was okay, so why do you say he's illegal?"

"Because I know he is. I got him here. That's what I do and I could use your help."

"So you're going to blackmail me into helping you?"

Andy shot Grant a look, and took a sip of tea. "I don't like that word. And who are you to judge? I'm just offering you a deal."

"That was a bad choice of words. I'm sorry. What kind of a deal are you offering?"

"I'm offering you a chance to make a lot of money."

That was the last thing Grant wanted to hear. "I already make a lot of money. In fact, I've made more than enough money. I'm giving this crap up and today is not a day too soon."

"I think you should hear me out. If nothing else, it's the least you could do. Grant agreed and Andy went on. I help bring in Chinese people who want to live the American dream. And they are not just any Chinese people; they are rich ones. Let's face it, we bring in a lot of boat people. Why not bring in a few yacht people? They have money—lots of it—and are willing to pay to come here. These people will invest in our country and work hard. They have a lot to offer."

"So why don't they just immigrate?"

"They don't want to spend years waiting to get to the top of the list. I just help the rich ones skip the waiting list and you could help."

"What exactly could I do?"

"We have non-stops from Hong Kong and Shanghai and I need someone to make it easier for our people to get onboard with the fewest amount of obstacles."

"It doesn't seem as though you have any problems now."

"Well, yes and no. Bringing them to Honolulu first just makes one more place for something to go wrong. We're talking a lot of money and I want to make it as smooth as possible. We'll still bring some through Honolulu, but we don't want that to be our only option."

"Was that passenger agent working for you?"

"Yes, and he's a good man. We just need to explore more options."

"I have to be honest with you. This trip today is the end of my drug smuggling. Well, not really smuggling, just helping a friend out for a few bucks."

"I don't even want to know how you're involved, but I have to say, you were extremely careless this evening."

"That might be true, but it's turning out okay."

"Did you ever think that might be dumb luck on your part? If it was anyone but me they would have had your ass."

Grant, realizing Andy was more right than wrong, wasn't sure what to say. "Just tell me what it is you want. And what's in it for me?"

"How does $25,000 per person sound?"

Grant didn't want to indicate how tempting that sounded. He couldn't believe he was even entertaining the idea. His greed was getting the best of him. But it sounded like a lot easier way to make a lot of money than his present endeavor.

Grant asked Andy for some time to think it over. He really didn't need any time. He just didn't want to appear too eager. They exchanged phone numbers and Grant promised to call with his decision.

It was around 3:00 A.M. when Grant pulled into his driveway. He was so preoccupied that he almost forgot the suitcases in his trunk. After returning to the car to retrieve them, he opened the front door and wondered, "Where do you hide $300,000 worth of coke?" His waterbed had drawers on both sides and a removable panel on the end. He put the two suitcases in there and replaced the panel.

Still too wound up to sleep, Grant went to his bar and poured himself another drink. He sat and watched the few planes that were landing at this late hour. It was 4:30 before he went into the bedroom, got undressed and turned out the light. In the dark, Grant noticed the message light flashing on his machine. He couldn't imagine who would have called so late, and felt a sense of concern.

Grant turned on the light and saw there was one message, sent at 2:15 A.M. He pressed the play button. "Grant, I need to talk with you, I really need your help, call me."

With his heart racing, Grant dialed Brian's number and got his machine. "Damn it Brian, where are you?" He redialed and got the same message. Still worrying about the possibility of the Feds listening in, Grant decided against leaving a message. He paced while trying to think what to do. Out of frustration, he tried Brian's number again. The machine picked up and Grant made the quick decision to leave a message. He hadn't finished the message when the phone was picked up. "Brian," Grant felt relieved. "What's going on?" There was no response. "Hello?" Grant felt panic starting to edge in. "Hello?" Grant could hear breathing. He yelled, "Brian? Are you there?"

Grant left the phone off the hook while he quickly got dressed. He held the phone to his ear. "Brian? Hello?" There was no voice and the breathing sounded shallow.

Grant decided to get in his car and drive to Brian's house. He was reasonably confident the suitcases would be safe under his bed behind the panel. But still, he was uneasy about it. It was more important to find out about Brian. Grant drove quickly down the hill to Highway 280 and headed south toward Hillsborough. Dawn was breaking when he turned onto Brian's street. Grant couldn't imagine what was going on, but knew something wasn't right. He felt cautious and decided to first drive by Brian's house. He kept the same speed trying not to look too suspicious.

Brian's gate was a car length back from the street and Grant couldn't see it until he was on top of it. As he passed, he could see that the gate was open. Brian had always been fastidious about closing it whenever Grant had been there. Something was wrong. Grant made a U-turn at the next corner and drove by more slowly this time. There were no cars or other signs of anyone being there. The street was quiet and there were only two cars parked along the way. Grant turned into the driveway and parked in front of the three-car garage. He went to the front door and rang the doorbell and then knocked. No answer. He walked around back by the pool and looked into the living room. He put his hands alongside his face and scanned the large room from left to right. His heart started racing when he saw Brian lying on the floor behind the coffee table. Grant could see the phone was off the hook. He knocked on the glass door, but Brian didn't stir. There was nothing else to do but break in. Grant grabbed a small garden figurine and broke the glass window next to the doorknob. The alarm immediately went off shrieking its warning. Grant reached inside and opened the door. Ignoring the alarm, Grant went straight to Brian. There was a pool of blood next to him. Brian's had one eye open and the other was glazed over. He seemed incoherent.

"Brian, Brian, can you hear me?" Grant asked breathlessly.

Brian's lips moved slowly but no sound came forth. Then his eyes closed. Grant reached for the phone and hung it up. It immediately started ringing. Thinking it might be Vicki, he picked it up. "Hello."

"Hello, Mr. Lasswell?"

"No this is Grant Guidera. I'm a friend of Mr. Lasswell's."

"This is the Oswalt alarm service, we show the house alarm was activated and we need Mr. Lasswell's PIN number."

"There's been a break in and Mr. Lasswell is unconscious, please send an ambulance, right away."

The operator said she would call right away and the alarm stopped. Grant untied Brian's feet and hid all the nylon ropes. He didn't want it to look like anything other than a burglary. Grant was relieved when he heard sirens approaching. It had only been a matter of minutes. He had tried unsuccessfully to wake Brian but couldn't detect a pulse. When he put his ear to Brian's mouth, Grant could tell he was still breathing. The pulse was too faint. There was banging at the front door but it was only a couple of young cops. Grant opened the door and heard another siren growing louder.

Two ambulance attendants came through the open front door with a stretcher. They moved the coffee table to make room and one of the cops said, "Don't touch anything." The other cop looked at him and then nodded to the ambulance drivers, "Do what you have to."

"Where are you taking him?" Grant asked.

"To the Peninsula Hospital emergency room."

Grant headed toward his car.

"Just a minute," one of the patrolmen said.

"What do you want? I want to be with my friend."

"He'll be there for awhile. We need to see some identification for our report."

Grant pulled out his drivers license and gave it to him.

"We also need your phone number and a description of what happened."

Grant was exasperated, but knew he had to be careful. He told them what happened starting with the message, but was careful not to say anything more. Then he asked if he could go. The cops thanked him and Grant was on his way to the hospital.

Grant walked to the open counter window in the waiting area at the hospital. Two young women were busy, but they looked up as soon as he approached the window. "May I help you?" one asked. Grant saw the nametag on her scrubs: Stephanie.

"Thanks Stephanie, my name is Grant Guidera. I'm here about my friend Brian Lasswell."

"He's in the emergency room with several doctors. He's lost a lot of blood. If you'll just have a seat, we'll let you know how he's doing and when you can see him. Dr. Kistler is a good doctor, so he's in good hands." The other girl smiled in agreement.

Grant waited for what seemed an eternity. He passed the time looking around the waiting room. He saw someone using the pay phone and it made him think of Vicki. She was due in on flight 180 arriving around 3:30 P.M. Grant called the office and spoke with the duty supervisor. He asked, "Can you have someone meet flight 180 out of Honolulu and tell Vicki O'Donnell, a deadheading flight attendant, to come to the Peninsula Hospital? Explain to her that her fiancé had an accident, he'll be all right and that Grant is with him." She promised to see that Vicki would get the message.

Grant would glance at the nurse's station from time to time, hoping Stephanie had some kind of word. She would return an understanding, sympathetic smile. Finally, Stephanie came out from the desk and sat next to Grant. He could see the other nurse looking their way with a concerned look on her face.

"Mr. Guidera, your…"

"Please, call me Grant."

"Grant, your friend is stable, but he has internal bleeding as well as broken ribs. They are taking him into surgery. He's in good hands, but it will be some time before we will know anything for sure. Maybe you would like to get something to eat? We have a nice cafeteria."

"I'm not really hungry. Is this the best place to wait?"

"Most likely he will be in recovery for some time after surgery and then be sent to a room. Darla and I don't get off until ten o'clock this morning, so we should be here when he gets out of the recovery room. One of us will let you know his room number as soon as we find out."

"Mr. Guidera… sorry, Grant, your friend Mr. Lasswell is out of surgery and in recovery. He will be going to room 530 after that. There is a waiting room on that floor if you would like to wait there." Darla interrupted Grant's thoughts. He thanked her and asked her to thank Stephanie who was on a break.

Grant told the volunteer on the fifth floor that he was waiting for Brian Lasswell. She took down his name and said she would keep him informed. After several catnaps and two morning talk shows, Grant asked the volunteer if she had any new information about Brian's status. She looked at her list and agreed that he had been in recovery an unusually long time. After a brief wait, she returned to Grant. "I'm sorry," she said, "It seems your friend's vital signs took a turn for the worse. They took him back into surgery and now he's in the intensive care unit. Seems there was some internal bleeding they didn't catch the first time."

"When can I see him?"

"I can take you back now, but the nurse says he's still sleeping. Wouldn't you rather wait?"

"I would like to see him now, if I may."

The volunteer told Grant to follow her. She walked away as he entered the room. The attending nurse was just leaving and cast Grant a brief smile. He walked over to a pallid and bruised Brian. Tears came to Grant's eyes.

He felt helpless and unable to speak. Grant knew Brian needed his rest. He sat there, hoping to see some improvement. Hours went by before Grant realized the time. He couldn't sit any longer, so he decided to go to the airport and meet Vicki himself.

Grant went to the gate for flight 180. He was explaining the situation to the gate agent when the 747 pulled into its designated spot next to the Jetway.

"Do you want to go with me while I pull up the Jetway and open the door?" she asked.

"Thanks, if you don't mind, I will."

"Just put on your identification badge and follow me."

After the door was opened, Grant stood back while the passengers got off. Most were either tanned or sunburned. Vicki finally deplaned with another flight attendant who had also been deadheading . They both had their street clothes on and seemed in a good mood. At first Vicki didn't notice Grant standing behind the agent, but when she did, her face lit up. She hurried over and gave him a hug. Grant could smell she had been drinking, which is not unusual when deadheading in first class. After the hug, Vicki stepped back and said goodbye to her flying partner. She looked back at Grant. "Grant, what's wrong? You look worn out.'

"Let's walk up to the boarding area."

"What's wrong? Has something happened?"

Grant put his arm around her as they walked to the boarding area. The majority of passengers were on the way to baggage claim. Grant pointed to some seats in back of the boarding area.

"What's wrong Grant, you're scaring me."

They sat, and she could see he had a tear in his eye.

"Grant, tell me what's wrong. Is it Brian? Did something happen?"

"Yes, something did. He's in the hospital, but he'll be all right."

"What happened?"

Grant started by telling Vicki that Renee had been her replacement on the flight. It took Grant several minutes to explain what had happened the day before. By the time he told her about getting to Brian's house, she was desperate to see Brian. So Grant finished the story on their way to the hospital.

Grant put his arm around Vicki as they walked past the other patients to Brian's room. He felt her tighten up as they turned into the room. To Grant's pleasure, Brian had his right eye fully open.

"See, I told you he would be fine." Grant was grateful that Brian's eye was open and observant. His eye even followed them as they walked around the bed. Vicki leaned over and kissed him on the forehead. He gave a slight half smile and closed his eye. Grant motioned with his head for Vicki to accompany him out of the room.

"Listen, I need to go freshen up and call Pat. Will you be all right here? What would you like to do?"

"I would like to have my car here if you're going to leave. Maybe you could drop me off at the airport and I could come right back."

"Either that or I'll come back a little later and get you"

"Why don't we get my car now and let Brian get some rest."

They both peeked in to make sure Brian was still asleep. They left the ICU and were walking toward the elevator when Pat emerged from the opening elevator door. Vicki started to cry and Grant tried to comfort her while telling Pat what had happened. "Brian's in intensive care. He lost a lot of blood from internal bleeding."

"Is he going to be all right?" Pat asked with a concerned expression on her face.

"He'll be fine. It's just going to take some time."

Pat put her arm around Vicki and quietly held her.

Pat wanted to freshen up before going back to the hospital. Grant dozed off while waiting for her on the sofa. She finally woke him around seven o'clock.

"Why did you let me sleep so long?"

"Honey, you were beat. I didn't have the heart to wake you."

"Let's go see Brian," he said.

Pat and Grant didn't say much as they headed to the fifth floor ICU. A deeply concerned Vicki greeted them. She went straight for Pat and they hugged. Grant asked, "How's he doing?"

"He woke up and we talked but not for long, and he fell back to sleep. They have him on a lot of pain medication, and it only takes a few words to tire him out."

"What have the doctors said? Have they been in to see him?"

"Yes, Dr. Kistler has been in two times and so has the respiratory therapist. They say he's doing as good as can be expected, whatever that means."

Pat asked, "Can we see him now?"

"It's only supposed to be relatives but his nurse is great. She told me I could bring you back with me."

The three friends walked into Brian's room, and to their amazement, he was wide-awake. Vicki almost ran to his bedside. His eyes followed her. He then glanced to his left at Pat and Grant and gave them a brief smile before looking back at Vicki, who leaned over and kissed him on the forehead. He grimaced. Vicki hadn't noticed the lump on his head.

"I'm sorry honey. I didn't see that lump."

Feebly, Brian spoke, "I feel like I have lumps all over. Grant, where were you last night?"

"I was at the airport." Grant gave a quick look around. "I got the suitcases."

"You're kidding. How did you pull that off?"

"I knew the guy who works in baggage claim." Grant didn't want to tell the entire story, at least not then.

"Was everything still in them?"

"Yes."

"What about the Feds? Didn't they check the luggage?"

"I was afraid they might, but they got sidetracked by some lost Chinese guy. I almost died when I saw the suitcase going around on the carousel. It was your conversation with the Feds that cleared me. What exactly did you tell them?"

"Just that I was concerned the courier boxes may have been damaged when they were loaded in Honolulu, and asked you to check. What did you say to them?"

"Just that you asked me to look at them, I didn't say why." Brian looked relieved and Grant could see Brian needed some rest. But before he dozed off, Brian said, "I need to call Romano and ask him to call off his dogs. I'll do that tomorrow."

Pat suggested that Vicki come home with them. She declined, saying she just wanted to go to her house. Grant asked, "Are you going to Brian's house or your apartment?"

"I'm going to my apartment, why?"

"I just don't think it would be a good idea to stay at Brian's until we can clear up this whole mess. I don't know where those thugs are and don't want to take any chances. I'm guessing this guy Romano must be their boss. Once this gets cleared up with him, I'll feel better knowing you are safe."

Vicki thanked Grant and said she was going stay a little while longer before going home. Pat and Grant parted with a hug from Vicki and a look back at Brian.

✈ ✈ ✈

Grant and Pat were tired, but he wanted to show her something. Pat reluctantly agreed.

"Where are we going?"

"To my house."

Pat looked perplexed. "This isn't the way to your house. Where are we going?" she demanded.

"I told you, to my house, my new house." Grant took the Hillsborough exit.

"When did you get a house up here?"

"A few months ago. I'm renting it out for the time being. I wanted to surprise you." Grant turned onto Mountain View Way and stopped in front of a large home with a spectacular entrance. It had wrought iron gates and a large hedge for privacy. The house needed a coat of paint and some yard work.

Grant explained, "I got a good deal because it needs a lot of work. I've given low rent to some bachelors in exchange for doing a lot of the work. I've given them six months. What do you think?"

"I don't know what to think. Brian's lying in the hospital and you could be next. How can you enjoy this with all the risks you're taking? Grant this is all too much for me. Let's go to your house. Your other house. We need to talk."

Grant was disappointed that Pat wasn't more enthusiastic about the new house. He sullenly drove home although he knew it wasn't fair to Pat.

"Grant, tell me what happened yesterday. I heard bits and pieces from some flight attendants. It scared the hell out of me. Why didn't you tell me about it last night?"

"I was afraid my phone might have been bugged, and I was going to tell you about it today. Then this happened with Brian."

"You know I've always been afraid something might happen, not with Brian, but with you. You could get caught, or hurt."

"It's been so simple. And I didn't think anyone would ever get hurt."

"For starters, it's hurting the people who are hooked on drugs. What do you think it's doing to their lives?"

"They would get it somewhere even if I weren't involved. Anyway, it's over. I told Brian I wanted out before all this happened. We just need to resolve some things."

"What about Renee?"

"I'd guess she's going to have some problems over this. In one way she was in the right, but it just looks like she was trying to get back at me. As far as anyone is concerned, I was only doing what a passenger asked me to do."

"What do you mean?"

"You heard Brian. He told the Feds that he asked me to check on the courier boxes, which is what I did. At least that's what they think I did."

"I know you're upset with Renee, but somehow this seems unfair to her."

"She's had more than her fair share of breaks. This is just a little payback. Between the union protecting the most worthless flight attendants, and the company CEO walking away with over fifty million, I don't feel all that guilty"

"Grant, I know Renee has caused you a lot of problems. I know the job is not like being a friendship service director. I know the CEOs are looking out for themselves. Is that any reason to get involved in criminal activities and risk the consequences?"

Grant knew this was no time to tell her about Andy. There would never be a right time.

Chapter 12

Grant woke up with Brian calling his name. "Grant, Grant, we need to call Romano. We need to call Romano." Grant had to get his bearings. He looked at his watch. It was 3:30 A.M.

Grant went to Brian's bedside, "Sure Brian, of course we'll call him. We'll take care of it."

Brian closed his eyes as the nurse came in. "What happened? I saw on the monitor his pulse went way up."

"He woke up distraught," Grant informed her.

"He seems all right now. Call me if he wakes up again."

Grant dozed back off and didn't wake up until 7:15, when the next nurses came on shift.

"Good morning, I'm Sonya. I hear you spent the night with Mr. Lasswell."

"Yeah, not that it made any difference. He only woke up once that I know of."

"That must have been at 3:30. The nurse I relieved, Carrie, said he woke up again around 5:20 and they talked for a while. That's a good sign."

"I slept right through that. A lot of good I am."

"Carrie said it made him comfortable to see you, so it was good that you were here"

Brian woke up with a smile. He looked alert. Sonya asked if she could raise his bed. He gave a nod. She raised his bed and adjusted his pillows.

"Good morning, sleepy head," Grant said.

"Excuse me. I was awake earlier and you were out like a light."

"Okay, you caught me." Grant smiled.

Those bastards really did a number on me."

"When you're up to it, we need to talk about a couple of things. Most urgently, what should I do with the suitcases? And how are we going to deal with Romano?"

"How do you know about Romano?"

"You said it last night—we need to call Romano. You said it twice. Why don't you think about it? I need to go home and get freshened up."

Vicki arrived just as Grant departed.

Grant took a shower since it was still early and then called Andy Park. Andy answered the phone sounding a little sleepy.

"Andy, this is Grant, I'm sorry if I woke you."

"That's fine, I need to get up. I'm glad you called. Have you given my proposal some thought?"

Grant was relieved that Andy didn't say anything more incriminating. There was still the possibility the Feds had given Grant a long enough leash to get careless.

"I have and I would like to meet with you to talk in person."

"Of course, when and where?" Andy asked. They agreed to meet the next day at 3:00 p.m. at Grant's home.

But first Grant had to get himself and Brian out of their present predicament.

Grant went back to the hospital just before lunch. Brian was eating, so Grant made himself a cup of tea and sat next to Vicki.

Grant smiled at Vicki, "He's making me hungry. How about you?"

"I had breakfast, but that was a long time ago. I could eat something."

"Brian, I'm going to take Vicki to the cafeteria. You're making us hungry."

"I'm sorry. Sure, you guys go have something to eat." Brain said, as he ate a spoonful of food.

Grant and Vicki sat and took their plates off the trays but didn't say anything for what seemed a long time. Finally, with moist eyes, Vicki said, "Grant, what are we going to do? We can't go on like this."

"Let's do this after lunch. We'll go back to his room. Why don't you say you want to go home and freshen up? That will give me a chance to discuss it with him, what do you think?"

"Let's face it. I know as much about all this as you and Brian. Why shouldn't I help?"

"I know you do, but I don't think he wants you to be any further involved. He's worried about you."

After Vicki left, Grant searched for a way to broach the subject. He made himself a cup of tea and looked out the window, "What a view."

"You have a good view from your house."

"This is so much closer than mine. Brian, we have to talk. Are you up for it?"

"Why don't you start, and I'll let you know if I am."

"First, I have two suitcases filled with coke. We need to get this resolved."

"Believe me I know. I just need to talk with Romano."

"How can you expect to talk to the guy who did this to you?"

"I don't think he meant for this to happen."

"What do you mean?"

"I think his guys are afraid of him. I can't believe he wanted this."

"What the hell's the matter with you? Just listen to yourself. Romano's what, a nice guy?"

"In fact he is. My uncle Joe used to tend bar for him. They went on gambling junkets together to Aruba, Las Vegas—they had great times. Romano and my uncle didn't pay for anything. The clubs knew Romano's losses would make up for it."

"Did your uncle have the kind of money to be included?"

"No, but Romano helped him set up an account. The clubs didn't care if you won. They just wanted to see activity with your account. I'm sure they would rather you lost. On trips where Romano would be losing and had reached his limit, he would borrow from my Uncle's account, it kept it active. Romano would always pay it back. Their accounts would be paid up and the invitations kept on coming."

"Well, that's all well and fine, but what makes you think he's going to be reasonable?"

"Two reasons: One, he's the one who loaned me the money to get into this business, and he is willing to buy it from me. Two, he knows I want out."

Grant was dumbfounded. "So, with that all said, where do we go from here?" Grant asked.

"I need to talk with him, and at this point, the sooner the better."

"Why don't you call him?"

"I will, but I need to think about what I'm going to say."

Grant reclined back on the couch. They were quiet, and Brian closed his eyes. Grant's eyes shut too and they both took a nap.

✈ ✈ ✈

Grant woke up when a nurse came in to check Brian's blood pressure. The nurse left and Brian told Grant to shut the door. Grant closed the door and made a cup of tea, hoping it would help to wake him up.

"Pass me the phone," Brian requested. He dialed a number. "Romano, this is Brian."

Grant could only guess what was being said on the other end

Brian continued, "Didn't you know? I'm in the hospital. Your two over-achievers almost killed me. I'm sure they meant to leave me for dead, and they weren't too far wrong. ... That makes two of us. I want to make this right and then I want out. You tell me what it will take. ... Yes, I have them now. ... No, I didn't when they were at my house. My friend from Universal made it happen. He's a good guy and a good friend. ... I think he might, but I don't want to put him in jeopardy. I'll discuss it with him. ... What about the money? ... That sounds fair, of course that would include the Honolulu operation too. ... Let me call you back. ... Thanks. I believe you. ... Yes, within the hour, I'll talk to you then." Brian hung up.

Grant couldn't wait and asked, "What did he say?"

"He thought I was dead, but there was nothing in the papers. Max and Roberto told him they did their best not to kill me, but I just wouldn't cooperate. He's pissed off at them. He said he wants to make it right too. He really needs the suitcases and the money from the goods. That money will help him buy me out. He's going to pay for the suitcases plus $300,000 toward my San Francisco and Honolulu franchises. You will get what I owe you for that last trip. In fact, I'm going to give you more after all you've been through. He wants you to meet with Max and Roberto to get the suitcases."

"You've got to be shitting me. I don't want to go anywhere near those two assholes. And what about the Honolulu operation?"

"Romano and a Honolulu businessman have been partners all through this."

"Are you telling me that Keoki and his Samoan friend work for Romano too?"

"Yes and no. Keoki and a few other guys work for the Honolulu guy. Romano doesn't know what's going on out there. He leaves it up to his partner. Romano trusts him."

"Who's the guy in Honolulu?"

"Let's not go there again. The less you know the better."

"Okay, what next?"

"I promised Romano I would call him right back. Here's what I'm thinking: we need to keep this in a public place. I don't want anything unexpected to happen with Max and Roberto. Are you willing to meet with them?"

"Brian, I don't like this entire idea. They dammed near killed you and I'm supposed to meet with them? I'll tell you what I would be comfortable with. First, I think we should only deal with one of those goons. And yes you're right—a public place is a must. How about this? Have Romano come visit you in the hospital and bring one of his jerks along with a suitcase and the money. Would you trust him to have the right amount?"

"I would, then what?"

"Then I bring in the two suitcases, and we exchange them here."

"That sounds risky to me, what will people think?"

"I've noticed people are taking suitcases in and out of here. Neither of the cases weigh that much. It will just look like someone is bringing clothing in and taking clothing out. I think it's perfectly safe."

"I'll call and see what he says. He might just like it. And he wants, or I should say needs, those suitcases. He's a few days behind. When can we do this?"

"This evening or tomorrow morning. I have a three o'clock appointment tomorrow."

"How long will that last?"

"An hour or two."

Brian picked up the phone and punched in Romano's number. "May I speak with Romano? Brian, just tell him Brian." Brian sounded annoyed. Whoever was on the other end must have asked for his last name. "Romano, Brian. ... Yes I think we can work this out. If you're in a big hurry we can do it this evening." There was a pause then Brian explained Grant's idea. "Okay that's fine. I'm in a private room. There are no particular visiting hours, but I think you should come during regular hospital visiting hours. Let's make it seven o'clock." Brian made it clear only one of Romano's flunkeys was to come with him to carry the one suitcase in and the two out.

Brian hung up and looked at Grant, "It's all set. What do you think?"

"If you really trust Romano there shouldn't be a problem."

"I do. He's really been fair to me, and he wants to put this behind us, as much as we do."

"Okay then, seven o'clock it is. Let's do this. I'll call Vicki and tell her what's going on. She can meet me in the parking lot and bring up one of the suitcases, and I'll bring the other."

"I don't want her involved."

"Why not? You said you trust Romano."

"I do, but I don't trust whoever he's going to bring. I just don't want her here."

"Don't worry. I'll work this out. Get some rest. It'll be fine."

Grant was deep in thought on his drive home. While he didn't like the idea of meeting Romano and company, he also knew he couldn't very well leave Brian alone with them and the suitcase. Grant walked in the door and went upstairs to his bedroom. He noticed the light flashing on his answering machine. It was Pat. "Hi Grant, just in case you come home, I have 129 tonight leaving at 7:25 P.M. I didn't want to call you at the hospital, but I'll stop by the hospital before I go to the airport." There was no way Grant wanted Pat anywhere near the hospital tonight. He called her back. The phone rang and just before the answering machine picked up, she answered.

"Hi honey, I just got your message,"

"Good, I was getting ready to leave. Should I meet you at the hospital?"

"No, today is not a good day to be there. Brian is going to meet with the guy who wants to buy him out. The good news is, it will soon be over."

"That makes me very happy. I'm dressed and ready to go. Let me stop by your house for a few minutes before my trip."

Grant agreed and then called Vicki. She answered on the first ring, "Hello?"

"Hi Vic, it looks like tonight is the night. Romano is getting the suitcases and leaving a big deposit for Brian's businesses."

"Both here and Honolulu?"

"I guess so. At least, that's what I understood."

"That is good news. Is he coming to your house?"

"No, we're doing this at the hospital."

"You have to be kidding? You're going to bring that much coke to a public place? Whose bright idea was that?"

Grant clenched his teeth and prayed that no one was listening in. "Thanks, I'll take the credit. That's the whole idea. Brian trusts Romano, but I'm not so sure. I just thought doing it in public would be safer. And it won't be as conspicuous as you might think. People are carrying suitcases in and out of there all the time. That's how I got the idea."

"What can I do?"

"If you're up to it, maybe you could carry one of the suitcases in. You could see Brian and then leave. That way it won't seem as strange as if I carried in two suitcases."

"How should we do this? Do you want me to meet you somewhere or come to your house?"

"Why don't you come here. You could even leave a little before me and spend some time with Brian before I show up."

"What time do you want me there?"

"Pat's going to stop by before her trip this evening. Her check in is at 6:20. I don't want her to see these suitcases. She knows about it, but it would still freak her out. Why don't you come around ten after six? She'll be gone by then."

"Okay, I'll see you then. I'll be so glad when this is over."

Pat showed up at 5:30, looking alluringly attractive in her kimu.

"Tell me it'll soon be over," pleaded Pat.

Grant didn't want to get into a lot of detail. He especially didn't want to remind her that he had a mint of coke in his possession. "Brian is selling his businesses, and it will soon be over."

"Not a day too soon. I can't tell you how happy that makes me." She gave Grant a hug and a warm kiss. Grant was wracked with guilt. If she knew what he was going to agree to do for Andy, their relationship would be over.

As soon as Pat left, Grant retrieved the suitcases from under his waterbed. He couldn't resist the urge to peek inside. The coke was wrapped tightly in cellophane. Grant was admiring the precise wrapping of the two bags when the doorbell rang. He put the packages on the other side of his tall bed. He looked out the window and saw Vicki's car. Vicki stood on the front porch. After a kiss on the cheek and a friendly hug, they headed upstairs. Grant got the two suitcases and set them on the floor in the living room.

"Do you want to take a look?" he asked with a smile on his face.

"I've seen enough of that stuff to last a lifetime."

"Sorry, I didn't think about that."

"How are we going to do this?"

"Like I said, you take one and leave now, spend some time with Brian and leave the suitcase in his room. Maybe in the closet if it'll fit. Just be sure to leave by 6:45 at the latest."

"That doesn't give me much time, I better get going."

Grant carried the suitcase down and put it in Vicki's trunk. He then impatiently waited about fifteen minutes and left for the hospital. He got a parking place close to the front door. Grant grabbed the suitcase, glanced around, and headed for the main door. Vicki was coming out just as he got there. They talked briefly. She told Grant that Brian was waiting for him and asked Grant to call her with news as soon as he could. He promised.

Grant walked into Brian's room with the suitcase and went straight for the closet. Before he got there, Brian said, "It won't fit. Put it under the bed, that's where the other one is."

Grant had just poured a cup of hot water when the man Grant presumed to be Romano walked in with a suitcase. Romano walked directly to Brian's side. He didn't seem to notice Grant. He just stood there looking at Brian then he leaned over and kissed him on the forehead. Romano had olive-colored Latin features. His black hair, graying at the sides, was slicked back, exposing a broad forehead. Under his aquiline nose was a stylishly thin mustache. He held Brian's hand, and looked up at Grant.

"Romano, I want you to meet Grant."

Grant noticed Romano's eyes were glistening with tears. Grant walked toward him and held out his hand. Romano shook it firmly, cupping their right hands with his left. "You've been a good friend to Brian. I want to thank you."

Grant wasn't sure what to say. "This shouldn't have happened to my friend," said Grant.

"You will have to believe me—it is too late this time—but it will never happen again. I've seen to that."

Brian told Romano the suitcases were under the bed. Grant expected him to take them and leave, but Romano surprised him.

"There is no hurry. I want to visit."

Grant wasn't sure if he should leave Brian and Romano alone so they could talk, so he found a distant corner of the room and turned his attention to the airport and the bay. Grant eavesdropped from time to time and decided that Romano sincerely cared for Brian. He was baffled how Max and Roberto could have misunderstood Romano's intentions, unless they did so deliberately.

Romano turned to Grant and asked, "Would you please take one of the suitcases out to Max? He knows to leave, and I'll take the other in a little while. I just want a few minutes alone with Brian. We came in two cars, and I don't want Max to come in here. You can't miss him. He's bald and probably the biggest guy in the waiting room."

Grant wanted it over with although he opposed the idea, so he took a deep breath and walked out with the suitcase. There were only three people in the waiting room, making Max easy to find. "Max?" Max wheeled around, and Grant saw that he had a bruised cheek and cut lip. "Romano must have been very angry," thought Grant.

"Yes, that's me." He was almost polite, clearly afraid to offend a friend of Romano's.

"This is for you. Romano said he would catch up shortly."

Max took the suitcase and headed for the elevator. Grant waited a short time before he went back into the room. Romano was sitting on the sofa, and Brian had his eyes closed. Romano whispered, "I think he needs his rest. I'll just wait a couple of minutes and leave. I want to thank you for being his friend. He said you are a very good friend."

"He's been a good friend to me too."

Romano shook Grant's hand and put his left hand on Grant's shoulder. Grant said goodbye as Romano quietly left the room.

It was still early enough to call Vicki when Grant got home. Even if it had been later, he knew she was waiting for his call, making him that much more concerned when she didn't answer. He let the phone ring, counting twenty rings before he hung up. He poured a drink on the rocks and took a sip, then another. The drink took away some of the tension of the evening but not his concern about Vicki. He was getting ready to dial her again when the phone rang. He picked up on the first ring, "Hello?"

"Grant, did you just call?"

Grant let out a quiet sigh of relief. "Yes, where were you?"

"I was feeling so good about Brian and getting out of this mess that I poured myself a glass of wine, lit a few candles and got in a nice hot tub. I forgot to turn on my machine, and then fell asleep. I thought I heard the phone ring, but I wasn't sure. I can't believe it. You should see me, I'm all wrinkles."

"Well, I think everything is fine. Romano seemed like a nice guy. He seemed genuinely concerned about Brian."

"I think he is. That's why I couldn't believe what happened."

"So you know him."

"Yes, before Brian's uncle Joe died we all went out on the boat."

"You sure kept that a secret."

"Brian didn't want me to talk about Romano to anyone. Romano had his name in the paper for a few minor run-ins, but nothing ever came of it. Still, he seems like an okay guy."

Grant woke up early, feeling refreshed, trouble-free and optimistic. It didn't take long for his mind to start racing though; how would this deal with Andy work out? What should he do about Pat? Should he tell her, or leave her out of it? What if she found out and he hadn't told her?

Grant tried to put those thoughts aside and went to a local coffee shop and had a nice breakfast. He knew most of the guys there and they knew he was an in-flight supervisor for Universal. Grant liked it when they asked questions about his job. He enjoyed telling them about all the girls he worked with and places he'd been. Grant stopped by the Sees Candy factory outlet on El Camino and bought two five-pound boxes of mixed chocolates on the way to the hospital.

Grant walked up to the nurse's station where three nurses were busy looking at charts. "Good morning ladies."

They all looked up and one said, "Good morning."

"These are for you. I can't thank you enough for all you've done for Brian. If you have some left over, could you leave some for the night shift?"

The nurses all thanked Grant for his gift. They promised to leave a box for the night shift. He was pleased by their warm smiles.

Brian was drinking a cup of coffee. His bedside table was off to one side. Grant walked over and lifted the cover off the breakfast plate. It was empty except for a half piece of toast.

"Looks like you have your appetite back."

"As hungry as I am, it still hurts to eat. Even to drink a cup of coffee."

Grant made his usual cup of tea just as one of the nurses came in to see Brian and fluff his pillow.

"Your very nice friend here brought us a large box of chocolates, so we have to take good care of you." She said with a teasing smile on her face.

"So Grant, you've taken to bribing nurses?"

"I want you to have the best."

"I don't see how they could get much better." Brian said with a smile.

It was still fairly early, and Grant wanted to talk with Brian before Vicki came to visit. "How did it go with Romano last night? How did you leave it?"

"When you were out in the waiting room, he asked if I thought you would be willing to continue helping with the Hawaiian shipments."

"What? Look, I told you…"

Brian interrupted Grant. "Relax, I told him you wanted out. I told him you wanted out a long time ago. I told him there was no question about it. I'm sure he understands. He does have a problem because he has dealers who will go somewhere else if he doesn't continue to produce. At least he has those two suitcases for the time being."

"When does he take over? How is that going to work?"

Grant realized he didn't want to know too much. On the other hand, he cared about Brian and wanted it to go smoothly.

"It's not really a big deal. Romano will still have the legitimate part of the business and the rest will be up to him"

"I'm sure he's not doing it for the legitimate part, is he?"

"Of course not, but that's not my problem. I'll help him with some ideas, but that's it."

"What kind of ideas? I hope not by giving him names…"

Brian interrupted again, "Let's do this Grant, we won't worry or even think about it. Romano has connections, he gets things done—let him worry about it. We're out and that's it, will that work for you?"

Grant could tell Brain was done with the discussion, and that was fine with Grant. It was over. Brian was getting better and Vicki was happy. They sat in uncomfortable silence for a while. Both Grant and Brian were visibly relieved when Vicki walked in. She looked great and was obviously in a good mood. She gave Grant a hug, then walked over to Brian and gave him a careful hug and a kiss. Brian let out an involuntary moan as Vicki hugged him. "I'm sorry honey. Do you still hurt?"

"It was worth it. And I'm feeling better. The doctor said I'll be able to go home in a day or two."

Vickie looked pleased, "I'll trade some trips and get the time off to help you. I can stay for at least a week if you need me."

"I always need you."

Grant took his cue to leave. He shook Brian's hand and the grateful look on his face was enough for him. There were no words, but everything was understood. He hugged Vicki and left.

Grant spent the rest of the morning thinking about Andy's visit. Andy showed up promptly at 3:00 P.M. They shook hands and Grant led the way upstairs. Andy walked to the window, and without turning said, "Wow, what a spectacular view. You have a better view than the control tower."

"Yeah, I like it. I never get tired of looking out the window. You should see it at night. Can I get you something to drink from the bar?"

"If it's not too much trouble, I would enjoy a cup of tea."

Grant put two cups of water in the microwave and set out a selection of tea for Andy. They sat at the dining table both facing the window and the enviable view.

"I know I've asked you before Andy, but I still don't understand why you need me. You seem to have it well under control."

"It may seem that way, but it's not always so. For example, a very wealthy Chinese man was stopped by an overzealous passenger agent in Shanghai, who could tell the man's passport and visa were forged. The agent turned the man over to the local authorities trying to make himself look good. The man didn't get in trouble. He just paid the authorities off and was told not to try again. We lost a customer, a very high paying customer. We are having a difficult time getting quality passports. We need someone like you, someone who is there to tell the passenger agent everything is okay, and then early board the men. Don't forget some of those agents also work for me."

"Why would you pay me so much for what is really not much more than a simple pre-board?"

"Sometimes it's not all that simple, but mostly it is."

Grant asked Andy how a Korean guy like him had learned to speak Chinese. Andy explained that his father was in the diplomatic service in Korea. His father had been assigned to China and later France. He spent enough time in both countries to learn the languages.

The two men sat quietly sipping their tea, and Grant wondered why Andy didn't have a better job. Why would he be taking so many chances with this illegal operation? Grant realized the answer was simple: Andy was probably making more money than most professional people.

Andy broke Grant's reverie and asked, "What is your schedule like? What trips do you have?"

"I've been flying mostly Honolulu, but that could change. I won't have the same obligations any longer."

Andy seemed to understand, but didn't say anything. Instead he asked, "When will you be going to Honolulu again?"

"I'm still on reserve for a few more days."

"We have a Chinese man who's been in Honolulu for two weeks and we need to get him here."

"This is where I don't see your problem. He's already in the States, and his papers are of no consequence at this point. Why are you concerned?"

"Maybe I should explain the Honolulu situation. First, you're right. There are fewer problems getting them boarded on a flight once they're in the US. On the other hand, they most likely went through a great deal getting to Honolulu. Some were smuggled over on container ships. Some came on China Airlines after paying off some of their people. These men have been through a great deal by this time and don't know what to think. They don't even think they're in the States until they arrive on the mainland. We have a nice place for them to stay while they're in Honolulu, but they can't stay forever. This guy is scared to death about getting caught. If we have a deal, I would like you to meet him at the airport. Our contact will call you at the Marine Surf when you get in and make arrangements to meet with you. You just have to help the man through security and the ticket counter. Then stay with him until you get him seated. I'll meet the flight as the Chinese interpreter. For that you get $15,000."

"I thought you said $25,000."

"I should have made it clearer. That's when you bring them here from Hong Kong or mainland China. Its $15,000 from Honolulu because most of the hard work has been done by then, and I pay in cash."

Grant wasn't sure if Andy was trying to do a bait and switch, but still, it was a lot of money. "Even at that, I'm not sure when I will be going to Honolulu."

"If you want to shake on our deal, you'll be leaving tomorrow."

Grant didn't bother to ask, he knew the crew schedulers were for sale. Andy was at the airport most of the time and knew all those people, probably better than Grant. Grant smiled, held out his hand and said, "Let's do it."

"I think you will be surprisingly happy to see how much you make and how easy it will be for you."

They talked for a short while longer. Andy thanked Grant for the tea and said he had to head for the airport. After Andy left, Grant gazed out at the bay and airport. The windows in Oakland were sparkling back as the sun was about to set. Since Grant had the third floor added on, he had the highest house in San Bruno. It was still a little early to have a drink, but Grant felt he needed to celebrate his new money-making scheme.

Chapter 13

Not even an hour had gone by when the phone rang. "Hi Grant, this is Joe at the crew desk. We need you to fly 97 tomorrow, leaving at 1:50 P.M. returning the next day on 96 at 2:30. Will that work for you?"

Grant wasn't sure what Joe knew or didn't know. He wasn't sure if "will that work for you" was sarcasm or just a polite question. "Sure Joe. That would be fine. I'll see you tomorrow."

"Not me you won't. I have the day off. Have a nice trip."

"Enjoy your day off."

Grant dozed off watching television and woke when the phone rang. It was Pat. She apologized when she realized she had woken him.

"That's okay. Hearing your voice is worth it. How was your trip?"

"It was nice—good crew, nice passengers, on time both ways. How is Brian doing?"

"He's doing much better. I saw him this morning. He's going home in two days."

"That's great news. How did it go with the guy buying him out? Is it really over?"

"It sure seems that way. I know it's over for me. I guess there are a few things that need to be worked out with Brian, but he seems up to it and ready to move on. He's made some good investments. I think he and Vicki will be fine."

"I was more worried about you. Are you in the mood for some company?"

"I would love it."

Pat arrived around eleven o'clock, wide-awake as she was still on Honolulu time which was three hours earlier. Grant dozed off while Pat took a quick shower to "wash off the airplane," as she liked to say. Her sweet fragrance woke him up long enough to make love before he was out for the night. He woke up to the smell of bacon and coffee wafting into the bedroom. Pat was using the electric frying pan on the bar top to cook breakfast. She looked into the bedroom just as he was opening his eyes.

"Can I get you a cup of tea?"

"Why the hell are you up so early?'

"I'm feeling especially good, and I love you."

"A cup of tea sounds good. What smells so good?'

"Some extra thick bacon I found, and eggs cooked to order when you're ready."

Pat was in an especially good mood, Grant could tell. He got a small knot in his stomach when he thought about his deal with Andy. More importantly, what Pat would do if she found out.

They had a leisurely breakfast and Grant told Pat, "I'll call you the day after I get in. I don't want to call too late tomorrow night."

"You mean like I did?"

"Kinda. But I'm glad you did. I want you to get your rest. I'll call you the morning after I get in."

Pat left, and Grant jumped in the shower. He didn't have the same kind of apprehension for the upcoming flight as he had moving drugs. Grant had a few concerns, but didn't anticipate any big problems.

The steaming hot water pulsated on the back of his neck and relaxed him. He toweled off and made a cup of tea. He didn't notice the light on his answering machine flashing until he started getting dressed. Grant pressed the play button. "Grant, Andy here. I just wanted to talk with you for a minute. Give me a call if you get this before your trip."

Andy answered on the second ring. He explained to Grant that the guy in Honolulu who would be calling was Bill Chen. At one time Bill worked for the airline, but now he was the "host" at the Chinese halfway house, as he liked to call it. "I'll meet your flight tomorrow night. Have a good one."

After the trip was over and Grant had called in his conversions, he sprawled on the bed listening to the cool air streaming from the air conditioner. His mind was so cluttered with thoughts he didn't even feel like going to Jamison's to unwind. He took refuge in the local news, which helped him to doze off. The phone rang. Grant was sure it must be Bill Chen. He muted the television and answered. "Hello."

Someone asked, "Is this Grant?"

"Yes, Bill?"

"Andy told me to give you a call to set things up for tomorrow." He had no accent.

"Sure, how do you usually do this?"

"It depends. Sometimes we have an agent working the trip who helps us. We can't depend on that, and that's where you come in. We just need to make these people feel comfortable with you and hopefully pre-board them without too many people looking at their papers."

"I don't really see a problem once they're here in Honolulu."

"That's why we call these easy money trips for the supervisors. The man you will be assisting tomorrow is a nervous wreck. I think he will feel better when he meets you and realizes you're in a position of authority. They pay a lot to come here, it's the least we can offer."

When Grant heard "supervisors," he didn't want to know.

Bill continued, "After your briefing, I'll meet you at the bottom of the escalator and take you to meet Mr. Lin Wong. He doesn't speak English, but I will explain more to him tomorrow when we are there. I'll look forward to meeting you tomorrow."

"Okay. I'll see you there."

Grant was a lot more relaxed in the morning. He leaned back and enjoyed the bus trip, sitting alone in the last row, just staring out the window at the casually dressed tourists walking in and out of the shops. The ride to the airport passed by quickly, and the lines were short through security. Grant was pre-occupied during the briefing. It didn't seem to matter—the Honolulu flight attendants didn't need or expect him to assist for the most part. In Grant's mind, he was still a friendship service director. He just wanted to sell tickets.

The spacious boarding area was crowded with passengers waiting to board their flights. Grant scanned the room. It wasn't long before a youthful, clean-cut Asian man walked up and glanced at his nametag before saying, "Grant, I'm Bill Chen."

Grant shook Bill's hand. "Nice to meet you Bill. Where is your passenger?" Grant wasn't sure how to refer to him. Passenger didn't sound right. Bill motioned with his head for Grant to follow. The boarding area buzzed with a steady background murmur punctuated with intermittent PA announcements. Bill walked to a remote corner and stopped in front of an anxious Chinese man. Bill said something to him in Chinese. Grant held out his hand. The Chinese man slowly and reluctantly held out his hand. Bill continued talking with the man while Grant stood by. Grant felt a little uncomfortable. He looked around and saw people looking back. Grant wasn't surprised. Most people recognized the uniform and knew people wearing it were employees of Universal Airlines. Grant just smiled back and nodded his head at those people looking at him. Bill explained to Grant that he had told Mr. Wong that Grant would be taking him onboard.

"Also I told him there was nothing for him to do but sit and enjoy the flight. He knows you have to walk around the plane and won't be with him. He also knows to wait for you to take him off the plane and introduce him to Andy."

Grant said, "That pretty much covers it. Where's his ticket?"

Bill handed Grant Mr. Wong's ticket. Grant excused himself and headed for the ticket podium. Grant knew all three agents working the flight. "Hi Gary, could you help me with a passenger? If you could check him in, I'd like to pre-board him."

"Where did you find this guy?"

"I got off the escalator and this man asked if I could help his friend. Is there a problem?"

"No, of course not. I was wondering if you were working the line."

"No, I just felt sorry for this guy's friend. He doesn't speak English, and this is his first trip to the mainland. There should be an interpreter meeting the flight. Could you check the manifest to see if that's there?"

"Wasn't it on your briefing sheet?"

"Don't embarrass me. I forgot to pick it up."

Gary walked up to the third computer at the podium and punched in his company code allowing him access. It only took a few minutes and Gary wrote a seat number across his ticket and told Grant there would be an interpreter meeting the flight. Gary handed Grant the ticket and said, "That's strange that an interpreter would be meeting the flight if he's not connecting to another Universal flight. He should have people meeting him."

"I'm not sure about that. Thanks for doing this. I'll get him and go onboard." Grant walked over to where Mr. Wong and Bill were sitting. "Okay, he's all checked in. Tell him to follow me."

Bill said something to Mr. Wong and they both nodded their heads. "He's ready to go. I told him to try not to worry. He said he likes you, so that's a plus."

Grant shook Bill's hand and motioned for Mr. Wong to follow. Gary saw Grant coming and walked to open the Jetway door. Mr. Wong looked scared when he saw Gary and then relieved when he just opened the door.

"Are we boarding?" the flight attendant by the main cabin door asked.

"No, this is Mr. Wong. I'm just pre-boarding him. He doesn't speak English."

Mr. Wong reached in his carry-on bag and tried to hand a large envelope to the flight attendant. It had Chinese writing on it and looked official. Grant shook his head and motioned for him to put it back. Grant handed Mr. Wong's ticket to the flight attendant. After Mr. Wong was seated, Grant involuntarily gave a little bow to Mr. Wong, which Mr. Wong returned.

The first flight attendant stopped Grant as he headed toward the upper lounge and asked, "How did you know about the Chinese guy? You left briefing before I had a chance to mention him."

"I didn't know. When I went downstairs the passenger agent, Gary, asked if I wouldn't mind pre-boarding Mr. Wong after the crew was onboard." That seemed to satisfy her curiosity, to Grant's relief.

Grant put his suitcases in the upper first class lounge closet after getting his tip sheet out of the briefcase. He went below and put together his tips when the passengers started boarding.

Grant checked on Mr. Wong a few times during the flight and patted Mr. Wong on the shoulder, hoping to make him feel comfortable. The last few times Grant walked by, Mr. Wong was fast asleep. Grant felt good. Mr. Wong couldn't be too nervous if he could sleep so soundly.

The trip went well and Grant's confidence in his new venture rose. When the flight arrived in San Francisco, Grant stood by the door thanking passengers with the first flight attendant. He looked out the Jetway and saw Andy waiting. Grant nodded his head affirmatively, and Andy smiled back. Grant escorted Mr. Wong off, telling the flight attendant he would be right back. Grant started to introduce Mr. Wong to Andy, when Andy bowed and started speaking Chinese. Mr. Wong handed Andy the envelope that he had tried to give to the flight attendant. Andy took the envelope and bowed to Mr. Wong.

Andy looked at Grant and said, "I'll take it from here Grant. Thanks."

Grant called in his conversions, did a little paperwork, and headed for the crew bus. He was the only passenger on the bus by the time it stopped near where he was parked. He opened the trunk and put his suitcases away. He got in the car and felt something under his feet. Grant turned on the interior light and saw a brown paper bag that hadn't been there before. Inside were three packages of fifty, one-hundred dollar bills. He couldn't believe his eyes. Grant turned out the light and took a couple of deep breaths. It disturbed him that Andy had found his car and had gotten in so easily. And he wondered why Andy would leave so much money without letting Grant know. He needed to talk with Andy.

Grant's conscience was the only thing that spoiled his wonderful day off with Pat. When Grant got home at the end of the evening, there was a message on his machine. It was the crew desk. He had another Honolulu trip the next afternoon. Grant had hardly finished listening to the message when the phone rang. It was Andy calling from the airport—Grant could hear the PA in the background.

"Grant, did you get a call from the crew desk?"

"Yeah, I have a Honolulu trip tomorrow. I guess you had something to do with that?"

"Yes, it was kind of a rush situation. I got a call this afternoon from Bill Chen. Someone showed up unexpectedly, and we need to get him here. It will be just like your last trip. Bill will call you and arrange for you to meet."

"When you say just like my last trip, will there be another bag full of money when I get back to my car?"

"Maybe, why?"

"I'm not sure I liked that. I felt uncomfortable knowing someone broke into my car."

"Lighten up Grant. Why don't you call the cops and tell them someone broke into your car and left $15,000? Seriously, I'm sorry if that bothered you. It was just too much to bring into the airport. Besides, I will use different ways to pay you each time. I don't want to set any kind of pattern. If you feel you can trust me, I will pay you a lump sum in cash after four trips. Does that sound better?"

Grant trusted Andy and agreed. He felt more comfortable with Andy's suggestion.

Grant walked into the briefing room for his Honolulu flight. He shook hands with the stewards, and kissed a couple of flight attendants on the cheek. He had just sat down when Shanda came walking into the room. She hadn't pulled her hair back, as per regulation, yet. She looked stunning and triggered vivid memories. Shanda smiled when she caught Grant looking at her. He felt like he had been caught doing something wrong and quickly looked away. She grinned. Grant reminded himself how much Pat meant to him, and how committed he was to her. Still, he struggled to control his memories of past trips with Shanda.

Shanda was working first class so she was close by as Grant prepared his tip sheet, almost too close for his comfort. Fortunately, she was getting ready for her passengers. Grant couldn't help but think that she had it all: beauty and a super attitude. They exchanged smiles as the first flight attendant announced the beginning of boarding.

Shanda leaned over, close enough for him to smell her hair and said, "Let me know if you have any possible conversions in first class and I'll be extra nice to them."

"Who are you kidding? You're nice to everyone. It's easy to get conversions when you're working the flight." Grant teased as the passengers started boarding.

There were a lot of open returns and a number of possible conversions. Grant was busy writing them down when he came to a familiar name, making his stomach leap—Mr. E. Romano. He doubted it was the same person. "Besides wasn't Romano his first name?" Grant wondered. Mr. Romano's ticket had an open return, so Grant wrote the seat number down. He shook off the possibility that it could be the same Romano. The agent made the final boarding announcement and Grant headed up the staircase to his favorite place, but not before casting a quick glance into first class towards 3A, Mr. Romano's seat. Grant could only see the top of a head over the plush tall seat. His black hair was gracefully graying. Grant continued up the staircase to organize his paperwork and thoughts until takeoff.

Once the seatbelt sign went off, Grant went into the cockpit to say a brief hello. At the bottom of the spiral stairs, Grant made his usual announcement, then leaned on the flight attendant's jump seat and watched Shanda and the other flight attendant working the beverage cart. When there was enough room to get by, Grant headed to the front of first class to start greeting passengers. Shanda gave him a suggestive smile as he walked toward her cart. When he turned at seat 1A, he looked up and saw Romano smiling at him. Grant excused himself before even saying hello to the passenger and went to Romano's seat. Grant shook Romano's hand and obeyed when Romano nodded toward the empty seat next to him and asked Grant to sit down.

"I saw the name Romano, but there was an "E" in front of it. I wondered if that was you."

"Romano is my last name, but everyone I know has called me that since I was a little boy."

Grant couldn't imagine Romano ever being a little boy. They chatted for a few minutes before Grant excused himself to do some work. Romano made Grant promise to come back and visit when he had time. Grant finished his rounds in first class, apologizing to the people in 1A, explaining he had spotted an old friend. Overhearing Grant's remark, Romano smiled.

The first flight attendant interrupted Grant's daydream in the first class lounge. He'd made all his sales, finding the most difficult to be a businessman in the lounge, and had finally sat down to take a break. Without meaning to, Grant's mind had wandered back to Shanda. The flight attendant asked Grant if he wouldn't mind taking an unaccompanied minor off the plane once the flight arrived.

"Only if you take the heat if one of the union girls says something," Grant said jokingly.

"Of course. But don't worry, this is a great crew and they all like you."

The first flight attendant had moved the little boy to a seat close to the main cabin door. When the flight arrived and pulled up to the gate, Grant sat down next to the little boy. He looked about nine years old.

"So, you're going to visit your dad?" Grant asked the precocious little boy.

"Yes, I'm going to spend two weeks with him on his fishing boat. He and my Mom are divorced."

"Well, I hope you have a wonderful time, and maybe I'll see you on the way back. The flight attendants said you are a very nice polite young man."

The little boy just smiled, but looked anxiously at the Jetway being maneuvered to the door. Grant took the boy close to the door and waited for it to open. The little boy even thanked the flight attendant before getting off the plane. The dad had blond hair and looked too young to be a father. Grant made sure the dad had the proper papers before turning the little boy over to him. Grant shook hands with the dad and patted the boy on the head.

"You have a very nice son here. The flight attendant said he has perfect manners."

"Well, thank you. He is a good boy."

Before heading back to the plane, Grant noticed a limo driver holding a sign that read: "Mr. Romano." Grant waded against the stream of eager de-planing passengers. Romano was just coming out of the cabin door when Grant got to the plane. "I saw a sign out there—your limo driver is waiting."

"Thanks Grant. It was nice talking with you."

"Have a pleasant stay and good luck with your business dealings." Romano had told Grant he was in Honolulu on business. Grant didn't want to know but certainly suspected what the business was.

When Grant got on the crew bus, most of the seats were taken. Shanda raised her eyebrow at him as he passed her row on his way to the last open seat. Grant tried to enjoy the ride but his mind was going faster than the bus. Shanda's hair was down and when Grant thought of the times they had shared together, he could smell her hair. Grant tried desperately to shake those thoughts out of his head as he stared aimlessly into the street.

Grant was the last one off the bus and into the lobby. He usually waited until the crew had their room keys before walking up to the desk. After checking in, Grant was surprised to see Shanda standing alone by the elevator. She smiled and asked, "What room did you get?"

Grant looked at his key and said, "724. What room did you get?"

"710. You got the room with a view."

Grant followed Shanda onto the elevator. She put her suitcase down and turned toward Grant. He just looked at her with an awkward smile.

"What's the matter Grant? You seem distant. Are you tired?"

The elevator stopped at the seventh floor. As they walked off the elevator Grant said, "I guess I am. It was a busy trip."

Shanda followed Grant past her room down the hall to his. Grant looked at her with a puzzled look before comprehension struck. He knew what was going on, but didn't want to admit it, not even to himself. Shanda didn't deserve his elusiveness. "Do you want to come in for a guava?" he asked.

Grant immediately crossed the room to the air-conditioner and turned it up to high. He then went to the mini bar and got out a couple of guavas. Shanda was sitting on one of the king size beds with her legs crossed. With the slit in her kimu, he could see all the way up to her silky thigh. Grant sat on the other bed, facing her. She patted the bed next to her and said, "Come, sit here."

Like a puppy, Grant obeyed and sat next to her. He was sure she knew something was wrong, but he didn't want to try and explain. Shanda set her guava down and leaned toward Grant and gave him a kiss, making him realize that she didn't. He responded half-heartedly.

"Is there something wrong?" Shanda asked, pulling back.

"No, it's just that I feel all sweaty and sticky." Grant lied.

"So, that's the way we usually end up. Just look at it like a head start."

Grant was tempted, but instead gave her an awkward smile and lied again, "I'm really not feeling well."

"I'm sorry, was it something you ate on the plane?"

"No, not really, I didn't feel well before I got on the plane."

"If there's nothing I can do, I'll go to my room and clean up. Do you want me to call you later?"

"Maybe I'll feel better if I take a shower and rest a little. Why don't I call you if I'm feeling better?"

With a skeptical smile, Shanda got up and left. Grant felt like an idiot. "Why couldn't I just be honest?" he wondered. Grant knew Shanda deserved better. After taking a cool shower and calling in his conversions, he dozed off. The ringing phone woke him. He was sure it was Shanda but was relieved when it turned out to be Bill Chen. Bill and Grant agreed to meet at the same place at the base of the escalator.

It was almost 7:30 P.M.. Grant was hungry and felt like having a drink. He felt ashamed when he walked passed Shanda's room on the way to the elevator. It was bright in the lobby and it took a few minutes to adjust to the dim light in Jamison's. He walked over to the bar and sat at the very end next to the wall. Lonnie was busy, but not too busy to smile and wink at him. Grant was sipping his Manhattan when he noticed Romano in a booth with Keoki and his large Samoan friend. Keoki was waving his hands around as he talked. He looked more Italian than Romano did. The large Samoan seemed oblivious to their conversation. Grant didn't want to be seen by Romano or Keoki.

Grant was getting ready to leave when Lonnie came over. She noticed Grant looking toward Keoki's booth and said, "I wonder what's with Keoki these days? I've seen him almost every night talking with any stewardess or supervisors who will let him buy drinks."

"You're asking the wrong guy. I haven't a clue what he's up to." Grant knew exactly what Keoki was up to. He just didn't want to be a part of it anymore. Worst of all, Keoki seemed very indiscrete. Lonnie excused herself to wait on a customer. Grant wanted out of there, but it was too late. Romano, Keoki and the Samoan had gotten out of the booth and were heading toward the glass door to the outside stairs. Grant turned toward the wall and hoped they wouldn't see him. They were arguing.

Keoki asserted, "Don't worry, I'll find someone."

As they walked past Grant, Romano said, "You better or I'll find someone to replace you."

Grant turned in time to see motion outside the door. The Samoan put his hand on Romano's shoulder and Romano knocked it away. Keoki jumped in front of the Samoan and looked around. He obviously didn't want anyone to see what had happened. Keoki said something to the Samoan and they headed down the side stairs to the alley. Romano went down the front stairs to a waiting limo. Grant's heart was pounding. Lonnie came back and stood by Grant. "It looks like Keoki and his new friend were having a difference of opinion."

"Have you seen him with that man before?"

"Sure. He was at Keoki's place a week or so ago. They were sure being a lot nicer to him then. I think he's somebody important."

Grant left it at that and had one more drink before he decided to talk with Shanda. He was still hungry, but this was more important. Grant said goodnight to Lonnie on his way out to the lobby elevator.

Grant knocked lightly on the door to 710. There was no answer, but he could hear the television going. Grant started to walk away when the door opened. Shanda had obviously been asleep. She looked radiant wearing a simple, long sweatshirt.

"I'm sorry. Did I wake you?" Grant asked sheepishly.

"That's okay. Come in. How are you feeling?"

"Mostly ashamed. May we talk?"

"Sure, what's that matter?"

"I should have told you before. Pat and I have gotten quite serious. I want to have an honest relationship. She and I need to trust each other." Grant felt like a hypocrite saying those words. He was afraid his honesty was a bigger issue than his faithfulness. He could be faithful to Pat, but he wasn't being honest.

"You should have said something. Did you think I wouldn't understand?"

"No, of course not. I don't know. I guess I was so tempted I really didn't want to say no. This is new to me. Just say you forgive me, please."

"Of course I do. You're kind of cute when you're in love."

They talked a little more and Shanda admitted she too would like to have someone all her own. The pilot she was dating wasn't that kind of a guy.

Grant asked, "Would you like to get a bite to eat?"

"Only if you promise not to try that informal hearing thing again."

They both laughed and Grant said, "It won't be easy, but I'll try." They went to the little Japanese sushi bar down the street and eased into their new arrangement as friends.

The next day, Grant left briefing a bit early and headed down the escalator to look for Bill Chen. Grant saw Bill when he was halfway down. Bill greeted him at the bottom with a firm handshake. They walked together to the same area as before, where a young Chinese man was sitting. Bill said something to him in Chinese and the man got up and shook Grant's hand.

"Grant this is Mr. Ling Wu." The young man started to hand Grant an envelope, as Mr. Lin Wong had on the last trip. Bill said something to Mr. Wu and he put it back in his carry-on bag. Bill and Mr. Wu sat and talked while waiting for the flight attendants to board. Shortly after they boarded, Grant went to the podium with the man's ticket and checked him in. Grant told the gate agent he was going to pre-board Mr. Wu. Grant said goodbye to Bill and headed down the Jetway to the plane with Mr. Wu in tow. There was no one at the door, so Grant took Mr. Wu to his seat and brought his ticket back to a flight attendant. "I pre-boarded Mr. Ling Wu. He's in 25C. He doesn't speak English. He'll be met in San Francisco."

The flight attendant walked back to Mr. Wu's seat and Grant followed. She smiled at Mr. Wu and welcomed him aboard, which prompted Mr. Wu to reach in his bag for the envelope. Grant shook his head and gently pushed Mr. Wu's hand back to his bag. Grant couldn't get over how young Mr. Wu was. "How could he be so rich and afford to buy his way to America?" Grant wondered. "Maybe his father paid for him?"

Andy was waiting for Mr. Wu in San Francisco. When they met, Mr. Wu handed Andy the large envelope that Grant assumed was full of counterfeit documents.

Grant's Honolulu trip was followed by two trips to Beijing and one to Shanghai, bringing three more Chinese men to Andy. Grant was unconcerned with the forged papers each man carried, as there never seemed to be any questions about the documents.

Arriving home from Shanghai, as usual, Grant briefly saw Andy. Heading for the office he wondered when Andy was going to pay him for the last four trips. He didn't have to wonder long. When he went to his mailbox in the crew office, there was an envelope with a key and note. "Grant, this is to a baggage locker on the B concourse by the shoe shine stand, thanks Andy. P.S. combo 747."

Andy had never let Grant down and he felt a bit guilty for wondering about the money. He rushed through his office work and anxiously headed for the locker. He could feel the adrenalin coursing through his body as he opened the locker and saw the briefcase which he knew held a small fortune. Realizing he had too many bags to carry, Grant rented an available locker and left his company briefcase to be picked up before his next flight. He went to the employee bus stop clutching the valuable briefcase, and with other employees, waited for the bus. If they only knew, he thought.

Grant put the case in his trunk and headed up the hill to his San Bruno home. He had to tell himself to slow down. He didn't need an ambitious cop looking in the trunk. Grant pulled into his driveway, went to the trunk for the briefcase. He jogged upstairs, flicking on lights along the way. Grant set the briefcase on the sofa and sat beside it. He dialed in the combination and lifted the top. The sight of so much money left him breathless. Grant closed the briefcase and poured himself a bourbon. He took a big sip, set the drink down, and started counting one of the stacks. There were eighteen bundles of one-hundred dollar bills, fifty to each bundle. He didn't count it all, but knew it was all there. He set the case on the floor and looked out the window at the string of lights from the planes landing at SFO.

The pounding in his heart subsided with the second drink. He took off his jacket and noticed the red light blinking on his answering machine. He topped off his bourbon, sat on the bed and pressed the play button. The first message was from Pat. "Hi Grant, I just wanted you to have a message when you got home. I love you. Call me tomorrow."

The next was from Gina. "Hi Grant, I guess you're on a trip. Call me when you get back. I have some good news. I love you."

The last was from Vicki. "Hi Grant. Please call me at Brian's house. I talked with the crew desk and they said you worked a Shanghai trip, so call us in the morning."

Grant decided it was too late to return calls and went back to the living room. He knew he wouldn't be able to sleep just yet and pulled his favorite chair up to the window. Grant was mesmerized by all the lights down the peninsula and across the bay, topped only by the reflection of the moon on the water. His thoughts finally started to slow down.

Grant was startled awake by the ringing phone. He was disappointed when he saw it was only 7:30 A.M.. He felt like he needed more sleep. "Hello," he mumbled.

"Grant, its Vicki. I'm sorry if I woke you."

"Me too. What's going on? Is Brian okay?"

"Yes, he's fine…well, not really. Can you come by this morning?"

"Sure, but what's wrong?"

"When you get here we can talk about it. What time do you think you can make it?"

"If there's no emergency, will ten o'clock work?"

"Sure, see you then."

It only took a moment for Grant to doze off again. He woke wondering about Vicki's call. It was 8:30 and he was anxious to call Pat. After his Honolulu trip with Shanda, Grant felt he'd made a true commitment of his love for Pat. But he didn't think she would find it as significant as he did. He had no plans to discuss it with her.

Grant walked into the living room, glanced at the briefcase full of money with his uniform coat draped over it, and put a cup of tea in the microwave. He took his tea back to the bedroom and sat down on the bed a little too fast. The motion of the waterbed spilled some hot tea on his bare leg. He ignored the burning and dialed Pat's number.

"Good morning," she answered cheerfully"

"Are you always this friendly so early in the morning?"

"Only when I love the person on the other end of the phone."

"How did you know it was me?"

"I didn't, I thought you were somebody else." She laughed, and they laughed together.

"Did I wake you?"

"No, I was hoping you would call. How was your trip?"

"It was okay. I slept a lot."

"Did you go out with any of the crew for dinner?"

"What is this, the third degree?"

"Of course not, I was just making conversation. You always ask me what I do."

"That's true, so how about lunch this afternoon?" They decided to have lunch at the dock in Tiburon.

"What time should I be ready? What are you doing this morning?"

"Vicki called and wants me to go see Brian, so how about a little on the late side, maybe twelve-thirty or one o'clock? Is that okay?"

"Sure, is Brian okay?"

"I'm not sure. She didn't want to talk on the phone."

"Grant, you are finished with that situation aren't you?

"Of course, you know that. We'll talk about it at lunch. I love you."

"I love you too. See you then."

Grant hung up, feeling guilty about the briefcase of money in the living room.

Next, Grant dialed Gina's number. Randy answered the phone and when Grant asked about the good news, Randy said, "I'll let Gina tell you about it."

Gina's voice came on the line. "Hi Grant, how have you been? It seems like forever since we've talked."

"You know how hard it is to get an appointment with doctors these days."

"I'll always have time for you. I love my little brother."

"I know you do Gina. I love you too. What's the good news? Can I guess?"

"Sure."

"You got a position as chief nephrology surgeon in some great hospital."

"Better than that. Randy and I are getting married."

"Gina, that's so exciting. When's the big day? Have you told Dad?" Grant was thrilled and could hear the happiness in Gina's voice.

"I spoke with him yesterday. He seemed happy but said he hoped I wasn't planning a big expensive wedding. I guess he doesn't have a lot of money these days. He seemed worried. I told him that wasn't important."

"I can't wait to tell Pat—we're having lunch today."

"What are you two up to these days? Any marriage in your future?"

Grant jokingly said, "Well, I was going to ask her, but I don't want to steal your thunder."

They shared a few more laughs before Gina hinted that she was curious how he was doing on making all his house payments. Grant was getting good at avoiding the subject and they hung up shortly thereafter.

After taking a quick shower and hiding the money, Grant was on his way south to Hillsborough. Vicki opened the door, They hugged, and as they separated, Grant saw her wet cheeks. "What's the matter? What's going on? Where's Brian?"

"I'm sorry. It's just that so much is happening at once. Brian is hurting in more ways than one. I had to give him a sedative earlier. He's resting and should be waking up soon. He wants to see you. Can I get you a cup of tea, maybe something to eat?"

"Tea sounds great. Tell me what's going on."

Vicki brought the tea to the kitchenette and they sat looking out over the rectangular pool. Grant took a sip of his tea before Vicki blurted, "Romano is dead. Brian can't believe it. He's not taking it well. I never knew how fond he was of Romano."

"What? I can't believe it. I just saw him the night before last. What did he die from?"

"He was murdered in Honolulu—we think last night."

Grant was visually upset by the news. His hands starting shaking so much he had to put his cup down. "I can't believe it. He was on my flight over. I sat and talked with him. I saw him in Jamison's. How did you find out?"

"Someone called Brian. I don't know all the details. I'll let him tell you. He should be waking up soon."

Brian came over the intercom. "Vicki, are you there?"

"I am honey and so is Grant."

"Could I have a cup of coffee? And could you send Grant in?"

Brian was sitting up, with his legs hanging over the edge of the bed. He asked Grant to help him sit at a small teak table near the window overlooking a picturesque garden. There were magnificent redwoods interspersed with clumps of crimson columbine and California birds of paradise. Grant shook Brian's hand, and then helped him to his feet. Brian gave Grant a bear hug that took him by surprise. Grant hugged him back.

"Grant, I have some terrible news. Romano was killed in Honolulu sometime in the last two days.

Vicki came in and set down a tray with coffee and tea and said, "I already told Grant. I just didn't tell him the rest."

"Tell me the rest about what?" Grant asked. Vicki asked if they wanted anything else. They both said no, and Vicki left the room. "What is the rest?"

"I got a call late last night from the warehouse."

"What warehouse?"

"My warehouse. It was Geoff, one of my ex-supervisors. He told me Romano was murdered."

Brian started to tear up and took a sip of his coffee to help fight back his emotions. Grant turned his gaze out the window, pained to see such heartache on his friend's face. Brian started to speak again, and Grant turned back to him.

"I'm really concerned. It wasn't just the local police that went to the warehouse. The FBI went there too. I guess because it's an interstate business they become involved.

"The FBI asked Geoff a lot of questions; How long had he worked there? How many owners did he work for? How long did Romano own the business? Et cetera. The FBI called this morning; they want to talk with me. Vicki told them I would have to call them as I'd been in the hospital and just got home to start recuperating. They didn't ask any questions, but said they needed to talk with me within a couple of days."

"About what? You couldn't be a suspect."

"I'm not sure, but they asked Geoff about our flight schedule from the mainland to Honolulu. They asked about other islands too. They asked him what air carriers we used and what was in most of our shipments."

Grant was apprehensive. The answers to some of those questions would lead right to him.

"Don't worry Grant. There is no need to mention you. I'm sure it's just routine stuff. If they know Romano was involved in anything illegal, and I'm sure they must, how was I supposed to know when I sold the business?"

"They could talk to those two goons who beat you up. Who knows what they might say. And what about the Feds showing up at our flight thanks to Renee? That's going to raise more questions." Grant's concern showed on his face, and Brian could see it. Brian tried to convince Grant that he had nothing to worry about. Grant knew Brian meant well, but it didn't help much. Grant didn't tell Brian that Romano was on his flight or that he saw Romano with Keoki and the Samoan. He didn't want to upset Brian any further. Brian was doing much better physically though, and Vicki seemed happy about it.

On the way out to Grant's car, Vicki admitted to him, "I'll sure be glad when this is over."

Grant gave her a knowing smile and another hug before leaving.

Chapter 14

The fog had already lifted from the coast, and it was a beautiful, clear day. When Grant got to the other side of the Golden Gate Bridge, he pulled into the observation area and looked back at the city. For a brief moment he felt calm. Suddenly, he realized it was past one o'clock and he had a date with Pat. She was standing in front of her apartment when he pulled up. He was happy to be greeted by her wide smile. He started to apologize but she put her finger over his lips and gave him a smooth kiss. Pat pulled back, looked at him and asked if he was all right. This was why he loved her so much. Pat was forgiving and caring. She knew seeing Brian wasn't easy for him.

It was a nice drive to Tiburon and Grant tried to put the events of the morning behind him. The Dock was slowing down from their lunch rush. Grant and Pat sat at an umbrella-covered outside table, overlooking Angel Island, San Francisco and the yacht club. Grant told Pat about Gina and Randy's engagement. He also told her about Gina's conversation with their dad and what he had said.

Pat sat quietly for a few minutes and then said, "Why don't we do the wedding for them? You should be in your Hillsborough home by then and we can have it out by the pool. Your dad could still give her away, and nobody would have to worry about the cost. What do you think?"

"I think you're amazing, but I'm not sure if they've made plans yet. His folks are well off and might want a big church wedding for their friends and relatives."

"Why don't you just ask and see if Gina and Randy like the idea? The house should be in beautiful shape by then. Let's face it—Hillsborough is one of the wealthiest areas in California. Who wouldn't be impressed?"

The more Grant thought about it, the more excited he got. He hoped Gina and Randy would feel the same. They had a tasty, relaxing lunch before going back to Pat's apartment, where Grant spent the night.

The guys renting Grant's Hillsborough home had done a fantastic job with the painting and redoing the garden area. It was spectacular. Grant was so impressed with their work he gave them each $2,000 and asked for a favor. "I want to have my sister's wedding here. It won't be for some time, but I need to make plans. First, I would like to move in as close to the end of the six months as possible. Second, would you mind if I had my sister and her fiancé up here for lunch very soon?"

The two grand did very little to hide the disappointment they must have felt. Their time was almost up living in such a fantastic house. Grant, feeling uncomfortable while waiting for their answer, asked if they had any plans as to where they would move. They looked at each other and shrugged their shoulders.

"Not really. We were hoping you wouldn't want to move in right away."

Grant felt uncomfortable. Then he came up with an idea. "How about this? You can move into my San Bruno home. It needs some work and I'll give you a break on the rent until it's done. Then I'll let you have it for $500 a month."

That seemed to give the tenants a lift. It wasn't Hillsborough, but it had a spectacular view. If they had to move, that would be a great home to go to. They shook on it. All Grant had to do was figure out when to have Gina and Randy to the Hillsborough house for a look or maybe lunch.

Pat's flight from Honolulu arrived at 6:40 A.M. Since there was no note from Grant in her mailbox, she knew he hadn't gone on a trip.

Grant was happy to hear Pat's voice when she called.

"It doesn't sound like I woke you. Did I?"

"No, in fact I was expecting your call. I checked on your flight and knew it was on time. Are you coming up before going home?"

I'm pretty tired. I won't stay long, if that's okay?"

"Sure. I'll make you a nice breakfast and maybe you could take a nap here."

"It sounds like you are in an especially good mood for this time of day."

"I am. Just get up here and I'll tell you all about it."

"Give me a hint?"

"Just get up here."

Grant couldn't wait to tell Pat about the tenants moving out, about the garden looking beautiful, or about his idea of having Gina and Randy up for lunch to show them the garden and ask if they would like to get married there. He blurted it all out while making waffles with bacon and eggs.

Pat seemed as excited as Grant about the lunch idea. "We could have an elegant table set out by the pool. I have some great menu ideas." And then her excitement was finally overcome by sleepiness. Pat took more than just a nap. She didn't wake until one o'clock- in the afternoon. She found Grant packing boxes in the basement.

"I'm sorry—I didn't mean to sleep so long."

"I do the same thing after that trip. I'm getting a head start on my packing. I can't believe how much junk I've thrown out."

Grant made Pat lunch while she showered. While they ate, they brainstormed about the important step of having Gina and Randy out to the Hillsborough house for lunch.

Later in the evening, Grant called Gina. "Are you and Randy available for a nice lunch the Saturday after next? Pat and I would like to take you somewhere special."

"I'm sure Randy is free. How nice. We'd love to get together with you and Pat."

Grant hadn't been assigned any trips for several days. He was also surprised he hadn't heard from Andy. He wondered if maybe Andy had brought someone else onboard. "Maybe that would be a good thing," he thought. He had plenty of money, real estate and stocks. It wouldn't hurt to get out.

Pat spent most of her time off that week planning the Hillsborough lunch. She called the tenants and took a trip out to see the yard.

Gina and Randy were punctual, as usual, for their Saturday lunch date with Grant and Pat. Grant headed out the door before they were out of their car. Gina rolled down her window, "Hi Grant. Where's Pat?"

"We're going to meet her. Let's take my car."

"Why don't we take our car? Hop in."

Grant liked that idea. Pat had her car at the house and Gina and Randy could just leave from there.

"Where to?" Randy asked.

"I'll give you directions as we go."

Randy and Gina gave each other a quick look. They seemed to know something was up. Grant told Randy to turn south on 280 but he was so excited he could hardly wait to give the next direction. "Take the Hillsborough turnoff."

Gina turned in her seat to look at Grant. "Where are we going?" she asked. "There's no restaurant up here."

Grant didn't answer. "Randy, turn left on Mountain View Way."

It wasn't far before Grant told Randy to slow down and turn into the next driveway. The gate was open and Grant had them park in an area overlooking the pool and peninsula. Pat saw them coming and walked out to meet them.

Gina asked, "Does Pat live here?"

"Not yet, maybe someday." Grant jumped out and opened Gina's door for her. Randy got out and gave Pat a kiss and a hug. Then he asked, "Do you live here?"

Before Pat could answer, Gina said, "This is beautiful. Whose house is it?"

"I'll let Grant tell you all about it."

"Well Grant, tell us all about it." Gina said.

"Let's go sit down and we'll talk."

Grant led the way through the garden toward the pool where Pat had set a beautiful table. Grant could see how impressed Gina and Randy were. Gina and Randy wandered around, soaking in the view, and returned to the table where Grant and Pat were waiting.

"What would you like to drink?" Grant asked. Gina and Randy chose wine, so it was wine all around. Grant held up his glass, "A toast to Gina and Randy. You are made for each other, wishing you both a lifetime of happiness." They took a sip and Grant continued, "I bought this house a few months back. I had to sell three of my houses to make this deal."

Pat shot Grant a look, she knew he had just lied to his sister.

Randy and Gina complimented Grant for his taste in houses and paused to tell Pat how wonderful the lunch was.

Grant went on, "This brings up our reason for having you here for lunch. Pat and I would like you to think about having your wedding here."

Gina and Randy looked at each other and then back to Pat and Grant. Before they could say anything, Grant went on with their plans. "We could build an altar here, maybe a large trellis over here. Put all the chairs here, just far enough from the pool. There's plenty of parking, and we can have it catered. There's a guy named Alvergue in San Bruno who does everything first class."

Grant didn't show signs of slowing down. His enthusiasm was palpable. Gina got up, went to Grant, put her arm around his shoulder, and kissed him on the cheek. "It sounds like you've given this a lot of thought. You're so special; both of you. We can't thank you enough." She stopped short of disappointing Grant, but did say, "Randy and I will have to give this some thought. But, it looks so beautiful."

Randy interrupted, "I think this could work fine if Grant really wants that large of a crowd here. I just wouldn't want to do any damage to the yard or house. There will be a lot of guests from my family's side."

Gina glared at Randy. Randy caught her look and added, in great attorney fashion, "Of course, Gina and I would like some time to think about this, but I have to tell you, I love this idea."

Grant was pleased and anticipated an affirmative answer from Gina and Randy. He just couldn't wait. The lunch finished with coffee and tea, followed by a short tour of the house. Grant explained he had tenants and didn't want to go into their bedrooms. The living and dining rooms were impressive with their high ceilings, accentuated by large mahogany beams. After the tour they all said their goodbyes.

Walking back to the yard, Grant said, "That was a spectacular lunch. I just know that will be what makes them decide to have their wedding here."

"I have to admit, I'm pleased with the way everything turned out. I was so worried. I knew how much this meant to you."

After clearing the table and doing the dishes, Grant and Pat sat outside and had another glass of wine to savor the success of their luncheon. It wasn't long before Pat asked, "Why did you tell Gina and Randy you sold three houses to buy this one?"

"What did you want me to say? I made lots of money working part time in the drug business? I did exceptionally well with my investments, but not good enough to buy this house and have the others too. Let's face it—if they thought I still had those other homes, I'm sure they would think something was up. Don't you?"

Just like Grant had hoped, the wedding was a wonderful event and even made the local society page. Grant didn't have anything to do with that, so he surmised Randy's parents were responsible.

There were over three-hundred guests, including many of Grant's and Pat's friends. One table alone had fifteen people from Universal Airlines.

Grant's ears burned as he walked by—the big topic of conversation at that table was Grant's financial success.

Grant continued to make a number of trips escorting the Chinese men to America. There were occasions where he would go weeks without one of those trips and he didn't mind being able to work a trip without the constant worry of getting caught. Grant toyed with the idea of retiring, only to realize that it would certainly send up a red flag if he left Universal at such a young age.

On one occasion, Andy came to Grant's house and they drank tea together. Andy had brought a large amount of cash with him to get Grant caught up with his payments. Andy joked that he had run out of clever ways of paying him. Grant trusted Andy so he didn't really care how he was paid. They enjoyed the visit and shared some thoughts of the future. Andy talked about wanting to go back to Korea. He had family there. Grant didn't have any big ideas or ambitions to share. He was comfortable for the time being.

Although Pat spent much of her time at Grant's house, she kept her apartment in Sausalito. When Grant was flying, Pat would mainly stay at her apartment unless she had some friends over to Grant's place for a swim or luncheon. Grant suspected that she wanted more of a commitment, but he was content with the status quo. As much as he loved her, it just wasn't time. He wanted to be free and clear of anything that would displease her.

Pat and Grant were dining together when he got an unexpected call from the crew desk assigning him to a Shanghai trip that night. While discussing his assignment, the phone rang again. It was Andy.

"Hi Grant. Did the crew desk call you?"

Not wanting to explain the second call, Grant tried to make it sound like it was the crew desk again. "Yes, Joe already called. Are you guys so busy you don't know who's doing what?"

"Okay, I understand. I generated your trip and I'll see you back here with my passenger when you arrive."

"Okay. You have a nice evening too." Grant was relieved that Andy understood his hint.

It was still fairly early and Pat hadn't been to her place in a few days. She seldom stayed alone overnight while Grant was on a trip, so she ironed a couple of Grant's shirts and headed for home.

It had been over six days since Grant had a trip, and he was actually looking forward to going. He missed the atmosphere in the crew area and his friends. He also enjoyed a certain respect from his co-workers. He didn't realize how much of that respect came from his financial success.

After chatting, Grant headed for the Shanghai trip briefing room. For him, part of the fun of being on reserve was the mystery of whom he would be working with. Of course, that was a double-edged sword. There was always the possibility of Renee or Betty, the redheaded union nightmare. Luckily, this time he walked into the briefing room to find a good-natured crew. There was still five minutes until briefing would start, and the room oozed with good energy. There were hugs all around as everyone started to settle down and get ready for their briefing.

The first flight attendant looked at her watch and said, "Let's give it a couple more minutes for the reserves to find our room."

A couple of stragglers came in looking a little sheepish, followed by Pat who had a big smile on her face. "Surprise! I'm going to Shanghai."

By this time, most of the crew knew Pat and Grant were an item. The crew also knew they seldom flew together. It seemed to Grant that everyone in the room was looking to see his reaction. He gave a clumsy smile and quipped, "There goes my anti-fraternization promise."

That elicited a few laughs and relieved the tension Grant felt when he saw Pat. As far as anti-fraternization, while it was never a problem, Grant and Pat tried not to fly together for that very reason—they didn't want management or other crew members to cause problems. They weren't the only supervisor-flight attendant couple, so they were all as discrete as possible to maintain peace with management.

Grant's mind went into high gear during the briefing. Grant dealt with several different people in Shanghai and always had to wait for their call to his room. He disliked the inconvenience of the language barrier. It always worked out, but of course Pat wasn't there. Then there was meeting with them in the boarding area before the flight. On most trips, he didn't attend the briefing, so he could meet with them and pre-board without the flight crew noticing. But Pat's presence complicated the situation. Fortunately, he had a long trip and layover to give it a lot of thought.

Like most of Grant's Shanghai trips, this one was uneventful. Grant found getting conversions a hit and miss proposition on his international flights. Passengers might have had a return on another carrier, but half of those possible conversions didn't speak English.

Pat worked the coach section and other than one break, she and Grant didn't spend any time together. They arrived at the Pu Dong Airport in Shanghai around noon the next day and sat together on the crew bus to the hotel. Grant was having a difficult time figuring out how to keep Pat from finding out what he was up to.

"Honey, why don't you get in line with the rest of the crew and get your own room when we get to the hotel? I don't want to flaunt our relationship." Grant suggested.

"You weren't that concerned on the other trips we've had together." Pat retorted.

"Well, I've heard some flight attendants mentioned to management the supervisor-flight attendant couples are not being discrete."

"Why didn't you mention this before?"

"Because we don't fly together that often. Why do you care?" Grant snapped. His anxiety and the 15-hour trip were taking their toll. They sat quietly the rest of the ride to the hotel.

Grant got his room key and waited for Pat who was toward the back of the line. She walked over to him and they exchanged room numbers. There was tension, but they had a 48-hour layover and Grant hoped it would be enough time to make it up to Pat. He didn't expect to be hearing from his Shanghai contact until the night before the trip.

"Why don't you drop your things off at your room and come to mine?" he suggested.

"Aren't you afraid someone might see us? And why your room? Why not mine?"

"Look, we got past the worst part. You got your own room and my room is much nicer. Wait until you see the view."

"Grant, do you really think these people are that stupid? Do you think my getting my own room fooled anyone? I'm tired. Why don't we go to our own rooms and take a nap. Call me when you wake up if you want to get some dinner."

"Okay, I don't feel like arguing. I'll call you around five o'clock, local time. How does that sound?"

Grant and Pat were the only people on the elevator and they kissed before she got off at her floor. It was a tepid kiss, but at least they parted on decent terms. It took Grant some time to get to sleep with Pat troubling his mind. He knew she had every reason to be upset.

The phone rang before his alarm went off. Grant was pleased that it was Pat and she sounded like nothing had happened. They both dropped the matter and met for dinner.

Grant thought maybe he was being too cautious. Helping a passenger shouldn't make Pat suspicious. He knew it must be his guilty conscience acting up. They spent the night in Grant's room and went sightseeing the next day. Not wanting to miss the call, Grant suggested they stay close to the hotel and more specifically, his room. Grant knew Pat would most likely be there when he got the call, so he tried to think it out. They watched movies and had room service sent up. It turned out to be a very romantic layover. They hadn't made that much love in one day for a long time. Later in the evening, the phone rang. Pat was closer to the phone, but let Grant answer. "Hello, this is Grant Guidera."

In very broken English, a voice responded, "Hello Mr. Guidera, I'm Wen Lin. We meet tomorrow with Mr. Hong Lu, okay?"

"Yes, what time and where?"

"We meet in boarding area, I'll see you in Universal uniform with nametag. "

"Okay, I'll do that. See you tomorrow."

When he hung up, Pat asked, "What was that all about?"

"The crew desk said passenger service has some papers they want me to bring back to our office."

"Why did you have to ask where? You know where the crew desk is."

"I don't know where the passenger service office is."

Pat slept in her room that night so there wouldn't be a problem fighting over the shower or sharing one in the morning. They would certainly have missed their bus.

The crew was in an upbeat mood the next morning. They had visited the traditional splendor of the Yuyuan Garden, the Jade Buddha Temple, and cruised the congested Huangpu River. Grant was satisfied with the cab tour of the city and romantic interlude that had been his layover with Pat. That was his idea of a good layover. He felt culturally challenged but content.

Grant parted from the crew, teasing that he knew they could handle briefing without him. He overheard Pat explaining he had to meet a guy from passenger service to get some papers. Grant wasn't in the boarding area long before a nice looking Chinese man with another younger man approached him.

"Mr. Guidera?"

"Yes."

"I'm Wen Lin and this is Mr. Hong Lu."

Grant shook Mr. Lu's hand and said, "It's nice to meet you Mr. Lu." Grant smiled and tried to make the men feel comfortable. They went to a corner of the boarding area and sat down. Mr. Lin gave Grant the tickets and waited until Grant came back with a boarding pass. When Grant got to the podium the same passenger agent was there who had been there on most of his other trips; making the process simple. Grant sat with Mr. Lin and Mr. Lu while he waited for the crew to board the plane. He tried to make conversation with little success. It was a wonder Grant had understood any of the short phone conversation the night before.

When most of the crew was onboard, Grant shook hands with Mr. Lin and motioned with his head for Mr. Lu to follow. Mr. Lu nodded to Mr. Lin and followed Grant.

The first flight attendant asked, "Are we boarding now?"

"No, this is just a pre-board."

Jokingly she said, "Why, doesn't he speak the language?"

"No smart ass, he's just very apprehensive about traveling and they asked me to escort him and help him get settled."

"I didn't see anything about that on the briefing sheet."

Grant had heard that one before. "It was a last minute situation. He'll be fine."

"Where is he sitting? I'll get the language-qualified attendant to take care of him, not to mention the other hundred or so who don't speak English."

Grant let that remark go without a response. For $25,000 he didn't mind putting up with a little sarcasm. "He'll be in 28C."

She wrote down the seat number, smiled and said, "Have a nice flight."

Mr. Lu seemed to understand. He smiled back and followed Grant to his seat.

Grant put his belongings away and went to the main cabin door to get ready for boarding. Pat was just getting on-board when the first flight attendant said, "You better be careful coming late. The supervisor might write you up." She said it with a smile but it made Grant uncomfortable. Pat apologized and explained that she had run into an old friend who came in on another trip. She hurried off to do her preflight check.

Mr. Lu slept most of the trip. Grant was sitting in the upper first class lounge during a movie when Pat arrived and sat down with him. He was happy to see her until she plopped a familiar looking envelope in front of him.

"Where did you get this? I should say--why do you have this?" Grant asked.

"The language-qualified attendant was somewhere else and when I asked Mr. Lu in 28C what he wanted for dinner, he handed me this envelope."

Grant didn't know what to think, and said, "I doubt it has his dinner choice in it."

"It didn't. It's just medical records, in English, and his passport."

"Why did you look in it?"

"I don't know. He just seemed anxious to give it to me. I didn't want to be rude."

"Well, leave it here, and I'll get it back to him."

Pat left mumbling, "That's why you make the big bucks."

The envelope got the better of Grant and he walked over to the spiral staircase to make sure Pat was gone. He opened the envelope only to find three other sealed envelopes. One said: "Medical Records." He took out the passport realizing it must be forged and admired how authentic it looked. The other two envelopes were blank and securely sealed. He put everything back in the envelope and bent the metal tabs over the hole in the flap. He asked the language-qualified flight attendant to give it back to Mr. Lu and to explain to him to only give it to the Chinese-speaking man who would meet him in San Francisco. Mr. Lu just nodded while the language-qualified flight attendant spoke to him.

Both Grant and Pat had the next four days off, so they spent them together at Grant's house. Pat was watching the morning news while making breakfast. Grant sat out by the pool with a cup of tea reminiscing about Gina and Randy's wedding. He was proud that he had a sizeable home and spacious garden large enough to hold such an elaborate wedding. His daydream was broken by Pat's shriek.

"Grant, come in here. Hurry, hurry! Look at this!"

Grant couldn't imagine what could be so important. He got in the kitchen in time to see Mr. Lu's face on the television. "What was that all about?"

"I'm not sure. He was found wandering on Market Street, bleeding, and he won't talk to the authorities."

"Of course he won't. He doesn't speak English."

"You dumb ass. They had Chinese officers trying to get information from him."

Grant wasn't sure what to make of it. They continued to watch the news, but it was late afternoon before the same story was replayed. The authorities were asking for information from anyone who might know the man.

Pat said, "We better call and tell them he was on our flight."

For a brief moment Grant considered it but thought better of it. "Let's wait and see if someone else identifies him."

"But why? We know when he got here and from where. Maybe that will help them."

"If we get involved, there will be reams of paperwork and who knows what else."

"I can't believe you just said that. I'm going to call."

Before Grant thought about it, he blurted out, "You can't, I could get in trouble."

"What the hell are you talking about? How could you get in trouble?" Comprehension dawned on Pat's face. "Grant, are you somehow involved? What do you know about this?"

"Before I answer, let me ask you something. After the boat trip with Brian do you remember me asking you 'Do you want me to become a rich international smuggler?' And you said, 'I guess the money would be nice to have, but I'll bet it's not worth the risk.' And then I said, 'So, you sound a little tempted?' And you said, 'Aren't you?' Well, the answer to that was yes.

"Grant, I know all about that. You did it and it's over. What does that have to do with this Chinese man?"

"I met a passenger agent because of the drug thing. At first I thought he was threatening me, but then he offered me what I'm doing now. It was some offer."

"Which was to do what?"

"I help bring rich, but illegal, Chinese men to America. They just get here a lot sooner than if they waited to get to the top of the immigration list. I don't think it's as bad as the drug thing and I couldn't believe the money."

"Because of that, you're going to just do nothing?"

"What can I do? Go to the cops and tell them I helped smuggle in guys with forged papers, lose my job, and maybe go to jail?"

"You can just say he was on your flight and that's it."

"You don't understand. I met him with the guy in Shanghai. He knows what I do and why. If he starts to talk, that's it. Maybe he got mugged and robbed. At least they found him and he's getting medical care."

That answer didn't seem to satisfy Pat. She sulked for a while and told Grant she was going home.

"To do what?" Grant asked, a little irritated.

"I need to think."

With that, Pat gave Grant a tepid kiss and left. he sat by the pool, Pat's disappointment weighed heavily on him.

In the meantime, Grant needed to find out why Mr. Lu was found in that condition. He called Andy, only to get his answering machine. "Andy, call me."

Grant didn't want to leave his name and was sure Andy would recognize his voice. It wasn't ten minutes before Andy returned his call.

"Andy, have you seen the news?"

"Yes I did, and I was going to call you."

"And?"

"And say not to panic. Those things just happen."

"What things just happen? People get mugged? Is that what happened to him? Where do you take these guys after you get them off the plane?"

"I turn them over to a sponsor, the Chinese people who set this all up. Just don't say anything and don't worry about it. It was just a bad break for him. Maybe he went for a walk in the wrong neighborhood. They found him in Chinatown. That's where it must have happened."

Andy made Grant feel a little better, but still, he felt Andy was withholding something. The worst part was Pat's disappointment. He decided to let her think about it.

Grant had never felt lonely before in his big house, but not knowing where things stood with Pat made it different. His depression made him sleepy, and he dozed off. It seemed only minutes before the phone rang, but the clock showed that it had been over an hour.

"Grant, Brian. How are you doing?"

"Hi Brian. I'm fine. Why are you asking in that way?"

"You know the case about Romano is still open. It's not high priority with these guys, but they don't let up. The guy working the case came by today and tried to stir me up."

"About what?"

"About you. I never wanted to tell you, but one time a couple of agents were here and mentioned that you were on a lot of the same flights as me when I was traveling to and from Honolulu."

"Why didn't you tell me?"

"I didn't want to phone, and I hadn't seen you. They didn't go anywhere with it and realized I made a lot of trips when you weren't on my flights. I admitted we had become friends because I was sure they already knew."

"So why are you telling me now? Aren't you afraid they might still be tapping your line?"

"I'm not calling from home. The reason I'm telling you now is because when he was here today, the agent said, 'Well, Mr. Lasswell, it seems your friend Grant's name came up again. He was on another flight where interesting things happened.' I told him I didn't have a clue what he was talking about. I told him that I'm sure a lot of things happen on other people's flights as well. They travel with hundreds of people every month.

Maybe some guys in first class cheated on their wives while on a business trip; maybe some mafia hit man was on his flight. Is that Grant's fault? He left with a shit-eating grin on his face, but didn't say anything more. I'm not sure what he was getting at. Do you?"

"Brian, come to my house. I don't want to talk on the phone."

"Sure, when?"

"The sooner, the better."

"I'll be there within the hour."

Paranoia was replacing Grant's depression. The hour waiting for Brian dragged on slowly. Grant left the gate open and Brian drove right up to the lawn in front of the pool where Grant sat, slightly slouched forward, waiting. When Grant saw Brian, he got up and walked toward the car. They met half way, shook hands, and hugged. Brian was looking good, even better than he had at Gina's wedding. Grant motioned toward a table by the pool.

"Grant, what do you think that Fed was talking about? Why would he have brought up your name?" Brian asked, taking a sip of his coffee.

Grant looked around before speaking. His paranoia was deepening. "Have you seen the news lately?"

"Yes, but nothing sticks out."

"Did you happen to see the story about the Chinese man, found bleeding wandering around Chinatown?"

"Just briefly, it looked like a mugging to me. The police just want to find a relative or a friend who knew him. He wasn't talking. Maybe he was in shock. What does that have to do with you?"

Grant looked around again. "I've been working for a guy who brings in wealthy Chinese guys.

"So, what's wrong with that?"

"Their papers, passports, they are all forged."

"What do you do?"

"I just make sure things work more smoothly. I keep the wrong people from looking at their papers or asking them questions."

"How long have you been doing this?"

"Since we gave up the drugs."

"And I was impressed with all you had done with the money I paid you. I was beginning to think you were some kind of a stock market whiz kid."

"I'm not sure what to do. What do you think?"

"If it weren't for that Fed talking with me, I wouldn't say anything. On the other hand, if the Chinese guy talks, and I'm sure he will in time, I'd try to cover my ass."

"And do what? If he tells the authorities I helped him, that's it."

"I hate to say this Grant, but it's not only that. I think the Feds are on to something about our drug smuggling. This agent who's been coming to my house has told me horror stories about the new guys who took over from Romano. They're blatantly trying to recruit flight crew members to help them."

"So why don't they arrest those guys?"

"This guy doesn't tell me everything, but I think they're looking for bigger fish to fry. He just tells me what he thinks will make me nervous, hoping I might say something. He's even had the balls to offer me a deal if I help him."

"What kind of a deal?"

"I don't know. I didn't let him get that far. I've stuck with my story. My business was legitimate. What they are doing now—I know nothing about. They don't seem to have anything to prove me wrong. To be honest Grant, I think they will come up with something sooner or later."

"What are you going to do about it?"

"I've sent most of my assets offshore. I would like to sell my house too, but I think they're watching and waiting for me to try."

"Then what?"

"Vicki and I have talked about it. We can live in Europe or some exotic island. We're not wanted for anything, so we have every right to leave. I just don't want the authorities to know when we leave or where we are."

"That takes care of you and Vicki. What am I going to do?"

"If I were you, I would call my brother-in-law. I'm sure he has some ideas."

"Gina would be so upset with me. I couldn't stand that."

"That's the lesser of the two evils. You're going to need a lawyer someday the way things are going."

"If I don't get caught about the drug dealings, what have I really done wrong? I've helped some rich people come to America. They will invest, pay taxes."

"That sounds good, but I'm not going to be on your jury. I don't how I can help, but I would do anything you ask."

Brian left and Grant was more confused than he was before Brian's visit. Grant moped around the house and after a couple of drinks, decided to call Pat. She answered the phone but sounded distant.

"Honey, are you still upset?"

"Grant this was not one of our disagreements. You've been lying to me all this time—stock market, my ass."

"And if I told you the truth, would that have mattered?"

"At least, I could have made a decision based on the truth."

"A decision about what?"

"Whether or not I wanted to be a part of your life and the things you've chosen to make money."

"Just tell me, in your mind what crime have I committed? Gangs and hoodlums are crossing our borders everyday and the government doesn't seem to care. I bring in rich, worthwhile people."

"Grant, I love you, but you're heading for trouble if you keep this up."

"So what should I do now?"

"If I were you, I would at least talk to Randy, maybe Gina too."

"Have you talked with Brian? He said the same thing."

"No, but that's two people who love you saying the same thing. Maybe you should listen."

They exchanged a lackluster "I love you" and hung up. Grant had a couple more drinks and for a while things seemed to make sense. Randy could help him. Randy would get him out of this.

Unfortunately, Grant's clarity was gone the next morning. He had tea and stared at the phone. "Why did it seem so simple last night?" he lamented. He sheepishly called Randy's number at his office in San Francisco.

"District Attorney's Office, how may I direct your call?"

"May I speak to Mr. Barrett?"

"Mr. Barrett is in a meeting, may I have him return your call?"

"Yes please. Could you have him call Grant Guidera at 415-555-1868?"

"Oh hi Grant, this is Melissa. I met you at the wedding."

"I met so many people. I was a wreck that day. Hope you had a good time."

"It was a spectacular wedding, and I loved your home. I'll have Mr. Barrett call you."

Grant felt like it was an eternity before the phone finally rang. His emotions were mixed, part of him wanted it to be Pat and the other part wanted Randy. It was Randy. "Hi Grant. Sorry for the delay. We have a lot of meetings here. I hope it's nothing important?"

"I'm not really sure, but I need to talk with you. It might not be anything, but I don't want to take any chances."

"What's going on?"

"Not on the phone. Could you come by?"

"Gina is working late again, so we took two cars. How about I stop by after work?"

"That would be fine. See you tonight. Thanks Randy."

Grant wanted a drink to calm his nerves, but knew better than to smell like alcohol when Randy arrived. The phone didn't ring the rest of the day, making Grant feel lonely and abandoned.

Randy pulled into the driveway much earlier than Grant had expected. Grant greeted Randy by the parking area and they walked toward the pool. Randy asked if they could sit outside, he'd been in a stuffy office all day. Grant was thrilled when Randy said he'd love a scotch. Grant made himself a double bourbon and Randy's scotch. They lightly touched glasses.

"What can I do for you?" Randy asked, before taking his first sip.

"It's kind of a long story and not one that I'm very proud of. By the way, is everything I tell you confidential?"

"Grant. I'm your brother-in-law not your attorney. In either case, I would never repeat what you have to say."

"I'm sorry. I just don't know how these things work." Grant went on, "I guess you've wondered how I've made so many investments on my supervisor's salary." Randy didn't say anything. "Well, I met a guy who was a courier."

"Brian?"

"Yes. He had a very legitimate business with a few exceptions: he was bringing in drugs from Honolulu. He offered me a chance to make some money. It didn't seem like such a bad thing at first. The drugs were already on the plane in his courier boxes, all I did was switch the drugs to suitcases that were later picked up in the baggage area."

Randy couldn't hide his astonishment. "Switch them how?"

"I would go into the forward cargo pit during the trip and take them from the courier boxes and put them in specially marked suitcases."

"Grant you might just as well have peddled them on the street. You're just as guilty in the eyes of the law. To make matters worse, there are most likely international laws that have been broken."

"We never left the States. It was just from Honolulu to San Francisco."

"Universal is an international carrier. I'm sure there are laws that cover cargo regardless where you fly. I'm not sure about that, but nonetheless, you've broken some serious laws. I have no doubt about that."

"Well, I quit doing that months ago, but that's not my problem."

"Maybe you don't think it is, but those things have a way of coming back. What other indiscretions have you been involved in?

"Well, a passenger agent found out about the drugs, and actually saved my ass, he then asked me to do something for him."

"Which was what?"

"He wanted me to help him get rich Chinese men into the country with limited problems."

"What's wrong with that?"

"Well, they all had forged passports and papers."

Looking puzzled, Randy asked, "He blackmailed you into doing this?"

"No, I thought that's what he was doing at first, but then he just offered it to me. I was getting out of the drug thing when I met him. It all sounded so easy and the pay was unbelievable. Besides, I owed him."

"And now, something went wrong and you're committing another felony?"

"I'm not sure. A Chinese man who was on my flight the other day was found bleeding in Chinatown. I think he was mugged."

"I can't believe what I'm hearing. He was on your flight?"

"Yes, what's so hard to believe about that?"

"Grant, if that man talks, you're in a world of trouble. He wasn't mugged—he had a kidney removed and later wandered away. We think from an illegal operating room."

"What are you talking about? How do you know anything about this? Why would he come here for a surgery?"

"Grant, don't be as dumb as I sometimes think you are. He didn't come here for surgery. He either sold his kidney or it was stolen. It was even mentioned in this morning's meeting. That's where I was when you called."

Grant didn't understand what Randy was telling him. He just sat, thinking. Randy didn't say anything waiting for Grant to understand. If Grant had any idea what Randy was talking about, it didn't show.

Finally Grant said, "What are you talking about? How could he sell a kidney? He just got here. They didn't say anything about that on the news."

"The authorities didn't want everyone to know what really happened. They want to catch whoever is responsible. Grant, I need to get some things done at home. Let me call Gina and we can both meet you here later and talk about this."

"Does Gina have to know just yet?"

"That's for you to decide. She's my wife and your sister. She cares about you and I think she needs to know."

"Maybe nothing will come of this. Why tell her now?"

"From what I heard at the office, plenty will come of it and you will be in the middle. Trust me; you're going to need some help."

Grant was alarmed at Randy's words. "Why would more come of it? And why would I be involved?" he puzzled.

When Randy got home, he didn't even hang up his coat before calling Gina.

"UC San Francisco." The receptionist answered.

"May I speak with Dr. Barrett please?"

"I'm sorry. I don't show a Dr. Barrett."

"Dr. Guidera-Barrett."

"One moment."

Gina picked up, "Hi honey."

"Hi Gina. What time will you be getting off?"

"I had a patient cancel so I should be leaving shortly. What did you need?"

"Grant called me today and has a legal problem. I stopped by after work and we talked. Why don't you meet me at his house and I'll explain then."

"What's this about? What kind of legal problem? He has a lawyer. Why didn't Grant call him?"

"We need to discuss this together. I'm sure he will contact another lawyer if he has to. In the mean time, he could use some support and input from us, together."

"I don't like the sound of this, but I can't talk now. I'll be leaving in a few minutes and I'll meet you at Grant's."

Randy arrived a little before Gina and found Grant sitting with a drink in the pool house watching the news. Randy's sudden appearance startled a jumpy Grant. "Where's Gina?"

Grant had no sooner asked when Gina appeared by the pool. They both walked out to kiss and hug her. Grant held on a little longer than normal, which he knew Gina sensed. Grant offered Gina and Randy a drink; they both accepted. Grant made himself another double and took them to the pool house. They all sat without saying anything.

After a sip of her wine, Gina asked, "What's going on that you wanted to see us?"

"Grant why don't you tell your sister what you told me?"

Grant was hoping Randy would relay the story and not make it sound so bad. He thought that's what attorney's do best, but that was not to be. He didn't know where to begin. If it weren't for the drinks, he would have hidden under the bed.

"You know my friend Brian?"

"Yes, of course," she said.

Grant explained how he had become involved in drug smuggling.

Gina couldn't hold back, "What were you thinking? I can't believe you let yourself get involved."

Randy chimed in, "He's not through, let him finish."

Grant divulged everything including how he met Andy and his proposition.

"He blackmailed you?" queried Gina.

"Just what I asked," Randy said.

"No, he didn't blackmail me. He offered me the chance to make a lot of money."

Gina was so astounded she had hardly touched her wine. "What did he want you to do?"

"He wanted me to help him bring illegal Chinese men here with as few problems as possible. They had forged passports and visas. In fact, they had an entire envelope filled with papers."

"So, where did they go after they got here?"

"They went with the passenger agent I told you about. He told me they were very rich and paid a lot to get here. That's why he paid me so much. I don't know where they went after that."

Randy interjected, "That is until today. A Chinese man, who was on Grant's flight, was found roaming around Chinatown, bleeding. In fact he passed out. They had to give him a transfusion."

"How is that Grant's fault?"

"Grant aided in smuggling that man here. The man had a kidney removed. The authorities don't know if he sold it, donated it, or if it was stolen. But they're going to find out. The man hasn't talked so far, but I don't think it will take long before he tells all. I'm sure he will tell them Universal Airline employees helped him. That's where Grant comes in."

Gina gave Grant a long look of disappointment. Her eyes were misty and her mouth drawn down in the corners. He couldn't tell if she was going to cry or yell at him. She'd never yelled before and he was hoping she wouldn't start now. She visibly struggled to calm herself, glanced at her wine and took a sip. Gina looked at Randy and asked, "What can be done? What will they do with Grant if and when they find out?

"It's not a matter of if—they will find out. I can't even guess how many charges they may level against him and that doesn't count his involvement in the drug business. I think with this passenger agent knowing about the drugs, it's going to come out too. What's his name?"

"His name is Andy. He's a nice guy and has always been honest with me."

Randy continued, "Grant you both might be nice guys, but you've both committed a very serious felony."

"How serious can it be to help rich people come to America?"

"And give up a kidney? You forgot to add that."

"I don't know anything about that. Why would someone come here to sell or have a kidney stolen? There are millions of people already here."

Grant should have known the topic was right down Gina's alley. "Grant you have no idea. There are people on waiting lists for a kidney that have been waiting for seven years. They may never find the proper match. Not only that, depending on their situation they may even be moved down the list. It's complicated. I can't even begin to tell you."

Gina and Randy finished their drinks and told Grant they would give it some thought and meet with him tomorrow. Grant still had three more days off.

It was getting late and Grant was surprised when the phone rang. His first thought was the crew desk. He hoped they wouldn't take away his days off. Much to his delight it was Pat.

"I didn't catch you napping did I?"

"Almost, I was getting ready for bed."

"Grant, I feel terrible. I love you. I want to support you. It's just that I was shocked, and of course, disappointed. And then you said something that made me feel you thought I would have approved of you making money illegally."

"I didn't mean to imply that. It's just that we talked about it after the boat trip. You never encouraged me. I made this mistake on my own."

"Did you call Randy or Gina?"

"Yes, Randy came over and Gina met him here. He heard about Mr. Lu in his morning meeting. He doesn't think the case will wind up in his office, but he can find out what's going on."

They discussed the situation briefly. Grant was newly apprehensive of the possibility of his phone being bugged. He was afraid if that were the case, the whole conversation would sound suspicious.

"I know it's late, but do you want me to come over?"

"I'd love that. I'll leave the gate open."

"I'll be there in forty-five minutes. I love you."

Grant woke up with Pat gently shaking his shoulder. He jumped up and gave her a long hug. She couldn't apologize enough for leaving the way she did. After they wore themselves out apologizing, they sat and talked for hours. Pat agreed it was a touchy situation but at least he was friends with Brian and didn't need to worry about him saying anything. Grant started to feel guilty when she mentioned Brian. He didn't want to tell her about the FBI's suspicions of his presence on certain trips. He had enough with the problem at hand. They were both too tired and distracted to make love and just fell asleep in each other's arms.

Grant and Pat were awakened by the phone and were shocked to see it was 10:00 A.M. Grant tried to clear his head so he wouldn't sound sleepy so late in the morning. "Hello."

"Grant, Randy, I talked with one of the detectives and he said the Chinese man still hasn't said anything."

"That's good isn't it?"

"For the time being. They're turning him over to the INS and the detective seemed fairly sure the INS would be able to get something out of him. I didn't want to ask too many questions. Our office doesn't have anything to do with this and he might begin to wonder why I'm so interested. So far, he thinks I'm just curious."

"Maybe Mr. Lu won't say anything about me."

"Maybe not right away, but I'll bet once he starts feeling comfortable, or uncomfortable, he'll talk a lot."

"So what should I do?"

Pat looked puzzled, Grant mouthed the word "Randy" to her. She nodded her head and made an expression, as if to say: "Of course, I should have known."

Randy paused. "I talked with my dad this morning and told him about the situation."

"Why would you do that? What is he going to think of me?"

"Don't worry, I didn't mention you. I worked it into our conversation about the Chinese man and his missing kidney. He said I would be hearing a lot more about it. Dad has a friend in the DOJ and they oversee the INS. Evidently, this is becoming a serious nationwide problem."

"Randy, I don't know what the DOJ is."

"The DOJ is the Department of Justice. The good news—the United States Attorney General's Office enforces the immigration laws."

"Why is that so good?"

"That's where my dad works. He's an Assistant Attorney General."

"If Mr. Lu's not talking, why should we do anything right now?"

"If you want my help, you need to let me talk with my dad some more about this. He can find out exactly what's going on with the situation here and what they're going to do with your Chinese friend."

"Can I think about this and get back to you?"

"Of course, but I wouldn't wait too long. If you are going to become involved sooner or later, and I think you are, it would look much better if you came forward, admitted he was on your flight and what you have been doing. You could tell them at that time you knew nothing about the kidney deals. That you honestly had no knowledge of that."

"And then what, go to jail?"

"Maybe not, just get back to me soon. If you really want help, I'll help you."

Grant and Randy said their goodbyes.

Pat couldn't stand the wait. "What did he say? What was that about going to jail? What was the DJ thing?"

"That was the DOJ—Department of Justice, and they're a step above the INS. Evidently, they know about this problem and are starting to look into it. He really thinks it will come back to me."

"What does he think you should do?"

"I'm not exactly sure. He said he could have his dad get some information. If it looks like this will come back to me he said I'd be better off coming forward before that happens. I'm not sure what to do."

"Whatever it takes to get this over with. I think you should listen to Randy."

"You're probably right, but what if that guy never talks? Who would know the difference?"

"Are you willing to take that chance? Isn't it better to let Randy find out what he can, rather than do nothing?"

Grant felt trapped. The worst part was he had no one to blame but himself. His feelings of success and satisfaction were diminishing with all the troubles it was causing the people he loved. Grant and Pat sat by the pool and had coffee and tea. Grant looked around the property, and admired the view. He was ashamed to admit it, but a part of him was still proud at what he had acquired. Grant was in no mood to enjoy the irony that most of what he had was because of good investments. The drug and immigration involvements just provided the seed money. "If only it had been honest money to have started with," Grant lamented to himself.

Grant knew what he should do, but couldn't bring himself to do it. "Just maybe, this will all go away." Grant wished. The phone rang, breaking his thoughtful silence. Pat was quietly lost in her own thoughts beside him.

"Hello."

"Hi Grant. What are you doing? Better yet, what are you going to do?"

"Hi Gina. What do you mean what am I going to do?"

"I just got off the phone with Randy. He wants to help you, but you have to allow him to."

"If he could be my attorney I would feel a lot more comfortable."

"Grant, listen to me. Randy will find out what needs to be done, if anything. And I'm sure he will find you an attorney who does this kind of work. The fact is, he knows a lot of criminal attorneys, the most experienced ones. But let's not get ahead of ourselves. Let him talk to his dad. Grant, I have to go. I'm due in surgery. I love you. Call Randy."

"I love you too."

Grant was relieved that although Gina was disappointed, she still wanted to help him. When he hung up, Pat asked, "Well?"

"I'm going to call Randy and tell him to talk with his dad."

"That has to be the best thing to do at this point."

Grant picked up the receiver and dialed. A very professional voice answered: "District Attorney's office."

"May I speak with Mr. Barrett?

"One moment please, I'll connect you."

There was a brief pause and then Randy's voice came on the line.

"Randal Barrett."

"Hi Randy, Grant here. Could you talk with your father for me?"

"Hi Grant. Of course I will. You must have talked with Gina."

"Yes I did. She's always been right when it comes to helping me."

"Actually, I called and told her to call you."

"I know, she told me. That's fine. I really appreciate you helping me. I am starting to see that I could be in a lot of trouble."

"Let's hope we can minimize whatever happens. I'll talk with you tonight."

Randy was just about to walk out the door to pick up Gina when the secretary buzzed his office.

"You have a call on line one."

"Randal Barrett."

"Randy, Dad. I spoke with Gordon like you asked. He did some research at the DOJ and just got back to me."

"What did he have to say?"

"Are you sitting down?"

"Should I be?"

"I'm afraid so. Grant is definitely on their radar and it's not totally because of this issue."

"What else could they have?"

"It seems Grant has been on a number of flights with some courier whose business was questionable. Gordon didn't have a lot of details, but it looks like there were some drug ties. They didn't have a lot of proof on that, mostly speculation. But between the FBI and the INS they found out this Chinese man was also on Grant's flight. Of course, you already knew that. Was anything going on that you know about?"

"Dad, I don't know what to say. I'm more concerned about the immigration thing. Can we work on one thing at a time?"

"What do you mean?"

"Grant was involved with Brian and had something to do with a drug situation for a while. He quit, and has been out of that business for some time. So has Brian. That part should be over."

"I'm not so sure about that. It seems the guy who bought Brian out was murdered. He had organized crime connections with some heavy hitters. There's an entire department working on that alone—not just because this guy was murdered, but because of whom he knew and did business with. Even he was on Grant's flight when he went to Hawaii and got killed."

"They don't think Grant had anything to do with it, do they?"

"I don't think so, but there are just too many coincidences with Grant's involvement. Son, he's going to need some real help. Do you know any good criminal attorneys out there?"

"Unfortunately, I've lost some cases to a few of them."

"Why don't you start thinking about that, and I'll have Gordon keep me up to speed. There is nothing wrong with him calling me about this; his department works on these things all the time."

Grant and Pat were having dinner when the gate buzzer rang.

"Who is it?' Grant asked.

"Grant, its Randy and Gina."

As Randy and Gina had become accustomed, they drove up by the pool and entered the house off the patio. Pat was clearing the remaining plates off the table.

"Have you eaten? We have lots of roast left." Pat offered.

Gina smiled. "It's tempting, but I think I'd just like a glass of wine and a scotch for Randy."

With drinks for Gina and Randy, Pat and Grant sat down. Randy took a deep breath and started on the conversation with his dad. Randy didn't stop until Grant and Pat's faces were nearly touching the floor. Randy took a sip of his scotch and waited.

Grant got up and made himself a drink. There was a long pause before Grant said, "So what should I do? What are my choices?"

"You need to get a good criminal attorney. I've been beaten by a few. I'm thinking Ray Neal—he's sharp and well liked by most of the judges. In fact, I get most impressed whenever I hear him argue a case."

"What kind of case would this be? Wouldn't it be federal?" Grant asked.

"It most likely will be, and he can handle federal cases as well. He has a good reputation at the ninth district federal court."

Gina looked at Grant. "Of course this is all up to you, but I think I would listen to Randy, and especially to what his father thinks."

"I'm going to listen to them, but when should I call?"

"Why don't you let me call him and see if he's interested?" Randy suggested. "I'll call you as soon as I know something."

Gina changed the subject. "May I change my mind about a little of that roast beef? Maybe a French dip if you have some au jus." Pat jumped up, at the same time asking Randy if he would like one too. It seemed getting things out in the open gave Gina and Randy an appetite. Grant's problems weren't brought up for the rest of their stay. When they left, Randy promised again to get back to Grant. Pat and Grant felt more comfortable now that a decision had been made.

Chapter 15

Ray Neal's schedule was quite full, but he was happy to extend Randy the professional courtesy of meeting with him and his brother-in-law.

Randy called Grant immediately.

"Grant, we have an appointment with Ray Neal tomorrow at 8:30 A.M. I'll pick you up at 7:45."

"Wow, that was fast. So he's going to take my case?"

"First, there is no case so far. And I'm not sure how far he will go with us. He's being kind enough to meet with us, so let's see where that goes."

Randy was at Grant's at 7:45 A.M. sharp and found Grant standing outside ready to go. Pat's car was still in the driveway. Randy asked, "Did you want Pat to come along?"

"No, I'd rather not get her any more involved. Her folks would die if they found out about this. They're already not too excited about me being slow to make a commitment. Besides, she has a trip this afternoon."

"I wouldn't get my hopes up too much about her folks not finding out. From what my father said, this situation is high priority and will certainly make the news one day."

Grant didn't like the sound of that.

Ray's office was in a prestigious building. The reception area had a view of the San Francisco City Hall and the Federal Building. When they walked in, Ray was making coffee. He explained that his secretary didn't get in until 9:00.

"Can I pour you a cup?" Ray asked.

Randy said he would love a cup and introduced Ray to Grant. Ray was a handsome man with dark, shiny hair, graying a bit at the temples.

"Grant would you like a cup of coffee?"

"Would tea be too much trouble?"

"Not at all—help yourself. Here's the tea and you can warm the water in the microwave. When you're ready, just come to my office. Randy, why don't you and I get settled? Grant can join us."

For being a senior partner, Ray's office was fairly modest. Besides a conference table it had a sofa and a small wet bar. His desk faced away from the terrific view. Grant was sure Ray must have swiveled around on occasion to enjoy where he was. Grant knew he would have, if it were his office. Ray and Randy sat across from each other at the conference table and left the end seat for Grant.

"Well Grant, Randy tells me you have a legal problem that I may be able to help you with. Why don't you start from the beginning?"

Grant looked at Randy and asked, "From the very beginning?" He took a couple sips of his tea and tried to organize his thoughts. He wasn't really sure what Randy meant. He started with, "I met a fellow who was bringing in illegal…"

Randy interrupted, "Grant, the very beginning."

Ray looked a little puzzled and glanced at Randy and then back to Grant. Grant started again.

"Well, I met a fellow who was on my flight from time to time who had a courier business. He was also dating a Universal flight attendant…"

Grant told the entire story. Randy glanced over to Ray on occasion as if to read his expressions. Grant ended with Pat's insistence that he call Randy.

Ray said, "Sounds like you have a smart girlfriend."

Randy confirmed that, as did Grant. Grant added that Randy's father had suggested he find a good criminal attorney. "And Randy thinks you're that person."

"Well, I'm flattered, and that is some story. I'm not sure I would be up to the task of a full-blown federal case over this. I've handled some drug cases and have even helped some people with immigration problems, but most of those cases were unchallenged. The other thing is this; I don't see where you are charged with anything at this point, so it's a bit premature to do anything. If that Chinese man doesn't talk, it could go away, but I would certainly advise you to discontinue any further criminal activities."

Grant appeared relieved and looked over to Randy, who said, "Ray, what Grant didn't tell you is that my father is an assistant US Attorney General. He talked with a friend at the DOJ who looked into the ongoing investigation regarding the Chinese man. The FBI is still investigating the murder of Romano and Grant's name keeps coming up. Grant is definitely on their radar, and I'm not sure how to move forward. I don't think we should do nothing."

"Well, that does put a different light on things. If you and your dad are sure, with no questions asked, that Grant might be brought in for questioning, you might want to take advantage of that information and be pro-active. What do you think Randy?"

"I agree, but I'm not sure how to go about it. I guess you could say that is the main reason we've come to you, for your opinion."

"I see a couple of problems. How do we move forward with what could only be called privileged information? They would know we knew something. On the other hand, if we just go to the local police and say the Chinese man was on Grant's flight, the police in turn might just give it to the INS. At that point, they may divulge what they know, giving Grant the opportunity to show he regrets his misdeeds without their prompting."

"What if they don't mention the kidney thing?"

"Then Grant says nothing. He doesn't and shouldn't know anything about that."

Grant spoke up, not liking the idea. "What if the Chinese man never talks? I would have turned myself in for nothing."

"From what Randy says, that's not likely. If they have an entire department working on this, I believe it's just a matter of time—time that is on your side to do the right thing. To get the most leniencies you should go to the authorities of your own accord. Of course, it's your choice. But I think it's in your best interest. You will know what they have on you and they will be more inclined toward leniency. That's one big thing on your side. It could be a gamble giving too much, but I seriously doubt it from what Randy is saying. We can take it one step at a time."

With that Ray looked at Randy and they both looked at Grant. The ball was clearly in his court.

"Okay, what should I do first?" Grant asked.

"I think maybe you and Randy should talk this over and get back to me. Under the circumstances, I wouldn't wait too long."

Grant replied, "I don't think we need to talk about it. I know how he feels and how much he trusts you. That's good enough for me."

Randy wore a tight smile. "I'm proud of you Grant. I think you've made the right decision."

Ray responded, "Well then, let's get started. I'll make up a statement. In fact, I'll make up a couple. One for the local cops who've asked for help on television and another for the INS. There's no telling how soon you will be contacted by them. Like I said, we'll take this one step at a time. I want to be sure it's in your best interest to tell what you know. I'll want you to read the statement and remember it. Don't stray from it or answer any questions unless we talk about it first. If you have any doubt, look at me. Let me work on this and if it's okay with you, I'll make an appointment with the local detectives working on this case."

"Won't they think I'm acting guilty by bringing an attorney?"

"Not at all. They know it's good thinking on your part. Are you free tomorrow?"

"I'm on reserve, but I can get some personal days off. Will a week do?"

"That should be fine for the time being. I'll call this afternoon."

The men shook hands all around and Randy and Grant departed. The secretary was now at her desk and smiled at Randy and Grant on the way out. They heard Ray over the intercom as they passed her desk, "Judy, could you come in here for a minute?"

Grant called the office and talked with Maryann about his personal days off. She said it wouldn't be a problem to take five days. She asked if everything was okay, without sounding as if she were prying. Grant said things were fine, he just had some personal matters to sort out. With a long day behind him, Grant was heading for bed when the phone rang.

"Hello."

"Hi Grant, this is Andy. What's going on with you?"

Andy's voice gave Grant a start. Grant was already trying to think of a reason why he couldn't take a trip for Andy.

"Not much, just enjoying my days off. I hope you're not calling about a trip. I just got some personal days off."

"No, as a matter of fact I'm not. I just wanted to touch base with you."

Grant didn't want to be obvious and totally ignore the topic of Mr. Lu, so he asked, "What was the deal with Mr. Lu? Did you ever find out anything?"

"I haven't heard anything since the other day. I'm sure it was just a mugging."

Grant wondered how much Andy knew about what was really going on. "Have you talked with the people you work with?"

"They've been surprisingly quiet. I haven't heard from them. I don't think it has anything to do with Mr. Lu, but you never know."

Grant was comfortable that Andy didn't seem to know any more than he did. Grant didn't want to mention anything else to Andy. He would find out soon enough what Grant was up to.

Grant had been awake for some time when the phone rang. It was Ray.

"Hi Grant, we have an appointment this afternoon at 1:30 with a Detective Moore. Will that work for you?"

"Right now would work for me. I want to get this over with."

"I'm sure you do, but we'll just have to wait until then. Why don't you meet me at 12:30 in my office, and we'll go in my car. You can park in our building. We'll validate your parking."

Grant thought Ray must have been kidding. That was the least of his worries. Grant wanted to ask a million questions but thought better than to waste Ray's time on the phone. He would have plenty of time in Ray's office and in the car to wherever they were going.

Grant got to Ray's office a bit early and the secretary was out to lunch. He had hardly sat down when Ray came out of his office. Grant rose and they shook hands. Ray told him to make himself a cup of tea. Ray was finishing a sandwich and organizing a file he had for Grant.

"Okay, here's what's going to happen today—we're going to meet with Detective Moore, who's been working on Mr. Lu's case. I'm sure it's been turned over to the INS. If not already, it will be soon, but Moore didn't say so. Maybe he's trying to get a little credit for finding out something more. I know him, but not that well. I'm sure he will be disappointed when he finds out we don't have much to tell him."

"Won't he wonder why I brought you?"

"He might act like it, but believe me he knows. After you've told him Mr. Lu was on your flight, unless it's a simple question, don't say anything more. Let me do any additional talking."

Grant and Ray arrived at the Hall of Justice at 1:15 and told the sergeant at the desk they had an appointment with Detective Moore. It was only a matter of minutes before a soft, haphazardly-dressed guy in wrinkled clothes came out of an office and shook hands with Ray.

"Hi Ray, haven't seen you in some time."

Ray smiled and introduced Detective Moore to Grant. Detective Moore's tie looked like an afterthought—the knot was loose and the narrow back stub hung to the side. He hadn't shaved for a few days. In fact, he looked as though he had spent the night in his office. Grant took comfort that Moore didn't look like a threat. Moore invited Ray and Grant into his office where he had two chairs sitting in front of a cluttered desk.

"Mr. Guidera, Ray says you have some information for us. What would that be?"

"Well, it's not all that much. It's just that I saw Mr. Lu's picture on television and the police were asking for any information. I'm a supervisor for Universal Airlines and he was on my flight a couple of days before I saw his picture on the news."

"And the flight came from where?"

"Shanghai."

"And why did you wait until now to tell us?"

Grant gave Ray a quick look and saw him nod in the affirmative. They had discussed this possible question.

"I thought you were looking for someone who knew him. I was sure you must have known where he came from. Then my brother-in-law, who's an attorney, said I should still give you that information."

"That was good advice because we didn't know where he came from."

Ray rose from his seat and said, "Well then, I hope the information helps."

Detective Moore interjected, "Is that all you have? Is there anything else you could tell me about this man?"

Grant wasn't sure what to say so he waited for Ray. Ray nodded to Grant.

"I don't think so. That's it. He was on my flight. At least now you know where he came from."

"Did you talk with him on the flight?"

"He didn't speak English. How could I talk with him?"

"How did you know he didn't speak English?"

Grant had slipped up. Ray had instructed him to keep his answers as brief as possible and not to give unsolicited information. There had been no need to mention Mr. Lu's lack of English skills.

"I think it was on the manifest."

"You must have had a lot of names on that manifest of people who didn't speak English."

Grant was suddenly worried that this man was a lot smarter than he had anticipated. He tried to compose himself without the detective noticing.

"You're right. That would have been a long list. It's just that I fly a lot of domestic trips and when someone doesn't speak English there is a note of it. Maybe it's because I saw the interpreter taking his meal order." Grant felt that he had gotten out of that one, albeit clumsily.

"Do you think the interpreter talked with him about anything besides his meal?"

"I have no way of knowing."

"If you remember Mr. Lu so well and didn't talk with him, maybe the interpreter will remember him more clearly. What was the interpreter's name and how can I get in touch?"

Grant began to answer when Ray interrupted, "You'll have to contact the company to get that information. I think that's about it from us."

"Are you saying I can't ask your client anymore questions?"

"I don't see any further purpose. He's told you what he knows and answered what you've asked."

"I think maybe he knows more than he's letting on. Grant, do you have something else to tell me?"

Grant's face flushed. He didn't know what to say and looked at Ray.

"If you think he has something to hide, why don't I see you making any offers to find out what that might be?" Ray interjected.

"What kind of offer would you be thinking of?"

"Protection from anything he tells you that may be incriminating."

"Are you saying immunity?"

"I'm saying, I don't want my client unknowingly getting in trouble trying to help you. I'm sure you understand."

"Ray, I'm just doing my job. I need to get as much information as I can."

"And I'm doing my job. I represent Mr. Guidera. If there's nothing else, we'll be leaving."

Grant felt relief wash over him. He also felt that he had said too much. They shook hands and Grant and Ray started to leave Moore's office. "One last question, did you know Mr. Lu had his kidney removed?"

"Why would I know that?"

"So, you didn't know?"

"No, no, I didn't."

When they were outside Grant looked at Ray, "Ray I'm sorry, he just asked the kind of questions that I couldn't refuse to answer. I didn't see any way out."

"You did fine, almost perfect actually. Remember, he already knew a lot more than he was asking you. He just wanted to see if he could add to that. He knows there's more. He's on notice that we want immunity for any further information. He can't grant that, so he'll have to get that from someone at the district attorney's office or maybe the INS. It depends."

"What do we do now?"

"We just sit and wait. I'm sure I'll be hearing from Detective Moore sometime soon. You have to remember, the important thing is, that you came forward to help. They didn't come after you. That alone will be worth something in your defense."

Grant thanked Ray and left. Grant wasn't sure how much of his involvement he wanted to tell the detective or anyone for that matter; the visit to Detective Moore's office was a hollow victory of sorts.

Grant called Randy as soon as he got home and told Randy about his visit with Detective Moore. Randy sounded impressed with how Ray had handled it. Randy knew Moore, adding that he found him to be more than competent.

"It sounds like you came out of the first round unscathed—good."

"How many rounds do you think there'll be?"

"There's no way of telling. You're in good hands. Just be patient."

Patience not being Grant's strongest suit, he wasn't sure how to cope. He usually waited until five to have a drink—however, he bent his rule on this occasion thinking of the old airline adage; it's five o'clock somewhere. The drink did the trick. Grant settled down and waited for the evening news. There was a tap on the patio door. He was thrilled to see Pat standing there in her kimu. She looked adorable with her hair hanging down, non-regulation. She was home much earlier than expected. Pat had used her gate opener to get in, but didn't have a key for the patio door. He went to the door, eager to let her in.

"Wow. You're home early."

"We had a tailwind, and I didn't go to the office. Not only that, I didn't have to wait but a minute for the crew bus. How did your meeting go with the attorney?"

"Why don't you take off your clothes and I'll tell you all about it."

Pat gave him a what-did-you-just-say look? He caught the look and knew exactly what she was thinking. "You knew what I meant. Get out of that uniform and into some comfortable clothes. I'll make you a drink." Pat went to change and Grant made her a Manhattan. She came back looking casually delightful in a tight t-shirt and jeans. He topped off her Manhattan with a maraschino cherry and picked up his drink. They touched glasses and said cheers. Then she asked, "How many drinks have you had?"

"This is my first."

"So tell me about your visit with the attorney. Did you like him? Was he everything Randy said he would be? How old of a guy is he? What did he say?"

"Slow down," Grant laughed. "Take a breath and a sip of your drink."

Grant told Pat the entire story and how he felt it went. "I have a good feeling about him. Ray, that is."

"Are you still on reserve? Do you have any trips?"

"No, I took some personal days off."

Grant and Pat were exchanging all the happenings of the last couple of days when the phone rang. It was Randy.

"Hi Grant, do you have a minute to talk?"

"Of course I do. You sound serious. Is something wrong?"

"I'm not sure yet. Evidently Detective Moore called our office and said he had spoken with the supervisor who was on Mr. Lu's flight. Moore said he thought this guy had a lot of information that would be a big help if we gave him immunity."

"How did you find out?"

"One of the guys in the office talked with Moore and told the DA about it. It just got around the office."

"What does it mean?"

"Well, it was good that Moore was willing to try and get immunity, but it's not really in our hands anymore. The DA agreed to let the INS handle it. It cuts the cost and workload to our office."

"Is that good or bad?"

"It could be good because maybe my dad can help. On the other hand, I felt I had to go to the District Attorney to explain you were my brother-in-law. I didn't want him to find out from anyone else."

"What did he say?"

"He seemed to understand, but was concerned about what I knew. I explained I just found out the other day and recommended an attorney for you. When I told him it was Ray Neal, he felt that was a good choice. I told him I went with you to see Ray, which he felt posed some concerns."

"What kind of concerns?"

"That it would have the appearance of impropriety on my part. Anyway, it seemed to be okay. And that was it for the time being."

"Could this be a problem for you at work?"

"No, the worst thing would be that I would have to resign. Don't you worry about it. I really want to help."

Grant sensed that Randy was being falsely lackadaisical about losing his job. Grant knew otherwise, but knew there was nothing he could do. "You said maybe your dad could help. In what way?"

"I'm not sure. Maybe he can let us know what the INS is planning. That would be a big help."

Grant and Pat made love just like the old days, before he had so many things on his mind. It was a wonderful night and a beautiful morning. Pat made a large omelet and they sat on the redwood-decked patio next to the pool. Grant wanted to talk about his situation, but Pat seemed too happy for him to spoil it. He wanted to ask her what she would do if he had to go to jail. He decided to wait. Besides it was her parents he was really concerned about.

Grant helped clear the table and offered to do the dishes.

"No, I'll do them. Why don't you take a swim?"

The phone rang while Grant swam his laps, so he didn't hear it. Pat came out of the house holding the phone in one hand and waving to get Grant's attention with the other. He finally noticed her.

"Who is it?" Grant asked, reaching for a towel.

"It's Mr. Neal."

Grant didn't bother to towel off. He got to the phone as fast as he could not wanting to waste any of Ray's time. He stood there dripping and trying to wipe himself dry and listen at the same time.

"Good morning Ray."

"Hi Grant. Did I catch you at a bad time?"

"Oh no, I was just swimming some laps."

"Well, I got a call early this morning from a Robert Higgins. He's an investigator for the INS. He would like to talk with you. Are you free this afternoon?"

"Sure. What time and where?"

"He said whenever we could get there would be good for him. I'll call and set it up and get back to you."

"Will this be where I tell my whole story?"

"It could be. I'm not sure. We'll talk about it when you get here."

Grant ran his hand through his hair and flippantly told Pat, "Well this looks like it. Maybe this is the guy who hears all my sins." She sighed and seemed relieved that the hard part would be over.

Ray called back. He had set up an appointment for 2:00 P.M. with Agent Higgins in the Federal Building. Grant met Ray in his office at 1:30 and they discussed what might happen at their meeting. Ray reminded Grant that the INS already knew about the kidney removal and the forged papers. They also, according to Randy's father, suspected Grant of a lot more than just a connection to the Chinese man.

"It's important you keep in mind, he knows the answer to a number of the questions he will ask you. He'll be watching for out-and-out lies. Let's test the waters and see how he decides to proceed. We still don't know if Mr. Lu has told them anything, just assume he did or soon will."

It was a short walk to the Federal Building. Ray seemed to know his way around, and they arrived promptly at 2:00. Ray stopped to inform a shapely secretary with a short afro: "Ray Neal for Agent Higgins."

She leaned back and pointed to a conference room with a large glass window and a man sitting at the table. "Go right in. He's expecting you."

Agent Higgins saw them heading his way and stood. He gave them a pleasant smile. Ray went first into the spacious room. He then introduced himself and Grant. Agent Higgins was a tall man with sparse graying hair. He looked in excellent shape for a man of about sixty. They exchanged pleasantries and Grant admired the view out the large window, like Ray's office, it had a view overlooking the Civic Center and San Francisco City Hall. Higgins offered them coffee and Grant, as usual, opted for tea. He felt that Ray was sometimes annoyed by his tea preference. Once again, Grant was directed to sit at the head of the large table with Agent Higgins and Ray sitting next to him and across from each other. Agent Higgins had a large file in front of him. Grant presumed it had to do with the case. It was intimidating to Grant.

Higgins looked at Ray. "If I may, I would like to ask Mr. Guidera a few questions."

"Please, call me Grant."

Ray nodded and Agent Higgins smiled.

"All right Grant, I would like to go over what you and Detective Moore discussed, just to refresh my mind." Grant took a quick look at Ray, who gave a slight nod.

"Now if I have this correct..." he looked at some notes before continuing, "You told Detective Moore you remember seeing Mr. Lu on your flight from Shanghai, and told him you didn't speak with Mr. Lu. Is that correct?"

"Yes."

"And then you told him you didn't speak to him because he didn't speak English. Is that right?"

"I didn't try not to talk to him because he didn't speak English, I just didn't try."

"Did you tell Detective Moore that you didn't talk with him because you knew he didn't speak English?"

"I may have said something like that, I'm not sure."

"I have to ask the same question; how did you know he didn't speak English?"

"Just like I told Detective Moore, I think it was on the manifest."

"Well Grant, I have a copy of the manifest. There are so many abbreviations that I don't understand everything on it, maybe you could help me?" With that he pushed a copy of the manifest over to Grant. Ray asked if he could see it first. He looked it over and then slid it to Grant.

Before Grant had a chance to look it over, Higgins said, "I couldn't find Mr. Lu's name anywhere. Shouldn't it be on there if he was on the flight?"

"Not necessarily. These are people with connections, seat assignments, special meal requests, and those needing special help. Also all the first class passengers." Grant knew Lu's name wouldn't be on the manifest. He just looked it over to stall for time and calm himself down. "I don't see it."

"I understand you saw the interpreter talking with him?"

"Yes."

"Do you know what they were talking about?"

"I have no way of knowing. She was, most likely, getting his meal order."

"Well, I've talked with Universal's Ms. Wong."

Grant wasn't sure why, but it was disturbing to him that Higgins had gone that far. Who else had he talked with? Grant panicked. Higgins' next statement helped to relax Grant.

"She didn't remember talking with Mr. Lu, but admitted she could have. I showed her his picture and she surprised me when she said, 'They all look alike.' I asked, 'You mean Chinese men?' and she said, 'No, passengers.'"

Grant laughed along with Agent Higgins. Ray smiled but interjected, "Well, Agent Higgins, I think that just about recaps the meeting with Detective Moore. Did you have some questions that Detective Moore didn't ask?"

"Please, call me Bob. Yes I do, but first let me be honest with you. I understand you asked for immunity for your client."

"That's not exactly what I said. I said protection from anything he tells you."

"Potatoes, patadoes. Do you have a problem saying immunity?"

"No, not if you like that word better. You know the responsibility I have to my client—that's my main concern."

"Well Ray—if I may call you Ray—you do it quite well. You have a good reputation for just that."

"I'm sorry if you have a problem with that—or should I say thank you?"

Grant was glad he wasn't a part of the verbal sparring. It seemed to him that the two men were vying for some sort of upper hand in the situation.

Maybe it was just posturing or a part of negotiating. Grant wasn't sure who was winning the confrontation, but Ray seemed to be holding his own.

"To be honest, I do have a problem when I see a good attorney defending some low life for drunk driving, drugs, etc. You know what I mean. I feel that's not the case here. I think Grant is a good person who just made some bad choices."

"Agent Higgins, let me stop you there. This may be going too far. Are you prepared to charge Mr. Guidera with something or are we here for a character assassination?"

"You didn't let me finish; please don't take offense to that. If Grant has something to offer us—and I think he does—I believe we can work something out to protect your client."

Higgins had put his hands up and made air quotes with his fingers when he said "protect." Grant had a feeling it was almost time to tell all. He wanted so much to get it off his chest, and with possible immunity, he was almost home free.

"No offense taken, what kind of protection did you have in mind?"

"First, I would like Grant to tell me everything he knows about this Chinese man and any others he may have been involved with. Then we would like Grant to work with us in…"

"May I stop you Agent Higgins?"

"Sure, please call me Bob."

"Before we get too far ahead with your assumptions, may I see what you have in mind for Mr. Guidera in the way of protection?"

Agent Higgins shuffled through some of the papers in front of him and then looked in his briefcase sitting on the chair next to him. He pulled out a folder that had Grant's surname written on the outside. He set it on the varnished mahogany table and slid it over to Ray. Agent Higgins got up and asked if anyone wanted a beverage. Ray said yes and Grant declined, instead asking where the bathroom was.

When Grant got back, Higgins and Ray were talking like old friends. Grant sat and Ray pushed the open folder in front of him to read. Grant hated contracts but knew this was important; nonetheless, he mostly glanced over it trusting Ray wouldn't let him sign anything that wasn't in his best interest.

A section of the document read; "Mr. Guidera will be given full immunity by the Department of Immigration and Naturalization in return for his cooperation in the matter of investigating the aiding and supporting the transportation of illegal persons into the United States. His cooperation will include continuing to work as a supervisor and as our agent. He will be willing to give a full deposition and possibly testify in any court proceedings that may be required in any action taken by the INS, using his information."

"Excuse me," said Grant, "I don't recall saying Mr. Lu was here illegally."

"Grant just keep reading," said Ray, "You are not admitting anything until you sign this and will be getting immunity at the same time."

There were a number of other legal terms that Grant didn't understand, so he pushed it back to Ray. "What do you think Ray?"

"I think it looks reasonable, but I would like to hear a little more of what they expect from you. You don't mind, do you Bob?"

"Of course not, I would expect nothing less from my attorney. First, we need to know how you are contacted, how plans are made, and what you do to help these aliens get into the country."

Politely, Ray said, "I'm sorry Bob, but I believe we need your signature under your directors."

"Sure, I'm sorry. I guess I was getting a little ahead of myself."

Agent Higgins signed two copies of the contract and handed them to Grant and Ray to sign. Ray took his copy and put it in his briefcase, as did Agent Higgins.

Grant told the entire story from the day he met Andy. He didn't tell Higgins how he met Andy, just that they worked together. Grant told how he had brought in the rich Chinese men to live and invest in America. He didn't think it would hurt to make it sound patriotic.

"How many would you say you helped into the country?" Higgins was taking notes.

"I'm not sure, some were already in the country when I helped them from Honolulu. Maybe thirty or forty."

"How much did you receive for each trip?

"Well, I..."

Ray interrupted, "I don't see the relevance."

"Okay, I understand. I'll leave that out for the time being, but I can't promise you it won't be brought up at a later date."

Grant finished his story and felt a wave of relief. Then Agent Higgins asked, "Did you know Mr. Lu had a kidney removed?"

"I heard about it, but I can't remember where."

"Does your sister, Dr. Guidera-Barrett, have anything to do with this?"

The question baffled and infuriated Grant. "What the hell are you talking about? Why would you bring my sister into this?"

"Well, she is a Nephrologist and she does kidney transplants."

"What does that have to do with anything?"

Ray was staring Grant down. He asked Agent Higgins, "May I have a few minutes with my client?"

"Sure, take all the time you need. When you're done, let's take a short break before we pick up where we left off." Higgins left the room.

"Grant, tell me the truth. Does your sister have anything to do with this?"

"Absolutely not. I can't believe you're asking. Why are you asking?"

"I believe as Agent Higgins and the police department do, that these men were brought here to have their kidneys harvested."

"I think Randy and Gina mentioned something about that, but I didn't understand. There are plenty of people in our country, why import more people for their organs?"

"I'm not even sure that's what they're doing, but it's a possibility I think they've considered. Do you have any idea what those papers were in the envelopes they all had?"

"Not really. I did look into one of the envelopes. There was a passport with visa and a couple of other sealed envelopes. What could they be?"

"If in fact they are being brought here for the purpose of having their kidneys removed, willingly or not, that envelope might have something to do with it. Just go along with Higgins and keep your temper down about your sister. He's just fishing. I'm sure he will find if his suspicions are in fact accurate about the kidneys, that it's just a coincidence about Gina, a big coincidence."

"Ray I swear to you, Gina has nothing to do with any of this. She is the reason I called you for help to turn myself in."

"I believe you. In that case, there is absolutely nothing to worry about. Just answer straightforwardly." Ray paused. "Let's take a bathroom break. We'll see where he's going with all this when we get back."

Agent Higgins was sitting at the table when they came back. Ray poured a cup of coffee before sitting down. Higgins spoke first. "Okay, let's get started. Grant, I have to be honest with you—I've talked this over with some of the other agents. We came to a consensus; if you are willing to cooperate, with immunity of course, we would like for you, as it said in our immunity agreement, to act as our agent."

Grant looked at Ray, who didn't appear concerned, "What exactly does that mean? What would I have to do?"

"Just what you've done before. Wait for a call from Andy, make the trip and do everything just like you've done on other trips."

"I'm not sure I understand how that will help you. What does that mean, agent? Isn't that the same as an informant?"

"That's just an expression. Here's what we are going to do. First, we will place a tap on your telephone and wait for an assignment from Andy. Then we're going to have one of our Chinese agents on your trip—not necessarily on the one going over, but definitely on the way back. We have to work out all the details, but for the most part you don't have to do anything. Our agent or agents will be in the terminal when you meet with your next Chinese passenger. If you are asked to do anything by an agent during the flight, you will cooperate." Higgins held up his identification badge, "They will have identification just like this. Do you have any problems with that?"

Grant looked at Ray, who was shaking his head. "No, I guess not. When will this all start?"

"We will have a tap on your line this afternoon. And just like you, we'll wait for Andy to call."

"What if he never calls?"

"We're betting he does."

Grant and Ray left the office after shaking hands with Agent Higgins.

On the way back to Ray's office, he said, "Grant, I think this is a good deal for you. As far as I'm concerned, we got exactly what I was hoping for. We planted the seed with Detective Moore and it came up with Agent Higgins. This will give you a new lease on life, one that I can only hope you appreciate."

"I do, I really do. My only concern is getting Andy in trouble. He's been honest with me and doesn't deserve what might happen to him on my account. Can he get immunity too?"

"Grant, Andy is not my client. You're my client. What happens to you, not Andy, is my concern. I hope you understand that."

Grant didn't want to be home free at the expense of people he knew. There needed to be a way around this. He had a lot of thinking to do. "Yes, I guess I do. There are just some aspects about this I don't like."

"You better not think about changing your mind. You've already admitted to what you were doing."

"No, of course not. And I appreciate everything you've done for me."

"Well, it's not over yet, but it's a good start. We don't need to be in contact for the time being. If you need to call, remember your phone is tapped."

The two men shook hands and parted.

Grant was on 101 South when he decided to take the Army Street turnoff and go by his old neighborhood. He couldn't believe the small unit where he had lived during his childhood. He parked across the street looking at the weathered brick building and remembered only the good times. Then Grant drove to 25th Street and parked by the phone company. He went to one of the enclosed booths and called Brian.

"Hello."

"Hi Brian. How are you doing?"

"Fine Grant. What are you up to?"

It dawned on Grant that he had better not tell Brian about his phone being tapped, on a phone that was most likely being tapped as well. He hemmed and hawed and then said, "Let's meet for a drink."

"Sure, why don't you come to my place. We can have a drink here."

Grant wasn't any more comfortable with that idea but agreed to meet Brian at his house anyway. When he got there, they exchanged small talk and then Grant, motioned with his head for Brian to follow him outside. They walked on the garden path and Brian asked, "What the hell's going on?"

"Plenty, I called to tell you my phone is going to be bugged and then realized yours probably already is."

"I'm sure it is, but how do you know yours is?"

"It's all part of me getting out of the new mess I'm in."

"You mean about the Chinese men?"

"Yeah, I made a deal with the Feds. I got immunity before I agreed to help them." Brian didn't say anything. Grant told Brian not to talk about any drug- or Romano-related subjects from his house phone. He explained there was a lot going on and apologized that he couldn't say more. Grant left feeling he did the right thing.

When Grant got home, Pat was watching television and pouting.

"What's the matter? Are you in a bad mood?" Grant asked.

"Where have you been? Don't tell me you've been with that agent and attorney all this time."

"Why not? There was a lot to talk about. Okay. I wasn't, I went to see Brian."

"So, why didn't you call me? What was so important that you had to see Brian all of a sudden?

"What did you have for breakfast, Carnation Instant Bitch?"

Pat grinned and Grant had to laugh at that one himself. "No, and I'm sorry. I've just been a wreck all day waiting to hear about your meeting. How did it go?"

Grant curled his finger in a "come-here" motion and then put it over his mouth indicating not to say anything. Pat followed and they went out the patio door.

"What's going on? Why are we out here?"

"For starters, the phone is being tapped."

"How do you know that?"

"Because I agreed to it. It's all part of a deal Ray got for me."

"So, why are we out here?"

"I don't know. Maybe they have the house bugged as well?"

"I think you're being paranoid."

"Maybe, but I just can't be too careful. Brian didn't question me when I asked him to go outside for the same reason."

"If you told them everything, what more could they find out?"

"About my working for Brian. I know they suspect it, but haven't mentioned it so far."

"So that's still hanging over your head?"

"All they know is that I was on some of Brian's flights. I think that's it."

For some reason Grant felt uneasy. There was something in the back of his mind that he couldn't quite put his finger on. They walked around the garden and sat on a bench and took in the ambiance. Pat didn't say anything. Grant finally told her about the entire agreement he made with the INS and Agent Higgins in exchange for his immunity.

"That's a good start, but that only covers the immigration thing."

"So far, but I think Ray can work that out too, if it comes to that. There's still the question of getting Andy in trouble, not to mention losing my job. What do I do then?"

"Grant, you have enough money, homes and investments. You could retire now and get by well enough."

"I have more than enough to get by. It's just that I don't want to just get by. I want to belong somewhere; to something that has meaning. There is a part of this job I need. I may have abused the responsibility and made a lot of money, but the most satisfying part is helping people. The passengers, the flight attendants, that means a lot to me. I'm afraid to lose that."

Grant had never described his work that way before. He had often talked about employees in his group and how he could help them with some of their personal problems. On some occasions he would have heated arguments with his operating managers because they wanted him to put a letter in the file of what he considered an outstanding employee for missing too much work.

On one occasion Grant had asked, "Why should I put a letter in her file?"

The operating manager retorted, "Because the computer says to."

"Then let the computer put the letter in her file."

Upper management wanted consistency in dealing with the employees. At one time, that sounded reasonable to Grant until he saw outstanding employees being treated the same as those Grant considered less desirable, even worthless. Pat knew about all this, but Grant had never put it like that before. She put her arms around him and gave him a long hug.

Grant and Pat weren't back in the house five minutes when the phone rang. It was Andy. "Hi Grant, before you get upset, I know you're on personal days off, but if you can change that, I'll make it worth your while. The trip has not been assigned and it's going to a reserve. I could see that you get it. I really need you."

"What could be so important that it can't wait a few days?"

"I'm not really sure, but I just know this guy must be worth a fortune. There's a bonus in it for me, and I'll share it with you."

"Let me call the office and get back to you."

Grant couldn't understand why Andy sounded so anxious. If the office would cooperate, Grant's agreement with the INS would be under way. Grant became nervous knowing this was inevitable, whether it be this trip or another to come. The more he allowed himself to think about it, the worse it got. Grant dialed the office number.

"Good afternoon, duty supervisor."

Grant recognized the voice on the other end. "Hi Dorothy, is Maryann around?"

"Hi Grant. She's in. I'll transfer you."

There was a pause then Maryann's voice. "This is Maryann."

"Hi Maryann, this is Grant. It's turning out I don't need all of those personal days off. Could you cancel the rest?"

"Are you sure? You have those days coming to you. It's up to you."

"I appreciate it, but if I could, I would like to save them."

"If you're just trying to get out of the house, I don't think you will be going anywhere. We have most of our trips covered."

Grant just thanked her and called Andy back.

"Okay Andy. I'm back on the reserve roster. What trip will I be taking?"

"You'll be on the 12:30 Shanghai trip day after tomorrow. You'll have the regular 44-hour layover and will bring back a Mr. Hui Liu, spelled H-U-I-space-L-I-U. Good luck pronouncing his name. I'm not sure who will be calling you in Shanghai, but he will call you at the hotel as usual and make arrangements to meet with you. The return flight leaves at 1:45 P.M. and arrives at 8:10 A.M. in SFO, so I'll see you then.

"Okay, I'll see you in a couple of days."

Grant got off the phone and Pat hugged him. Grant could see the concern in her face and tried to soothe her.

"Honey, don't worry, it's almost over. You go on your trip tomorrow and try not to worry. I've done this too many times for anything to go wrong."

"But, you weren't double-crossing anyone those times. Could these people be dangerous?"

"I really don't think so. I haven't seen anyone who looks the least bit dangerous. In fact, most of the people I've met have been very pleasant. They treat these rich guys with kid gloves."

"Well I'm going to make us dinner and then go home early. I have a lot to do before my trip tomorrow."

"You can't go home now. I won't see you for four days."

"I have to get a clean uniform and layover clothes and pay some bills. I'll call you when I get to the airport in the morning. You know I'll be thinking of you all the time."

Chapter 16

Pat called before her briefing and woke Grant up. Fortunately the conversation didn't go too far before he remembered the phone was tapped. He kept it simple, and apparently Pat remembered too. Grant didn't want Higgins or whoever was listening to know Pat had knowledge about his upcoming trip. He even thought it was too much when she said, "I love you." Grant just replied, "Me too." He told her to have a nice trip and not to get too much sun. He didn't want Agent Higgins knowing how much he loved Pat, thinking somehow that might involve her further.

Before Grant started his day, he called and left a message for Agent Higgins. He wanted to tell Higgins he had a trip for Andy. In hindsight, he realized Higgins was probably already aware of it.

Grant had a full day to get ready for his trip, laying out his uniform and replenishing his briefcase. He put what information Andy had given him in a small pocket in the lid.

Grant ran a few errands and got home around three o'clock. He was listening to a message on his machine from Ray when he was startled by the buzzer at the front gate. He looked out the window before opening the gate and saw Randy and Gina's car with another car behind them.

"Hi Randy. Is that other car with you?"

"Yes, it's an Agent Higgins, and Ray."

Grant pressed the button to open the gate and watched as the cars pulled up to the front of the house by the main door. He opened the front door before they rang the bell. Grant couldn't help but think Gina and Randy with Agent Higgins and Ray all standing there looked like dinner guests.

"What's going on, Gina? Why are you all here?"

Ray said, "Sorry Grant, I tried calling you about this. Did you get my message?"

"I was just listening to it when you drove up."

"Is there a place where we can sit?"

Almost as a second thought, Grant gave Gina a hug and shook hands with the others. He led them into the dining room and moved the fruit bowl, making room at the extendable teak table. Agent Higgins looked around, giving Grant cause to wonder what he was thinking.

Ray interrupted Grant's thoughts about Agent Higgins. "Bob called yesterday after our meeting. He is certain these Chinese men are being brought here for their kidneys. Whether they know it or not is another story. If they are unaware, that is possibly another criminal matter altogether. I called and talked with Randy explaining our visit with Agent Higgins and the conclusions he and his colleagues came to. Randy's office may get involved. I was surprised to learn how much Randy knew about kidneys and the rarity of a match between donors and recipients. Of course, he told me about Gina and the fact she's a Nephrologist. I explained that Agent Higgins already knew and wanted to know if she could possibly help. That's why she's here."

"I'm sorry Gina. I never wanted to get you involved."

"Grant, we all need to do whatever it takes to get this over with," Gina said, with conviction in her voice.

"What can you do? I don't think there is any reason to get you involved."

Agent Higgins spoke up, "Grant, here is what we are planning and we need you to cooperate." Higgins looked at Ray as he spoke. He obviously wanted Ray's support, which he got.

"Grant, you have to listen to Bob." Ray said.

Higgins continued. "Your sister will not be on your flight going over. She will be on your flight coming back."

Before Grant could say anything, Higgins went on. "As will several of our agents. Gina will be traveling under the name Dr. Barrett without the Guidera in front of it, to avoid suspicion." Randy smirked and Grant knew it was because Randy hadn't wanted Gina to hyphenate her name after the marriage, but Gina insisted, wanting to make their father proud. "We will need you to somehow get the envelope you mentioned from Mr. Liu."

Grant was about to ask how Agent Higgins knew the name of Mr. Liu and then it dawned on him that Higgins must have listened to his conversation with Andy.

"We want you to bring the envelope to your sister who will be in first class, maybe two envelopes."

"What do you mean two? Why two?"

"One might be from our agent. I'll explain that later. We want Gina to look through the papers to substantiate or refute our suspicions. Do you think you could do that?"

"That shouldn't be a problem, they always seem eager to hand over the envelope. What about opening the sealed envelopes inside?"

"We have others that we'll give to Dr. Guidera," he said, using Gina's maiden name. His remark wiped the smirk off Randy's face.

"If she can't reseal the envelope, she will use a new one after taking notes."

"Taking notes? What kind of notes?" Grant asked.

"Whatever she deems important; mostly to confirm if he is traveling here for one reason only—to donate his kidney."

Grant was struggling to comprehend how serious the authorities were about organ trafficking. It just didn't seem like a logical explanation to why the Chinese men were being smuggled into the country to him. He just didn't grasp how difficult matching kidney donors to recipients could be.

Agent Higgins continued, "We will have agents at the terminal when you meet with Mr. Liu. Two Chinese-speaking agents will follow whoever brought him to you. While we have no jurisdiction in that country, we can go through diplomatic channels at a later date. We can only hope they are willing to cooperate without political pressure. At this point, the agents will only be gathering as much information as possible. When you take Mr. Liu onboard as you normally do, we will need an empty seat next to him for our agent."

"How will I know who your agent is?"

"I'm getting to that. He will come onboard and introduce himself and show you his identification. Here is what I want from you; I want you to call your reservation desk and get a seat assignment for Mr. Liu and have them keep the seat next to him open. Can you do that?"

"If the plane has lots of open seats, that won't be a problem. But if it's full, it won't work. Can you request a seat when you call in the reservation for your agent and then give me the seat number and name he is traveling under?"

"I can have that before you leave tomorrow."

"Good, then I will call ahead and get the seat next to him for Mr. Liu."

"Good, I think that will work. Our agent is pretty sharp and in fact, was born in China. He can start a conversation and see where it goes. But there is a chance they won't have a conversation about why they are coming to America. That's why I would like you to have your interpreter ask them both for their papers. Our guy will also have the envelopes as you described. That might help their conversation along. Do you think there might be a problem with the interpreter doing as you ask?"

"No that part should be fine."

"Well then, I think we have a good plan so far. Any questions?"

"If Mr. Liu does confide in your agent and thinks he's coming for the same reason, won't he be suspicious when we get to San Francisco and I bring Mr. Liu to Andy and your agent doesn't come with me?"

"Good question. First, we don't know if our agent can get Mr. Liu to discuss why he's coming to America. If that's the case, and Mr. Liu doesn't think they have anything in common, it won't be a problem."

"And if they do discuss why they are coming?"

"We think Mr. Liu will be so overwhelmed when he gets here, he won't give our agent a second thought. Our agent will try to tell you what's going on if he can. If he needs more help from you, he will let you know."

No one else had any questions. Ray and Agent Higgins left together after Ray briefly talked with Grant. Ray stressed that Grant had a good deal going and asked him to do his best to cooperate.

Gina, Randy and Grant went into the family room and had a drink to relax.

Gina broke the ice: "Well Grant, you sure make life interesting."

Grant wasn't sure what to say, so he apologized for getting them involved. He thanked Randy for finding Ray. "I think he's doing a good job. I might not have gotten this far if I had the wrong attorney."

The three talked a short while longer before Randy and Gina had to leave. It seemed everyone had something to do, especially Grant.

After Randy and Gina left, Grant felt alone. He slumped down in his chair with his drink, thinking about his upcoming trip. He dozed off, only to be awakened by Agent Higgins' phone call.

"Grant, our agent, Bill Lee, will be sitting in 35J. I understand that is a row with only two seats, which should make it a little easier to encourage a conversation. What do you think?"

"I think you're working late. I'm sorry, let me get a pencil. Give me that again."

Higgins apologized for having awakened Grant and gave him the agent's name and seat number again. Higgins thanked Grant again for his cooperation and told Grant it would have been a lot more difficult without his help. Grant felt immunity was a fair exchange for what they expected on the upcoming trip.

Grant walked into the briefing room for his Shanghai trip. He absorbed the atmosphere. It seemed to get better as time went on. He had a good reputation, knew most of the crew and enjoyed the hugs and smiles. He didn't want to think about how many more trips he would be taking, or wouldn't be. He didn't think he could realistically keep his job when his involvement got out. He appreciated that Pat hadn't said anything, knowing she already would have thought of such an eventuality.

The trip to Shanghai was surprisingly productive as far as sales went, remarkably uneventful otherwise. It kept Grant busy and took his mind off the return trip. The flight arrived in Shanghai at 6:15 P.M the next day. After a quick shower, he called reservations to confirm his sales. While he was on the phone, he told the agent he needed a seat assignment for a Mr. Hui Liu on the San Francisco flight.

The agent hesitated and asked, "How did you arrange this for Mr. Liu? I don't show he was on your flight over."

Grant was beginning to impress himself with how fast he could think on his feet, when needed. "I had a note in my mailbox that a Mr. Bill Lee will be on the Shanghai to San Francisco flight the day after tomorrow, and he wanted to be seated next to Mr. Liu. Do you show Mr. Lee in 35J?"

"Yes, I do. Should I give Mr. Liu 35H?"

"Perfect, that should make them happy. Thanks for everything, that does it."

Grant's body clock was on San Francisco time—2 A.M.—and it finally took its toll. When he woke at 4 A.M. local time, starving and he couldn't believe he'd slept almost eight hours.

Grant thought about Gina coming over on today's flight and leaving the next day. At least she would be able to sleep on the flight. How he would love to meet her flight and have dinner with her. He wasn't told not to, but was sure it wouldn't be appropriate under the circumstances. He was confident he was being watched. No doubt Higgins had thought of everything.

Grant had turned down an invitation to go sightseeing with some of the crew. He enjoyed an early walk instead. He hoped one day he and Pat would come and spend some time enjoying the city with its sights and restaurants.

Grant watched a movie and took another nap before ordering room service. He had just finished his last bite when the phone rang.

"Mr. Guwedeyra?" asked a voice in broken English.

"Yes, this is Mr. Guidera."

"I meet you tomorrow, same place with Mr. Liu, okay?"

Grant recognized the man's voice, although he didn't know his name. "Yes, I'll see you tomorrow, same place as before."

After a restless night, Grant knew the trip shouldn't be any different than the others, but of course it was.

Skipping the briefing, Grant went to the boarding area and the same man he had met a number of times before once again found him first. He appeared out of nowhere. "Mr. Guidera, I'm Yi."

"Yes, I remember you." Grant shook Yi's hand and then followed Yi to where Mr. Liu was sitting. Yi introduced Grant to Mr. Liu. Grant went through the same routine he always used—he took Mr. Liu's ticket to the podium and checked him in. Then he went back to Mr. Liu and told Yi to have Mr. Liu follow him onboard. Yi and Mr. Liu nodded and said their goodbyes.

As usual, the first flight attendant asked, "Are we boarding?"

"No, I'm just pre-boarding Mr. Liu. He's very nervous about crowds and lines so they asked me to bring him onboard." Grant took Mr. Liu back to 35H, relieved that the seat assignment next to Bill Lee had worked out. Grant asked the interpreter to stop by and say hello and see that Mr. Liu was comfortable. Grant tried to treat this like any other trip and stood at the cross-aisle to put his tip sheet together. He watched the passengers getting on and tried to guess which was Agent Bill. Grant's heart jumped when he saw Gina get onboard and head for first class.

"Good afternoon," Grant said with a big smile. Gina smiled back. He was startled when someone tapped him on the shoulder.

"Sorry, I didn't mean to scare you. Here's my identification." It was Agent Lee. Grant was glad he hadn't introduced himself out loud and was sure that Agent Lee was glad Grant didn't say his name as well.

"Thank you, if there's anything I can do for you, please ask. You did get seat 35J?"

Agent Lee glanced at his boarding pass and said. "Yes, yes. I did. Thank you."

With that Lee went to his seat. Grant had a good list of possible conversions, but just didn't have his heart or mind on sales. Besides Agent Lee, Grant was sure there were more agents onboard. He didn't understand why they hadn't just stayed in San Francisco and followed Mr. Liu from there. That thought made Grant think about the two agents who were going to follow Yi when he left the airport.

With Grant's 747 going east and the sun going west, it got dark fast. Grant had already talked with most of the first class passengers. He walked through the coach cabin on the aisle opposite of Agent Lee and Mr. Liu. They didn't seem to be talking when he first looked, but when he came up their aisle on the return to first class he could see they had started talking and making hand gestures. Grant hoped it was a good sign.

Agent Lee had started the conversation by introducing himself to Mr. Liu, who seemed concerned, but willing to talk. Lee started by asking in Chinese, "Is this your first time to America?

"Yes it is, and you?"

"I was there before, but only on a tourist visa. What about you? Are you visiting or are you staying?"

That was too much for Mr. Liu and Agent Lee could see that. Mr. Liu looked outwardly nervous but said, "I'm visiting friends, but maybe I would like to stay some day."

Agent Lee purposely looked nervous and excused himself. He headed toward the front of the coach section looking for Grant. In perfect English he asked the flight attendant, "Would you please tell the flight supervisor I would like to see him?"

"Of course, I'll be right back."

In a few minutes, Grant came through the curtain and looked around to make sure no one was listening. "Can I help you with something?" Grant questioned with a surprised look on his face.

"I think this would be a good time to have the interpreter ask us for our envelopes. I want him to think we are both going to America for the same reason, whatever that might be."

"I'll have her do that shortly."

Agent Lee went back to his seat and Grant went into first class to get Gina. Her seat partner was sleeping so Grant motioned with his chin toward the stairs. He waited by the spiral staircase and let Gina go up first. There was no one else in the lounge and Grant took that opportunity to give his sister a hug.

"Gina, I can't thank you enough. Why don't you sit at this table? It's my favorite. If you spread out some papers, people will seldom sit here with you. Do you want me to have the flight attendant bring you something?"

"I think I'd like a cup of tea."

"I'll have her bring you one, and then I'm going to have the interpreter get the envelopes."

Grant had the flight attendant who was working first class take Gina a cup of tea and then went looking for the interpreter. The interpreter, Cindy Lou, was in the aft pit taking a break when Grant found her.

"Cindy, when you get finished here, would you do me a favor?"

"Sure Grant, what is it?"

"Would you please go to seats 35H and J—there are two Chinese-speaking men there. Ask them for their traveling envelopes and bring them to me in the first class lounge."

"What's a travel envelope? I've never heard of that."

"I was told to check their tickets, and make sure they have everything they'll need to travel in the states. They'll know what you are asking for. I've done this before."

Grant went back to the first class lounge after getting a cup of tea. He sat with Gina and waited for Cindy to bring the envelopes. It took longer than Grant thought it should. But he knew he was just getting anxious to get this over with. He heard someone coming up the spiral staircase and it was Cindy. She saw Grant sitting with Gina and hesitated.

"Thank you Cindy. Did you get the envelopes?"

"Yes, but it was the strangest thing."

"What was?"

"I went to seats 35H and J and saw the man who was looking for you earlier. He spoke perfect English, but when I saw him in his seat he acted like he didn't know what I was saying. I asked the other man in 35H for his traveling envelope in Chinese and they both gave me envelopes. It was so strange."

"Well, you got the envelopes. That's all I needed. I'll check them over and bring them back myself."

Cindy left looking a bit bewildered. Grant gave the envelopes to Gina. She opened one before realizing it was the wrong one. It was the dummy envelope belonging to Agent Lee. She set it aside and opened Mr. Liu's envelope.

After speaking with Cindy Lou, Agent Lee said in Chinese to Mr. Liu, "I see you have the same envelope as me. Maybe we are doing the same thing?"

He said it in a way as to imply they were both doing something wrong. Mr. Liu raised his thin eyebrows, and his forehead furrowed. It was a pained expression of anxiety.

Agent Lee again mimicked Mr. Liu's concern and asked, "Maybe there is something wrong with our papers. Do you think that is why they wanted our envelopes?"

"I have done nothing wrong. I'm just coming to America to work. Those are my work papers."

Agent Lee made a bold guess. "Yes, those are my work papers too, but I'm concerned about my passport."

Mr. Liu's features eased slightly. Lee had earned his trust. "My passport is not real, but my work papers must be. I am promised a job."

"Me too, but I don't know what kind of job. Do you know?"

"They just said if I was healthy enough, they would pay me money in advance to give to my family. I will work in the US and pay back what they advanced me."

Agent Lee was well briefed by Agent Higgins on the suspicions of the INS and the demand for black market kidneys. Bill Lee just smiled at Mr. Liu. Lee knew Liu's reference to being "healthy enough" referred to a blood test for compatibility.

Grant left Gina alone with the envelopes. She was so focused that she didn't notice him leaving. He wandered around the dark cabin and tried to stay out of the way of the movie-watchers, the few that were still awake. He noticed Bill Lee and Mr. Liu having a comfortable conversation. Grant wasn't sure how much time Gina needed, but there seemed to be no need to hurry.

Gina was still alone and just putting the two smaller envelopes back into the larger one, when Grant returned.

"Did you find what you were looking for?"

"I sure did. Maybe more than I wanted to find."

"What do you mean?"

"Your Mr. Liu has definitely been tested for blood type and cross matching. Not only that, he has a very rare blood type to match."

"So he is selling his kidney?"

"I'm not sure if he's selling it voluntarily. I guess it depends on what the agent sitting with him finds out. But he's definitely been tested for donor compatibility. I had to use two new envelopes, I damaged the others when I opened them."

"Can I give these back to them now?"

"Sure, I've copied all the information. I'm not sure what it can be used for. It only says he's been tested for blood type and his is rare. If he says he is voluntarily selling his kidney the only crime is that he's coming here illegally. I'm afraid to guess. About his passport, I'm no expert but it looked good to me. I'm going back to my seat to take a nap. Will you wake me in an hour or so?"

"You can sleep a little longer than that. We still have five hours to go. You can use seat 7A. There is no one in the other seat. You can sleep and drool all you want." Grant gave Gina a hug. "Gina, I love you so much. It's a wonder you even talk to me."

"I love you too Grant. You know I've always wanted you to be happy. I only hope this will be over with soon and you can go on with your life. I just don't know how this will end. Let's just pray this is it."

Grant took the envelopes and went down the staircase before Gina. He informed the flight attendant working first class that he had told Dr. Barrett she could use seat 7A.

"I took her meal order. Will she be sitting there for breakfast?" she asked.

"I don't see why not. Ask her when she wakes up."

Grant found Cindy. "Cindy, when you get a minute, would you please return these envelopes to the gentleman in 35H and J?"

"Sure, is there anything you want me to tell them or just give them back?"

"Just thank them and let them know the passenger agent will also need to see the papers in San Francisco."

Cindy walked the two envelopes back to 35H and J. She handed Mr. Liu his and said in Chinese, "Thank you and keep these available in San Francisco." Then she handed Bill Lee his and said in English, "Thank you and keep these available in San Francisco."

Mr. Liu looked confused as Agent Lee asked in Chinese, "I don't understand what you said. Should I do the same as Mr. Liu?"

Cindy nodded her head and walked away smiling a bewildered smile.

Grant started to feel apprehensive about what would come next and how he would be involved. Grant just sat in his favorite seat, gazing out the window until he saw the lights of San Francisco on the west coast. It was becoming daylight far too soon for Grant—too soon to land, too soon to end what had been the best part of his life. There was no way out and he knew he had done what he had to do, but hoped at least he and Pat could have a fresh start.

After the flight landed, Grant went down the stairs and stood across from the door. He tried to see Mr. Liu so he could introduce Andy. Grant looked down the rows of seats, now mostly empty, and saw Agent Lee still sitting next to the window. He was surprised to see Mr. Liu coming up the aisle. Andy was standing on the Jetway smiling at the passengers as they got off. Mr. Liu was close enough to Grant that Andy knew who he was. Before Grant had a chance to introduce Mr. Liu to Andy, Andy started talking in Chinese and reached out for Mr. Liu's envelope.

Mr. Liu said something to Andy, prompting Andy to ask Grant, "What other Chinese man is he talking about?"

"I would guess he's talking about the man who was sitting next to him."

Andy thanked Grant and headed up the Jetway with Mr. Liu in tow. Grant went back for his two cases, passing Gina who was on her way out. They both smiled.

"Thanks Gina. I'll call you later" Going up the Jetway, Grant was thrilled to see Pat standing there in her kimu.

"I have to rush and get on my flight. I just wanted to see you. How did it go?"

"I think okay. The Chinese guy just left with Andy. He's definitely selling his kidney, or having it stolen. I don't think I'll know much more until tomorrow, if even then."

"Call me tonight if you hear anything. If not, I'll see you tomorrow night late. Is that okay?"

"Sure, I'll see you then." They both looked around and seeing they were alone, sneaked a short kiss.

Outside the terminal, Andy and Mr. Liu talked until a station wagon pulled up with two men inside. The man sitting on the passenger side got out and opened the back door for Mr. Liu. There was no formal introduction. Mr. Liu nodded to Andy before getting in the car. Andy turned and went back inside the terminal. The station wagon was followed off the airport by three cars, each carrying two INS agents.

Each car stayed behind the station wagon for short intervals to avoid being detected. There might not be a second chance if the tail cars were discovered. The plan was easy on 101 north, as there was heavy traffic. The cars crossed the Golden Gate Bridge and continued north to San Rafael. After the San Rafael turnoff, the first car followed for four blocks before turning off and letting the second car take over. The second car followed six blocks and turned off, allowing the third car to move up. Then the third car radioed the two other cars with the location and direction of Mr. Liu's escort. The INS agents took side streets and were able to beat the station wagon to an intersection, where the first car took over again. The first car followed for only a short distance, until the station wagon turned into an underground garage that required a key card to enter. The sign on the building read: Marin Medical Center. The three INS cars met a block away and the six agents discussed a plan of action. It became apparent they needed further instructions from Agent Higgins. Agent Bill Lee had informed Higgins that he was sure Mr. Liu didn't know he was about to donate a kidney, so Higgins instructed the agents to stand by and assist the local police when they got there. He was sure there was about to be an illegal surgery that had to be stopped. The immigration crime could wait.

Unsure if he was being followed, Grant went to a phone booth on the concourse. Against his better judgment he had to do what he thought was right. He had been bothered by nagging concerns most of the return flight. Grant had the airport operator page Andy Park.

"Hello, this is Andy Park."

"Andy, Grant. I have to tell you something."

"Where are you? Let's meet. What's going on?"

"I can't. It's possible I'm being followed. Listen, there's not a lot of time to explain. The INS knows about the Chinese men we've been bringing in. I'm sure they're following you and Mr. Liu. They know about the kidney business."

"What are you talking about? What kidney business?"

"Those men are being brought here to have a kidney taken, and they don't know it."

"What the hell are you talking about?"

"Those men have rare blood types that make their kidneys valuable. That's why they're here. They're not rich guys like you and I thought." Grant was sure Andy didn't know about the kidney trafficking.

"I can't believe this, but it's making sense now that I think about it. They were in an unusual hurry to get this guy here. But how do you know about all this?"

"It started when I saw Mr. Lu on the news. The news didn't mention, or maybe they didn't know, but his kidney was taken. He didn't talk, at least not at the time. When I told my brother-in-law, who is an attorney, he told me about Lu's kidney being removed." Grant explained the details quickly to Andy. Grant could hear his apprehension.

"You did what? You told him about us—the money, everything?"

"Yes, that's why I'm calling you. Get out of town. You said you wanted to go back to Korea, well, now's the time. I got a lawyer and he made a deal for me. I don't want you to get in trouble. You need to leave."

"Grant, I don't know whether I should be pissed or thank you. I want to retire from Universal before leaving town. I've sent most of my money home but I'm sure I have enough to get by. On the other hand, I'll lose my retirement and social security. How long do I have?"

"I hate to guess, maybe today or tomorrow. I don't want you to get in trouble because of me."

"I guess this had to end some day, but I didn't think it would be like this."

"I'm sorry Andy. This is the best I can do."

Grant was sure he would have had to give Andy's name, if and when, he had to testify. And unintentionally, Grant was also protecting himself. Andy was the last person who could have revealed Grant's involvement in drug smuggling.

Agent Higgins had the San Rafael Police meet with him and his agents to explain what he thought was going on. Since whoever was running the show seemed in such a big hurry to get Mr. Liu to America, Higgins didn't think they would waste a lot of time before removing his kidney.

Two plainclothes detectives, one thickset and the other with an athletic build, went into the medical center with two INS agents.

The athletic detective said, "This is your show, tell us what you want us to do and we'll support you."

One of the INS agents looked over a large medical directory for a clue as to where Mr. Liu might be. Finally he spotted what he was looking for; kidney specialist. "Sixth floor, let's go."

The four men walked into a large reception area with a number of doors leading to other areas. One read: Dialysis Department. There were three receptionists sitting behind a long sterile white counter. One of the INS agents showed his identification and asked if there was a patient named Mr. Liu in the office. The other three men walked around, looking through the small glass windows leading into other rooms. The receptionist said she needed to talk with a supervisor before she gave out any medical information. One of the plainclothes detectives spotted a man on a gurney being wheeled into a large generously lit room. He called for the agent standing at the desk to come and take a look.

The receptionist called after them, "Gentlemen, you can't go back there."

The lead INS agent peered in the little window and opened the door. The others followed. The flustered receptionist followed behind them, "You can't go back there. That's a sterile area."

"Please stop," the agent said sternly to the lean, middle-aged man pushing the gurney.

"Sir, you can't come in here," the man protested.

Two men wearing surgical scrubs and masks came out of the brightly lit room. The large double doors swung open behind them and the agents could see there was a person on an operating table under the bright lights.

There were two people still inside the room, also with masks and scrubs who looked up at the disturbance. One of them demanded, "What the hell is going on? This is a sterile area. Get out!"

The lead agent showed his identification and asked, "Who are you?"

"I'm Dr. Fallen. Why are you here?"

Just then the other INS agent cried, "Look here." The lead agent walked away from the doctor to get a closer look at the person on a gurney the agent was indicating. He matched Mr. Liu's description.

"What is this man's name?" the agent asked Dr. Fallen.

"I don't know and you must leave. We are about to start a critical surgery."

"If this man is Mr. Hui Liu, you won't be starting anything—other than jail time."

The doctor pulled his mask down and asked, "What are you talking about?"

"This man is in the country illegally and has not given his permission to have a kidney removed. Doctor, you're in a lot of trouble."

Chapter 17

Grant was surprised that he wasn't taken out of service and made two trips before he returned early one morning from an all-nighter only to find Maryann waiting at the end of the Jetway. "Grant we need to talk. Let's go to my office."

Grant didn't bother to ask why, instinctively he knew. He couldn't help but wonder how Maryann found out and how she was going to deal with it.

The pair walked into Maryann's office and she closed the door behind them. She was composed as she put the San Francisco Examiner on the desk in front of him, front page up. "Grant someone brought this morning's paper to my office."

The headline read: "Illegal Kidney Harvesting Ring Uncovered." The blood drained from Grant's face.

"Go ahead, read it, out loud."

Obediently Grant read the first paragraph: "With the help of a Universal Airline employee, the Immigration and Naturalization Service has aided local authorities in exposing an illicit kidney-harvesting ring. The alleged criminals lured Chinese nationals to the dream of a better life in the United State—only to subject them to a nightmare where black marketers provide kidneys for wealthy, difficult to match recipients."

So far, it read well to Grant. He continued: "The INS and local authorities discovered that the kidneys were stolen from Chinese men with rare blood types. The men, carrying forged passports and visas, were brought into the country with the help of Universal Airline employees. One of the culprits, Grant Guidera, an onboard supervisor for Universal, has been given immunity in exchange for his cooperation. Mr. Guidera has admitted to helping approximately forty men enter the country illegally. Mr. Guidera claims he was unaware of the kidney-harvesting ring. Mr. Guidera's sister, Dr. Gina Guidera-Barrett, a kidney specialist, assisted in identifying medical records that revealed the intentions of the smuggling ring. Arrests have been made in Marin County in what, according to one racketeering expert, 'is just the tip of the iceberg' in the bay area's illegal kidney-harvesting business."

Grant couldn't believe the article's detail. He was angry with himself for not including an agreement with Higgins to leave Gina's name out of his mess. Grant set the paper on Maryann's desk and sat back. Maryann didn't say anything. Grant just sat there staring at the paper. He knew it would get out one day, but he hadn't imagined it would be like this.

Finally Maryann spoke. "Grant, I'm more disappointed than upset that you would have allowed yourself to become party to such a terrible business. And to use your position of trust with Universal only adds to my disappointment. Do you have anything to say?"

"Yes. First, why didn't you ask me if any of this was true?"

Maryann looked chagrined. "You're right. Okay, tell me, is any of this true?"

"Yes, yes it all is. Are you happy?" Grant was upset. His predicament made him terse and rude.

Relieved her initial feelings were correct, Maryann overcame the embarrassment of presumptiveness. "Grant I'll notify you of a time and place for a company hearing. Until then, you will be suspended without pay."

"Why don't I save you and the company any further embarrassment; if you agree not to take any further action against me, I'll resign. The company will have to agree not to take any legal action against me regarding my job as a supervisor or as a company employee. Wouldn't that be best for all concerned?"

"I can't authorize such an agreement, but I will take it to the manager, and I'm sure it will go to our legal department. I'll let you know. I want you to take any personal papers you may have and leave your briefcase here with the tickets in it."

Maryann was stern. Grant was feeling weak in the knees. He rose from his seat and looked at Maryann before turning to leave.

"Maryann, I'm sorry. I can't begin to tell you how sorry I am. Please, just believe me when I say I'm ashamed."

"I'm sure you are, and you should be."

Grant left Maryann's office and went to the small cubical that held the supervisor's mailboxes. He put all the mail in his suitcase among his dirty clothes and walked through the larger outer office, cheeks burning under the gaze of gawking employees. He wondered if they all hated him. A few smiled and one even followed him out of the large office to ask if it was

FELONY AT 40,000 FEET

true. Grant didn't feel like talking. He just said, "I'm afraid it is," and kept walking.

When Grant arrived home, there were a couple of reporters parked outside. He ignored their questions as he waited for the gate to open. He was relieved that none tried to follow him beyond the gate. He had imagined reporters were more aggressive.

Grant hadn't taken off his coat when he noticed the light on his answering machine blinking rapidly. He couldn't count the number of messages. He started listening and erasing most of them. They were from reporters and other curious people. One lady wanted to know if he could help her husband get a kidney. Finally, one was from Pat who simply said, "Call me."

Before calling Pat or listening to the rest of his messages, Grant called Ray. "Ray, I don't understand why they had to use my sister's name. Who gave them all this information? Why was it even in the paper?"

"Grant, that's the least of our problems. The DEA has become involved. They want to meet with us."

"About what?"

"About the drug business. It seems the INS shared some of their information with the DEA."

"I thought we had a deal with Agent Higgins."

"We did and still do. I don't think it was his fault. Remember Randy's dad saying you were on their radar?"

"Only because I was on the same flights as Brian, and they still haven't proved anything there either."

"That's true. All they say is that they want to talk with you. Maybe it's nothing. And then again, maybe they know a lot more than we realize. I think it's the latter."

"When do we have to go?"

"It's up to you. So far it's a voluntary visit. What's your schedule like?"

"You're kidding right? Do you think I still have a schedule or a job after that newspaper article?"

"I guess not. Let's talk about that tomorrow when we go to the DEA. I'll set up an appointment."

Grant took his suitcase and went to the laundry room. He had forgotten that he had put his company mail in there. After putting his clothes in the hamper, he took the mail to the family room to sort through. There was the usual company bullshit, which he tossed on the floor, and sorted out what appeared to be personal letters. There were a few from friends and a couple of anonymous notes saying things like;

"Now we know how you got that nice house and Jaguar. Do you think you could loan me a few bucks?"

"Grant, you sly dog. I'm sorry to hear about your problems. I wish you well."

One with only his name on the front was at the bottom of the pile: "Dear Grant, We are so sorry to hear about your problems. We can only sympathize with you and what you will be going through. We've chosen not to let that happen to us. We're sure you will continue to be questioned and who knows what they will do to get you to tell all. We want you to know, we are not leaving because of that possibility, but had already decided to leave the country. We're sorry for not warning you, but the house is sold and we needed to leave. Do whatever you must to get out of this dilemma. According to this morning's paper you have immunity, so maybe you're not in that much trouble. We do hope to see you someday. Give our love to Pat and stay well. It's been wonderful knowing you, Love, B & V."

The next note was from Pat: "Honey, after I called you this morning and left a message, my folks called and wanted me to come and stay with them. They heard about this morning's paper, so I'm flying down to be with them. My supervisor gave me a leave of absence. It would be better if you didn't call me there. They seemed very upset. I'll try to call if I can. I love you, Pat."

Grant's world was falling apart. First, Brian and Vicki are gone, and then Pat. He didn't know what to do. He was alone. Grant dialed Pat's number in Sausalito, just to hear her voice. He left a brief message hoping she would check her machine.

"Hi honey, I don't know what to say. I'm so sorry that your folks found out from the Examiner. Please call me when you can. I love you. I'm sorry for the trouble I've caused."

Grant didn't like his message and wished he had thought it out first.

Ray called and said they had an appointment in the morning at 9:00 A.M. Grant hoped the meeting would somehow stop the anguish he was feeling. He was terribly worried about Gina and how upset she might be. He hesitantly dialed her number. Randy answered.

"Hi Randy." Grant couldn't stop himself and blurted out, "I'm so sorry about today's paper, I had no idea they would find out about Gina. That is so unfair. She must be very upset, I …"

"Calm down Grant, she's not upset. You know how much she wants this over with. She expected it to happen. Actually, other than you being her brother, the people at the hospital were impressed with how she helped the INS and local authorities."

"So they felt sorry for her because I'm her brother?"

"I guess that didn't come out right. What I'm trying to say is—lots of families have problems. They understand." Randy tried to comfort Grant and assured him Ray was doing the best job possible.

The next morning, Grant woke up early and his first thoughts were of Pat. He had hoped she would have called. He left the house to meet Ray and was surprised to find a couple of reporters and photographers still waiting outside his gate. They snapped pictures, only to have Grant shield himself with his hands up and head turned. He kept going.

The DEA was in the same government building as the INS. Ray once again told Grant not to say too much and to remember they knew the answers to most of the questions they would ask, especially the ones they would start with. Along with his recommendations, Ray gave Grant a disclaimer: "Grant, we were lucky with the INS. They gave you immunity because you agreed to help and possibly testify. I also think maybe, just maybe, Randy's dad had something to do with it. I'm not sure, but I can't count that out. I don't know if we'll be that lucky this time."

"Ray, you're scaring me. You don't have the same confidence as before."

"Let's just see where this goes. Maybe they don't have anything." His voice lacked conviction.

The two men walked into the large, bustling reception area with lawyers in their look-alike suits and slim ties hustling in and out. Ray walked up to a beefy brunette receptionist with glasses balanced near the end of her short nose.

"Good morning, Ray Neal and Grant Guidera for Mr. Sloan."

"Yes, Agent Sloan is expecting you." She pressed her stubby index finger on a button. "Agent Sloan, Mr. Neal and Mr. Guidera are here."

Ray and Grant were looking the wrong way when Agent Sloan entered the reception area.

"Good morning, I'm Mark Sloan." Agent Mark Sloan was a tall, striking, curly-haired man in his mid-forties. He was dressed very much like the others in his office, only he looked fitter than most. Ray shook his hand and introduced Grant. Agent Sloan had them follow him and pointed to a couple of chairs in front of his large desk. The chairs were comfortable but were much lower than Agent Sloan's, making Grant feel like a child in the principal's office. It wasn't enough he was a nervous wreck.

Ray politely asked, "If we're going to be looking at papers, maybe you have a conference room we could use?" He grimaced at Grant, and Grant knew he had noticed the chairs too.

"This should do fine for now. I just want to ask Mr. Guidera a few questions."

Grant appreciated that Ray had at least tried.

Agent Sloan started. "The reason we asked you to come in, is because your name kept coming up in connection with Brian Lasswell and his girlfriend Vicki O'Donnell. It appears you know them fairly well. Is that correct?"

"Yes, I know them."

"Would you say you are good friends?"

"Somewhat. He's been on some of my flights."

"And Vicki O'Donnell?"

"We've flown together a number of times, and I've had a drink or two with both of them on Honolulu layovers."

"What about here on the mainland?"

"I've been to his house, and I went to see him in the hospital."

"It sounds to me like you are friends."

"You asked if we were good friends. I wouldn't say so."

"Did you know he is suspected of trafficking drugs here from Honolulu?"

Ray interjected, "Excuse me Agent Sloan, may I ask how far you are going with this line of questioning?"

"I'm just trying to find out how much Mr. Guidera knows before I go further."

"In my client's interest, why don't you tell him what you know first and then ask your questions?"

"I've already told you what we know. Mr. Guidera's name kept coming up in our investigation. I was hoping not to have problems asking a few questions."

Agent Sloan's combativeness toward Ray left Grant feeling helpless and unnerved. He didn't know what to expect next.

Ray spoke, interrupting Grant's disillusioned thoughts. "I feel we are here as a courtesy, and I expect you to treat my client in a way commensurate with that spirit."

"Mr. Neal, I do agree you are here as a courtesy, and I am trying my level best to accommodate your client. So far I've asked very few questions. Since Mr. Lasswell is no longer available, Mr. Guidera is our main person of interest."

"What do you mean Mr. Lasswell is no longer available?"

"I was hoping your client could shed some light on that."

Agent Sloan looked at Grant, who looked at Ray, who asked, "Grant, do you know anything about Mr. Lasswell leaving town?"

Grant lied, "I don't know anything about it. I've been on a trip and just got back yesterday. I haven't heard anything."

"Let me ask you Agent Sloan—if my client has information that could help this investigation would you be willing to offer him immunity?"

"It depends on what kind of information, of course. Don't forget there is more to this than smuggling drugs; there was a murder related with this situation. The man who was murdered was on Mr. Guidera's flight on the way to Honolulu and was also seen in the same hotel bar where Mr. Guidera stayed. We understand Mr. Guidera was seen in the bar the same time as Mr. Romano, the same night he was murdered."

"You're not implying Mr. Guidera had anything to do with Mr. Romano's death, are you?"

"No, of course not—at least we don't believe so at this point. If your client has any information that would help with this investigation, there is the possibility of us granting immunity to match what Bob Higgins and the INS gave him."

"If I may, I would like to talk with my client."

"Take as much time as you like."

Sloan started to get up and Ray stopped him. "No, not here, not now. I would like to go back to my office and talk this over with my client, and I'll get back to you."

"How soon will that be?"

"No later than this afternoon."

Agent Sloan agreed. They parted, shaking hands all around.

Although the elevator was empty, Ray didn't say anything. Grant didn't know what to think. They didn't talk all the way back to Ray's office. Ray seemed to be deep in thought and Grant didn't want to disturb him. The meeting had come up so suddenly that Grant had forgotten to mention Brian's absconding to Ray. He thought better of broaching the topic now, while Ray was focused elsewhere.

Grant followed Ray into his office. Ray told his secretary to hold his calls. Grant was relieved when Ray finally spoke. "Grant, I can't decide where we are. Agent Sloan won't give you immunity unless you have some information that will help. You would actually have to admit you were a part of the drug trafficking business. You would have to testify in open court."

"What difference would that make, if I have immunity?"

"I don't think admitting you were a part of it is enough to get immunity. They'll want a lot more. In order to bargain with them, you would have to tell more than I care for. We need to show them you have something to offer, something they want, without showing all our cards."

"Like what?

"Names, places that could help them. Speaking of names, what do you know about Brian's disappearance?" Grant hesitated. "Grant, what are you not telling me?"

Is this between us?"

Ray snapped at Grant, "Of course! All information between a lawyer and his client is privileged. But in order to best protect you, I need to know all relevant information."

"Sorry, of course. I got a note from Brian and Vicki that I read last night. They've left the country."

"Where did they go?"

"I swear to you, I don't know. He did say to do whatever it took to stay out of trouble."

"So, you would be willing to use his name."

"I guess that's what he meant. Yes, I could do that."

"That might be something to work with. I'll call Sloan and tell him you have names and insight on how the drug trafficking worked, without saying you were involved. But, you will have to admit you were a part of it if he promises immunity."

"Yes, I understand. I just don't like having to involve Brian."

"It sounds to me that's what he wants you to do. In fact, I think you should tell Agent Sloan about Brian's note if you get immunity."

"I already told him I didn't know anything. Won't he be upset?"

"No, technically you only told me, although unfortunately, in front of him. But, if the note isn't dated, maybe you got it today or tomorrow as far as he and I know."

Ray's secretary's voice came over the speaker, "Ray, Agent Higgins is on line one."

Grant was surprised. Ray had told her to hold his calls. Grant understood the importance she and Ray put on that call.

"Hello, this is Ray. Yes we did... No, not yet... I can't say, but I'll ask him... I don't think he would have... Of course I understand, but I'm sure he had nothing to do with it. We have an agreement, and I'll expect you to honor it. You still have a strong case without him and mainly because my client helped you."

The conversation ended and Ray relayed Agent Higgins's questions. "He wanted to know if we had met with the DEA and if they had given you immunity. Also, he wanted to know if you told Andy about the INS investigation. He's threatening not to honor our agreement. Did you say anything to Andy about the INS?"

Grant couldn't bring himself to tell Ray, so he lied: "No, no, I didn't. Why are you asking?"

"Because Andy's nowhere to be found, and Agent Higgins thinks you had something to do with it. Higgins has a good enough case with the help you've given him. I think he's just bluffing to see if you said anything to Andy. We need to talk more about the DEA and what you have to offer them, any ideas?"

"It seems to me they don't really have anything. With Brian gone they have even less, so why should I tell them anything?"

"You could take that chance, but I don't think they'll give up until they find information that will lead back to you. Let me tell you how I've seen these things work; if you don't come forward and they find some other person who was involved, who offers information in exchange for immunity, you won't be needed and most likely become the main defendant. Whoever gets there first with the most, wins. Considering you did what you did, are you willing to take that chance? It's up to you."

"I need to think about this. When do you have to know?"

"You heard me. I told him I would get back this afternoon."

"I would like to talk with Randy. Is that okay?"

"Sure, but I need a decision soon."

Grant left Ray's office and used the payphone in the hall to call Randy. He was in an important meeting, so Grant left a message asking Randy not to leave the office. Rather than take his car out of the garage at Ray's building, he hailed a cab to the San Francisco Hall of Justice on Bryant Street. The squat cubic building with its fan-shaped windows featured very imposing architecture. Randy's office was on the second floor.

Grant approached the secretary. "Hello, I'm looking for Randy Barrett. I'm Grant Guidera."

"I see one of the other secretaries left a note for Mr. Barrett that you would be coming in."

Just then Randy came out of his office. "Hi Grant, I've been waiting for you. Do you have time for lunch?"

"I have the time, but I'm not too hungry. I really need to talk with you."

"Your timing is perfect, I just got off the phone with my dad. Let's grab a sandwich and go up to Coit Tower and talk. The restaurants are far too noisy around here."

The sandwich shop below Coit Tower was always busy during lunch. The shop's business was flourishing. The servers spent the morning making sandwiches using full loaves of the well-known San Francisco sourdough bread. They had shelves filled with sandwiches, each clearly marked with its contents.

Grant wasn't hungry when he got there, but it was too appetizing to pass up. Randy ordered Italian salami and cheese and Grant selected a ham and cheese with slices of pepperoni. They each chose a half loaf, Grant's treat.

It was a beautiful, clear day over the bay. Randy and Grant stayed in the car as most of the places to sit were either taken and there were too many tourists wandering around, some looking through the coin-operated binoculars.

Randy spoke, "Why don't you start and then I'll tell you about my dad's call."

"I don't know what to do. I got immunity from the INS thinking that was it. I did everything they asked of me. Then Ray called and told me the DEA wanted to talk with me. We went there this morning and have to get back to them this afternoon. Ray is trying to make a deal with them for immunity, but it would include me confessing to everything I've done as far as the drug business goes. And since they don't have anything so far and Brian is gone, they just might not have a case. I would be confessing for nothing. What do you think?"

"Where is Brian?"

"He left the country, he and Vicki."

"And he left you holding the bag?"

"No, that's not it at all. He told me to do whatever I needed to keep out of trouble. I guess that means I can tell the Feds what we did, for how long, and how we did it."

"Before you make that decision, let me tell you about the call from my dad. Unbeknownst to me, he's been watching this case and your situation. He got concerned when he found out Brian sold out to an organized crime figure. It seems the FBI, DEA, and INS will all be sharing your testimony."

"As long as I have full immunity, why should that make a difference?"

"I'm sure they would be asking you to identify some of the people associated with the drug business; Brian, Romano, and the list goes on."

"Why should that be a problem?"

"Let's just say you identify some people as being associated with Brian and Romano. They may have been connected with Romano's death and the drug business. You will have helped put them out of business and their investment will be lost, not to mention criminal charges they'll be facing.

Remember, Romano was connected with them and they killed him. What do you think they will do to you?"

"I'm not sure what you're saying. Don't testify? Don't get immunity? What do I do?"

"I'm saying, while it's the right thing to do, I'm scared you might be in grave danger if you testify against those people."

"Should I tell Ray not to make a deal with them? I need to tell him by this afternoon."

"It's a tough call. You're the only one who can make it. Your testimony might just end this, but you may put yourself or others close to you, in danger."

Grant couldn't finish his sandwich—his stomach was in a knot. This conversation seemed to affect Randy as well. For a few moments, they stared out over the bay and the passing ships. Randy broke the ice. "What does Ray think?"

"He must think it's a good idea because he's trying to get me immunity. He just doesn't know what your dad knows, although I think he suspects it. Can I tell him what your dad said?"

"Sure you can tell him, but I wouldn't want him to say where he got that information."

Randy dropped Grant off at Ray's office building and repeated his advice. "Grant, think it over; think it over carefully."

"That's what I've been doing. I was hoping you could help. If I don't do anything with the DEA, do you think they might not have a case against anyone?"

"I wouldn't count on that. If one of the other small fry involved gets nervous and agrees to testify, you're out." Pretty much what Ray had said.

Grant thanked Randy and went to Ray's office. The reception area was even more hectic than earlier. Ray's secretary recognizing Grant, said, "Hi Mr. Guidera. Mr. Neal is still out to lunch. Would you like a cup of tea?"

"Oh, no thanks, I just had a big lunch. I'll just wait over there." He pointed to a cozy armchair beside a magazine rack near the reception area.

Grant was sitting on a sofa facing away from the office door when he heard Ray's voice and turned to look. He was surprised to see Agent Sloan with Ray.

"Hi Grant. Come with us to the conference room."

Agent Sloan said, "Why don't you two go ahead and talk. I need to make a couple of calls."

"You can use the phone in that office," Ray said, pointing to an empty office.

Ray and Grant walked into the conference room and sat.

"Grant, I just had lunch with Agent Sloan. I called him and asked if we could talk over lunch. I think he's a reasonable guy and immunity is a possibility. He also mentioned, without using names, that they have their eye on a couple of other guys who just might testify with enough pressure. He said, and I believe him, he would rather have you as their witness. He thinks you would be more credible. It's up to you. How do you feel about that?"

"Not great. I think you and I have known, without saying, that Romano was killed by some of his competition in the crime world. If I testify, my life could be in danger. Randy just confirmed that over lunch. His dad had called and told him that was, in fact, the situation. And he'd rather keep that source between us. "

"Of course. You being in danger is a tricky call. You might be, or you might not be. If they get these guys with your testimony, you're home free."

"And if they don't, it's my ass."

"That's why it's your decision."

"What if they never prove I was working with Brian or helping him in any way? I would be putting myself in this dangerous position for nothing." Grant still hadn't clued in on Randy's warning that those near him might also be in danger.

"That's the chance you would be taking. If you're right, that's one thing. If you're wrong, it could mean a great deal of jail time for drug trafficking and you still could be a threat to the organized crime guys. They have friends in most prisons."

"You mean they kill people for keeping quiet? What happened to honor among criminals? You seem to think I would be better off testifying."

"It looks like your best chance to me. I believe if you don't step up, someone else will."

"I just had lunch with Randy and he seems to think like you, just not as strongly. I trust you both, so I don't really have a choice."

"Of course you do. It's just that Randy and I have been here. We have a good idea of what could happen. We both want to avoid that. What'll it be?"

"Like they say, why pay for an attorney if you're not going to listen to him? Does Sloan have the immunity agreement with him?"

"I don't know. Let's just tell him you're willing to testify."

"Ray, I have to tell you, I did warn Andy. He went home to Korea."

"I thought maybe you did, your loyalty is what made you lie—it's understandable, not a good thing, but understandable."

Agent Sloan appeared in the doorway and hesitated before Ray told him to come in.

"Grant and I have talked it over, and he would like to testify in exchange for his full immunity."

Agent Sloan shook Grant's hand. "Grant you won't be sorry, trust me. We do appreciate your willingness to help."

Grant hoped that was promising. He just smiled back and responded, "I think it's the right thing to do."

Sloan went to his briefcase and pulled out a stack of papers for Grant and Ray to sign. Ray looked them over and slid them down the table to Grant, who just signed them after a nod from Ray. Sloan thanked them both and left.

"Ray, I don't understand. He didn't ask what I knew, what I could testify to…"

"Trust me, he knows what you can testify to, and his eagerness to give you immunity tells me that. Any names you might provide associated with Romano could help with the murder investigation and be a bonus. I have no doubt they've thought this out."

"I'm not sure I would be much help there."

"You might be surprised. They can make a lot from little clues, clues they expect to get from you."

Grant was deep in thought as he drove south on 101 toward home. He was trying to recap where he was and where he was going. He hoped he was almost at the end of this gut-wrenching episode. He'd lost his job and disgraced himself with the story in the paper. He wondered what it would be like when the rest of the story broke. He thought of the sign off of popular newscaster, Paul Harvey: "Now you know the rest of the story." Grant tried to think of the positive side of his situation. He had a great deal of money and hopefully, in time, Pat's folks would get over what he'd done. He and Pat could get married. His father would surely forgive him, knowing how easily it is to fall from grace. "It's not all bad," thought Grant. It seemed almost worth it.

Grant pulled up to his gate and there were still reporters and photographers sitting in their cars. They jumped out as soon as they saw Grant's car. A couple of photographers took pictures and another couple of reporters thrust tape recorders under his nose and started firing questions at him.

Grant tried to be nice and said, "If you put those away and quit taking my picture, I'll talk to you. Of course, it will have to be off the record."

That did the trick. The tape recorders and cameras disappeared. One guy with a potbelly hanging over his belt asked, "How many men did you bring here to have their kidneys taken?"

"I didn't know that's why they were coming here. That won't be happening again."

"Are you going to testify to that?" another reporter queried.

"Yes, I am."

"Are there other people at Universal who are a part of this? What's happening next?"

"To be honest, I don't know what's next, and since it's an ongoing investigation I can't say anymore." Grant didn't know exactly what that meant, but he'd heard other people say it when being hounded by reporters.

He pulled forward into his driveway while looking in the rear view mirror. The reporters seemed to respect his property line and stepped back when the gate closed. The house seemed larger and emptier than ever. Grant poured himself a bourbon. When he sat down to enjoy his drink, he saw the red light on the answering machine blinking. Grant was sure it was mostly news people and decided to check later. Minutes later, he gave in hoping one of the messages would be from Pat. To his disappointment, there was none. Grant drowned his self-pity in bourbon and fell asleep in his chair, before waking and going to bed at three in the morning.

The next morning when he checked his mail, Grant was pleased to see there was only one lone reporter sitting in his car in front of the house. To be nice, Grant smiled and waved hoping his kind gesture wouldn't encourage him. Fortunately, it didn't seem to.

There was a great deal more mail than usual. There was mail from Newsweek, Time and several other magazines wanting to buy his story. They were polite, formal sounding offers. There was one letter that just had "Guidera" printed on the front, with his address underneath. Grant's stomach sank when he read the note: "Keep talking with your Fed friends and you're a dead man."

Grant wasn't sure what do think. Out of desperation, he called Ray. Ray warned him to expect more of those kinds of letters from nuts who read the papers.

Grant called Randy for a second opinion about the note. Grant's anxiety was apparent, so Randy offered to stop by later to put his mind at ease.

"Grant, I think you knew this kind of thing would happen. We discussed it." Randy sighed

"I know we did, but do you think it's serious or someone being a jerk?"
Most likely it's a bluff, but you can't be too careful."

Grant pondered the matter carefully. He was beginning to doubt Randy and Ray. Their advice ran counter to logic. They had both agreed there might be a danger in Grant coming forward, and yet they both played down the possibility of the anonymous threat representing a real danger. It seemed far-fetched to suppose that an uninvolved person had taken the time to deposit the threat in his mailbox just to upset him, a perfect stranger. Grant could only conclude that they were trying to baby him.

Breaking into Grant's thoughts, Randy added, "Speaking of which, it doesn't hurt to be careful. Make sure you're not being followed. Keep track of who's sitting outside your house, things like that." Speaking carefully, Randy told Grant that Gina was going to remove the Guidera from her name, as she had been called and harassed already. "Even some of her patients asked if she was related to you."

Exasperated, Grant blurted, "What are they, stupid? It was in the paper." Immediately, he regretted his outburst. Grant began to realize how threatened those close to him were. He wondered what he could do to protect those around him. He worried for Pat. His selfishness had brought danger over the heads of the people he loved the most.

Grant changed his mailing address to a P.O. Box, and got another unlisted phone line. From a pay phone he called Pat's number everyday, hoping she would be home. He had become so used to the answering machine he was shocked when she answered.

"Pat, when did you get home?"

"I just walked in the door."

"Have you been at your folks all this time?"

"Yes, and it hasn't been easy. I'm concerned about them."

"Concerned how? I don't blame them for being upset, but they'll get over it."

"I'd like to think so, but it won't be any time soon. I've never seen them like this."

"Well, you are their little girl. I can't blame them."

"I'm glad you understand. I'm still worried about you. Could you end up in jail?"

"I guess that is a possibility, but I don't think so. Ray is doing a good job."

"I got a note from Vicki in my mailbox, I can't believe she just gave up her job, her pension, everything."

"I'd like to think she's happy with Brian and they have a good life. At least they have each other." Hesitantly, Grant asked, "Can I come and see you?"

"Grant, I told you how my parents feel. Give me some time to think this through. I couldn't love you more, but I love my parents too. I know they would be upset if I saw you."

"You promised you wouldn't see me?"

"They didn't make me promise, but I know it would hurt them."

Grant was silent. He stood in the neglected phone booth with rude graffiti scrawled over the windows. His money was becoming more worthless by the minute. "Why don't you unpack and get organized, I'll call you later. Would that be all right?"

"Could you call me tomorrow? I need to think."

Grant reluctantly agreed. He didn't have any other choice.

On the way home, Grant was sure he was being followed. When he got to his house, Grant kept going. The car pulled in and parked out front. When he came back and opened the gate, Grant noticed it was the same car that was there the other day when he got his mail. While Grant was annoyed, he was also impressed that the reporter had called his bluff by pulling up when Grant had kept going

Grant sat home thinking of Pat while watching the light blink on his answering machine. He just couldn't take it—he was torn between respecting her wishes and wanting to see her. Grant hoped that maybe if she saw him, she would feel differently. Against his better judgment and out of selfish frustration, Grant took a shower and headed north on 280.

As Grant expected, the reporter wasn't far behind. Grant had to be careful not to drive too fast in his green Jaguar. He'd gotten several tickets and was sure cops loved stopping his car. Grant timed his speed just right to catch all the green lights on Nineteenth Avenue. The reporter, staying a good distance behind, wasn't so lucky and got stuck at a red light. Trying to lose him, Grant turned right off Nineteenth, went up a couple of blocks and continued north for about ten blocks before getting back on Nineteenth, headed for the Golden Gate Bridge. Grant paid the toll clerk and looked into his rearview mirror. He didn't see the reporter, but just to be sure, he pulled off at the scenic area and watched for the familiar car.

Grant took a moment to admire the bridge and beautiful downtown San Francisco, before a black two-door Mustang coupe pulled alongside the Jaguar. Grant casually glanced to his left, just in time to see a man pointing a gun at him.

Grant ducked down as a bullet whizzed past and pierced the passenger side window. He was afraid to sit up, so he just pressed down on his horn to scare off his assailant. Then there was another shot but it didn't hit his car. Grant heard two more shots, then silence. Grant lifted his head up to see the reporter's car next to the coupe. The reporter seemed pre-occupied looking in the other car; Grant started his car, leaving a spray of gravel. He looked back through the cloud of dust to see the reporter pointing a gun at a man standing next to the coupe.

Grant's heart was racing as he headed down the hill into Sausalito. He drove around for a few minutes to make sure he was alone before going up the hill to Pat's house. He parked his easy-to-spot Jaguar a block away and walked to her apartment, keeping a cautious eye out. Grant was apprehensive as he pressed the doorbell, not knowing how she would feel to his showing up unannounced. His heart was pounding heavily, a combination of being shot at and concern over how Pat would react.

At first Pat seemed excited to see him. "Grant, what's wrong? You look a mess."

"I guess ducking bullets doesn't become me. Not only that, I think all the blood left my face." Grant was pale and disheveled.

Pat motioned with her arm. "Get in here! What happened?"

"I was being careful not to be followed, so after I crossed the bridge I pulled into the scenic area to make sure." Grant told Pat the entire story as she sat there shaking her head in disbelief.

She had a million questions, none of which Grant had an answer for. "Why would a reporter have a gun? Why would he be willing to help you? Who was the guy who shot at you?" Pat was way ahead of him. Grant had been blinded by his self-interested ambition to be with her. His face reddened with shame.

"Honey, I'm sorry, but I better go home. My car is a block away, and it's too easy to spot. I don't want any of those people to know where I am or who you are. I need to do something about this."

"Like what?"

"I'm so sorry I came. I didn't mean to upset you. I had no idea how serious this was. Please forgive me?"

"I'm glad you came, but this scares me. I have to think, please understand."

"Honey, I do, and until I get this worked out, I promise I won't come here again. I love you too much to let you get hurt or frightened."

Grant and Pat hugged a long time. Neither wanted to let go. It broke Grant's heart when he saw Pat's eyes flooded with tears. "I'll fix this. I promise."

Instinctively, Grant headed home. He still hadn't seen the bigger picture. Pat's pertinent question about the mysterious reporter slipped past his consideration. He concentrated on his few options to resolve his self-created mess. Grant could not just testify and hope they would leave him alone. That was wishful thinking. The people his testimony would implicate had everything to lose and killing him would only brighten prospects for them. The only other prospect for him was jail, where he would still be in danger.

There were no better choices. His only real choice was to work with the Feds, in hopes of getting rid of the people threatening him. Grant had to know Pat would be safe and secure with him before he could go on.

The shooting burned vividly in his mind, Grant was even more paranoid—justified though it was. The wind blowing noisily through the bullet hole in his car's window reminded Grant to continually check his mirror and be cautious of speeding cars pulling alongside. Grant apprehensively glanced over at the scenic area as he approached the bridge. The reporter and other guy were gone, as were their cars. It seemed to take forever to get home. He was relieved to see there were no cars parked outside his house. For a moment Grant thought of Pat's question. Why would that reporter come to his rescue?

Not caring if his phone was bugged, Grant called Ray. "Ray, I was shot at today. The bullet just missed me and went through my passenger window. If it weren't for some reporter shooting at the guy who shot at me, and then holding him, I would have been killed. I can't take much more of this. What am I supposed to do?"

"What reporter? What are you talking about?"

"He's been parked outside my house for days. In fact, he's the last reporter still hanging around today."

"Grant, I'm concerned. Let me look into a couple of things and get back to you. It might be a couple of days. If the police don't provide security, which is unlikely, we could hire security to stay outside your place. Can you handle that?"

"What choice do I have?"

"That's what I'm going to look into."

Grant spent the better part of the next few days drinking and becoming more paranoid. He was wallowing in self-pity and instead of a clear head and increased vigilance, he got lost in a cloud of boozing. Grant kept the lights turned down when he should have done the opposite, since criminals don't like brightly burning lights. Pissed off at the media intrusion, he refrained from answering his phones—another foolish decision, no doubt aided by his alcohol-induced stupor. Grant failed to consider that his lawyer might be trying to reach him. He should have been more concerned about Pat and Gina.

Grant was startled when he heard the buzzer at the gate. He looked out and saw Randy's car. Randy was alone. Grant was thankful Gina wasn't with him. He knew he looked as bad as he felt and was sure his drinking would be obvious. Grant opened the gate and ran a comb through his matted hair. He took a quick look in the hall mirror. He didn't like what he saw. Randy was at the door before he could make any further improvements. Grant opened the door before Randy rang the bell. He reached out to shake Randy's hand, only to have Randy step back and look him up and down.

"Grant, you're looking more than a little rough around the edges."

"Well, thank you. I would have cleaned up if I knew you were coming."

"I'm sorry Grant. It's just that I've never seen you looking like this. What are you doing with yourself?"

"Well, I guess you can say I'm being a law-abiding patriotic witness for the government. Why don't we go to the family room and I'll make you a drink."

"It's a little early for me, but I'd love a cup of coffee."

Grant put on a pot of coffee and made himself a Bloody Mary. He always thought it was more acceptable to drink Bloody Marys earlier in the day, an opinion he wasn't sure Randy shared.

Randy took a sip of his coffee and began speaking. "Ray called and wanted me to come by and talk with you. He told me about your conversation and how you were shot at. He too, has been getting threats. I think he's somewhat used to getting those kinds of calls though. On the other hand, he's taking the threats to you extremely seriously. You have him worried. There doesn't seem to be any doubt now—the remnants of Romano's régime are a very well-connected crime family."

"Other than sitting around, scared shitless to leave the house and drinking too much—what choice do I have?"

"That's why I'm here. You do have a choice."

"Like what?"

"Ray and I discussed it, and he thinks it would be in your best interest."

"What would be in my best interest?"

"The witness protection program. Gina is sick about the idea, but if it keeps you alive, you should consider it."

"What do they do? Have someone from the INS or FBI live with me?"

"Well, actually that would be a part of it in the beginning, but there is a lot more to it if you're accepted."

"What do you mean accepted? Do I have to be interviewed?"

"My dad can help with that, but I think you need to be serious and I don't think the drinking is helping. In a way, you do have to interview to be accepted into the program. I'm sure you could work through Ray. He should be able to get you considered. The process begins when a state or federal law enforcement agency submits a request for protection. After you work out all the details with Ray he could ask the INS, DEA or FBI, or maybe all three, to submit a request which will be given to the Office of Enforcement Operations. They will decide if your life is in danger as a result of your testimony against drug traffickers and the Chinese gangs who have been bringing in the immigrants."

"And if we prove that, then what?"

"The OEC will arrange for a preliminary interview with the Marshal's Service so you can find out what to expect of life in the program. Here's the best part: the final authority to enroll a witness into the program belongs to the US Attorney General's office. That's where my dad can help if need be. I don't think we will have to get him involved. You have good enough reasons to be in the program without his help."

Grant's head was swimming with everything Randy told him, but it just wasn't sinking in. He poured another drink and stared out the window at the pool before speaking. "You said my new life in the program. What new life? Don't these guys just stay with me before and during the trial?"

"That's part of it, but not all of it. Maybe we should talk about this when you're not drinking?" Randy looked concerned.

"I'm fine. Just tell me what the hell you're talking about." Grant's immature self-pity was unbecoming. Randy's words were a cruel reality check.

"Look Grant, you are my brother-in-law and I like you, but you really have to get a grip on yourself. Your actions have affected a lot of people, and a lot of people are trying to help you. I suggest you pull yourself together and take responsibility for your actions. You might not be the only person in danger because of what you have done. Have you thought about that?" Grant had no response. "If you go into the program, you will have to move, get a new identity, and not see or be in contact with any family or friends."

"I can't see you or Gina...or Dad? What about Pat? What about her?"

"You and Pat could get married so she could be with you in the program. You could have a good life and most importantly a safe life."

"How long would I have to stay away? What about my houses and stocks? Could we come back some day?"

"Grant, I think it would be best if you discussed those details with Ray. I just wanted you to know you have options and that you don't have to fear for your life forever. I'm not excited about this, and I can't begin to tell you how Gina feels. She's been doing a lot of crying lately, especially since I've mentioned witness protection. But even Gina thinks it might be the best way to go. She told me she would rather not see you and know you are alive than the alterative. Why don't you just think about it? Talk it over with Ray. By the way, who is that guy sitting in the car across the street?"

"I didn't know there was anyone there now." Grant peered out the window. "I think he must be a reporter."

"Well, be careful. You never know. I'll stop by his car when I leave, so watch out the window just in case. I'll call you and let you know if I find out anything."

Grant left the gate open as Randy left. Randy pulled out of the driveway, parked, and walked over to the car. Grant saw Randy show what must have been his identification from the DA's office. The two men talked for a few minutes before Randy left and Grant closed the gate.

Grant switched to his favorite bourbon and tried to contemplate the witness protection program. He was ambivalent. One moment, it sounded like a good thing—moving, getting a new life, and feeling safe. He even thought of where he would like to go if he decided it was a good thing to do. It was a place he once visited, it was just outside of Eugene, Oregon, along a beautiful stretch of river. He remembered thinking at the time what a wonderful place it would be to live if he didn't have to work. "Well hell," he thought after a couple more bourbons, "I don't have to work anymore."

Grant didn't get much thinking done before falling into a drunken stupor by two o'clock. He could hear the phone ringing and people leaving messages. But he was too lazy to get up and turn off the ringer on his old line. Grant had no intention of answering it.

He woke up at midnight and finally gave up trying to fall back to sleep around three in the morning. He pressed play on the answering machine and heard Randy's voice. "Grant, that guy sitting in front of your house is a reporter. I also talked with Ray and he said all he needed was your permission to get started with witness protection program request. He agrees it would be the best way to go for you, and he mentioned Pat too. You need to call him in the morning."

It seemed like forever until it was time to call Ray. When Grant did call, he wondered if Ray had been waiting.

"Hi Grant, I've talked with Randy, Agent Higgins and Agent Sloan about the possibility of you entering the witness protection program."

It had been several hours and bourbons since Grant had thought it was a good idea. He was still groggy and wasn't sure what to think. He also didn't want Ray to think he didn't appreciate the effort, even though Grant hadn't asked for his help with this.

"Wow, you and Randy don't waste any time. Do you really think that would be the smartest thing to do? What are my choices?"

"I've dealt with a lot of small time defendants who weren't threatened, and even they were in danger if they testified against their former partners-in-crime. To answer your question, your choice is to live in constant danger or enter the program. I do think it would be the smart thing to do. Did Randy explain how it works and what is expected of you?"

"He kind of told me how it works, but he didn't say anything about what is expected of me."

"After you're accepted into the program, you will have to report once a year to your contact. You will also have to check in with local police wherever you decide to live. They want to be sure you aren't a threat to the community or start up with your old ways. Of course, you will have a new name. They say it's a good idea to keep the same initials and maybe even your first name. That's pretty much it."

"What about my houses, my stocks, my savings and most importantly, Pat?"

"Those are all things we can negotiate, but you would have to sell everything. I just need your go ahead before I formalize the request."

"Can I think about it for a few days?"

"Of course you can, but I wouldn't waste too much time."

Chapter 18

G rant frowned in contemplation of what would be best; he imagined a new life. Through the lens of a few bourbons, the decision had seemed easier last night. In lieu of trying to clarify it once again with the help of a Bloody Mary, Grant decided to call Pat. He had promised Pat he wouldn't go to her house again unless it was safe, but there was no rule against calling. Grant had lost track of Pat's days off and called repeatedly hoping to tell her about what he considered great news. Finally he heard, "Hello?"

"Hi honey, where have you been? I've been calling for hours."

"I just walked in the door from my trip. Where are you calling from?"

"From my new phone line at home."

"I thought you were worried about that line too?"

"Not really and besides, I have some good news."

"I've been worried about you since you haven't called. Why haven't you?"

"I got the impression you didn't want me to. I just wanted to wait until I had something good to tell you."

Skeptically Pat asked, "And what is this good news?"

"Are you sitting down?"

"How good can it be? Yes, I'm sitting."

"Ray is going to apply for us to get into the witness protection program."

"Us!? What are you talking about? Have you been drinking?"

"No, not now I'm not, I swear." He went on, "If I'm accepted into the program, we could get married, move, and be totally safe living somewhere else." Grant compounded his presumptuousness. "I have a place all picked out."

"And where might that be?"

"I'll tell you about that later. How does it sound?"

"It sounds crazy! I don't understand. Are you saying I would have to give up my job, move, and not see my family, for God only knows how long?"

"Yes, sort of. It might be over one day when everyone is caught. We could come back or maybe we would like our new home."

"Grant, there is not going to be any our new home. There is no way I want to give up my job and not see my parents."

"Pat, I love you more than anything. I thought you felt the same."

"Grant I do, but there is no 'us' anymore, especially since you take it upon yourself to make all the decisions without consulting me. And you keep making dumb choices. First the drugs, then bringing in those poor Chinese men, and now this …" She paused. Grant interrupted,

"Wait, how fair is that? Do you think I would have done it if I knew?"

"That's the point Grant. You just don't think things through. Have you thought this witness protection program through?"

"Well, not exactly, but it seems my choices are to enter the program or end up dead. What's there to think about?"

"How about the future? Family? Could we ever live a normal life? You need to think about those kinds of things."

"That's my point—I don't think I will have a future if I don't listen to Ray and Randy and enter the program."

"Grant, I'm tired and I don't know what to say. I can only say I love you, but let me get some rest. Call me later."

Grant couldn't have been more discouraged. He thought Pat would have been open to a new life, maybe even her parents would have been happy for her—no, even he couldn't believe that one.

It was still early enough to call Ray. There was no doubt in Grant's mind. He knew he had to enter the witness protection program. Ray was out of the office, so Grant left a message. It was only a few minutes before Ray called back.

"Hi Grant, I told my secretary to page me if you called. How are you?"

"What do you mean, how am I? My life is a mess and I'm trying to do the right thing."

"Forgive me Grant, but if you did the right thing in the first place, this wouldn't have happened."

"Please Ray, I'm getting that from Pat, Randy and now you. I'm very aware of what I've done. I just want to get past it. What do I need to do?"

"Okay, here's the deal. Randy and I talked about the incident by the bridge and the witness program. I talked with Agent Sloan, who also knew what happened by the bridge."

"How did he find out about that?"

"Evidently, the fellow who saved you was a US Marshal and was assigned to protect you. He took the shooter into custody."

"Randy checked him out the other day and said he had identification from a newspaper. At least I thought that was the same guy."

"Grant you're being naïve. After all you've been through, how hard do you think it would be for a federal agent to get any kind of identification he wanted? He needs to keep a low profile. Just be thankful he was there."

Grant wondered why the marshal hadn't just informed him of who he was.

Ray seemed to read Grant's thoughts as he explained that in order for the marshal to maintain his cover, it was necessary for Grant to act naturally toward him. It worked and Grant did, thinking he was a reporter.

Grant felt a little embarrassed and tried to move on. "About the witness protection program, I think I want to do that."

"I'm happy to hear you say that. Sloan really thinks you're in a lot of danger. Even if you don't have to testify in open court, your depositions will do a lot for their case."

"Randy thinks I should, you think I should, and it doesn't sound like Agent Sloan thinks my life is worth much at this point. What do I have to do?"

"I think Randy told you. To get in the program, we need a state or federal agency to submit a request for protection. We're in good shape there. In fact, Sloan suggested I tell you about the program. If you're sure that's what you want, I'll get things started."

Grant hesitated, thinking of Pat, then said meekly: "Yes, I think I should do that. Let's do it."

"I want you to keep in mind once we start this, there is no turning back. It will take a lot of work to get you everything I ask for."

"Ask for, what are you going to ask for?"

"Since you are not being charged with anything, I'll ask that you be allowed to liquidate your assets and put the entire proceeds into an escrow account to be transferred to your new locale. In exchange, I'll say you don't want the usual salary that is given to participants in the program. I also want a federal marshal to stay with you before, during, and after the trial. If there's anything else you can think of, let me know now."

"What about Pat? Randy said I could bring her?"

"Of course, that's not a problem. It's just a matter of names on the paper work. Are you getting married before you go or after you get there?"

"I'm not sure. I'm not even sure if she will want to come with me." Grant exaggerated. "She's thinking about it." He paused then continued, "Can't we just leave that open until I work it out?"

"It would be nice to know but I'll work around it. Keep in mind, they move fast on cases like this. I would like to come to your house this evening with the paperwork for your signature."

"Wouldn't you rather I come to your office?"

"Grant, I want to get this done. I'm convinced, as is Agent Sloan, you're in a great deal of danger. The sooner we set the wheels in motion the better."

Despite all that had happened—despite being shot at—Grant doubted he was in as much danger as everyone kept telling him. The fact that a federal marshal was assigned to sit outside his house and most likely saved his life should have been enough proof, but he still held out a little hope it was all a bad dream.

It was quarter past five before Ray arrived at the house. He was all business and Grant sensed the urgency in Ray's no-nonsense manner. Ray laid all the papers on the dining room table. He methodically explained each one before sliding it over for Grant's signature.

"Can I call Pat before I sign these papers?"

"Would that really make a difference?"

"Ray, I think I would rather die than live without her."

"Are you listening to yourself? That just might happen if you don't enter the program."

"Okay, pass them over."

The final piece of paper was for Grant to fill out and give to the federal marshal's office. It had to do with where Grant wanted to live while in the program.

"Why can't I give this to you to handle?"

"Because they want as few people as possible to know where you've chosen to live. That is an important part of the program. For the safety of your friends, family and, yes, even your attorney, it has to be between you and the OEC. When they determine your life is in danger, and I don't think that will be a question, they will assign marshals to your case and make arrangements for you to enter the program."

Grant felt good that he made a decision. He only hoped Pat would be pleased and accept what he'd done. He called Pat and tried to put a good spin on it. "Honey, Ray just left. I've signed most of the papers. It's a good deal all things considered. Have you thought about it?"

"I've thought of nothing else. I love you so much and it all sounds good: a new life, a fresh start, but… I don't think I could do it. It would break my parents' hearts. And give up my flying job? Grant, you should understand."

"Are you saying no or maybe?"

"I'm sorry, Grant. I guess I'm saying I don't think so."

"I just signed the papers. I thought you would change your mind after you got some rest."

"You did the right thing, the right thing for you. But I'm not sure it's the right thing for me. I'm sorry." Pat was sobbing as she said goodbye.

It only took a day for Grant to receive a call from a Mr. Ernie Hansen, the OEC representative. He made an appointment to come to Grant's house that very day to discuss the witness protection program. He explained to Grant the same details as did Randy and Ray, only now Grant sensed the importance of the appointment. He was now in the program.

After Hansen arrived, he carefully laid out how Grant would have a federal marshal stay with him and explained, until Grant's assets were in a government escrow account, Mr. Hansen would be the liaison between the marshals and Grant. After that was accomplished only one marshal would be with Grant until he relocated. It would be that marshal who would deposit Grant's money into an account in Eugene, Oregon, Grant's desired city of relocation under his new name.

With Grant's information confidential and secure, Hansen asked, "Do you have any further questions?"

"How long will this take?"

"The sooner we get this done, the sooner you can testify and be safely out of town. That about does it. Oh, just one more thing. I have a federal marshal waiting outside. He'll be staying with you until you testify and relocate. Let me get him." Hansen introduced Grant. "Grant, this is Marshal Bob Neal."

Marshal Neal was a gentle-looking man of about five-foot-eight with a twinkle in his eye and a ready smile. Grant had expected a marshal to be much taller, but he certainly had an air of confidence about him. "Nice meeting you Marshal Neal. My attorney's last name is Neal also."

"Please, call me Bob."

Grant paused. "Why do you look so familiar?"

"Well," Neal said with a smile, "I've been sitting outside your house for some time and you tried to lose me one day when you crossed the bridge."

"That was you? You're the guy who saved me that day?"

"I guess it was fortunate I caught up with you."

Grant held out his hand and thanked Marshal Neal.

Hansen and Neal talked briefly before Hansen left. Grant showed Neal around the property and then to a guest room next to his.

After eating together, playing cards and sharing stories for several days, the two men became fast friends.

The phone rang and Grant prayed that it was Pat. Neal saw the disappointment on Grant's face as he held out the phone: "It's for you."

Marshal Neal had a brief conversation and then turned to Grant. "Well, we need to get downtown. There will be a car here to take us in about thirty minutes."

"Where are we going?"

"We are meeting some attorneys at the Hall of Justice for depositions."

"Why the Hall of Justice?"

"They also have some prisoners they want you to identify."

That sent a chill through Grant.

Grant's trepidation showed and Neal assured him, "Don't worry. They can't see you. It's a one-way mirror, just like on television. It's safe."

Grant went to his room to get ready and picked up the phone to call Pat. It rang once before he hung up. He didn't know what he could say that he hadn't already said.

A van with dark windows pulled up to the house. Neal looked around carefully before waving Grant into the van.

"I'm sorry for the drama Grant. I just need to be careful."

At the Hall of Justice, the van went down a driveway and waited for a gate to open. It looked very secure. The van was met by two uniformed San Francisco policemen who took them in an elevator to the top floor.

Grant was thrilled to see Randy standing among several men with briefcases. Randy came over as soon as he saw Grant.

"Hi Grant, I've been waiting for you."

"Who are all those guys?"

"They're attorneys; one from the DEA, another from the INS and a couple from my office."

"But there are six of them."

"A couple of them are defense attorneys."

"I'm sorry Randy. This is Bob Neal. He's a federal marshal. Bob this is my brother-in-law, Randy Barrett. He's a deputy district attorney." Randy and Bob Neal recognized each other from Randy asking who he was, when sitting outside Grant's house. Neither made mention of that.

"Mr. Neal. Nice meeting you. I heard someone was taking good care of my brother-in-law."

"I'm enjoying being with Grant. I'll miss him when he leaves."

"Any idea when that will be?"

"I guess it depends on how this goes today."

It sounded too quick for Grant, but he knew this day would have to come.

"Are you working on this Mr. Barrett?"

"No, far too much conflict for that. I'm just trying to stay close by for Grant."

A man walked up, said hello to Randy and then turned to Grant.

"Mr. Guidera, I'm Agent Schmitt. Please come with me to the interrogation room. Randy, you can come too, if you like."

Grant, Neal, and Randy walked into a dark room with a large glass window. The room behind the window was well lit. The attorneys were sitting in back, one row up.

Agent Schmitt again addressed Grant. "Mr. Guidera, I'm here with you today because the primary investigators are not allowed. I want you to be comfortable and take your time. The men in today's lineup cannot see you. We will be using what's called a sequential lineup. We will bring in one person at a time. You will have as much time as you need before we bring in the next. The goal of this lineup is to identify defendants and build crucial evidence. Do you have any questions?"

Grant looked at Randy and Neal. There were no questions he could think of. "No, no, I don't."

"If you come up with any, please feel free to ask them."

Agent Schmitt spoke into a microphone, "Bring in the first man." A door opened and an unsmiling man with an unshaven face came into the room accompanied by a police officer who stood off to one side.

"Face forward," agent Schmitt said into the microphone. "Now face left. Now right." Schmitt looked at Grant, "Anything?"

"He looks kind of common to me, but I couldn't say for sure if I ever saw him."

"Send in the next man."

Grant's heart leaped. "That's him, that's Max, Max Payne."

"Are you sure? Where have you seen him before?"

"At the hospital. He came with Romano."

"No question about it?"

"None."

"Send in the next man."

Grant looked at him for a while. "Nothing."

"Send in the next."

Grant took his time, waited and looked some more.

"What is it?" Agent Schmitt asked.

I've seen this guy, but I can't place where."

"Take off your jacket," Schmitt ordered the man.

Grant looked intently. "This is driving my crazy...I know. I saw him outside the baggage area. I think it was the day the FBI was there."

There were a couple more guys, but none of them looked familiar.

"Thank you Mr. Guidera. We have some pictures to show you and we'll be done."

Once outside the room, Neal said to Grant, "The first guy was the guy who shot at you. But don't worry about that, I've already identified him."

"I think I was ducking at the time."

Neal smiled.

Agent Schmitt led the group into a large conference room where Grant identified pictures of Keoki, the Samoan who was with Keoki most of the time, Brian Lasswell, Vicki O'Donnell, and Andy Park. The last three photos made him uncomfortable. They were, after all, friends of his. There were two more pictures to look at. One was of Max Payne and the other the guy Grant had seen outside the baggage area. It was Roberto. Grant knew that was where he'd seen him, and he thought again outside the Hilton hotel with Brian.

After Grant identified the pictures, the attorneys started milling around the room, some going out to the hall. The two defense attorneys seemed upset.

"Randy what's going on?" Grant asked.

"They're waiting for Ray. They can't take your deposition without him."

When Ray came he apologized and explained he had to take a last minute call.

The depositions took over an hour and a half. Ray didn't need to say anything. Grant was a wreck and thankful when it was over. The prosecuting attorneys seemed pleased with Grant's testimony.

As they walked out of the room, Randy put his arm around Grant. "You couldn't have done better."

Ray agreed and Neal gave a smile of approval. They all got in the same elevator. When they got to Randy's floor, he held the door open. "Ray, thank you so much for all you've done for Grant. Agent Neal, it was nice meeting you. Grant, call me as soon as you know something. Gina wants to come over and spend some time with you."

Ray's car was also in the basement parking lot, where they parted. Grant thanked Ray and reached out to shake his hand. Ray looked at his hand and put his arms out to give Grant a hug. Grant swallowed hard. It was a somber ride home.

Grant spent day's playing cards with Neal and leaving messages on Pat's answering machine.

"Your deal," Neal said. "She's still not home?"

"Either that, or she doesn't want to talk to me."

"It has to be difficult for her too. This will change both of your lives."

"I'm still not sure it's worth it. If those guys are put away, why would I be in danger?"

"I guess you have to understand these people. It's all about one thing, money. And there are secret rituals, complicated rules, and family loyalty."

"But these guys aren't related. They're not family."

"They are more like family than most families. You cross one of them, and they are honor bound to defend their family."

The phone rang. It was Hansen. "Grant, your deposition was fine. After some interrogation the men you identified started talking. They are facing more danger than you now."

"From who?"

"They were just low-level family members. They gave the names needed to solve Romano's murder and put a stop to the drug trafficking. They won't even be safe in jail. The case with the doctors and Chinese men is being handled by Marin County's DA office. I'm sorry to say, you might have to actually testify in court on the Romano case."

"I thought my deposition was good enough."

"I thought so too, but because we are in charge of your safety, the federal attorney's office notified me that it's a real possibility. May I speak with Marshal Neal?"

Grant handed the phone to Neal and thought how he would give back every penny if he could start over. Neal got off the phone and didn't look pleased. He tried to put a good spin on it. "Grant, if you do have to go to court, we'll have a lot more time together." Grant's eyes stared back blankly. He felt his voice grow hoarse. "As much as I like that idea, I just want this over with."

A court date was set.

The federal attorney, immaculately dressed in a charcoal suit with a blue silk tie, first established Grant was in the same bar as Romano the night Romano was killed. He then leaned on the rosewood railing in front of Grant and asked, "Mr. Guidera, is the person you saw arguing with Mr. Romano on the night of his death present in the courtroom?"

Grant nodded. "Yes."

Straightening himself, the attorney looked over to the jury box and took a few steps. His shoes clacked on the parquet floor. With a dramatic sweep of his right arm he requested, "Would you please point out that person for the ladies and gentlemen of the jury?"

"That man in the second row with the tan suit and black tie," Grant replied, with his right arm raised and index finger extended.

"Would the transcript please note that Mr. Guidera has identified Keoki Hiapo?"

Keoki sprang from his chair. "You're a dead man Guidera!"

The bailiffs rushed to restrain Keoki, who flung one bailiff aside, before the other managed to pin Keoki on the floor. Some members of the audience stood to better see, as a faint murmur rose to a dull roar throughout the courtroom.

Rising from his bench, the bearded judge banged his gavel sharply on his desk, almost displacing black-rimmed spectacles delicately perched near the end of his nose, and barked, "Order in the court! Bailiffs escort this man from the court!"

On his way out, Keoki threatened Grant, "You'll regret this day you Haole bastard!"

Cross-examination became irrelevant and the judge called it a day.

Chapter 19

Neal's time with Grant was at its end. "Grant it looks like you gave the authorities all they need. We'll be leaving tomorrow afternoon. Your attorney has been informed of your departure date."

Grant didn't like the sound of the inevitable. It was happening and all too quickly. Grant became aware of his rapid heartbeat. It beat with an eerie, unnatural thud. "I want to see my sister, but I'm concerned about her safety. Is there any other way?"

"Of course there is. I'll get the van to pick them up and take them home. Along with the van will be another car to make sure they're not being followed to and from here."

Grant was impressed with his new friend and only wished they had met under different circumstances. "I don't mean to push it, but could you do the same for Pat if she would be willing?"

"I'm sure that can be arranged. Give her a call and ask if she wants to come here. I'll take care of the rest."

Grant had a good feeling for the first time in days as he dialed Pat's number.

"I'm sorry, the number you dialed is no longer in service. If you feel…"

Grant hung up and dialed again, reaching the same recording. The phone released itself from Grant's unfurled hand and landed sideways on the cradle.

"What's the matter?" Neal asked.

"Her phone's been disconnected. I don't understand."

Neal surmised, "Maybe she just changed her number."

Neal's words kind as they were meant to be, didn't slow Grant's spiral into depression and panic.

The hours became minutes. Desperation enveloped Grant. The sounding of the gate's buzzer lifted Grant's spirits momentarily. With mixed emotions, Grant realized it was Gina and Randy. He opened the door to see Gina with tear-filled eyes. A glistening bead rolled slowly down her right cheek. They hugged in silence.

Grant swallowed hard. With a hoarse throat, he mumbled softly: "I'm so sorry things have to be like this. It's not what I planned in life Gina. I hope you can forgive me."

"There's nothing to forgive. You've made some mistakes and you're paying dearly for them. I can only hope you can forgive yourself and have a safe, happy life. There could be better years ahead."

Randy spoke without conviction. "Come on you two, this doesn't have to be forever. Maybe someday this will be over. We'll just be apart for as long as need be."

"It wouldn't be so bad if Pat were coming with me."

Gina tilted her head slightly, in that way that shows care. "Grant, I wish I could say something to stop the hurt you must be feeling, but I'm not sure I understand. I know Pat loves you. It just has to be something to do with her parents. They're a close family, and believe me; I can well imagine how they must feel. I'm sick about you leaving too, but I want to know you're safe, and for that I'm willing to accept what has to be. I don't think her parents are thinking like that. Pat's not in any danger unless it has to do with you. You have to try and understand and accept her decision."

"I don't know if I'm more angry or hurt. Don't you think I have good reason?"

"Grant, don't make me say it. Just try, try to see how her parents must be feeling. If she was your daughter, wouldn't you feel the same way and want to protect her?"

There were sobs, more tears rolled down already moist cheeks. The room lights couldn't disperse the gloom. Hours passed, as did too many drinks for Grant.

Neal pulled him aside. "Grant, we have to leave around noon tomorrow. I hope I'm not being out of line, but maybe you should cut back on the drinking. You wouldn't want your sister to remember you as inebriated, would you?"

"No, you're not out of line. I wish you had been with me when I was making other decisions. I wouldn't be in this mess." Neal sighed calmly in response.

Grant spent another hour alone with Gina and Randy before Neal said, "Well, I think we should be taking your sister and brother-in-law home."

Grant hugged Gina. It was in vain to hold the tears back any longer; the tears flowed freely.

"I love you Grant. Be safe."

"I don't want to leave you Gina. I'm so sorry."

Grant put his hand out to shake Randy's, which was gently pushed aside. They hugged warmly. Grant's hand clenched the back of Randy's wool blazer.

Grant threw three large suitcases into the trunk of an unmarked cream patrol car. They drove through the late evening traffic listening to pop hits on the local station. Dusty Springfield's mellow voice sang "Spooky." It did nothing to encourage Grant, but it matched his mood. Grant focused on conversation instead. "How did you get them to have a plane waiting for us?"

"It's a chartered business jet. We'll be leaving from the San Francisco executive terminal."

Suddenly, there was the sound of screeching tires and a black Chevrolet rammed the patrol car in the rear passenger door. The patrol car fishtailed around and came to a stop pointing the opposite direction. The side and rear window had shattered and pelted Grant with the sharp glass. He felt warmth and his eyes rolled back.

Two masked gunmen darted out from the Chevrolet, now curled around a leaning streetlight. A third jumped out a moment later. He ran into the street and shot the occupants of the marshal van following the patrol car, prompting his demise as it careened out of control over him.

Neal rolled out the driver's door, pistol drawn. The two gunmen fired. Neal focused and hit one gunman squarely in the chest. The impact knocked the man off his feet and onto his back. Neal sprawled behind a fire hydrant, propped himself up on one knee, and scoped the area.

"You bastard," screamed the other masked man from behind a telephone post. He fired off three shots. One hit Neal in his left shoulder. It knocked Neal off balance. The shooter, sensing Neal's vulnerability, jumped out with his gun aimed and ordered Neal to drop his gun. Neal hesitated, then released the gun from his grip. The shooter, forehead beaded with nervous, wild sweat, strode angrily over, spat, and glared at Neal. "You killed my brother, you bastard." As the gunman raised his gun, the patrol car's passenger door started to scrape open. The movement distracted the assailant just long enough for Neal to quickly retrieve his gun. He rolled and fired in one motion. The disoriented shooter reeled back but raised his gun again. This time Neal let two rounds rip into the middle of the shooter's chest.

✈ ✈ ✈

When Grant came to, he found himself in a hospital bed with a concerned-looking Gina and a fatigued-looking Randy sitting at his bedside, brows furrowed, eyes glazed, faces etched deeply with concern. Grant's stirring brought them upright in their seats and put a tentative smile on their faces.

"Grant, we're so relieved you're okay," said Gina.

Grant didn't grasp what had happened. He looked down at the bandages covering parts of his torso and right arm. "Please get me a mirror."

Gina held open her compact. Grant's forehead was also bound and he had superficial gashes on his left cheek and a deeper gash that had received nine stitches on his upper right cheek, just below his eye.

"What am I doing here?" And then he remembered the crash and the rain of glass. "What happened to Bob?"

"Bob's okay," answered Randy, "He received a bullet wound to his shoulder but he's okay. He's outside. I'll get him."

"He's okay?" Grant asked Gina for confirmation.

"Yes. Apparently, someone got wind of you being transported from the house and you were ambushed on your way to the airport. Bob took down two of the attackers."

"That's twice he saved my sorry ass," winced Grant appreciatively as he shifted in the bed.

The door opened, and in strode Neal, twinkle in his eye and his left arm in a sling.

"Hey mister, careful, a cat only has so many lives," Neal joked.

"Who said I'm a cat?" laughed Grant, relieved to see his guardian wasn't too badly injured. "I can't say how lucky I am to have you looking out for me."

"That goes for us, too," added Gina.

"That's just my job," said Neal humbly. "Besides, whether Grant knows it or not, he saved my life when he tried to open the car door. It distracted my would-be killer just long enough for me to take him down."

A tall physician with wispy, graying hair and a goatee entered. "I'm Dr. Navarro and you my friend, are one lucky man to be here rather than the morgue. You have many lacerations to your chest and right arm but none are too severe. You took a serious beating in the collision. You are lucky to not have more serious wounds. There appears to be no serious trauma either. We'd like to keep you overnight for observation though. So if all goes well, you'll be on your way home tomorrow morning."

"That's great news doctor," said Grant.

The doctor put a needle in Grant's IV. "A little something for the pain. See you tomorrow morning."

"We'll discuss tomorrow, tomorrow," chuckled Neal. "I'm going to get home and get some rest. There is a guard posted outside your door and limited admittance to this wing with strict scrutiny of all people entering. You should sleep soundly."

Grant would have felt better if he knew Neal were staying, but he knew Neal needed his rest too. "Thanks. Sorry about the arm. Sleep well my friend."

Neal smiled and winked.

"Great guy," said Randy.

"Yeah, and we better go too so you can get some rest. We'll see you tomorrow."

They both hugged Grant carefully and Grant watched them leave through the door.

Grant closed his eyes; his thoughts were elsewhere. He wondered about Pat. He was told that she had been unreachable. It was just as well. To be near him now was to place oneself in danger.

After a brief examination the next morning, Dr. Navarro released Grant from the hospital. Neal was already there and informed Grant they would be going straight to the airport. The jet was on standby.

"What if they ambush us again?"

"Grant, three died trying yesterday. It is highly unlikely they will try anything again so soon. For that reason, it's in your best interest that we put you out of harm's way as quickly as possible." Grant couldn't argue with Neal's logic.

It was a crisp, sunny morning, and the ride to the airport proved to be uneventful, but it didn't completely ease Grant's worries. "So what's stopping someone from finding out where they're taking me?" Grant asked Neal.

"Don't worry, not even the pilots know where they're taking you until I give them a flight plan and the door is closed."

Grant and Neal arrived at the San Francisco executive terminal twenty minutes later. When they pulled up front, two federal marshals approached the van. They opened the door and took Grant's bags to a waiting business jet. The sleek Cessna Citation looked so inviting with a pilot standing by the small stairs, and natural lighting from the cabin beckoning as they approached. Circumstances, however, tinged Grant's observations. He imagined himself like a condemned man walking his last mile.

"Grant, wait!" screamed a hard-breathing, familiar voice from behind. As Neal continued toward the waiting jet, Grant turned to see Pat running with an escorting police officer in tow. Grant ran to her. They embraced, unashamedly sobbing. Pat's milky complexion was stained by streaks of mascara down her cheeks.

Grant's heart leapt. But then he noticed something. "Pat, where are your bags?"

"I'm sorry Grant, but I'm only here to see you off. I'm not coming. I couldn't let you slip off without saying good bye and telling you I love you"

"But, but, I did all this for us," Grant sputtered, confused.

"Grant, don't ruin this. You know full well why this came to be. I love you, but maybe not enough. Just like you didn't love me enough. Love is about sharing and not about keeping secrets from each other. You lived a part of your life without including me. This is the result, and I'm sad. I wish you all the best and I want to part on good terms."

Grant faced the inevitability, kissed Pat gently, and smiled weakly as he stepped back. "Goodbye Pat. I'm sorry. I'll always love you."

Grant turned and trudged to the awaiting Cessna. Neal stood by the airplane stairs and as Grant approached gave an envelope to the co-pilot. He turned toward Grant and it was obvious this was not easy for him either. He put his arms out and he and Grant embraced. It was a long embrace, but no words were spoken, there didn't need to be.

Once in the plane, Grant ducked quickly into the cockpit and said a brief hello. Ordinarily, the dials, colored lights, and instrumentation of the cockpit would spellbind Grant, but there was no retrieving Grant from his despair. The outer door closed and Grant could see the pilot flipping overhead switches as the engines gained the RPM'S needed for ignition— sights and sounds Grant normally would have enjoyed. Looking out the small window, he could see Pat standing outside the terminal with her arm up in a half wave. He kept his eyes on her as long as he could as they taxied away.

Grant's emotions soared and dipped as the engines on the small plane revved for takeoff. Grant sat up straight so he could look through the open cockpit door and see down the runway. The pilot released the brakes and the forward thrust put Grant back into his seat. He felt the tires thump as they rolled over the cracks in the runway. Then lift off.

Grant was a single, lonely passenger deep in thought as he watched, without seeing, the plane rise toward the horizon sandwiched between the starry sky and the gleaming lights of San Francisco. The lights were mostly a blur through Grant's tear filled eyes.

The small plane hadn't crossed the Golden Gate when a short man with greasy hair and a cigarette dangling from the right corner of his mouth, walked into the back room of a North Beach restaurant. He removed his cigarette and whispered in the ear of the plump man sitting at the head of the table; who in turn dismissed the greasy visitor from the room with a nod. The plump man then looked at the other men around the table, first to the left and then to the right. "Gentlemen, Grant Guidera is on his way to Eugene, Oregon."